Lost Colony

The Hennepin Island Murders

A Novel

STEVE BERG

Evots Publishing LLC

THIS BOOK IS A WORK OF FICTION. The story and characters, except for some well known historical and public figures introduced to create a sense of authenticity, are products of the author's imagination. Any resemblance to persons living or dead is coincidental. The title, "Lost Colony," refers not to Roanoke Island in North Carolina but to a figment of the fictional Kron family's imagination: that Hennepin Island, between Minneapolis and St. Paul, Minnesota, is a "lost colony" of the seventeenth-century Swedish empire.

Library of Congress Control Number: 2023909288

- Ebook ISBN: 979-8-9883637-0-5
- Paperback ISBN: 979-8-9883637-1-2
- Hardcover ISBN: 979-8-9883637-2-9
- Audiobook ISBN: 979-8-9883637-3-6

EVETS PUBLISHING LLC, NEW YORK. ASHEVILLE.

To Sawyer and Ingrid

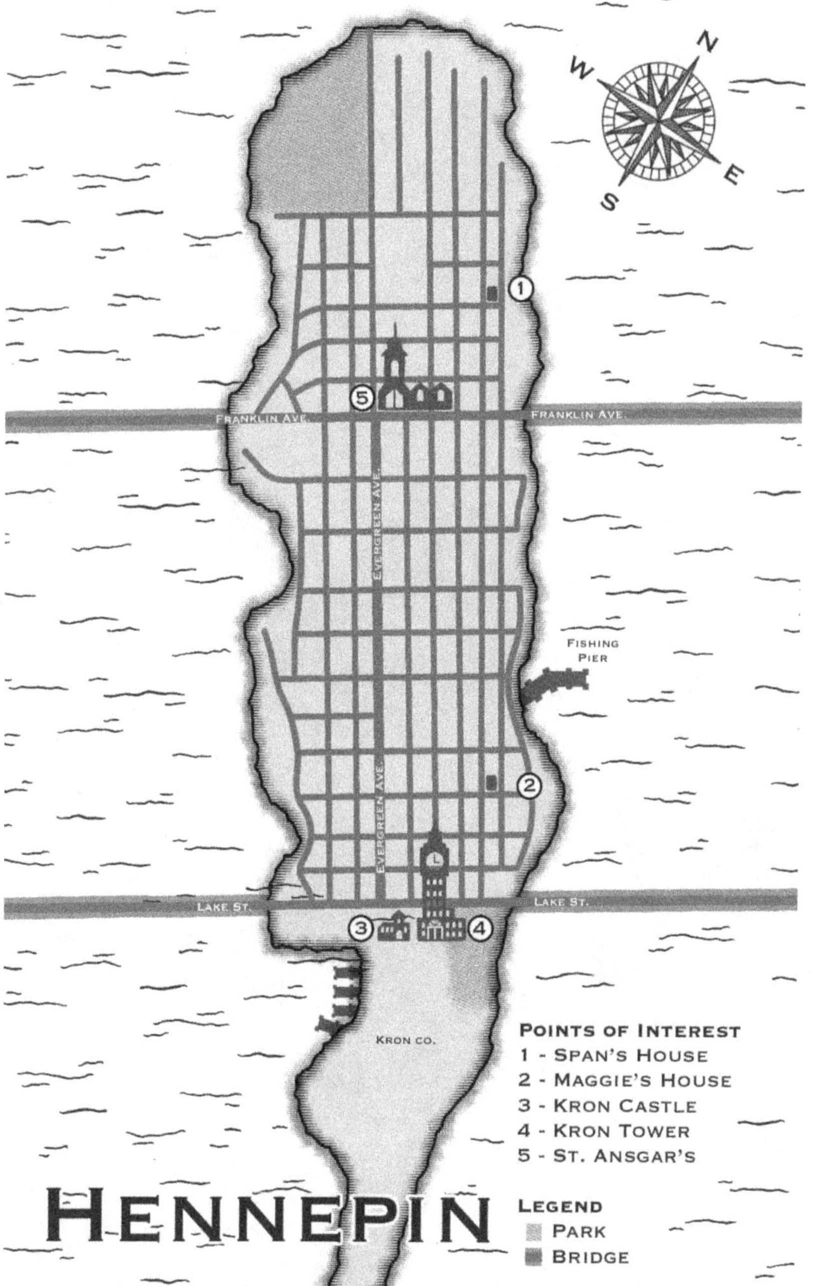

Hennepin Island

Part One

The Reporter

PROLOGUE

Stockholm, Sweden
Friday, February 28, 1986, 11:30 p.m. local time

By the time Jaan's pace had slowed from sprinting to loping to jogging down Tunnelgatan, then up the stairway onto a darker, narrower street, the young man was gasping for breath. A car door opened and he slid in beside the driver, his chest heaving, his brow damp with sweat despite the chilly night.

The palm of a meaty hand emerged from the back seat and Jaan immediately surrendered the Smith & Wesson three fifty-seven Magnum. The arm retracted, revealing dark outlines of the rest of the massive man who filled the entire rear of the small car. He sniffed at the barrel, then clutched the revolver to his considerable midsection, rotating the cylinder and peering into the chamber.

"Two bullets fired," he pronounced in accented Swedish. "To the head?"

"Yes," Jaan replied, his panting rapidly fogging the windows, the car catapulting suddenly from its parking spot into the street, heading at a just-above-legal speed toward the harbor.

"Who saw you?"

"She saw me," Jaan gasped. "Some other people were around, but they did not do anything. Nobody followed me."

It occurred to Jaan that four bullets remained and that the Big Man had control of the pistol, which he pointed vaguely in the direction of the front seat as he asked his next question.

"Is he dead?"

"Has to be."

Actually, he was. There were not two bullets through the target's brain as the Big Man had instructed but rather one slug through the prime minister's back and a second one that sort of got away from Jaan, grazing the shoulder of the prime minister's wife. Jaan's aim had not been as cool and precise as he claimed.

Nevertheless, at forty minutes before midnight, at the moment Olof Palme's head cracked against the icy pavement, the prime minister of Sweden, was, for all intents and purposes, dead. The official announcement came later, after forty-five minutes of chaos that included a frenzied and futile ambulance ride that failed to change the harsh reality. For the first time since Gustav III in 1792, a Swedish head of state had been assassinated.

Bodyguards? Well, there were none. These were days of innocence. Palme quite often strolled amongst his people unguarded. This was, after all, Scandinavia. This was, after all, his hometown, almost his home neighborhood. This was familiar turf. The prime minister's privileged childhood had unfolded in the posh Östermalm district, not far from the street corner where, in his last seconds, he sprawled face down in a pool of his own blood.

As for the lack of security, that could easily be explained. The movie was a spur-of-the-moment kind of thing. Palme had been under a lot of strain. His wife, Lisbeth, had thought it would be relaxing to meet their son Mårten and his girlfriend at the Grand cinema to see the popular comedy "Bröderna Mozart" ("The Brothers Mozart"). By the time Olof had agreed, he'd already dismissed the security staff. It would have been cruel to call them back to work.

No matter. This was cozy, reliable Stockholm. The cinema wasn't far away. The glamorous couple slipped on their coats and headed for the Gamla stan metro station for the short ride uptown, not noticing among the clutches of fellow riders who greeted and chatted with them a hefty man in a gray overcoat who followed at a medium distance. At the third stop, the Palmes emerged from the Rådmansgatan station a block from the Grand. The stout figure in the gray overcoat didn't follow them into the cinema but waited outside, stomping his feet against the cold, at one point choosing to sit for a time in a VW beetle with two companions, the three of them warming themselves by passing a flask, checking the gun, waiting for the proper moment when it would happen, not really thinking about the aftermath when a prominent politician would assert, "This must be the work of a lunatic."

Chapter One

Thirty years later
Minneapolis, USA
Monday, June 6, 2016, 5:30 p.m.

Slouching at his desk in the far corner of the Star Journal's vast newsroom, Span Lokken needs to get this straight in his head while there's still time, before the clutter sets in, before events begin to cascade, as they always do when murder is involved. He needs to imagine as vividly as possible what Margaret Lindberg saw in those first terrible moments this morning. No. Not just what she saw. What she experienced.

Only then can he hope to "move the story forward in terms of understanding," as one of his geek editors told him, or "get to the bottom of this hole," as Her Majesty, Carla, instructed him, although Carla, poor child, hasn't the foggiest notion of how far it can be to the bottom of the human heart. Span must concede, though, that Carla's own black little heart, even at its tender age, knows almost everything about the depth of human ambition. She'll be running this paper one day soon, God help us. Or she'll be running whatever big-city newspapers turn out to be.

Margaret Lindberg, on the other hand, although not much older than Carla, has seen a lot more of life — and of death. And, given the events of this morning, death is what's weighing most keenly on her mind.

Was it only this morning that these things happened? To Span it seems longer ago. So how to begin imagining her day? He closes his eyes.

Her alarm goes off at seven. Maggie Lindberg is one of those blondish, fine-featured girls who probably looks good even a few seconds after being jolted awake. She stands beside her bed now in T-shirt and bikini underwear scratching her head then stretching her long arms toward the ceiling. She's a tall girl, over six feet, with tanned skin, long legs and the slender but strong build of a volleyball player, which she had been in college. Span calls her a girl. She seems like a girl to a guy his age even though she's what? Thirty-four years old.

OK, truth is Span doesn't know what Maggie sleeps in or what she looks like half dressed. He's just trying to imagine for the sake of the follow-up story he's trying to write. He needs to be clear about this point in his mind: He's way past his woman-chasing years, if he ever really had any woman-chasing years. He's, let's see, twenty-four years older than she is, and his pausing to describe how she looks, or might look, has nothing to do with lust and everything to do with art appreciation. Anyway, there's the unfortunate collar thing.

After a shower she jumps into her Monday morning attire: slim black jeans, stylish black sneakers and the long-sleeved black shirt with the never-more-unpopular clerical collar – you know, the kind priests wear – and finally the orange slicker/windbreaker, the kind cyclists wear, because June is rain month in Minneapolis, and surely by late afternoon there'll be a shower or two. Then, let's see, she steps across the hall to peek in on Petra, who appears to be still asleep. A stream of sunlight intrudes below the window shade, revealing the eight-year-old's bare feet poking from beneath her coverings. Suddenly she stirs and squints and greets her mom with a sleepy, gap-toothed grin. "Summer vacation," is all she says.

"That's right, Cubby," Maggie says, bending down to kiss the child. "Go back to sleepy town. Nori is coming to look after you today. I'll be back at 5:30. Maybe I'll bring your favorite sushi roll and we'll celebrate summer." But Petra has already turned over and drifted off.

Nori is tapping on the front door by the time Maggie gets downstairs. After hugs and a few instructions for her kid sister, Maggie makes for the door. This is the second summer she has tapped Nori as a sitter. Nori seems happy to have incorporated Petra into her life. She's a welcome diversion, perhaps, from Nori's obsession with painting the same stupid bird over and over again. Besides, Maggie pays money, a commodity that every starving artist needs but tends to forget she needs.

Happiness happens when you're too busy to notice it, which pretty much describes Maggie. She's busy and happy, and she's actually astonished to find herself in the religion business. As a child, she had accepted the religious customs of her Swedish immigrant grandparents as normal. Lutheranism was the default, more a habit, perhaps, than a belief. By her teens she had grown indifferent to spirituality until, well, things happened in her life and she fled to a church out of desperation, at least that's the way she thinks about it now.

She's happy, too, that Petra has so easily adapted to their new situation and to Maggie's old surroundings on Hennepin Island. Leaving L.A. and coming back home without her husband felt like the right thing to do, and still does. There is something cozy and timeless about the island.

Only recently have things begun to change a little, but it's still easy to recognize the streets she knew so well as a happy kid. The island is a soft, fuzzy security blanket. Or was, until today.

Down the steps and onto the narrow shady street lined with trees and with modest two- and three-story row houses, all nearly identical to the one she rents, and nearly identical to the one she grew up in. Two blocks to what might soon be a Starbucks but still survives as Joe's Cuppa Joe. The rhythm of a workday morning is resuming along Evergreen Avenue, the old commercial strip that runs the length of the skinny island. Delivery trucks line up along the curb, casting dark shadows that block the sharp-angled glare of the early-morning sun. Squinting people hurry off to work, although missing from the usual scene are the clumps of kids on their way to school, blocking the narrow sidewalk space between the stores and the street.

By the time Maggie elbows her way to the counter at Joe's Cuppa Joe, her usual order — double dark roast with an inch of creamy foam on top — is already steaming and ready for her. Her designer glasses fog up as she sips and scans the Star Journal's headlines on her phone, then she hears the clank and chime of Old Yeller approaching. Old Yeller is the local name for the small fleet of 1940s-era streetcars that still rattles the length of the island, from the Kron rock quarry on the south end to the Franklin Avenue crossing on the north. The city insisted in the mid 1950s that the Krons dismantle the tracks and scrap the streetcars to make room for more autos along Evergreen, but the family refused, (nobody can make the Krons do what they don't want to do) and even now, sixty years later, the State Historical Society and the metro transit agency continue to operate the streetcars reluctantly, constantly griping about their stubborn popularity and their horrendous maintenance costs.

Maggie rides Old Yeller almost every weekday for ten blocks along Evergreen, absorbing the bumps and jolts that the cars have always delivered and peering out the dirty windows at the blocks and landmarks she long ago memorized: the Roxy Theatre (still operating), the Swedish bakery and deli, the bowling alley, the Bluebird Bar and Grille. And the newcomers, too; the yoga studios, nail salons and real estate offices with photos of apartments in their windows.

Nearly all the buildings have been built with the tan limestone cut right here on the island. The rows of narrow houses and most of the commercial structures had gone up in the 1890s as a company town of sorts for the stonecutters who worked at the quarry. Bigger houses had been set aside for the office workers and, of course, for the Kron family, which still maintains an impressive compound near the island's south end. As for the main street, there's nary an evergreen on Evergreen. But looking to the south end, there's the imposing stone clock tower on the Kron Industries headquarters near the foot of the Lake Street Bridge, next to the idle quarry with its four idle smokestacks spelling out K – R – O – N. The stone business gave out maybe thirty years ago, but the family by then had transitioned to big construction on a global scale.

Pivoting to the north, Maggie sees the tall, slender spire of Saint Ansgar, the sizable church on Franklin Avenue where the streetcar line ends and where she climbs off. The old Swedish church is an imposing pile of golden limestone blocks, darkened by air pollution over the years but still beautiful in the bright morning sun.

Maggie slips her plastic card into the slot in the iron fence and the church's gate slides open. Then comes the first clue that something is not quite right. She steps over the debris of a discarded lunch: a KFC box, several empty paper cups, chicken bones, cigarette butts and an empty pint of cheap vodka. It's the kind of mess that's not unusual in front of the church, but it's something that Henrik would have swept up by now in preparation for the weekly 9 o'clock staff meeting. The church's meticulous sexton is a man of rigid predictability, a neat freak who lives by the clock. It is nearly 8:30.

When Maggie tries the door to the vestibule, the space separating the church itself from the offices and other rooms of the parish house, it is inexplicably locked. Maggie uses her key and, once inside, turns right toward the offices. The lights are on, but there's an eerie silence along the hallway. Always by now there's the piped-in music and the affected voices from Minnesota Public Radio's classical service. Always there's the inviting scent of coffee, an aroma that's mandatory for any gathering of Lutherans. And always there's Henrik's deadpan greeting. "Top of the mornin,' Father Maggie," he likes to say in a fake Irish brogue that mixes poorly with the accent of his native Estonia. Then he chuckles at the joke that he started and never tires of. Everyone calls her Father Maggie now, and she takes it as intended – a term of endearment. But there is none of that today. Where is Henrik? Why no music? No coffee? No greeting?

Henrik has been known to take a drink or several. He's probably not a devout person, but who really knows about those things? She's never known him to take communion or sing a hymn or comment on one of her homilies or even to talk about religion, especially to Saint Ansgar's legendary and venerable pastor, one Matthias P. Hammar. Maggie has the impression that Henrik is a little intimidated by Matthias, and who isn't?

But the sexton is always here, always with a new feeble joke to tell and never failing to have the offices sparkling. Now, surrounded by an empty and slightly messy office with the lights on and the roar of silence rushing in her ears, a sick, sour feeling begins to mount in Maggie's stomach. She calls out, "Henrik! Henrik, where are you?" Silence. Maybe she should check the janitor's tiny apartment down the back stairway, attached to the undercroft of the church. Maybe she should check the church itself.

She's floating now, down the silent corridor, then through the vestibule entrance to what should be a darkened narthex. But when she opens the door, the lights are on. The sweetness of incense from yesterday's festivities hangs in the air. An artificial coolness envelops her. Someone has turned on the air conditioner. Or forgot yesterday to turn it off. She hears the motor's hum as a backdrop against the muffled sounds of morning traffic passing outside, along Franklin Avenue. A chill overtakes Maggie. She feels herself quiver.

Rounding the corner to the center aisle of the nave, she sees on the stone floor a pool of drying brown liquid at the base of the baptismal font. And lying nearby is Henrik. He has gone too far this time, she thinks. This prank isn't funny at all. He's dressed in his Sunday outfit – gray slacks, white shirt. A broom lies alongside him. His long blondish-gray hair is matted, and Maggie notices two black holes, perfectly round, just behind Henrick's left ear. He has struck a very still pose. Is this a painting?

Her ears are ringing now. She listens. Nothing. Her eyes are drawn down the long center aisle, rows of empty pews on each side, to the steps and a tall, magnificently carved backdrop behind a main altar that has been draped in red and gold fabric, traditional colors for yesterday's Pentecost feast. Maggie feels her feet moving forward now.

There's something odd about the cross that thrusts upward from the base of the backdrop. For Lutherans it's most often an empty cross, a symbol of Christ's resurrection, but this cross is occupied. There is a cruciform figure attached to it, far too plump to be Jesus, and with close-cropped hair and a clean-shaven face. The figure is slumped and covered with massive amounts of what appears to be dried blood that has run down both outstretched arms from hands that have been punctured by spikes, and from feet punctured also by spikes, and from a massive fleshy hole in the stomach, where some bone, possibly ribs, are poking outward.

Matthias Hammar is naked. His head has flopped to his left side, his bloodied mouth is open and missing perhaps some teeth, but he is silent. There is no movement in Matthias. His bright red chasuble lies rumpled on the floor of the raised chancel along with a heap of other clothing. His blood has pooled around the base of the altar and has flowed down the steps so that it touches the toe of Maggie's sneaker.

She feels herself running now, back down the aisle toward the narthex. Deep breaths. Long, deep breaths. She fumbles for her phone as she throws open the big doors to the sharp brightness and street noise beyond. 9-1-1.

Chapter Two

Nine hours earlier
Monday, 8:30 a.m.

Span is a dog person, always has been. He talks to Max more than he likes to admit. He prefers to believe that they have a mutual understanding about many things, and that Max shares the joys, sorrows and routines of his so-called life. Although Max's routines, Span confesses, aren't always understandable to him. Like now, on their Monday morning walk, he can't in the slightest relate to Max's pressing need for excessive sniffing and strategic peeing.

Span feels no compulsion to mark his territory. He's lived here on this island for twenty years, ever since the paper moved him back from New York and closed the New York Bureau. Actually, Span was the New York Bureau. They closed him. Shut him down. Explained that it had nothing to do with his work, but that they needed him back here to cover a crime wave that, in the mid 1990s, the Times and CNN had christened "Murderapolis," much to the horror of the local civic establishment. "Cover the crime wave" wasn't quite the right term of art. The Star Journal had a hungry crew of young crime reporters to handle the individual homicides, assaults and episodes of general mayhem. Span was supposed to explain them. Why, suddenly, in this land of Sky Blue Waters and Minnesota Nice, why in a place where the corporations were home-grown and civic-minded, where all the children were above average and where Scandinavian smugness prevailed, were African-American drug dealers shooting each other on the streets? Why were black teenagers, whose mothers had drifted in by the thousands from the South Side of Chicago looking for better lives, suddenly joining violent gangs and practicing their drive-by marksmanship skills? To the Minneapolis way of thinking, this was all just a big misunderstanding. If only we could grasp the root causes and sit down over coffee and cake to discuss this thing, together, surely the shooting would stop.

It did stop eventually. Or, at least it diminished, although Span couldn't say precisely why. By the turn of the new century, the Star Journal had diminished, too, along with all the other big papers across the country. And Span's role had diminished, although he still hangs on bravely, some might say pathetically, as the staff "explainer." What he is trying hard to do now, on this particular morning, with Max straining against his leash as they march westward down Franklin Avenue toward their turnaround point at Evergreen, the sharpness of the Monday morning sun at their backs, is not to think about his upcoming piece on the pluses and minuses of lower gas prices and the "human element" that Her Majesty, the metro editor, claims is missing from his first draft. What he's really thinking is that Max is almost human but doesn't give a rat's ass about gas prices.

"Max! Slow down!" Span scolds him. "Max!"

And it occurs to him that Max, although he clearly knows his own name, doesn't know Span's name, doesn't have a clue.

Span could tell him, "My name is Span Lokken and a lot of people in this city, well, a lot of people over fifty in this city know my name and my byline." And if he were to tell Max all about himself and his fading status at the paper, Max wouldn't comprehend. He'd just stare at Span with his big brown eyes and pant. Span mumbles almost out loud, "Can we really be best friends if he doesn't even know my name?"

Maybe it's the siren – actually more than one of them – and all the commotion ahead that causes Max to tug so hard. Span has an aversion to sirens and commotion and the sealing off of a "perimeter" with yellow police tape because to him it signifies work, and, at this point in his so-called career, at this juncture on his gently sloping glide path, more work isn't what he's looking for. But now it's staring him in the face and he can't quite avoid it. He counts two, four, no, six squad cars and two ambulances, and now a K-9 unit just pulling up in front of St. Ansgar's. This unfortunately smells like news. 8:45 on the Wells Fargo time/temperature sign across the street. He's shouting into his cellphone now.

"Carla, it's Span," he tells the editor, his voice cracking. "Shitload of police activity on Hennepin Island in front of Saint A's, the big church at Franklin and Evergreen. Better send one of the cop shop boys and a photog ASAP. Call me." Her Majesty's line probably rolled over to voicemail because she's already on the case. Let's hope so because the TV trucks are already pulling up and suddenly there's a helicopter, no, two helicopters hovering overhead.

"Looks like we're gonna be here for awhile," he tells Max.

Now they're pawing their way through the gathering crowd, Span looking for a familiar face among the cops — but he doesn't see one. So he approaches a stout young patrolman — C. Novak, according to the nameplate on his tunic.

"Officer Novak? Lokken of the Star Journal," he announces, flashing his press card. "What's happening here?"

Novak gives him the once-over. "Not at liberty, sir." Then he looks away, disinterested.

Hmm. This is an approach that works in the movies, Span's thinking. Maybe there's something wrong with his getup – faded purple Northwestern sweatshirt over drooping gray sweatpants. Maybe it's the fact that Span is trying desperately to manage Max while hoping to look "official." Maybe it's the coffee breath and the three-day beard. Maybe he should have tried a trench coat and fedora like Jimmy Stewart in "Northside 777." C. Novak, of course, would have no inkling of Jimmy Stewart, no recollection of film noir, no appreciation for the Star Journal and what it means, or once meant, to this city. He's what? Twenty-three, twenty-four?

Hold it. Through the bars of the tall iron fence that runs along the front of Saint A's, Span catches a glimpse of Bender and his entourage from the Crime Scene Unit walking briskly into the church. Span has this love-hate thing going with Bender, and him with Span. Recently up from lieutenant, he's now Captain Larry Bender, deputy honcho of detectives, homicide bureau. Span knows he's not thinking quite clearly now due to his excessive consumption of red wine last night, but still he's able to grasp two sharp concepts: One, there has been a murder here. Two, it must be a helluva big murder if Larry Bender has been lured from his new corner office before 9 on a Monday morning.

Just as he's about to take another crack at Patrolman C. Novak, his cell vibrates – Her Majesty – wondering why he hasn't tweeted. Carla knows Span doesn't tweet. He's aware that the paper has provided him something they call a Twitter account, and, actually, he's not against technology. Not really. He just forgets to use it. Or forgets how to use it.

She tells him that the radio room picked up a nugget on the police feed indicating that there are "two down" in the church, but that's all we know. Efforts to reach Saint A's pastor, the Reverend Matthias Hammar (she spells it out), have not been successful. And Hammar's associate, the Reverend Margaret Lindberg (she spells it out), is said to be on her way. Calls to the church office are being fielded by a cop with "no comment." Wait. Now she tells Span that the police commissioner will have an "availability" at 10 at the church and that two young hot shots will cover it and write the daily story, whatever it is. Span? He should be ready to write the "atmospherics" and the "why piece" if that's what it comes to.

This doesn't surprise him. Nor does it excite him. He's written hundreds of stories "off the news," as they say. By the time he gets Max home and fed and locked in for the day and gets back to the church for the commissioner's dog-and-pony show, the bodies are coming out. He sees them now. Two of them, one on each gurney, each zipped into a gray bag, each loaded into a separate ambulance, doors now closing, both vehicles gliding west along Franklin, toward the bridge, toward downtown, toward the county ice box.

As if on cue, the police commissioner, a slim, dignified-looking African-American woman, Vivian Harlow by name, appears in the church doorway. She walks toward the opened gate in the iron fence and up onto a small riser with a podium and M.P.D. logo that has appeared suddenly on the scene. Bender, wearing what looks like a new suit, is a pace behind her, then stands almost at her side. She's wearing her dress blues with tie, white shirt and sunglasses. Her manner is less that of a cop than an Ivy League professor.

She leans into the microphone. "I regret to inform you of two deaths. Henrik Piedela (she spells it out), white male, age fifty-five, parish custodian." She pauses. "And the Reverend

Matthias Hammar (she spells it out amid gasps and murmurs from the gathering crowd), pastor of St. Ansgar's, age sixty-six. Both appear to have died yesterday afternoon under suspicious circumstances. An investigation is under way. No arrests have been made at this time."

A flurry of questions yields no more useful information, fueling the usual journalistic dark humor and speculation. Especially popular is the murder/suicide angle with, of course, homosexual implications. As Harlow retreats to an unmarked sedan, Span's fellow scribes start pecking on their mobile devices, now coming up with news that this priest, or whatever he is, this Hammar (suddenly known as The Hammer) may or may not have been feuding with a local Somali warlord over the church's refugee program. (It's always nice to toss in the Muslim angle, Minneapolis being home to more Somalis than almost any place outside of Mogadishu.) Now, a woman from Channel 11 says The Hammer has an alienated son back in Philly who hates his guts. Span has enough experience to take none of this seriously, but he admits that somewhere deep inside he feels a faint stirring of the old journalistic juices.

His cell again. It's Marion the Librarian telling him he's emailed him a shitload of background stuff on The Hammer, a person quite well known in religion circles, Marion says. Those are circles Span hasn't traveled in since well before his last days at Jesuit High on the north side of Chicago more than forty years ago. He has some catching up to do, he tells Marion. Marion is a reporter's dream, a kind of Radar O'Reilly of newspaper librarians. If he likes you (he likes Span), he'll send you information before you realize you need it.

The crowd is thinning out now. The TV trucks are pulling away. The CSU van will be here for hours, perhaps days, its crew sifting through every possible shred of evidence. It's after 11. Span needs to get down to the paper. He needs to start phoning and writing. Just as he's turning to go he catches a glimpse of Bender leaving the side door of the church with a tall blond woman dressed all in black, except for the orange rain jacket slung around her shoulders like a shawl. Even at this distance, Span feels he has seen this woman before, and admired her. But he can't quite place her. She bends almost in half climbing into the back seat of a patrol car as Bender holds the door and scans the thinning crowd, seeing Span straining at one of the yellow barricades. He walks toward him now.

"Coming in for confession, Lokken? Feeling guilty for all the fuckin' lies you printed about me over the years?"

"How's it going, Larry? I mean Captain Bender. How'd you get promoted to captain? Got to be a new low for the M.P.D., don't you think?"

Bender smiles without showing his teeth. "Seriously, Lokken. This tall blond fox I got in the backseat, we're going downtown for a couple hours. Gonna show her a good time. See if she likes my new office. Maybe try out my new couch."

"Who is she, anyway? Looks kinda familiar to me. She a witness? A suspect?"

"That's for you to find out, smart guy."

"Gimme a break, Larry. Ain't we pals no more, now that you're a captain?"

Bender sighs, looking down at his shoes. "Name is Lindberg. She works here. Found the bodies. Girl priest. Believe that? I never seen legs that fuckin' long. She can give me absolution anytime."

"You're a sick man, Larry."

"Face it, Lokken. You're past your prime."

"C'mon, Larry. We go way back. You gotta throw me a bone here."

"I'll tell you this," Bender says, leaning in. "It's a goddamn blood bath in there. Never seen anything like it." Then, looking

Span square in the eye, "Hey, Genius. We never had this little chat, OK? Point is, on all the official shit, spell my name right. I'm in charge here. This is my case. Capeesh?"

"How come you're so good to me, Larry?"

Bender lowers his voice to a whisper. "Look, Lokken. I'm taking this fine, young clergy person down to my office for a couple hours, show her my new leather sofa. Maybe she'll get lucky. Anyways, about two-thirty, we're gonna drop her back at her house on the island, not too far from your house. Get my drift? About two-thirty."

"Thanks, Larry. You're still a pal after all."

Fumbling for his Camels, Bender comes up empty. Then, turning his back and walking toward a squad car, he flings the empty pack into the street.

Chapter Three

Monday, 2:30 p.m.

Span's mid-afternoon drive from the paper to Hennepin Island ends on Connor Street at the address he'd scraped off the internet, an address barely eight blocks from his own house. There he waits. Bender said he'd be delivering Margaret Lindberg back here at two-thirty. Ten minutes go by. Span, sitting in his car, stares at a screen shot of her he'd snagged from the church website, while going over in his mind the brief digital plunge he'd taken into the life of Margaret Louise Lindberg.

Born Minneapolis 1982, graduated 1999 from Redondo Union High School in southern California and from UCLA in 2003. There she was, pictured in a volleyball uniform with a notation that she'd made all-conference — "all PAC-10 in her senior year." Impressive. But then a gap. Nothing. Nothing until she turned up back in Minneapolis as a pastor at St. Ansgar eleven years later, in 2014, with Facebook photos of a smiling, curly-haired daughter, Petra.

Finally, at a quarter to three, a cop car pulls up, Lindberg emerging with a two-uniform escort, Span approaching on foot from the curb.

"You Lokken?" one of the cops asks, obviously suspicious.

Span nods.

"Captain says you can ask her a question," the cop says, motioning to his partner and grabbing a house key from Lindberg. "We'll be checking the premises," he announces, the two cops going around back, leaving them alone on the porch, Lindberg and Span.

They looked at each other head on, Span knowing right away that they weren't entirely strangers. They'd rarely spoken, but had seen each other occasionally on Saturday mornings, perhaps a ritual for the both of them, at the Whole Foods on Lake Street. She, sometimes with a child, sometimes not. Always in some kind of athletic gear, looking, how can he say it? Appealing, in the way a woman jock can be appealing. Span? Not so much appealing-wise, he supposed. Seeing her now standing on her porch in black shirt and clerical collar was more than a little jarring, leaving him momentarily tongue-tied, giving her a chance to break an awkward silence.

"Still deep into Brussels sprouts?"

It's true. In the produce section they'd once had the basic Brussels sprouts conversation, the one about how the world is divided into two groups, those who love them and those who hate them. Span had gone on and on about the benefits of this particular vegetable. He was surprised she remembered.

"Didn't know you worked for the Star Journal," she says.

"Didn't know you worked for the Big Guy," he answers, pointing a thumb to the sky and trying a smile at the corner of his mouth.

"I could use a drink," she says. "Maybe two or three."

That's how it starts. With the two cops still parked out front, and with Lindberg's daughter with a sitter, Span sits in the living room admiring the way Margaret has decorated the place. Fundamentally, her row house is identical to his, with the crown molding and the historic woodwork, the hardwood floors, even the floor plan. But, unlike Span's pile of neglect, Lindberg's place is spotless and artfully spare. She has tastefully blended modern furniture, wall hangings and photos of her daughter to make the house simultaneously contemporary and cozy. One link to the past is a 1940s era Philco radio sitting on a bookshelf. It's the same one Span's family had in their kitchen when he was a kid. While he takes mental notes on the décor, Margaret Lindberg is in the kitchen poking in the freezer, emerging finally with a frosty bottle of fruit-flavored Absolut and two shot glasses.

As she pours, her cellphone, charging on a side table, vibrates, Span taking a peek at the screen. Incoming call – somebody named JAMES RINCON. Photo of a handsome Latino face. Thirtyish. Lindberg picks up the phone, glares at the image and quickly hits ignore, turning the phone on its face.

"I didn't expect you to invite me in, considering the circumstances," Span stammers, watching as she perches herself and her long legs on the edge of the sofa. "I have only about a thousand questions."

"Me, too," she says, taking off her glasses and rubbing her remarkably green eyes until they're puffy and red around the edges.

Her cellphone buzzes again. This time she leans over and answers. "Hi Cubby ... No, stay with Aunt Nori this afternoon ... just a problem at church. Talk tonight. Love you."

Her account of the day unfolds then, not in the frantic, emotional way a citizen would tell it, but in perfect sequence, like a cop would testify in court, or maybe like a girl priest might tell it. But Span wouldn't know anything about that. Nothing in his vast background as a reporter or as a human person has prepared him for Margaret Lindberg. Except for a wedding or a funeral now and then, Span hasn't darkened the door of a church in more than thirty years, the dreary religiosity of his childhood buried deep in a pile of stuff that he'd filed away as contemptuous or irrelevant. For him, this rangy, blond, pony-tailed girl in a collar hovers somewhere between absurdity and allure.

Then there's the hideous crime itself. Step by step, she spills out the details of her discovery of the bodies and her matter-of-fact description of the bloodied victims. Until today Span had barely heard of Matthias Hammar and never grasped his prominence or his status as a controversial figure. Turns out, the man was a titanic defender of the poor and powerless, according to his research. And his words, so admired by his followers, often infuriated the city's elites. All of this Lindberg confirms.

"Apparent cause of death," she tells Span, speaking of Hammar in a calm, clinical voice, "extensive loss of blood from a series of deep lacerations in the midsection compounded by punctures through both hands and feet and blunt force damage to the jaw. The perpetrators, had to be at least two of them, maybe more, went to a lot of trouble hauling down a heavy wooden cross, maybe fifteen feet high, and somehow managing to strip off the victim's clothes while holding him down and driving spikes into his hands and feet and then hoisting him back up apparently with a pulley. Never imagined a crime scene so, um, theatrical as this."

"Yeah," Span blurts. "But how did you feel about it?"

He instantly regrets the question. It's one of those insipid TV news questions meant to draw an emotional response, the kind of question that makes a real reporter want to puke. Still, Span's intention is clear. The young, eager cop-shop reporters would have all the gory details. What he needed from Lindberg was the deeper stuff.

"What I mean," he says, trying to recover, "is that I know you're trying hard to be professional about this and, perhaps as a pastor, describe the scene with a certain ... detachment. But this victim was your friend, your boss, maybe your mentor. You worked with him every day. This is different, isn't it?"

Lindberg freezes for a moment. She sets her glass on the table and stands up, her eyes moist. The veneer is peeling off. "I loved them both," she says, then turns abruptly and walks into the hallway. Span hears a door click shut. Then just a clock ticking and the distant muffle of a riverboat's horn. He sits there awkwardly for what feels like five minutes. Is the interview over? He doesn't know. Is he an intruder? Probably. He gets up. Walks into the hallway. Hears what he thinks is quiet sobbing from behind what must be a bathroom door. He stands there, not quite knowing what to do. Finally, he knocks softly. The door clicks open.

"I'm sorry," she says, trying to compose herself, tears still on her cheeks.

"I should go," Span says.

"No, please. It's just that I don't know who I'm supposed to be."

She walks back into the living room and pours herself another drink. "What's my obligation? What's my role? In my heart I can't deny that I want to get the assholes who did this." She sighs. "Am I a pastor? Yes, and I'm supposed to be concerned less with revenge, less with anger, less with justice, than with comforting the people of our parish and restoring some sense of stability for them." She takes another swallow. "Am I a mother? Yes." And she begins to cry again. "I can't imagine how I'm going to tell my eight-year-old daughter about what happened, and why it happened." She sets the glass down. "Do you have kids?"

"No."

"Span, who did this? I know Matthias made a lot of people uncomfortable, but who did this? Why did they do it?"

"That's what I'm hoping to find out," Span says.

"And what about the rest of our church staff?" she asks. "Are we targets, too? Bender doesn't think so. He thinks this is all about Matthias. He's probably right, but I've got two brothers-in-blue out there just in case," she says, peering out the front window at the patrol car sitting by the curb.

"Brothers in blue." A curious phrase for her to use, he thinks. The two of them talk a while longer. Span is surprised she isn't eager to get rid of him. He asks her more questions about Matthias Hammar. What was he like? Who were his enemies? What were his connections to the immigrant and refugee communities? What had he done recently to offend people?

He asks Lindberg about herself, too. Hadn't she spent time in California?

She's reluctant to talk about herself and her circumstance, always steering the conversation back to the victims. "We lived out there for awhile, then I came back" is pretty much all she says about the West Coast. She also skirts questions about what she's discussed with Bender, questions about evidence and police theories, although Span gets the clear impression that she knows more about the crime than she lets on.

Span even finds the right moment to ask about the whereabouts of her daughter's father. But again, Lindberg's answers are vague.

Once more her phone vibrates and Span notices the image of JAMES RINCON calling and notices, too, that Maggie quickly declines the call and shuts down her phone.

Of all the questions Span asks, the one that seems to intrigue her most is about the symbolism of Hammar's elaborate and ghastly crucifixion. "What message were these creeps trying to send?" she asks at one point.

They talk for almost two hours. Twice a cop comes to the door to ask if she's OK – a not-so-subtle intimation that Span should leave. But she dismisses them. Despite her evasiveness on some things, Span gets the impression she is relieved to have somebody to unload on, and that, for some odd reason, she trusts him. Maybe when it's your job to listen to other peoples' troubles all day long, you're grateful for a shoulder to cry on when you have troubles of your own, especially when there's no husband or boyfriend around and no mentor to lean on. He doesn't know. He just has the feeling as he gets ready to go, stumbling over how to address her ("Please just call me Maggie."), that this won't be their last conversation and that, despite the tragedy and sorrow of this day, Maggie Lindberg and Span Lokken have the makings of an odd sort of friendship. At least he hopes so. And he hopes that she hopes so, too.

Chapter Four

Monday, 6:35 p.m.

Rain falls harder as Span splashes his way down Marquette Avenue, sans umbrella, darting beneath awnings and dodging the last wave of afternoon commuters squinting for the numbers on a long line of buses inching along the curb. Now, finally, he's ducking into Buster's where the pounding rain is replaced by the din of a damp bar crowd. By the looks of them, these are Cubs fans — one plump guy in a T-shirt saying, "I can't wait another century" — up from Chicago for a rare series against the Twinkies.

Although it's nearly game time, these people seem to have sensed a rainout and settled into Buster's for the evening. Just as well. Span looks for a dark, quiet booth against the back wall. He sees no one he knows. Buster's used to be a newspaper bar. Star Journal reporters and a fleet of copy editors taking their dinner break once dominated the place at this hour. The night supervisor, Lucas Cornell, long since retired, would stroll in with his entourage holding up three fingers, and within a minute three frosty Beefeater martinis appeared before him. That was dinner.

For now, Span is hoping for a beer and a burger and more time to digest the day's unlikely string of events before he meets later with his old friend, Stephanie Levin, a downtown lawyer with an uncanny knowledge of what goes on in the upper layers of this city, and sometimes the lower layers too.

It's after 8 when Span spots Stephanie picking her way past the crowded bar. She isn't hard to notice. With her dark suit, high heels, Florida tan, black hair pulled back tight in a bun, and trademark oversized glasses, Stephanie looks nothing like a drunken Cubs fan.

She plunks down her sleek leather briefcase and slides into Span's booth. "Jonas Kron is a psychopath," she says, barely looking at Span while scanning the bar for a waitress, obviously hoping for a martini. Soon.

The first thing Span had done after leaving Margaret Lindberg late in the afternoon was ponder her answer to a question he'd asked about Hammar's enemies. Among others, she had mentioned a long-festering feud between the murdered clergyman and none other than Jonas W. Kron III, keeper of the Kron family fortune, eccentric industrialist, toast of the country club set and self-proclaimed Lord of Hennepin Island.

Span had never met the man. But he knew Stephanie's law firm was knee-deep in the business affairs of Kron Industries. And he knew Stephanie. On a news day like today, she'd be unable to – how can he say this politely? – restrain her massive and obsessive curiosity. So he called her, told her he'd heard rumors of a possible feud between Kron and the brutally murdered Hammar, and asked her to meet.

This wasn't the cruel trick it might seem to be. He's known Stephanie for thirty years and loves her dearly. And she dearly loves to, shall we say, use her type A instincts to develop these timely tidbits that he sometimes feeds her. She's not really a gossip. She's a compulsive gatherer, sorter and storer of information about everything from the trivial to the essential. Ask her to recite the names, titles and hobbies of the British royal family. She knows. Ask her about the key players on the 1994 New York Rangers Stanley Cup team. She knows. Stephanie is one of the few people in the world who can explain the Higgs boson while keeping meticulous track of the hookups of Hollywood starlets.

But her specialty is the city's upper crust – not just the old families that made fortunes in timber, flour, railroads, banks and department stores, but also the new swashbucklers in technology and advertising. Span gets the impression that Stephanie made partner at Gleason Stone Olyphant less because of her considerable legal ability than her talent as a data sponge. If there were an inside scoop on the bad blood between Jonas Kron and Matthias Hammar, Stephanie would know it, or find about it in short order. For years she and Span have traded favors, not just to bolster their careers but to enhance their friendship.

"I don't say psychopath lightly, but, by the fourth generation, the blood is running so thin it doesn't really nourish the brain, if you know what I mean. Thanks, Sweetie."

The "thanks, sweetie" is meant for the waitress who delivers a frosty glass of gin, straight up, with (in Stephanie's words) "an essence of vermouth and two olives," although Stephanie never bothers to look at the waitress, absorbed, as she is, in telling her tale.

"So, it begins somewhere around 1880," she tells Span, "when this young kid of nineteen, maybe twenty, arrives in America from Sweden. This is no Ellis Island, huddled masses kind of thing. This kid, Andreas Kron, is loaded. If he's not exactly nobility, he's close. The family is into shipbuilding, big time, in Stockholm. But his older brother has the inside track on running the business, so young Andreas takes the plunge across the pond to, you know, make his own fortune. And guess where he ends up? Where there's, like, mass quantities of Swedes, which is here. These are mostly, you know, poor farmers, carpenters, laborers, not really his class of people. But they speak the language and make for a potentially good labor pool for whatever he decides to do. After a few years he ends up buying this small rock quarry on the south end of the island. He's building barges down there and floating slabs of limestone downriver."

The island Stephanie refers to is, of course, Hennepin Island. In the 1880s it wasn't much more than an overgrown weed patch in the middle of the Mississippi River between Minneapolis and St. Paul. The island is slender, less than half mile wide and two miles long, although it was longer back then, before the Kron family took all the stone from its south end.

Nowadays, the island is just another neighborhood in Minneapolis, although it's largely an afterthought, a noirish kind of place that hasn't changed much in sixty years. More than anything, neglect has given the place a certain charm. Film crews sometimes ship in old cars and use the streets for period shots. Two structures dominate the island: the Kron headquarters with its clock tower and St. Ansgar Church. Though a mile apart, the two structures face each other as in a standoff – although guess which family donated most of the money to build the big church.

"So, it's Andreas Kron in the 1880s who gets the empire rolling in America," Stephanie continues, "but it's his son, Jonas One, who stokes the furnace. He's the one who builds the family compound — this is just before World War I — and he's the one who uses the railroads to extend the stone business coast to coast. But here's the thing: Much more than his father, he has this creepy fascination with the old country.

He was born here, but he travels to Sweden constantly and fancies himself as a kind of, you know, Old World aristocrat, even starts referring to himself as Count Jonas Kron. There are old pictures of him wearing a sash across his chest and medals. And even now, if you go into the Kron mansion, you'll see swords and suits of armor and family crests and old pictures of Jonas One with the King and other big shots, including guys in flowing gowns and those pointy bishops' hats."

"You mean miters?" Span asks.

Stephanie cracks an ironic smile. "Whatever. Christianity isn't my strong suit, but I have a good excuse, right? Like Woody Allen said, 'When your people were enjoying all those rich sauces, my people were getting raped by Cossacks.' Or something like that. Anyway, I'm told that Jonas One was absolutely obsessed with the traditions of the Swedish church, you know, the ceremonies and so on. He was a terrible snob about it. And he had this disdain for the, I don't know, simpler folk religion that the commoners were bringing to this country. And that's why he poured so much of the family fortune into building St. A's. This is after World War I, maybe in the early twenties. I've never been in that church, but I'm told it's quite ornate for a Protestant church. So, hold that thought, because it's going to be important."

Stephanie orders another drink. The bar is quieter now. The Cubs fans who were standing and shouting are now sitting and talking. The big TVs are showing mostly women's World Cup soccer from Canada.

"Now let's cut to the next Kron," she says, "which would be Jonas Two, born around 1920. Compared to his father there's not much to say. He doesn't like the spotlight. His big contribution is realizing that the stone supply is running out so he transitions the family into construction and general contracting. He moves his household out of the compound and into a big flashy place on Lake Minnetonka, where he has sailboats and hangs with the country club set, and apparently lacks all the eccentricities of the previous Krons. He dies young, in his forties, when Jonas Three, the Kron we all know and love, is just a prep school kid. That would be around 1965."

Span is fidgeting now and giving Stephanie his best deadpan. "Ah, this is absolutely fascinating, Stephanie. I'm on the edge of my seat. But seriously, there's been a little thing here called murder? When do we get to the feud between Kron and the Hammer? Why is Kron a psychopath? What does this, um, history lesson have to do with two bodies, one of them crucified?"

Stephanie adjusts her oversized glasses. "Patience is a virtue, my dear Spaniel."

Span has never liked his nickname. Nicknames were mandatory in the Chicago neighborhood of his childhood. "Spandex" came much later in life. For a short period of time in grade school he was "Spicken" and then, inevitably, "Spaniel." When he went back to his high school's fortieth reunion last summer, he was still Spaniel, the good and faithful dog.

"As a kid, Jonas Three was a lot closer to his grandfather, the Count, than to his father. After the father dies, the grandfather, who's over eighty by this time, becomes an even stronger influence in the kid's life. He's constantly filling his head with – what would you call it? – lore about the Vikings' conquests and then about knights and castles and the Crusades and the Thirty Years War and the glories of the Swedish empire back in, when? The 1600s? Anyway, there apparently was an empire that covered part of Russia, Finland and most of northern

Europe. You get the picture. But most of what the old man believed was grossly exaggerated and overly sentimental, the same kind of mystical 'folk' bullshit that Hitler spewed out about the purity and superiority of the Germanic people and the Nordic tribes."

Span, impatient, asks: "So Jonas Kron is a Nazi?"

"No, no. I'm not saying that. What I'm saying is that these fairy tales were planted in his demented little brain early in life, and maybe they went dormant for a while. But now that he's in his sixties and losing his grip on the company and maybe because he lost a ton of money in the '08 recession and maybe because he got addicted to the internet, he's reverting to this craziness.

At board meetings, for God's sake, he's talking about how the government is using vapor trails, you know, from airplanes, to spray chemicals on the American people to make them more submissive. It's a new take on the old fluoride-in-the-drinking-water thing. And he's into all these conspiracies about the U.S. government manipulating all kinds of events like nine-eleven and AIDS and autism, and how the deep state and the media are controlled by six families, all Jews of course, who don't want people to find out the truth about what's really happening, especially the pedophilia rings that the liberal elites are running. This is a relatively smart, very rich man who's, like, riding through life in a black helicopter."

Stephanie is getting revved up.

"The conspiracy that really consumes him, though, is that these powers that be, as he calls them, are using Norway and its oil money to systematically humiliate, dominate and ultimately colonize Sweden. Okay, I know this is loony tunes, and even if it were true nobody would care. These are remote, obscure countries. Who gives a shit, right? But to Kron, this is major league stuff. This is what keeps him up at night. He's living in a bubble.

Nobody to really talk to. Never married. No heir. Consumed by his job until the last few years.

"Now he's moved back into that musty old mansion on the island. Picks fights with board members. Can't keep a staff. The line between reality and conspiracy getting very thin. He loves to talk about how the six Jewish families used Norwegian oil money to bankroll the purchase of Volvo by the Chinese, you know, another humiliation for Sweden. Sweden playing the victim. He won't shut up about that. And, get this: He's convinced that our deceased friend, the Reverend Mathias Hammar, is — or rather was — some kind of agent or maybe an unwitting instrument in this ongoing conspiracy against Sweden."

Span flashes a look of disbelief. "And this is a man who runs a multibillion-dollar business?"

"Well, like I said, he's losing his grip. He's apparently able to operate on two levels. He's got a veneer that allows him to pass as almost normal, but the other part comes bubbling up more and more."

"And so The Hammer was a foreign agent? This obscure priest in Minneapolis? I don't think so."

"Well, as best as I understand it, Kron thinks that Hammar betrayed the Kron family. The family spent millions to build and maintain this big church as a showcase for Swedish culture and tradition, and, you know, all the music and ceremonies and smells and bells. And the family worked hard to get Hammar to come here from Philadelphia. And once he gets here he turns into this flaming liberal."

"That's kind of thin stuff. Not really a motive for murder, is it? I don't think so. What did Hammar say specifically? What did he do specifically that pissed off Kron so much ?"

"I don't know the details. Maybe he let the homeless into the church. Who knows? All I know is that Kron felt betrayed, and maybe felt embarrassed by all the shit he had to take from his country club buddies about all the liberal do-gooder shit that Hammar was doing."

Span's clicking on his phone now, pulling up Kron's Wikipedia page, studying a portrait of the man, seeing what he looks like.

Chapter Five

Tuesday, June 7, 7:15 a.m.

Span slept maybe three hours total last night, and now the fog in his brain matches the fog that crouches over the island on what must be, let's see, only a Tuesday morning. Max and he have come to a complete stop along the river parkway, just short of the Lake Street bridge. The pavement is damp and the sun is barely evident just above the treetops and pointy roofs across the water on the St. Paul side. The fog seems to muffle the hum of traffic on the bridge overhead. Looking up, neither dog nor man can quite see the shapes of the cars on the bridge, only the low beams of their headlights.

Fewer than twenty-four hours have passed since the grisly discovery at St. Ansgar. The Star Journal splashed the story all over page one this morning. Span's quickie profile on the gruesomely crucified Mathias Hammar played below the fold and jumped to the top of 8A. It was nice stuff, but it didn't really move the story forward. Without a stronger link, Span couldn't, for example, mention the feud between Hammar and the creepy industrialist Jonas Kron. That's a path he'd like to explore starting today. Indeed, after his abbreviated walk with Max, there's a long list of phone calls for Span to tackle on what's surely the most sensational crime case to hit this city in decades. Already, old-timers are comparing it to the Thompson murder-for-hire in 1963 and the Piper and Kronholm kidnappings in the early seventies, all cases involving prominent families. Prominence might figure in this one, too, if Kron is implicated, which seems more than likely.

Already the crime, routinely called the "church murders" has gone viral and coastal. All the networks have stories on their morning news shows. The blogosphere is churning with outrageous theories that add extra juice to the spectacle. The New York Times has budgeted a piece for tomorrow, meaning that a Times reporter has already parachuted into town to join the local stringer. Both will probably be present at Bender's 10 o'clock briefing at City Hall, a fact that reminds Span to get Max locked in and get himself in gear.

Even at this early juncture, Span knows that he has two, maybe three advantages over the competition: a special pipeline to Maggie Lindberg who has supplied him with, among other things, insights into the complex character of her murdered mentor; and a pipeline to Stephanie Levin, who can get him details of the festering Kron-Hammar dispute.

A third possible flow of exclusive information runs from the newly captainized Larry Bender. Bender has been curiously chummy, especially after all they've been through. Span still cringes at the memory of Bender throwing a chair at him after a critical story he'd written maybe ten years ago, and another time grabbing him by the neck, his cigarette/Juicy Fruit breath hot against Span's face, threatening to put out a contract on him unless he stopped pursuing a story about a corrupt thumper on his detective squad. Why Bender is suddenly Span's best pal is a deep mystery that Span doesn't quite trust. Maybe it's finally occurring to Bender that upward mobility in the department is easier with a "friend" at the paper, even if the friend is Span Lokken.

The 10 o'clock briefing turns out to be a zoo. The usually ample City Hall media room is crammed with cameras and commotion. Bender is in his element, delivering a hard-boiled cop performance without giving away too many specifics. The lead is that the police are treating this as a possible religious hate crime given the gory details of Hammar's death. As for the suspects, there are two of them. They are white, Latino or Middle Eastern, one medium-build, the other stocky with a dark beard, identities unknown. They fled the scene in a white van. The vehicle has not been found. There's a possibility — at one point Bender says a *probability* — that the suspects have fled the country. That point touches off all kinds of intriguing speculation. The FBI hasn't formally joined the case but may do so as the case unfolds.

Span lingers as the room clears out, a young woman officer he's never seen before approaching him saying, "He'd like to see you in his office."

It's a two-block walk to the police department's once-elegant building. Bender's new digs are on the third floor, a corner office with two big windows. Not much of a view, but what do you expect at police headquarters? He's got a battered leather sofa and a conference table with gashes in it. The only decoration is a bulletin board with maps and stickpins that hangs behind his littered desk. By contrast, Bender is sharply tailored in yet another new suit. He meets Span at the door, then sloughs off his suit jacket and throws it on the sofa.

"You see the legs on that Lindberg babe?" he says, grabbing his crotch. "Lokken, I think I'm in love."

"So, making captain has already made you a classier guy, I can see that."

They sit as the same young female uniform brings in bad coffee in paper cups. Then she wheels in an aging TV monitor. What Bender tells Span over the next half hour and what he shows him from surveillance footage near the church, Span will combine with bits and pieces soon to be gathered from his friend Chuck at the Coroner's office, from more conversations with Father Maggie, from other interviews with members of the church staff and a few talkative parishioners, and from the official stuff that's been released by those whom the media generally refer to as *the authorities*.

He will also sift through the flood of "alternative facts" spilling out over social media. He will reject, for example, the "eye-witness account" that an Angel of Death had executed the pastor and janitor as punishment for their homosexual relationship. Also to be cast aside is the government coverup of a mysterious helicopter landing on the church parking lot shortly before the murders. (In another version, a submarine in the Mississippi River had dispatched a team of black-clad frogmen seen running toward the church.) Being a reporter nowadays is harder than it used to be.

Still, by putting all the credible stuff together, a picture is beginning to emerge:

At 12:02 last Sunday afternoon a white van pulls into a parking lot of the Wells Fargo branch across the street from the church. Images from the bank's surveillance cameras aren't all that clear, but the van appears to be a Chevy Express Cargo model, vintage 2005, with Midway Plumbing & Heating in red and black letters. Turns out, there is no Midway Plumbing & Heating and the phone number and website painted on the van are bogus. The van's license plates appear to have been stolen off a Toyota pickup in south Minneapolis earlier that morning. The van itself had been reported stolen after it had vanished from a driveway in Hudson, Wisconsin, on the previous Tuesday.

It's unclear from the footage how many people are inside the van. At 1:24, the camera shows the van departing the bank parking lot, turning west briefly on Franklin, then taking a right into the parish house portico across the street. Only a portion of the van is visible at this point. But at 1:36 two figures dressed in gray coveralls and baseball caps and wearing dark glasses appear at the back of the van. They unload a large trolley carrying what appear to be a sizable ladder and several cases of tools. It's a bright sunny day and shadows from the portico obscure many details of their faces, but the two figures appear to be men, probably of European, Latino or Middle Eastern origin, one of them perhaps, the stockier one, with a dark beard. At 1:45 they enter the double doors, which puts them in a hallway just outside the church offices.

The building is quiet and all but deserted. A service attended by more than three hundred people had concluded about 12:15. Fifty or so worshippers had stayed for a coffee hour, but a warm, sunny afternoon beckoned and the crowd had thinned out rather quickly with only a handful remaining by 1 o'clock. Father Maggie had left with her daughter Petra shortly after 1 in order to stop briefly at home, then join friends for lunch in Linden Hills before spending the afternoon on the beach at Lake Harriet. She had a solid alibi as far as the cops were concerned.

By the time the suspects enter the church, only two occupants are thought to have remained: Hammar and the sexton, Henrik Piedela. The two intruders steer their trolley right down the corridor, through the vestibule and into the church itself where they encounter Henrik with his broom, tidying up around the large baptismal font, which stands at the head of the center aisle.

From Henrik's point of view, the visitors' sudden appearance is cause for confusion. Has he ordered workmen today? No. Maybe these guys are lost. Maybe he can help. But there's no time for words. One of the men places the barrel of a nine millimeter handgun to a spot just behind Henrik's left ear, and pulls the trigger. Twice. Henrik has no time, really, to reflect on his life as a lonely Estonian immigrant who loved a sociable drink now and then but kept pretty much to himself in his apartment in the church undercroft where he delighted in dreaming up jokes for Father Maggie and the rest of the staff. The bullets pierce Henrik's skull and pass through his brain before emerging from the other side of his head and lodging in the wood of a nearby pew. By the time he hits the floor Henrik's life is over, his blood beginning to pool on the highly polished concrete floor at the base of the font.

The bangs echo through the cavernous church, drawing alarm from The Reverend Matthias Hammar, who is in the sacristy, a room just to the side of the altar, up near the front of the church. Apparently he's in the process of unlocking a storage closet in which he intends to store his red vestments, a stole and a chasuble, garments that wouldn't be needed again for several months. He has them in his arms when he leaves the sacristy to investigate the noise, perhaps dropping them in a heap at the side of the altar when he encounters two men, one armed with an automatic pistol and the other pushing a cart with bloody wheels up the center aisle. The conversation that might have ensued cannot be known. Neither can it be known if Hammar recognizes the intruders. What is known is that over the next half hour, Hammar endures the worst and the last moments of his life.

The exact order of events is unclear. But at some point early in the process Hammar's face comes into repeated contact with the fat end of a baseball bat. His nose, jaw and left cheekbone are shattered. Nine of his teeth are knocked out. A large ladder is erected and the wires holding up a highly polished, sixteen-foot wooden cross are severed. The cross, weighing several hundred pounds, crashes down eight feet onto the stone altar, then skids flat onto the floor of the chancel.

Patterns of blood on the floor indicate that at some point Hammar is kneeling near the fallen cross, his clothing having been removed. Black socks and shoes, gray cotton slacks, a long-sleeved black shirt with clerical collar, a white t-shirt and boxer shorts, all spattered or smeared with blood, are scattered nearby. A naked but still alive Hammar is then placed on the cross. How this is managed isn't known. Hammar is six feet tall and a flabby 210 pounds. His skin, except for the streams of blood flowing over his chest, is exceptionally pale, his reddish-gray hair closely cropped. His face, with its once prominent nose and jutting jaw, is, by this time, goo.

Six-inch, zinc-coated steel spikes are driven through his hands, attaching them to the arms of the cross. His feet are fastened with two identical spikes. A rope is looped around his shoulders for extra support. A large hook is embedded in the top of the cross. A line launcher shoots another rope over the top of an overhead beam, and a pulley is employed to hoist and tie the cross and its battered occupant to almost its original position.

Hammar's bladder and bowels empty themselves onto the altar, almost on the exact spot where hundreds of times he has transformed ordinary wafers and wine into the extraordinary spiritual gifts of his Lord's body and blood. The ladder is adjusted and one intruder climbs up to insert the blade of a large sword into Hammar's left side, just below the rib cage. It's not known whether the pastor cries out. The blade severs the mesenteric artery and pokes a gaping hole in the aorta. Blood spurts from the wound in great gushes, and with it flow the last moments of Hammar's life.

It cannot be known how the pastor greeted his attackers. Did he curse them? Did he forgive them? Did he know why he was being murdered? Did it occur to him that their ritual slaying of him seemed to mock the killing of his blessed Redeemer? Did he have time to reflect on the accomplishments of his life? To regret, perhaps, some of the bold stands he had taken? Did he ponder the wrath he had drawn from so many people, or the admiration he had gleaned from many others? Did he regret the loose ends he'd left behind? Did he pray for himself? For his parish? For his murderers? Did he think about his beloved and long-dead wife? Or about their estranged son? Did he know the fate of his friend Henrik? Was he afraid? Did he wonder if the promise of heaven was just an invention of wishful thinkers?

At 2:39, cameras show that the doors to the church portico open from the inside and two dark-haired men emerge, wearing t-shirts, jeans and gloves, carrying two large black plastic bags, and pushing the loaded cart. One has extensive tattoos on his left arm. They load the stuff, jump into the van and drive immediately off camera. Since the van doesn't reappear on screen, it has apparently turned right onto westbound Franklin Avenue, destination unknown.

Chapter Six

Tuesday, 12:40 p.m.

As Span heads to the elevator opposite the homicide bureau his cell vibrates — again. All through Bender's detailed recitation, Span's phone had been tickling his pocket. This latest caller's prefix indicates somebody at the Star Journal, although Span doesn't recognize the number. This is the caller's third try in the last ten minutes. Somebody wants him bad.

"Span Lokken," he answers, hearing his voice echo in the spare corridor.

"Samantha Iverson, circulation." He recognizes the name although they've never met. She's the circulation manager, a top executive at the paper.

"I'm pretty sure my subscription is paid up," he says.

She ignores the crack. "Sorry to bug you. I know you're busy, but one of my carriers just heard something on the news and he's driving me bonkers wanting to talk to you. Something about a white van."

A half hour later, Span has driven back to the island, picked up Margaret Lindberg at her house, crossed the Lake Street bridge and now hurries south on River Road toward the Minnehaha Park light rail station. Two blocks from the station, in a heavily wooded ravine just off 51st Street, that's the spot where the newspaper carrier said he saw the van. Saw it twice. Saw it Monday morning while delivering his papers. Saw it again this morning. Odd, he told Span over the phone. He notices a lot of parked cars early in the morning. Comes to know where they all belong. But a commercial vehicle off the street in a clump of trees? Doesn't fit. Then there was this morning's announcement on TV. Cops are looking for a white van from a plumbing company. "I think I seen it," the man, name of Cedric, told Span on the phone.

"You report it to the police?" Span wondered.

"Hell no. They all the time hassling me when I'm on my route. My contract is with the Star Journal, man. I'm calling you."

The van is right where Cedric said it was. Chevy Express Cargo model with red and black markings from Midway Plumbing & Heating.

"Don't get too close. Don't touch anything," Maggie tells Span as they tramp through a small, damp patch of woods, coming in the back way, getting to within maybe ten feet of the van.

Span fishes for his cellphone. "You calling Bender?" Maggie wonders. "We should call him."

"Calling photo," says Span."First things first."

Keeping a ten-foot distance from the van, as Maggie insists, is torture for Span. Every bone in his body wants to get up close and personal to this vehicle, wants to inspect it, describe it, discover the bits and pieces that might lead to unraveling this trail of tragedy. Maggie's instincts are the opposite. Patience. Wait for the cops. Wait for the lab crew. Secure the evidence.

Don't violate a space that might be important in proving a court case against two barbarians and those who may have hired them.

"Don't you dare walk up there," she tells him, pulling him by the arm. "Don't screw this up."

Now he's again on his phone talking this time with Her Majesty. Carla is delighted that Span has found the van. But it's not enough for her.

"Yes, Carla, there's a religious dimension to the story, but..."

The young metro editor is obsessed with the gory crucifixion of Matthias Hammar. She wants Span to pursue "the ritual nature of this crime." Span argues that it's more important first to track down the killers. There will be plenty of time later to analyze their motives, which may indeed include religious hatred. Span instructs her as if she's a child.

"First things first," he tells her. "This is a newspaper, not a magazine."

There's an awkward pause. Carla tells him she deeply resents his condescending manner. He's not the boss, she tells him. She's the boss, and Span will write what she tells him to write.

"Don't patronize me, Lokken," she snaps. "I know it disappoints you, but I'm the editor and you're not."

Span disconnects, holding the phone at arm's length, staring at it for a long moment – then staring at Maggie. "I thought that went extremely well," he says, failing to hide a slight smile. Maggie smiles, too, then, over Span's shoulder, watches a car pulling to the curb and a man with camera gear jumping out and tramping through the woods toward them. Immediately, she rings Bender.

"Found the van," she reports, reciting the location. Not ten seconds later she and Span hear sirens. Within three minutes, two squads from the Third Precinct pull to a stop on 51st Street. Within fifteen minutes the patch of woods has been sealed off and forensic crews are combing the van and its environs. To his irritation, Span fails to get closer to the action; he actually gets pushed farther away.

The cops, of course, want to know who found the van and how. A sergeant, name of Haskell, is all over Span and Maggie with questions. "I got a tip," is pretty much all Span tells him. "Anonymous."

"We decided to check it out," Maggie explains.

"We?" Haskell says. "You two a team or something?"

"Maybe," says Maggie.

Amid the whirl of cop conversations, Maggie twice overhears snippets: "What about the airport?" And "snafu at the airport." And "wild blue yonder." When she asks Haskell about the airport chatter, she gets only a shrug.

Catching up with Span at the edge of the gathering crowd, she says, "Maybe Bender is right. Maybe these two creeps did flee the country. They dump the van here, hike two blocks to the rail station, hop the Blue Line to the airport. Poof! They're gone."

"So we go to the transit cops and get video of the station platform about three on Sunday afternoon," Span says. "We see if two dark-haired creeps get on a southbound train."

But Maggie is already jumping ahead. She's remembering a parishioner, Sylvia somebody. Sylvia is a TSA supervisor at MSP. Sylvia Kraskie. It's a long shot, but maybe Sylvia knows something. Maybe she's worth a try. She fiddles with her phone, checking the parish directory. Then she punches in Sylvia Kraskie's work number. "It's Margaret Lindberg at St. Ansgar's. Please give me a call," she says, turning toward Span.

"Something's not right about this whole thing," she says. "If these guys did flee the country, then why does Bender have the whole force out turning over every garbage can looking for them?"

She and Span walk toward the car, Maggie trying to scrape mud off her fancy black sneakers. "I hate that we couldn't get a look inside the van," Span says. "I know you're right about preserving evidence. But it's frustrating. We're the ones who found the van. We should get a break on the contents. We've got to lean on Bender on this."

"Yeah," says Maggie. "He owes us something, whether he'll admit it or not."

They're back in Span's ancient Audi now, rattling north down River Road, back toward the island, toward St. A's. Maggie has a meeting with the bishop and the vestry. Lots of crying and praying to do. Funerals to plan. Arrangements to make, even in the grip of tragedy and fear, even when your heart is breaking.

Span dictates into his phone a short story for the website to go along with the photo of the newly-discovered van. He makes clear that it was the Star Journal that discovered the van and that the van's contents could constitute a "break in the case." But he's careful to butter up Bender, too, mentioning that Bender is in charge of the investigation, dropping a quote into the story from this morning's briefing, Bender saying that the department is "exhausting every resource to apprehend these two gentlemen."

As Span pulls up in front of the church, Maggie's phone chirps. "Margaret Lindberg."

"Pastor Lindberg, this is Sylvia Kraskie at TSA calling you back."

Chapter Seven

Tuesday, 8:30 p.m.

Turns out that Sylvia Kraskie doesn't have much to say. Quickly and nervously she turns the conversation toward sympathy and grief for the parish and for all those who loved and admired Matthias Hammar. But no, she couldn't say anything about the two suspects who must have cleared a TSA checkpoint at the airport on Sunday afternoon heading probably for an overseas destination.

Had the police inquired?

Sylvia pauses. "They have," she says. "But I don't have any first-hand knowledge."

With Maggie's long shot fizzling out, she goes off to her staff meeting in the church. It is an emotional experience that leaves her drained and feeling overburdened, not only with grief and anger but with the sad details of arranging a funeral mass for Matthias that was sure to draw wide attention.

Then there is the anxiety of explaining the tragedy to Petra. Her school and teachers had been helpful. But to tell an eight-year-old how sick, violent and horrific life can be, well, Maggie does the best she can before tucking into bed the most important, the most loved person of her life. Dealing with a call from James is tough, too. She thinks of him as her former husband. He's out of sight, out of mind, and out of her life most of the time. But not entirely out of her heart. They've never gotten around to divorce, although it seems inevitable. And it would probably be best for all concerned.

"I'm coming out," he announces. "On my way to LAX."

"Oh, great," Maggie says to herself. "Just what I need."

"Please don't come," she tells him. "Not now."

All of these events are swimming in Maggie's mind when her phone chirps. She doesn't recognize the number. The voice is a woman's and a familiar one from earlier in the day. Sylvia Kraskie's voice.

"This isn't me," the voice says. "I'm not making this call. I'm not calling from a number anybody knows. You deserve to know what I'm going to tell you. The police came by yesterday to inquire about two suspects. They had descriptions: Two men traveling together cleared the south TSA checkpoint in Terminal 1 just before 5 o'clock on Sunday afternoon, showing U.S. passports and economy tickets on a Lufthansa flight to Frankfurt. Names: Duane Daniel Hajinlian (she spells it), born 1982, Milwaukee, five-foot-eight, two hundred and thirty-five pounds, black/brown (with a beard), and Richard Anthony Reznik (she spells it), born 1983, Ferris, Minnesota, six-foot, one-sixty, black/brown. Both had criminal records. Both did time, but neither is on parole or probation at the moment. No outstanding warrants."

"Do we know what happened at the other end?" Maggie asks.

"Funny thing. We checked with the airline, right? These passengers never checked in at the gate, never made the flight. Looks like there was an incident at one of the bars on the international concourse. These guys might have been involved."

"Which bar?"

"Coast to Coast, B Concourse."

"What happened to these guys?"

"Good question. It's more than embarrassing. We don't know. Airport police don't know. They thought these guys were just a couple of drunks. Kicked them out of the building. Last time observed, they were standing outside by the curb on the baggage claim level."

"You're kidding."

"No. Look, this isn't me talking. We never had this conversation. This is privileged, OK? I'm confessing this to you."

"And the cops know who these guys are and that they still might be in the city?"

"I'm not saying any more."

"Did they check any luggage? Did their bags go to Germany?"

Silence on the line. Maggie waits.

"I heard that they had checked bags, but I don't know what happened at the other end."

"Let me understand," Maggie says. "So the Minneapolis police think these guys are still in the city and that their bags went to Frankfurt."

"Flight left on time at 8 sharp. They never got on. I'm not sure about the bags. All I know is that we don't have them."

Chapter Eight

Tuesday, 8:45 p.m.

Span is of the age that, after an exhausting day and after letting Max out to do his nightly business, all he wants to do is slump before the TV with a glass of red wine, tune in an old black-and-white movie, and slip into a coma. He's well on his way to unconsciousness when his cell vibrates and Maggie's number flashes into foggy view. Any other number he'd ignore, but he has to admit that he's not the hardboiled newsman he tries to portray when it comes to Maggie. For her, he's a pushover. And not mainly because of her green, green eyes or short blond ponytail or her uncommonly long strides. There's an X factor to Maggie Lindberg that Span can't quite identify. There's an improbable tug between the two of them, at least from Span's side of things.

"This better be good," he says, trying to sound as grumpy as possible.

"We gotta go to the airport. Now."

"What time is it?"

"Quarter to 9."

Ten minutes later they're in Maggie's old blue Volvo, Span tapping on his phone trying to find the two cheapest airline tickets available, settling on two Delta one-ways to Las Vegas departing at 10:45.

"Maybe we should really go," he says.

"I'd lose all our money," she quips. "Clergy and blackjack, um, don't add up to twenty-one."

The two e-tickets allow them to pass through the south TSA checkpoint in Terminal One. This being a Tuesday night, foot traffic is fairly light. Most travelers are getting off flights and heading home, skipping a drink at the bar.

The Coast to Coast cocktail lounge is halfway down Concourse B. It's a sleek kind of place, trying hard to look like early '60s International Style. Lots of chrome, mirrors and faux black leather. Lots of indirect lighting. Miles Davis on the speakers.

"Looking for Travis," Maggie tells one of the waitresses. She cocks her head to the right, indicating that Travis is the young black guy in the red vest at the far end of the almost empty bar. Maggie and Span grab a couple of seats. "Travis?" she says as he approaches. "I'm Margaret. We talked on the phone. This is Span Lokken from the Star Journal."

Handshakes are performed and drinks are ordered and delivered. Yes, Travis was working Sunday afternoon when the commotion took place. Yes, he remembers the two dudes who started the ruckus. How could he forget?

"Look at this," he says, showing them his bandaged left wrist. A deep cut from broken glass, he explains.

Turns out Travis is working his way through the U. Drama major, he says. Taken him five years so far, but still coming up short. He remembers these guys coming in late Sunday afternoon, after 5.

"They start throwing down Maker's on the rocks. One of them, the skinny one, clean-shaven, is mixing the drinks with some kind of prescription medication. Not being very discreet about it either. I lose track of how many drinks I'm pouring for them. One guy, the skinny one, says they're drinking because the fat one is afraid of flying. I do remember asking what time was their flight, but, by this time, they don't seem to know or care."

Travis remembers them getting louder and more aggressive in commentating on some NASCAR race they're showing on TV. And other customers, he says, start complaining about their volume and their profanity.

"At one point one of them starts making loud comments about a woman who comes in and sits at the bar, you know, like 'Whoop, whoop! Nice rack!' and 'I got a present for you over here, baby,' shit like that. And that's about when the woman's boyfriend shows up, and there's a shoving match and some drinks are spilling onto the floor and some glasses are breaking."

Travis shows his bandaged wrist again. "So, by this time my manager, he's seen enough and calls the cops. Two airport cops show up and the two guys get escorted out of the bar."

"And so the next night," Maggie interrupts, "that would be Monday, the city cops show up with some pictures for you and your manager to look at. And that's when you I.D. these two geniuses as (she looks down at her notebook) Richard R-e-z-n-i-k and Duane H-a-j-i-n-l-i-a-n, Reznik the skinny, loud one and Hajinlian the fat one with the beard who's afraid to fly."

Travis, looking surprised and flashing a smile, gives Maggie a look. "How did you know?" he says.

Maggie smiles back. "So, did you ever find out what happened to these guys on Sunday, you know, after the airport cops took them out of the bar, here?"

"Yeah, my manager, he went along with the cops. They took

them down to the baggage level and led them out the door. They didn't arrest them. They just basically kicked them out of the terminal."

"Do you remember if these guys had any luggage with them?"

"Didn't see any."

Maggie and Span are walking back down the concourse now, Span pulling Maggie over into an empty departure lounge the first chance he gets. They sit. Span stares at her, smiling.

"I know you people deal in miracles," he says. "But how the hell did you get those names? And how did you know they got drunk and never made their flight and got kicked out of the airport, for God's sake? This is getting a little creepy!"

Maggie laughs out loud. "Nothing creepy about it."

"But how did you know?"

"Let's just say I hear things."

"Bender tell you?"

"No. He's gone cryptic on me. I don't think he trusts me, probably since I've been hanging around with you."

Span scratches his head. "And so Bender has known for a whole day the names of these two bozos and that they never left the country? So why doesn't he tell us? Why does he want to mislead the public on this?"

"Two reasons, maybe. One is that he wants the bad guys to relax," Maggie says. "Thinks maybe they'll show themselves if they think the police aren't looking for them. Two, he's embarrassed."

"Embarrassed?"

"Yeah. These guys mess up. They don't get away. And probably they're still here. But the cops still can't find them. Makes the cops look like morons."

"What I'm thinking now," Span says, "is that you and I

should be flying over to Frankfurt tonight to look in those bags. But I'm going to have enough trouble with my expense account explaining our tickets to Vegas."

Chapter Nine

Wednesday, June 8, 9:05 a.m.

Span's desk is a tiny cubicle in a sea of cubicles on the Star Journal's eleventh floor. That's the floor that houses what's still called the city room, although today's version holds none of the rumpled charm of days past. Long gone is the clatter of typewriters, the rhythmic ticking of teletype machines, the boisterous banter among white men in wrinkled white shirts with loosened neckties. Gone, too, is the blue cloud of tobacco smoke that hung over momentous arguments about which story should lead the bulldog edition.

Today's city room is antiseptic by comparison, eerily quiet, diverse by gender and race, orderly and mannerly by disposition. The relentless pressure of putting out a daily newspaper has, if anything, intensified, what with the constant need to feed the twenty-four-hour news cycle via tweeting and updating the website. But today's stress rarely breaks out into tantrums of fist-pounding and name-calling. It is, instead, closely held, internalized, accepted as a hazard of the trade, showing up mainly in the astonishingly high consumption of caffeine and the early onset of outrageous blood pressure readings.

The walk from the elevators across the long expanse of the city room to Span's desk near the far end takes him past a stretch of windows that line the east and west sides of the 1960s-era building and past the curved metro desk with its wall of flat-screen monitors where the diminutive Carla, Her Majesty, holds tightly onto her journalistic turf. Already the newest crop of millennials – ear pieces attached to their heads – are tapping soberly and diligently on their keyboards.

The place looks extra corporate and tidy this morning, the much unloved "Order Patrol" having just made its monthly sweep, capturing all the excess paper, plastic cups, pizza boxes and other debris that tends to accumulate in a news operation. That's why the plain white envelope perched on Span's keyboard next to his uncommonly neat desk gets immediate attention. "Span" is hand-written on the outside. Inside, there's a short note on a scrap of paper:

Meet me on the Stone Arch Bridge at 11:30.

That's it. Not signed. Not dated. No clue as to who wrote it or why. Maybe it has nothing to do with the church murders, but Span doubts it. Still, he has a story to knock out, so he tries to push the note out of his mind as he plunks down into his chair to recount the evidence to this point.

Yesterday afternoon and again last night, Span led the paper in adding fresh details to the fast-moving story. It had been a good day for the Star Journal, and a good day for Span Lokken. His younger colleagues are eating his dust.

Thanks to Maggie, he had found the getaway van near a light rail station only three stops from the airport. Then, thanks to Maggie again, he'd come up with the actual names of suspects Reznik and Hajinlian and broken the news that these bozos missed their flight to Europe after instigating a disturbance in an airport bar. Span's late-night report lit up the website in time to crack the end of the 10 o'clock newscasts, forcing all the stations to credit the reporting of the Star Journal. The AP also picked up the item and spread it nationwide. Span's late disclosure sent the news desk into a frenzy, forcing a complete makeover of page one for the metro final.

In recounting all this, Span had been careful not to step too harshly on the toes of the police. He quoted Bender extensively. The police, while not entirely happy about Span's squashing of their narrative (that the suspects had probably fled the country), were thankful that Span's reporting didn't make them look like total idiots.

Span also pondered the bad guys' plot, coming to almost admire it — that is, up to the point of getting drunk and missing their flight. It takes eight hours to fly from Minneapolis to Frankfurt. Reznik and Hajinlian would have landed and cleared customs long before the bodies were discovered at the church and long before their names would have hit the worldwide criminal alert system. Real pros would have stayed sober while slipping quietly onto a new continent while obtaining new identities and, probably, a nice chunk of change. Reznik and Hajinlian are clearly not pros.

Or are they? This was a well-timed, intricate operation. They went to a lot of trouble to steal the van, get a phony paint job on it, crucify Hammar, and get to the airport. This murder required planning, skill and execution. Something's not right about this. And what's the motive?

Glancing at his watch, Span begins to quickly type out a summary of the crime's details known so far, starting with the van. Stolen a week ago Tuesday from an exurban driveway just across the Wisconsin line. Nine similar vans seen on traffic cameras crossing the freeway bridge over the St. Croix River into Minnesota over the next three hours. Van's paint job (the bogus plumbing company) performed the following Friday by a moonlighter working regularly at a paint shop in Columbia Heights, but doing this job freelance, in his garage, for three thousand cash, untraceable bills, paid by a young, plump, brown-haired woman, anonymous, wearing a gray U of M hoody, claiming to be a graduate student. No fingerprints on the bills. Day of the crime, Minnesota license plates lifted from a car parked within five miles of the crime scene and fastened to the van. Discarded Wisconsin plates not recovered. Abandoned van discovered yesterday, 43 hours after the crime, in a wooded ravine near a light-rail station two miles from the airport. Loaded with fingerprints matching those of the suspects.

Also in the van were plastic trash bags containing blood spattered coveralls, caps, gloves, shoes and other equipment, including rope, hammers, spikes, goggles, a ladder and a cart. But no weapons. No sword. No nine-millimeter pistol. Those have vanished into thin air. At least so far.

Span stops typing and stares into space. One puzzle is the relatively scarce DNA evidence at the crime scene. Hardly a drop of sweat or a gob of spit detected, or a discarded cigarette butt or drink cup or beer bottle found. Just a few hairs — pubic hairs, oddly enough — with no immediate DNA match. It may take weeks for Lorette Dolittle, the MPD's queen of forensics, to sort it all out. "Never seen anything like it," she told Span, off the record.

Actually, the harvest was understandably complex. Less than two hours before the gruesome crime, hundreds of worshipers had occupied the space. In the van, too, there were DNA traces matching the Wisconsin owner and his family and friends, but only a few marks from the suspects. The discovery of protective clothing in the van, together with the bloody tools of murder, explains some of the problem and adds to police confusion over whether these were sophisticated or sloppy killers, professionals or amateurs. Given that the police have ID'd Reznik and Hajinlian, DNA evidence may not be vital. But it's good backup for the DA to have.

At this point it's not the *who* that's so mystifying. It's the *why* and the *whereabouts* that drives the story. And the notion that, more and more, this is looking like murder-for-hire by somebody with a big grudge against Hammar.

The cops and the district attorney have been silent on motive. But social media have filled the void with speculation. An obvious religious hate crime? Muslims involved? Payback for a child molestation by Hammar? A homosexual thing? Some kind of right-wing nativist group upset with Hammar's liberal politics? Hammar's estranged son?

There has been no mention by the authorities or the media of Hammar's feud with Jonas Kron. That's fine with Span. Kron is high on Span's list.

The meaningful stuff that Span knows has come largely from "background" and "off the record" conversations with Bender as well as interviews with the forensics expert, the airport bartender, Stephanie Levin, Chuck Bennett at the coroner's office, members of the congregation and others. Off the record means Span can't use it unless verified by two other sources. Background means he can attribute the information to "unnamed sources close to the investigation."

Then there's Maggie. She has been an obvious gold mine. She and Span have talked every day. For some reason she seems to have selected Span as a sort of partner. She almost assumes that they're working together on this. He's puzzled about her reasons, but he's not complaining. He hopes she doesn't see him as a father figure, or detect his fading career. But as he starts to write today's lede, he can't help but feel that Maggie Lindberg is writing the story with him.

Span stops typing to jot down a few key questions on his

note pad: "What's in luggage? German cops? FBI getting into case? Motive against Hammar? Who are Rez and Hajin? Background? Why theatrical murder? Talk to Kron. Kron might be key."

Span checks his watch. 11:10. He looks again at the note on his desk. *Meet me on the Stone Arch Bridge at 11:30*. Maybe he should take a short walk, maybe grab a bite of lunch.

Chapter Ten

Wednesday, 11:30 a.m.

The Stone Arch Bridge was built in 1883 by the railroad tycoon James J. Hill to carry his fleet of transcontinental passenger trains over the Mississippi River and into the city's busiest station. Today, the historic bridge is one of downtown's most popular gathering spots. Lunchtime strollers pause to gaze over St. Anthony Falls and the downtown skyline just beyond. Span grabs a salami sandwich and a can of soda across the street from the paper. By the time he gets to the center of the bridge, the sandwich is half gone.

He's leaning against the railing looking down at the churning water when someone sidles up next to him, looking down at the river, saying nothing. Ten seconds go by, maybe twenty. Still nothing. Span has known Chuck Bennett since his early days on the paper in the 1980s. Back then, before he was deployed to New York, Chuck and Span used to chase little white balls around green hillsides and then join up with other frustrated duffers in the clubhouses of various public golf courses across Minneapolis and St. Paul for cold cans of Grain Belt, Rolling Rock and other popular brews. Those boisterous sessions sometimes spilled into neighborhood bars and lasted longer than the eighteen holes they'd just completed.

Chuck was fresh out of med school in those days and pulling graveyard shifts at the coroner's office where, over the decades, he developed a stellar reputation for knowing his way around a murdered corpse. He also had a fondness for opera, baseball and the newspaper crowd, taking refuge in the irreverence and snarky commentary so prevalent among scribes. That Chuck was openly, although not overtly, gay only added to his status among a group that liked to celebrate its liberal leanings.

Chuck exhales, long and loud. "I've done a bad thing." His voice is barely audible above the crashing of the falls.

"What?"

"I almost told you yesterday on the phone, but I didn't. I've done an unethical thing. I'm not proud of myself."

"What did you do, Chuck?"

"We've known each other for a long time, Span. I figured I'd rather tell you than anyone else, but I have to tell somebody. It's probably going to cost me my job, maybe my career. I'm not ready to retire. I'm ashamed about this."

As a reporter, Span has learned that when somebody gets to this point, it's best to shut up. So he just keeps gazing at the water below, knowing that Chuck is hurting, and, because they're good friends, he's kind of hurting, too. But — and Span is embarrassed to admit this — he's also excited because he's thinking that his story is about to get better.

"I tampered with evidence."

"You what?"

"Well, I didn't exactly tamper with it. I just didn't include it. I left it off my report. My intentions might have been good. But it's been eating at me all week."

Silence.

"So, I've decided to tell you."

More silence.

"There was semen in Matthias Hammar's mouth."

"What?"

"You heard me."

Chuck hands Span a small package, explaining that it's a slide containing a sample harvested from Hammar's saliva suitable for DNA testing. Span slips the package into his pocket while trying to process this information as deliberately as he can, standing there on the bridge, peering down into the churning water.

So, one possibility occurring to Span: that moments before this horrific murder Hammar was having a sexual adventure with the janitor? He doubts that. Not immediately after mass, not during the coffee hour when there were dozens of people around. Or was he doing one of the parishioners in a quiet room off to the side? He's trying to picture a man with pants unzipped and Hammar in his clerical garb, down on his knees, sucking away. No way. Hard to believe. Or maybe this was part of the murderous assault on this man, part of his humiliation, part of his mutilation, part of his gruesome crucifixion, part of the horrific bit of theater performed on him, a performance that was sicker and more hateful than anyone had so far imagined.

"This wasn't from Henrik Piedela," Chuck interrupts, naming the murdered janitor. "Nothing on his body or on Hammar's body indicated sexual activity at the time of death, or just before."

Two questions, then, are tugging at Span's brain. Whose semen is it? And why did Chuck withhold this information from the coroner's report?

He's focused on Chuck now, Chuck not looking so good, Chuck seeming suddenly older, more wrinkled around the eyes and mouth. Not the usual carefree version of Chuck, not the guy with the witty patter, none of the playful irony, none of the old nonchalant air about him. Span doesn't know quite how to take this new Chuck. He's a slender, good-looking guy with thinning blondish hair and dark-rimmed glasses. He's wearing his customary Hush Puppies-type shoes. They are walking now toward a bench in Water Power Park, at the downtown end of the bridge. Now they're sitting, looking at each other.

"I'm trying to figure out why I did this," he tells Span. "I was raised Catholic, you know that."

Span wonders about the relevance, answering, "You know that I was, too," Span says, hoping that this uninteresting fact will make Chuck feel better.

"No, but with me, it stuck. I'm what everybody now thinks of as an anachronism. I actually still practice my religion. I don't like to talk about it. But I need it. I go every Sunday. It's like an addiction. Maybe it's because I deal with death every day. Dead bodies. There's got to be more to life than dead bodies. I very much need to believe in a spiritual life, in a dimension that somehow hovers over dead meat on a slab, something that transcends my daily routine. The fact that I'm a doctor, that I know pathology, that I know biology, makes this, I don't know, *striving* for spirituality even more important, more urgent." He looks out at the river. "I'm sounding like a crazy person."

"No, I think I get it."

"Anyway, long story short, I know that Matthias Hammar was straight as an arrow, he wasn't one of us. He wasn't a queer. My brother told me. My brother and Hammar were close friends. You know my brother? Teaches theology at St. John's. He's a big admirer of Hammar's books and sermons. He was impressed by Hammar's, you know, liberal activism. My brother calls Hammar a throw-back. He looked like right out of the fifties, pudgy, crew cut guy, but the look was misleading. He was a radical. He knew how to throw the real Jesus at the evangelical crowd and the big-business crowd, and they hated him for it."

Span wasn't quite following. "What's that got to do with Hammar being 'straight as an arrow'? Why, Chuck, did you not include this evidence you found?"

"I admired Hammar, too. My brother and I have gone to hear him preach a few times. Didn't want the public to remember him with an asterisk next to his name."

"Asterisk?"

"Yeah. No offense, Span. But if the cops and the media found out about the semen in Hammar's saliva they'd have a field day. You know there'd be speculation galore. It would be a smear job. It's just simple reality that this bit of news wouldn't help his reputation."

Chuck pauses. "I'm a pretty quiet gay person. Not out on the front lines, so to speak. But this is a brutal murder that's getting a lot of attention. I guess I don't want *us* to look bad for no good reason."

Span sighs. He and Chuck talk a while longer. With a deadline looming, Span needs to get back to his desk. Already the lunchtime crowd along the river is thinning out. Chuck Bennett has joined the exodus, leaving Span alone on the bench.

Span stares out at the river. What to do with this salacious bit of information? Chuck obviously wants him to print it or he wouldn't have told him about it, and certainly wouldn't have given him the slide. But he worries about Carla. This is the kind of stuff Her Majesty would love to exploit, would love to use to further sensationalize the case. To Span's way of thinking, the new evidence should be treated carefully. In his story, he'll suggest that the coroner's office didn't withhold the evidence, but rather delayed it. And he'll emphasize the likelihood of Hammar being a victim of killers who were more sadistic than previously imagined. To him, the semen sowed even more confusion about what kind of killers these are. Are they the cold-blooded assassins, the professionals, who planned this crime down to every intricate detail? Or, given their barroom behavior and their missed flight and now the semen in Hammar's mouth, are these killers reckless perverts?

Whatever Chuck's motivation for withholding the evidence, it's not relevant to the story, Span decides. Chuck is his friend. His good friend. Like everyone else, Chuck is a victim of his own context. He's a medical doctor and an officer of the court with an obligation to present homicide evidence in a fair, complete and unbiased manner. But he's also a human being who's apparently embarrassed by his church's priestly sex scandals, who's sensitive about protecting the gay community, and who doesn't want to risk tarnishing the memory of a bravely radical Lutheran clergyman whom he admires. Chuck's name, Span decides, won't be in his story. Chuck will be, as they say, "an anonymous source close to the investigation."

Chapter Eleven

Wednesday, 9:30 p.m.

Span has been spending so much time at the paper this week that he feels like a stranger in his own home. Max seems to regard him that way, too, seeking affection at every opportunity and now, with expectation in his eyes, staring at Span from across the room. The room itself seems suddenly shabby to Span, especially after seeing Maggie's living room, a space of identical dimensions yet exuding so much more, how to say it? Charm? Maybe it's his stained and threadbare furniture (unnoticed until now) or the stacks of paperbacks on the floor under the front window, or the dust on the mantle, or the "art collection," consisting mainly of decades-old, cheaply-framed newspaper award certificates, or his most prized piece, displayed on a plastic pedestal: a yellowed baseball autographed by his childhood hero – "Ernie Banks #14."

Span can't deny that it's been a good week. He's had page-one stories every day and has happily soaked up the accolades from his colleagues. Even the publisher singled him out on the elevator this morning. Span likes to pretend he's outgrown the satisfaction you get from that kind of praise. He likes to pretend that he's embarrassed by it. But, candidly, he admits that it's good to swim again in the waters of notoriety.

For this he can't help but feel indebted to Maggie Lindberg. She's his unofficial but essential partner. Span is aware of the spell she's cast over him. He can't quite explain it. He can't seem to separate his thoughts about the big story from his thoughts about her. He's thinking now about the two phone calls she uncharacteristically avoided on that first afternoon they talked, calls from the man with the good-looking Latino face, James Rincon. Twice she had pressed decline. But Span had noted the face, the name and the 213 area code.

Without leaving his sagging old leather recliner, Span reaches for his laptop. He punches in *james rincon los angeles*. Dozens of men pop up, along with some photos. But none of them looks like the guy. So, with a dose of trepidation, he types in *margaret rincon* — and then *margaret lindberg rincon los angeles...*

And, whammo, there she is!

Span goes a little numb when he sees her photo. He had no idea she's a cop. Or *was* a cop. But there she is, blond and pony-tailed with the green eyes and a serious expression on her chis-eled face over the top of a blue, LAPD uniform, the photo ID'd below as Officer Margaret Rincon.

Headlines pop up, too. *Officer Resigns After Shooting Flap Suspension* (from the Los Angeles Times, September 16, 2011). The officer in the story is Margaret Lindberg Rincon, 30, of Redondo Beach.

A month earlier: 2 *Suspects Killed, One Officer, One Bystander Wounded in Foiled Liquor Store Holdup* (Los Angeles Times). Span's eyes race down the screen. The gist of the piece is that cops had been tipped to a possible robbery near Figueroa and 59th, but the three robbers, one in a car and the others on foot, failed to surrender and began lighting up the neighborhood with gunfire. This was at about 4 in the afternoon, just in time for the evening news. The police shot and killed two of the robbers and captured the other as he drove away. Major Peter Lindberg, 62, was listed in fair condition with a gunshot wound. The story failed to explain why a high-ranking police administrator had been on the scene. A clerk at the liquor store was also hospitalized, listed in critical condition.

The next day: *Wounded Police Official on 'Field Trip' When Shot.* Quoting a police spokesman, the item reported that Major Peter Lindberg, head of the department's Analytics Unit, was taking a first-hand look at police crime-reduction tactics when he was felled by a shot fired by one of the gunmen, who later died. More than three hundred rounds were expended in the brief gunfight outside a liquor store on South Figueroa, the paper reported.

A week later, the Times noted that the liquor store clerk had died from a wound inflicted by the robbers while inside the store. Two months later, a small item reported that Major Peter Lindberg had been released from County General and would retire "with honors."

Deeper into his dive Span ran across a story from 2001: UCLA's "dynamic" outside hitter Maggie Lindberg had been named to the All-PAC-10 volleyball team. The 6-1 senior from Redondo Beach averaged 5.1 points per set and had a 4.71 kills average. A photo showed a youthful Maggie suspended in mid air, her right arm behind her head, her blond hair flying wildly behind her.

Span is stunned. He thought he knew Maggie Lindberg, but apparently not. Up until now he had dismissed her vague answers to his questions about her past and her family, and especially about her time in California. He thought she was just trying to be modest and to shift their conversation in a more appropriate direction, toward the tragic deaths of her two friends. Now, she looks like a puzzle with a lot of pieces missing.

Chapter Twelve

Thursday, June 9, 5:10 a.m.

It's no secret that Minnesota is a northern state. Minneapolis is fully two-and-a-half degrees farther north than Canada's largest city (Toronto). In summer, the early morning consequences can be devastating if you don't have the proper window shades, and Span doesn't. After an almost sleepless night, just as he's drifting off to dreamland, the sun is blazing in his eyes and the goddamn birds are shrieking.

Strong coffee is the only solution. Span's rattling around in the kitchen fails to arouse Max who snoozes in the corner. The papers won't plop on his doorstep for another hour at least, so Span begins to graze online, first the Post, then the Times, then the Star Journal. Span's story about the semen in Hammar's mouth didn't make the paper, thank God. Yesterday afternoon had been a shit storm at the office. Carla was super hot to print the story immediately, even if it exposed Hammar to all kinds of lurid speculation. Span objected, arguing that the paper should wait for the lab analysis to see if the discharge could be traced to the DNA of one of the two bad guys, thus telling readers more about them and their motives.

"The focus should be on the perpetrators, not the victim," Span told Carla.

Her Majesty didn't bother to look up from her computer screen. "Last time I heard, Lokken, you're just a reporter," she said in a blunt tone, a vein clearly visible on her young forehead. "*I* get to decide what runs and what doesn't run."

"Yeah, but don't put my byline on a story like that," Span retorted, escalating the dispute by adding, "Sometimes I wonder whatever happened to responsible journalism."

Carla removed her glasses and made direct eye contact with Span. "How is it responsible to hide important information from our readers? You say it invites *speculation*," she said, making quote marks with her fingers. "I say it builds interest in a story our readers are hungry for."

Before the next words spilled from his mouth Span regretted them. "I remember the days when this paper was run by adults," he said.

Carla rose from her desk and looked at Span as if he were a fresh log of dog shit. "That's it, Lokken," she said. "You're crossing the line now."

"What if we let Daley decide?" Span said, referring to the Star Journal's dignified, paternalistic and aging executive editor, Timothy J. Daley II, who is widely thought to be grooming Carla as his successor. Daley's office is a glass cube near the center of the city room. From there he surveys his landscape with a light touch, preferring to rely heavily on the judgments of his top assistants, including Carla. After listening to both arguments, Daley sided with Span. Span wasn't surprised. Carla was.

She pouted, and took out her frustrations on Span, ordering him again to probe the ritualistic nature of the crime. Her theory (without any real foundation as far as Span can see) is that these two miscreants are members of some bizarre white nationalist cult that hates blacks and hates white religious goody-goodies like Hammar. She listed recent church attacks in South Carolina, Virginia and Indiana, none of which victimized majority white congregations, and none of which had the gruesome theatrics of the St. A's crime.

"If you want to go after that angle you might consider tapping the religion reporter," Span replied.

Carla glared at him.

"If you want to explore more likely avenues, you might send reporters to the hometowns of the suspects," he said. "Dig into their backgrounds. Maybe talk to guys who did time with them. Who are these guys? How did they get like they are?"

Carla continued to glare.

"Me, I'd rather go after the luggage. That has a better chance of locating these two creeps. Locating them is job one. That's my view anyway, for what it's worth."

Carla sat down, looked at her screen, and began to type. The conversation was apparently over.

Span considers the luggage a huge loose end. Two bags, according to Maggie's source at TSA. But other details have been hard to come by. Bender's not talking. The D.A.'s not talking. Customs is not talking. Nobody's talking. Maybe the bags went to Germany. Maybe they didn't. Maybe they came back. Maybe they didn't. The fog makes Span all the more curious about what's inside.

That was one of the things looping through Span's mind all last night, keeping him churning, keeping him awake. That and yesterday's commotion with Carla. And, perhaps most of all, the shock of discovering Maggie's "secret life" at LAPD.

Not even multiple cups of morning coffee clear his mind. By 8 he's at the paper, tucked into his cubicle. Again he punches

Maggie's number. Again he leaves a message. He has sent texts, posted emails. No response.

By 10 he's pacing up and down the long rows of desks, dropping by the cafeteria for yet another coffee, then pacing some more. He calls Bender, the DA's office, the Customs Service at the airport. He leaves messages. The toughest days for a reporter are the ones spent making calls that never get returned, days filled with lots of questions but no answers. A writer can't write without answers, and a writer who can't write is a miserable bastard.

He calls Maggie again. Again she rolls to voicemail. Finally, he calls the church.

"St. Ansgar. May I help you?" answers Gwen Gray, the parish administrator.

"Pastor Lindberg, please."

"I'm sorry, she's in conference until 11, then she's out of the office for most of the day. Would you like her voicemail, or may I take a message?"

At least Maggie is in. Span makes for the elevator, then the parking garage. By 10:55 he's sitting in his ancient Audi in the Wells Fargo parking lot across from St. A's. He has spotted Maggie's old blue Volvo in one of the "Reserved for Church Staff" spots on Franklin Avenue. At 11:05 Maggie appears at the door, all in black, in her priest's collar and slim pants, blond ponytail swaying side to side, taking long strides toward her car. She pulls into traffic and heads west across the bridge toward downtown.

Span follows.

What the hell is he doing? He's *stalking* his partner? His friend? What has this to do with the story he's supposed to be working on? He knows this isn't quite right. He should be working on the luggage angle, not this. But his curiosity won't let go. He has to know who Maggie Lindberg really is, and what she's up to. She's had time to answer his calls and texts, but she hasn't. Why not? She's a partner he can't seem to do without. But can he trust her? Can he trust a former cop who wants to keep her background a secret?

Ten minutes later, Maggie pulls into a parking lot in the Loring Park district on the edge of downtown. A sign on the 1950's-era building says "Twin Cities Council of Churches." Span lingers at the edge of the lot. Maggie parks, strides to the door and disappears. Span begins to tap on his phone. Looks like this is an office building for a whole collection of local Protestant denominational headquarters – Episcopalian, Lutheran, Presbyterian, Methodist, and so on, as well as various charity organizations. As far as he can tell, it's a little like a labor temple, a place where all the bosses of various unions can hang out in the same building for the sake of solidarity and cheap rent.

Span considers following Maggie inside and confronting her, but thinks better of it. Patience, he tells himself. Patience and tolerance. These are virtues he's grown to appreciate during his declining years at the Star Journal. And he's a happier man for it. He has purposely steered clear of the chronic complainers who seem to dominate every newsroom, people who take joy in making everyone else miserable. Their central complaint, as Span sees it, is that their editors are idiots. Sometimes that's true. Carla, for one, is a crackpot. But a newsroom is, on the whole, like any other workplace. It's a bell curve. A few journalists are exceptionally talented and energetic. A few are incompetent and lazy. Most are middling. They celebrate small triumphs and suffer mild defeats. When Span was a young reporter he cared a lot. He sought perfection. He set high standards for himself and his colleagues. But on his gradual descent, on his gently sloping glide path, he's mellowed out. He's more accepting of human frailty.

Until now. Until this story. Something about this story has

changed him. More than he likes to admit, he cares again. Quite suddenly he's more like the old Span, and he's not sure he likes the old Span.

He checks his watch and waits for Maggie to emerge from the building. Has she betrayed him? Maybe. Is he feeling a little paranoid? Maybe.

Suddenly at 12:10 there she is, and he can't believe his eyes. She's walking alongside a man. And the man is Minneapolis Police Captain Lawrence A. (for asshole) Bender. Bender! What's Bender doing in the Council of Churches building? The two of them stop alongside Maggie's old blue Volvo, talking. Bender turns and walks to a nearby unmarked black sedan that Span hasn't noticed. Bender is bending, talking to the driver, probably one of his gofers. Then he rejoins Maggie, climbing into the front seat of her car. Off they go. Span is more than a little numb. He slips into gear and follows.

Maggie drives west, then south on France Avenue to a burger joint in the Southdale district, name of Shake Shack. Span's thinking he could use a burger himself to settle his stomach. Maybe there'll be a chance meeting inside. "What in the world are you two doing here?" he might say. And so forth. "What a coincidence! I've been trying to reach you all day!" he might say.

Span waits five minutes before he goes in and loiters around the ordering counter, scanning the tables. He doesn't see them. It's a large restaurant with an outdoor patio in back. They're probably back there.

"Order number 42, Larry, ready for pickup," comes the announcement. Span ducks quickly into the men's room.

He ends up with take-out and sits in his car chewing and stewing. Confronting Maggie in Bender's presence — not a cool thing to do anyway. Pretty soon the couple emerges at the far end of the parking lot. Hands are shaken and backs are slapped.

Buddies. Bender heads off to the black sedan, which has just now reappeared. He gets in. Maggie stares down the line of cars – directly at Span! Instinctively he ducks down like a coward. Has she seen him? He doubts it.

When he sits back up, her car is on the move again, turning south on France. He follows. She turns into the Best Buy parking lot. Should he go in? He debates with himself, deciding against it. After a brief shopping excursion, she reemerges with a small plastic bag, sliding back into her car and driving east on the Crosstown Expressway, then north on Cedar to a small house on 47th Street near Lake Hiawatha. Span pulls to the curb several houses away, barely able to see Maggie through several clumps of shrubbery. She's climbing from her car, clutching the plastic bag, then hugging a small dark-haired girl who runs to meet her. Span's guess is that this is Maggie's daughter, Petra. He can't see her features, but, over all, she's a good match for photos of the curly-haired child that dominate Maggie's living room. Span's guess is that the woman on the porch is Maggie's sister, Nori.

Minutes later, Maggie, toting a grocery bag, is on the move again, this time driving west on the Crosstown. For the next thirty minutes, suburbia blurs past Span's windshield, the roadside terrain turning greener and hillier. Lake Minnetonka, with a hundred and twenty-five miles of shoreline, is the city's largest lake, and home to its most affluent districts. Excelsior is a leafy, well-tended enclave on the lake's south shore. The village's main street is pleasant, but not overly cute. Affluent, in these parts, doesn't necessarily mean opulent. On a modest hillside overlooking the lake, where you might expect a resort hotel, is instead "Villa Maria, an Eldercare Community." This collection of low-slung brick cottages appears to be Maggie's destination. She pulls into a spot outside something called the Welcoming

Center, then, looking over her shoulder, strides through the front door, the grocery bag in her left arm.

Span's workday is wasting away. It's already past two. He parks the ancient Audi and makes for the door to the Welcoming Center, expecting a medical atmosphere. Wrong. Looks more like an extended-stay hotel. There's a fake stone fireplace with plush sofas on one end of the spacious lobby and a faux movie theater (marquee and everything) at the other. Between them is a reception desk. Everyone he sees is old. Half are in wheel chairs. The two youngest people in the area are seated at the reception desk. Both young women appear to be of West African origin. One is on the phone. The other smiles as she sees a disheveled Span walking briskly toward her. Span is suddenly self-conscious. No one else in here seems to be in a hurry, no one else is moving nearly so fast.

"May I help you?" The young woman's name plate reads "Clara."

"Sorry," Span says, out of breath. "The clergy woman who just came in here, tall, blond, ponytail? I'm trying to catch up to her. She, uh, dropped something out by her car."

"Oh, do you mean Pastor Lindberg?"

"Yes, maybe."

"She is here to visit her father. She comes every Thursday. Never misses. What did she drop?"

"Oh, nothing. I, I can pick it up and put it on her car. No problem. What room is her father in?"

"Sorry, I cannot release that information. Anything else I can help you with?"

"No. I guess not. Thank you," Span says as he backs away from the desk, bowing slightly, then turning and walking back to his car. Her father? He's here? This would be Peter Lindberg, former LAPD? He wouldn't be old enough to live here, would he?

Span's cell chirps as he slides into the front seat. About time his calls get returned. Calls, yes, but no real answers. Customs can't comment on the luggage. Airport management doesn't know anything. Span's snitch at the FBI isn't talking.

When Span looks up from his phone, he sees Maggie Lindberg striding directly toward his car, looking directly at him. She's not smiling. Way too late to duck.

"You're lousy at surveillance," she says. "You have nothing better to do than follow me all day?"

"What do you mean, all day?"

"You think I'm stupid? How many faded, lime-green 1998 Audis with a dent in the left front fender do you think there are in this town?"

"Probably one."

She smiles. "Look, I'm on a tight schedule. Tonight, 7 o'clock sharp. The gazebo in Longfellow Park." She pounds her fist on Span's car, turns and walks briskly toward her car at the other end of the lot, turning back toward Span briefly, smiling slightly, flipping him the bird.

Chapter Thirteen

Thursday, 7:00 p.m

After a flurry of sniffing at shrubs and tree trunks, Max has reclined on a shady spot of grass in Longfellow Park, a small patch of greenery near the south end of Hennepin Island, only pitching-wedge distance from the Kron compound. Maggie and Span are sitting nearby on folding chairs. There's still enough sun in the western sky to produce a dappled pattern all around them, but Maggie sits entirely in lengthening shadows that seem only to accentuate, as Span sees them, her long legs and stunning green eyes. It's an effect that lowers his IQ by at least fifty points.

Add to that his sheepish feelings about his miserable performance as a spy and the ease with which Maggie unmasked him. Span is, after all, a male person, and male persons generally dislike being the butt of female amusement. It's safe to say that Maggie does seem more amused than angered by Span's antics. The result is that his stern accusations about her failure to disclose her police background are easily shrugged off. Maggie just laughs.

"That part of my life is over and done with," she says.

"Well, apparently not. Hanging with Bender? Having lunch with him?"

Maggie's thinking that maybe Span's got a point. Maybe she owes him the whole story, or a good part of it. "There's so much I'd like to tell you," she says. And so she begins. Her days are crammed, she says. Meetings with the bishop and, yes, the cops. A delicate and difficult sermon to deliver on Sunday. Two funerals to arrange and manage. Parishioners to comfort, a daughter to love, an absent husband to deal with, and a stunning murder case to make sense of. And yet, Span notices, she seems not to focus on her own burdens but on those of others, including his. There's so much he should know, she repeats, starting with her furlough from the church, her arrangement with the cops, a tantalizing bit of information from the Frankfurt airport and her emerging doubts about the evidence in the case.

Span feels suddenly like the junior partner in their enterprise. He's all ears.

She starts with this morning at 9 when her cell chirped and she heard the bishop on the other end asking her to drop by his office at 11:30 for a chat, and then, seemingly out of the blue, uttering the word *hiatus.* The first thing Maggie did was to say, "Yes, of course. I'll be there." The second thing was to Google "hiatus def." She'd associated the term with the Hollywood film industry, but wasn't sure what it meant in a wider context.

"An interruption in time or continuity," Webster explained. "A period when something (such as a program or activity) is suspended or interrupted."

Arriving at the bishop's office in the Council of Churches building, Maggie was astonished to find Captain Larry Bender sitting in one of the bishop's padded leather chairs, the two of them, like buddies, sipping coffee out of fine china cups with actual saucers, obviously at the tail end of cooking up something. Each had a pleased-as-punch grin on his face as she walked into the room.

The mood turned quickly solemn as the bishop explained their plan. Margaret will go "on leave" from St. A's over the summer. During her "hiatus," the bishop will install a clergy tag team from national, namely a man and a woman who specialize in grief and crisis situations. "This is what we have here, a grief and crisis situation," he informed Maggie, as if she were a dim-witted child. In addition, he said that the Reverend Ernie Gruendal, who for more than thirty years had been St. A's specialist in hospital visits and ministering to the elderly, would stay on to provide, as the bishop called it, "institutional memory." Maggie would continue to draw half-salary from the parish while drawing the other half from a consulting contract she would sign with Bender and the Minneapolis Police.

"Captain Bender, here, thinks you possess unique knowledge and skills with regard to this tragedy," the bishop had said, adjusting his glasses and glancing at the clock. What he meant was that, as a former homicide cop and a current parish pastor, Margaret Lindberg might offer special insights into catching the bad guys who had so horrifically profaned the church and who continued to embarrass a police department that, as Bender admitted, "hasn't got a clue as to the whereabouts of these two psychos."

"You'll be reporting directly to me," Bender had said, revealing a bit of information that didn't exactly thrill Maggie. To this point, her meetings with Larry Bender had convinced her that he was a good enough cop, perhaps an exceptional one. But he gave her the creeps. The way he looked at her. The way he deferred to her, consoled her, touched her shoulder. She didn't trust him.

Neither did she fully trust the bishop's rather odd decision to push her out of the way at this critical moment. Maybe she was paranoid, but she detected Jonas Kron's fingerprints all over this new arrangement. A power grab by Kron now that Hammar, his nemesis, was dead? Why not?

"I can't say I'm comfortable with this," Maggie had responded. "I left the force for a reason."

Her remark was greeted with silence. Clearly, she had no choice in the matter. Two powerful men had decided her short-term future. She absorbed it like just another blow to the gut. "I'll try my best," she managed to say.

As the meeting ended, Maggie got a question from Bender. Could they have lunch and could she come over to his office for another meeting at 4?

Maggie's narrative has Span's full attention. He knows Maggie was once a cop. Maggie must assume that he knows. He lets it pass. "You're not going to like working with Bender," he tells her. "I'd be suspicious about the arrangement."

"He sees me as a consultant," she explains. "Someone who knows the church and someone who has experience investigating murders. Hard to find that combination, he told me."

Span's real worry – and Maggie detects it easily – is that Maggie's new tie to the MPD will supersede their own journalistic partnership. "We'll still talk," she reassures him.

"Does Bender know about our arrangement?" Span wonders.

"What arrangement is that?" she says, smiling.

Then she starts again. The trip to Best Buy was to pick up a cellphone she had ordered for Petra, she explains. "My sister, Nori, has promised to teach her all the ways to use it. Well, not *all* the ways."

"Is it normal for an eight-year-old to have a phone?" he wonders.

Maggie says that, considering the frightening incidents of

recent days, "maybe it's just wishful thinking, but I'd like to have her just a click away."

Span glances over at Max. He's dozing under a tree.

Explaining her trip to the elder care facility in Excelsior is harder for Maggie. It forces her to pretty much tell her life story. Span knew she had grown up on Hennepin Island, but he didn't know the details. Her grandparents had come to the island as immigrant kids from Sweden about the time of World War I, she tells him. Over the decades, they grew up here, went to school together, got married and lived in a well-tended duplex, Grandpa working on the railroad and spending way too much time at the local taverns, and Grandma, the steadfast one, cultivating flowers and baking cookies, as Maggie remembers it. "I hung around for the cookies," she tells Span. Maggie says she withstood quite a lot of good-natured teasing from Grandma, who called her "Gänglig," which means lanky. She said it aggravated her self-consciousness about being the tallest kid in class.

Span is surprised to hear Maggie talking about herself. Until now she has shown nothing but reluctance. Maybe her memories of an idyllic girlhood on this island are a diversion from the recent butchery and from the realization that her gauzy island refuge isn't as safe as she thought it was. Who could blame her for wanting to call a timeout from reality?

She describes in detail her girlhood home at 27th and Ogden, less than a mile from her grandparents' and fewer than four blocks from where Span and Max currently reside. She had two older brothers and one younger sister. Her mom was a clerk at a bank downtown. Her dad, a sturdy man with blondish hair and glasses (she shows Span an old picture in her wallet), had been a naval officer in the Shore Patrol in the Philippines during Vietnam. When he got out he became police chief in several suburbs before taking a desk job downtown at police headquarters.

"He was a numbers guy, a fanatic with computers and maps, always figuring out strategies," Maggie says. "Playing a game of chess with him was always a bad idea unless you liked to lose."

She remembers her dad more as an analyst than a cop. "He figured out how to staff precincts and how to schedule training exercises, that kind of stuff. When they came up with these 'Broken Windows' policing theories, you know like arrest people for the little crimes and the big crimes won't happen, Dad was on it."

"That would have been the '80s?" Span asks.

"Yeah, I was a little kid. But he was the one who designed the 'Flood the Zone' strategy for Minneapolis, where you use data to predict where and when crimes will occur and then you concentrate your forces in that area. New York transit cops were doing the same thing about the same time. It's old stuff now, but it was a revolutionary thing back then, and they got a lot of bad guys off the street by doing that."

Span interrupted, "It also got out of hand when a lot of innocent people got stopped and frisked and neighborhood people started seeing the cops as an occupying army. There are a lot of stories going around about certain Minneapolis cops who love to beat up on black folks."

"I guess I shouldn't be surprised," she says. "But to be fair to Dad, he never intended for his strategies to be so aggressive and, you know, paramilitary. Maybe he was naïve. He thought neighborhood people would welcome a crackdown on the bad guys. He didn't know cops were going to be so indiscriminate and that so many of the neighbors were going to side with the criminals."

Span asks how she landed in L.A.

"One day Dad gets a call. It's Daryl Gates, the Los Angeles chief at the time asking would he be interested in joining LAPD. This wasn't totally out of the blue because he'd been out there several times giving seminars — what he called his map-and-clap show."

The family didn't want to move, she says, even though her mom had relatives in California. But eventually everyone caved. "It was mostly about the weather," she says.

Span sips at a plastic water bottle and tells his own story. "My Dad, he had this fantasy. Every winter we were on the brink of moving to Florida. 'This is the last damn snow I'm ever going to shovel,' he'd say. But we never left the north side of Chicago, rarely got across the city line. For him, Waukegan was a long trip."

Both of them laugh.

"For us, there was some big-time complaining about the move," Maggie says, especially from her brothers who were in high school at the time. "I'm in like fifth grade and thinking maybe this won't be so bad. I'd been watching these shows like 'L.A. Law' and 'Baywatch' and I'm thinking this California thing might be pretty cool. Truth is, I also thought there was a chance they appreciated tall girls out there. Sounds ridiculous, but I was a kid with a hang-up and maybe I was looking for a fresh start."

Maggie's phone is chirping like a cricket. She's talking now to her daughter, then, afterward, explaining that Petra was making a test call. "She's my whole life now," Maggie says, allowing a blank moment to be filled by the sound of an indifferent river flowing nearby and allowing Span to absorb more completely Maggie's overwhelming devotion to Petra. Having no kids himself, he realizes he can't fully appreciate the magnitude of the parent-to-child attachment. It's something he'll never completely grasp.

"Were you never married? Never had kids?" she asks, already knowing the answer.

"So, California," he blurts.

"It wasn't like on TV," she resumes, describing the family's modest three-bedroom rambler in Redondo Beach that came with two lemon trees but no pool, her brothers sharing one bedroom, she and Nori sharing another, all the kids having to walk more than a mile to the beach, everybody assuming she was into volleyball because she was tall. She wasn't "into it" at the time but quickly took to the game – both the beach and hardwood versions — because it gave her a special identity. By high school she was pretty good, good enough in her senior year to get scholarship offers, finally settling on UCLA, where she didn't play much at first, but made all-Pac-10 in her senior year.

She gets a little carried away, telling Span that you have to jump with both arms in the air, meeting the ball at the highest point possible, then, in front of your hitting shoulder, snap your wrist downward (she demonstrates) to give topspin and a powerful downward trajectory to your shot — and don't forget to follow through.

Maggie stops suddenly, wondering why she's telling all this to Span. Sounds trivial and self-centered, she thinks. "Sorry, I get carried away," she says.

Span figures it's a release for her to talk about herself for once. After all, she has been consumed with taking care of others – of Petra, of course, and of her parishioners who need her now more than ever. Maybe the hiatus will relieve some of the pressure, pushing her into old, familiar territory – finding the bad guys.

Maggie rises from her chair and walks toward the gazebo. Span follows. The low sun shines through the trees accentuating Maggie's impressive silhouette. Span can't help but wonder if attractive women know how attractive they really are. Some plainly do. He doesn't think this one has a clue.

They step up onto the gazebo, into the welcome shade, Maggie leaning against a railing. "After Mom died and Dad got hurt, Nori moved Dad back up here, and I came back, too. Now I visit him every Thursday," she says, her face flushing, her eyes tearing up. "He claims not to recognize me, claims not to know me. He had like three strokes. He's in a wheelchair. They have to feed him. I go see him because I miss him so much. I don't miss who he is now, I miss the guy he used to be. I idolized my dad."

Maggie's eyes are green puddles. "I don't have the words to tell you about my memories of him," she says. But she tries. Maybe she loved him because he was home so rarely during the impressionable years of her childhood. The touch of his padded hands, the masculine scent of him as she sat on his lap, the shine of his uniform buttons and badge, the brightness of his eyes – she can still feel, smell and see him as he was thirty years ago, she says. "I knew we had something special together, the specialness that fathers and daughters can have. I knew I was his favorite. Except for Petra" she says, "I've never loved anyone as much as I loved my dad."

Even through her teen years, the two stayed close, she tells Span. "He could somehow see into my innermost feelings without making me embarrassed. About eighth grade, boys started to hang around, some of them catching up to my height. Dad told me — this *was* embarrassing — that I was pretty and that I had to cope with that. I didn't really believe him. But he was my dad and he was trying to send me a message to keep my feet on the ground and to let me know about his high expectations for me, you know, keep me on an academic track.

"In college I decided I wanted to be a criminal lawyer, maybe a prosecutor. But afterward I decided to postpone law school and enroll in the police academy. It was my decision, not Dad's."

"How did you do at the academy?" Span wondered.

"Um, near the top of my class," Maggie said with some

embarrassment, adding that her status as a woman cop and as Pete Lindberg's daughter put her on the fast track to stardom within the department. Peter Lindberg was a well-known, much-admired figure at Parker Center, then at LAPD's spiffy new headquarters on West First Street, she explains. "There were plusses and minuses about being his daughter, but mostly plusses. I admit that I was seen as a rising star," she says. "Then came the bullet that ended Dad's career."

"Bullet?" Span asks, hiding the fact that he'd peeked into the newspaper archives, stumbling across several L.A. Times stories about the fateful incident from 2011, including the wounding of Major Peter Lindberg.

"Dad was hit during a shootout at a liquor store robbery, and um, he never recovered," Maggie tells Span, staring down at the river. "I'm the reason."

Span is stunned. "You? You're the reason? How could that be?"

"Pride. You know what they say – 'Pride cometh before the fall.'" Maggie confesses that she was excessively proud of her job performance and wanted to show her dad first hand. So, she told him he should be there to see how she had used his analytics to get intel on when and where this particular robbery would take place and how the arrest would go down.

"So, things got pretty chaotic pretty quickly. Dad was behind a dumpster and rounds were flying everywhere, and one ricocheted off something and got under his flak vest and went through a kidney and lodged near the spine. That was pretty much it. His career was over," she tells Span. "Turns out mine was over, too, but that took a little longer to happen."

Span's questions begin to spill out, overtaking a narrative that Maggie is obviously struggling to lay out. "I think we should stop with my story," Maggie interrupts. "There's more important stuff I need to tell you."

The momentum has clearly shifted. Span is thinking that maybe this was never really his story. It's Maggie who is directing traffic here. It's Maggie who's the leader of this journalistic enterprise. Span is feeling less like a reporter than a typist.

She wants to skip ahead in her story to this afternoon when she had confronted Span in the parking lot of the elder care center in Excelsior. From there, she tells him, she had driven downtown to meet with Bender again. At 4, she walked into his office, nodded to him and two other Minneapolis detectives she had met on the day of the murders, then shook the hand of Special Agent Mel Thurber, FBI.

"Thurber's got a present for us," Bender announced. "Could be up for an Oscar nomination, best picture." Bender's secretary, Cyd, handed out Styrofoam cups and poured bad coffee, then dimmed the lights.

On Bender's large screen, up came what looked like a grainy video poised for motion. Thurber clicked and the screen came to life. This looked like surveillance footage from an airport terminal. An information kiosk in the corner of the screen carried a Lufthansa logo. At the bottom of the screen these letters and numbers were superimposed: FLUGHAFEN FRANKFURT AM MAIN - TERMINAL 1 06.06.16/08.23

Passengers in summertime dress streamed past the camera, wheeling and toting luggage. A yellow sign "Zollkontrolle" pointed back toward where the crowd was coming from.

Thurber then picked up the narration. "This is Frankfurt Airport on the morning after the St. Ansgar homicides. These are people carrying bags offloaded from Lufthansa flight 431 and having just cleared customs. This is the flight from MSP that Reznik and Hajinlian were booked on but never made. They checked two bags. Those bags were never claimed in Frankfurt. We asked the German customs authorities to impound those bags and to look inside. They found forty thousand American dollars in neat bundles and a white envelope containing five thousand euros sewed into the lining.

"OK," Thurber continued. "Now check out the guy standing next to the information booth. He's the one in the knit shirt with the tattoo on his left arm and the black baseball cap. Notice the sign he's holding."

Indeed, a hefty man is holding a sign that says: WILLKOMMEN HR. PUUSEPP.

"He's obviously waiting for somebody," Thurber continued. "Look at him looking at his watch. OK, the tape jumps ahead now. Time goes by. He's still waiting. Now he's walking over to check with the information clerk. Several times he does this. He's waiting for somebody who never comes. Who is he waiting for? Who never comes?

"When the German police questioned the information clerk, she remembered the man as agitated, speaking German with an accent, maybe Russian. He asked repeatedly about the flight from Minneapolis and told her he was waiting for two friends. You can see him here talking to her, gesturing, and then walking out of the camera shot.

"OK, a little time goes by. Now from a different camera we see him outside the terminal talking on a cellphone, stuffing the sign into a trash barrel and, OK, just now, getting into a car that pulls up to the curb, then driving off camera.

Bender chimes in. "Questions about the movie? Comments? How many stars do you give it?"

Maggie had questions.

"Who is this guy? Does the FBI know him?"

Thurber cleared his throat. "We're running him through the facial recognition protocol, but the baseball cap and the shadows make him hard to ID. No sure matches at this point, but we're still working it."

"White Sox baseball cap? Does it mean anything?"

"Maybe an extra prop for Reznik and Hajinlian to notice aside from the sign with the name, what was it? Velkommen Hr. Puusepp?" Thurber spelled out the name.

"That name?" Maggie wondered. "Somebody's real name? Or maybe just a code?"

"It's an Estonian name," Thurber said. "Means carpenter. But it's pretty common in Finland, Russia, Sweden, Germany, the Baltic countries, that part of the world."

"So, there's nobody on the flight manifest by that name," Maggie said, "and maybe this guy was at the airport to meet our two friends and then got frustrated when they didn't show up?"

"That's what it looks like," Bender said.

"Maybe this is obvious, but they must have been stupid to stash that kind of cash in their bags," Maggie said. "Customs would be asking a lot of questions about that."

Nods all around.

"So even more than before, this looks like murder for hire," she concluded. "These guys are hit men who screwed up. And now they're extra pissed because they lost their money when they didn't make their flight. And the guy at the other end is pissed because they didn't show up and he doesn't know where they are. Sound right?"

More nods.

"What about the car?" Maggie wondered. "Any leads on that?"

Thurber looked at his notes. "It was a gray Opel SUV, a model called the Mokka X. German cops checked the plate. Turned out it was lifted from one of the airport parking lots. Owner was on vacation in Spain. Recovered late that same afternoon on a street in downtown Frankfurt, close to the railroad station. No helpful prints."

Bender stood as if to emphasize a point. "We saved the best

for last," he announced, clicking his remote. On the screen flashed a close-up of the white envelope containing the five thousand euros, some of the bills poking out of the top. Engraved on the upper left corner of the envelope:

KRON INDUSTRIES CREDIT UNION

45 Lake Street, Suite 603, Minneapolis, MN 55408-1399

Chapter Fourteen

Thursday, 8:15 p.m

As Maggie shows Span a photo she's captured on her phone, a photo of the incriminating envelope, she's also thinking about what she's not going to tell him. And that's this: After her meeting at police headquarters, upon leaving Bender's office, she found herself alone in an elevator with Special Agent Thurber.

"I wonder if you know anything about this," he asked her. "Maybe a month ago I get a recorded phone message from the Reverend Hammar who wonders if I've got time to meet with him. Nothing urgent, he says. By the time I call him back, he's on vacation. Some time after that he and the janitor turn up dead. So, that's a pretty remarkable coincidence, don't you think? I'm just wondering if you have any idea why Hammar might have wanted to meet me, might have wanted to share something with the FBI?"

Maggie was puzzled, telling him she can't imagine a reason.

"I'm hoping you'll keep this quiet for now, maybe discreetly ask Hammar's secretary, what's her name?"

"Gwen Gray."

"Yes, her. Could you maybe ask her discreetly if she knows anything about why her boss wanted to see me. This is an embarrassing loose end for me. Seems like an amazing coincidence that's a little too amazing."

Maggie agreed. And from that moment, she's not stopped thinking about why Matthias would want to have a talk with the FBI.

She'd like to tell Span, she admits. But the FBI has asked her to be discreet. So she will. Span knows about the envelope from the Kron credit union. That should make him happy. Considering Kron's strong ties to St. A's, it doesn't make her happy.

Dusk is approaching. The lights in the park flick on.

"I think we should go see Kron. Now," Span says. "We're what? Two blocks from his house?"

"Not sure that's a great idea," she says.

"Why not? Cops must consider him a prime suspect. Looks a lot like murder for hire to me."

"Maybe a little too convenient, don't you think? An envelope with Kron's name on it? A little too obvious, maybe?"

"Maybe. But we've got to confront him before he gets lawyered up. We need to ask him about it. If we want to print it, the part about the envelope and the five-thousand euros, we've got to give him an opportunity to respond."

Maggie reluctantly follows Span and Max out of the park, walking now down Lake Street, past the ominous Kron Industries complex, along the big stone wall, past the headquarters gate, past the tall clock tower, finally to the separate iron gate in front of the Krons' personal castle. Max sniffs the lush greenery beyond the iron bars. Span leans in, peering at the mostly dark mansion beyond, watching the windows. No movement. Alongside the gate there's a glass door with a camera overhead. Inside, there's a polished brass speaker with a buzzer. Maggie hangs back, holding Max's leash. Span buzzes.

No response.

He tries again. Without warning, two muscular mastiffs trot into the gate area on the other side of the bars. Span is startled. Max whimpers quietly.

"Oh, hey. Is Mister Kron home?" Span asks, stupidly. The dogs emit a low, gravelly growl, their sunken eyes focused on Span, their jowls quivering. Max cowers. Span and Maggie move back. "Well, tell him we dropped by," Span says, as the three of them retreat down the sidewalk. Turning back, Span notices the orb camera panning with them. His eyes narrow.

"Nice guy, this Jonas Kron of yours," Span says to Maggie. "Very hospitable."

Chapter Fifteen

Saturday, June 11, 8:15 a.m

One way to intimidate Span is to place a fishing rod in his hands, which is exactly what Maggie is doing in her garage first thing Saturday morning, Petra standing watching with a slight smirk on her round face. Span, despite growing up less than two miles from Lake Michigan and despite being more than fifty years old, has never been fishing. Petra can plainly see that he, a grown man, doesn't know how to properly grasp the rod or operate the reel. This is going to be a long morning.

Maggie, faced with delivering tomorrow's sermon one week after the gruesome deaths of her friends and on the very spot where the murders occurred, needs time to ponder and prepare, needs to fortify herself against emotional breakdown, needs to emerge as a compassionate but strong leader for a damaged community.

Span volunteered to hang with Petra today. He can use a break from the frustrations of yesterday. Again he had failed to connect with Jonas Kron. Again he had asked Bender about the luggage, this time getting him to confirm that the German authorities had indeed sent it back to Minneapolis but declining to discuss its contents, refusing to confirm or deny information about any cash or any envelope that might or might not have been recovered. He even refused to say whether the FBI had become involved in the case despite the obvious national and international implications. Thanks only to off-the-record confirmation from Maggie's friend Sylvia Kraskie at the TSA was Span able to write a story quoting sources "at the airport" saying that police were examining the contents of the returned luggage that may lead to the arrest of the two fugitives "and others who may have been involved in a conspiracy" to kill Hammar.

What Petra wanted to do today, perhaps to settle her own nerves, was to revert to the routine that she and her mom followed often on Saturdays, and that was to tramp down to the fishing dock on Longfellow Parkway and drop a line in the mighty Mississippi.

The rocky bottom near the dock, coupled with the remains of several concrete piers that once supported a large boathouse (long since demolished), forms a perfect feeding ground for walleye, sauger, crappie and large- and small-mouth bass, it is said, while big catfish lurk in the deeper, muddier waters immediately downstream. It is eight-year-old Petra delivering this information to Span.

She's standing by the door with her gear, decked out in shorts, sneakers and a wide-brimmed fishing hat that struggles to cover her unruly mop of dark, curly hair. Adults describe Petra as "adorable" and Span can't argue with that. But he doesn't know Petra as a person. And he doesn't really know how to be around children, having never had siblings — or kids of his own. All he knows is that he likes children, potentially. But he's also afraid of them. What if they cry? What if they want things that he can't immediately supply? What if they get bored? What do kids talk about anyway?

The sight of a person or persons walking down the street all decked out for fishing isn't uncommon in Minneapolis, and certainly isn't unusual on Hennepin Island. But Span never imagined he'd be one of them. Petra, on the other hand, seems to relish her role of showing Span the ropes. She leads him east from Connor Street on the short four-block walk to the bait shack now coming into view amid the trees. "Got your license?" she asks.

License? Maggie never mentioned a license. The bait shack is more like a kiosk operated by the parks department, selling hooks, lines and sinkers, along with sunscreen and other assorted necessities like nightcrawlers, minnows, leeches, frogs and various artificial lures. Fishing licenses are also available.

Span fills out a form and forks over fourteen dollars, plus an extra ten for bait. The dock isn't a single platform but a series of wooden structures extending out over the east channel. Petra marches directly to a favorite spot, plunks down on a bench, reaches into the bait pail, and hooks a squirmy chub onto her jig. Then she looks at Span, expecting him to do the same. It takes him several attempts before he's able even to hold the slippery minnow properly in his hand. Finally, Petra steps in to bait his hook. She shows him how to lower the line into the water and how to find the bottom before cranking it up a few feet. Then she performs a nifty underhand cast with her own rod, a move that makes her look like one of those fishing guides on TV.

Span is impressed. But he doesn't know quite what to say. "How's school?" he finally blurts.

"Summer," she says.

"Right. I know. But when you're in school, well, how is it?"

"Fine."

What grade are you in?"

"Gonna be fourth."

"Back when I was in fourth we had Sister Genevieve. I don't think she liked children." Petra reels in her line, then sends out another cast to a slightly different spot. "What's the biggest fish you ever caught?" Span wonders.

"Don't know," she says. "Maybe about a foot. Mom had to help me because I was only six. A walleye."

"Do you like to eat 'em?"

"We get them from the store. We don't eat them from the river. We do catch and release."

Span watches an empty barge chug quietly by, heading upriver for a load of something. On the opposite bank a line of trees partially obstructs his view of golfers on a manicured fairway. Overhead, a long queue of passenger jets lines up to land at the airport, one filling the sky with a shadow and a roar every few minutes. This is no wilderness fishing spot.

"Ever been to Disney World?" he asks.

An hour goes by without an apparent bite on either line. "Maybe we should try over there," Span suggests. "You want to move? I mean we're not catching anything."

Petra appears to be watching some birds circling overhead. Indeed, the sounds of birds and jets fill the air.

"Catching fish isn't really the point," she says, showing a smile beneath her sparkling brown eyes.

By early afternoon, the two new friends have gathered up their gear and are sauntering toward home. "I guess the fish weren't hungry today," Span says, "but me, I could use a chocolate milkshake."

Petra looks up at him, smiling. "Me too," she says.

The Dairy Queen on Lake Street requires a four-block detour. As they approach, Span's phone tickles his pocket. "Catching your limit I assume," Maggie says.

"Our arms are aching," he says.

"Petra behaving?"

"Of course. Actually, we're celebrating at Dairy Queen."

What Maggie fails to mention is her call this morning to Gwen Gray, the parish administrator. Casually, in the midst of discussing other details, she asked if Hammar had recently had any long private conversations with Henrik. She asked if Hammar had ever called the FBI, or had any calls from the FBI or traded correspondence of any kind?

Gwen had reminded Maggie that Hammar was a controversial figure and, yes, threats had been made against him. But she could recall no recent contact with the bureau. As for private conversations with Henrik, yes. Over the last month, the two had had several long, closed-door meetings in Hammar's office. The two had never discussed serious topics. Gwen considered the meetings "mysterious."

Chapter Sixteen

Sunday, June 12, 9:15 a.m

Avoiding churches was Span's religion. So it was perhaps extraordinary on Sunday morning, less than twenty-four hours after the police removed yellow tape from the premises, that he decides to check out the crime scene by attending the 10 o'clock service at St. Ansgar. Anticipating a large crowd, he plans to arrive a half hour early, thus curtailing his usual morning excursion with Max. The dog sits now at the kitchen door, pouting, looking at Span with a mix of scorn and wonder. Even Span considers himself a kind of traitor.

Outside, Span drinks in the fresh, bright morning. Streets are quiet. It's strange that no best friend tugs at his arm. Occasionally, a whiff of frying bacon floats between the houses as he walks along. Occasionally, dogs bark from backyards and mourning doves coo from wires overhead. It should take less than twenty minutes to reach the church. Along the way, he can't help but notice the regiment of front porches, all of a similar style, each attached to a similar stone house, most houses sharing a wall with another stone house. His fellow islanders have gone to great lengths to individualize their porches so as to make them their own.

This one has an oversupply of red geraniums, this one a collection of vintage metal lawn chairs of the type popular in the fifties, this one a red flag with a white W signifying intense loyalty to the Wisconsin Badgers. A porch across the street displays a green and white Wellstone campaign sign, a memorial to the feisty, youthful senator who died in a plane crash fourteen years ago.

Green plastic bags stuffed with the Sunday Star Journal rest on some of the porches – along with a few blue bags containing the New York Times. Span feels grateful that old habits die slowly, that some people still go through the ritual of groping their way to the front door, bending down, picking up and leafing through the Sunday paper. The newspaper was a great invention, he muses.

His big weekend story had been online for eighteen hours before readers saw the print version. His story had led the local 10 o'clock newscasts last night. He's old fashioned enough to still get a thrill from the thought that his stories this week have been "news" to his neighbors, that Wednesday's headline especially, was memorable. "*Church Killers Missed Flight, Local Manhunt Intensifies*" dominated the top of page one, and the subheads were loaded: "*Debacle in Airport Bar,*" "*Getaway Van Discovered*" and "*Pastor Was Sexually Violated.*"

Span's not ashamed to confess a small dash of pride in the work that he's done. He's had plenty of front page stories in his time, but this one strikes close to home with an almost comic absurdity: two highly skilled assassins turning into fuck-ups when it came to their getaway, and, more than that, the outrageously gruesome, sick nature of the crime itself —and its proximity to his own home.

Span has covered tragedies in other places — a volcano in Washington state, floods and tornados throughout the Midwest and South, a riot in Los Angeles, a terror attack in New York. He's sat with families of murdered loved ones in this city and felt their anguish, or thought he had. But he's also felt guilt. He knows why people hate reporters, because they waltz into horrific situations of rape, slaughter and mayhem, and make a spectacle of people's agony and grief, and then they depart to the safety and smugness of their own lives. Reporters have an escape valve; victims do not. Span has a close friend, Gilbert, whom he met during his years in New York. Gilbert is a war correspondent for the BBC and has been many times to dangerous places like Iraq, Afghanistan and Chechnya, and is constantly haunted by the reality that "what makes life horrible for others makes life better for me."

Span can't get this line out of his head as he crosses Franklin Avenue, turns west and begins to see along the sidewalk a progression of white ribbons tied around street lights and parking meters. And now, as he approaches St. A's, he sees bouquets of flowers, hundreds of them, tied to the iron fence that fronts the church property. And not just flowers but more white ribbons and homemade signs, some in Spanish, some in Somali, as well as hand-written notes, photos of families with the slain pastor and a few pictures of the janitor, too, along with crucifixes and teddy bears and burned-out candles. While the church itself had been taped off, people apparently needed some way to express their grief.

From a wider perspective, these gestures have come to seem common, trite and sentimental. But, as he's now discovering, it's somehow different when the terrible thing happens just around the corner *from you*. These people now descending on this big church from all directions, these hundreds of people joining Span along the sidewalk and near the entrance to St. A's are his neighbors. The media keeps calling this thing a "theatrical" crime, and so it was. But theatrical is all about pretending, and this is not pretending. The reality shows on the hollowed out faces of these people, in the quiet, shell-shocked manner in which they negotiate this place. A week ago it was their sacred refuge. Now it's a place where anything can happen.

Span enters St. A's through a large iron gate, then crosses a small courtyard before passing through one of three huge double doors, each now propped open. Immediately ahead is a heroic statue of Ansgar himself, "Apostle to the North," who, the inscription explains, was a ninth century German archbishop and missionary to the Nordic countries. This is news to Span, of course, but not very interesting news.

Turning left, Span enters a long narrow narthex that rests directly below the church's tall slender tower. Here, he encounters earnest, well-dressed people with carnations pinned to their jackets or dresses, handing out paper folders, the cover showing a colorful abstract image of triangles and a headline that reads: Feast of the Holy Trinity. Despite all the tearful hugs, all the haunted faces, this is not a funeral, not really. It's an effort to restore normalcy to a place marked forever by torture and murder. This passes for the regular Sunday morning ritual, or tries to.

Entering the main room of the church, Span immediately confronts a large stone baptismal font, intricately carved. He recognizes it from the police photos. This is where Henrik Piedela, the sexton, broom in hand, died when one of the intruders put two nine millimeter slugs through his brain. Span stands briefly on the spot where Piedela fell, then he's swept into the flow of the crowd, moving forward, finding a seat on the right aisle, half way up, giving him a good overall sense of this soaring crime scene.

This is a bigger church than he was expecting. The altar area, where Matthias Hammar was assaulted, tortured and murdered, is still a good distance from Span's pew, but he recognizes it clearly from the police photos. The large cross, to which Hammar was so crudely nailed, has been repaired, cleaned and reattached to its moorings. It looms over a carved stone altar pulled away from a back wall that's filled with eight carved figures, each gazing upward at the cross. From the high Gothic ceiling hang rows of brass lanterns flanking a single huge chandelier that hovers over the chancel. Two tiers of stained-glass windows dominate the sides of the nave, which is finished in the same tan colored stone as the building's exterior. There's a small wood-carved lectern to the right of the altar, the altar where Hammar spent his last conscious moments. To the left there's an impressive stone pulpit from which Hammar delivered the sermons that so impressed Span's friend, Chuck, and so angered and alienated so many of the city's business elite.

At the back of the church, from a gallery above the narthex, a large pipe organ kicks in, gently at first, then powerfully, filling the somber place with sound. The grim crowd sits quietly. Some cry softly. Some kneel with heads bowed and eyes closed. Four white-clad children have begun to light candles. None of this is foreign to Span. It's part of his past, a distant past that he's rejected as "nonsensical hocus pocus presided over by smarmy hypocrites." Yet, he's somehow moved by the atmosphere and by the faces of these damaged people. He wants to place himself apart from them. He's a reporter, after all, conditioned, trained to hold himself at a distance, to look at situations from the outside in, to cast himself as an independent, impartial observer. But these people are more like him than he's ever imagined.

His thoughts are interrupted by a lone figure, a tall slender man with a mane of gray hair, in a tailored dark suit, walking forward down the center aisle to the front row, dropping in a genuflect to one knee, then taking a seat on the opposite side just below the pulpit. Quickly he's joined on either side by two younger men in business suits. This is someone Span hadn't expected to see today. He recognizes the slender man as Jonas W. Kron III, the newly-minted "person of interest" in the murder of the Reverend Matthias Hammar. This is a man Span needs badly to meet. This is a man who needs to answer some questions.

Looking around, Span sees no one else he recognizes. Somewhere in this crowd are politicians, civic leaders and maybe some other reporters whom he would know by sight, but he doesn't see them now. Would Bender be here? He doubts it. Now, suddenly, everyone is standing and turning to face the back of the church as the organ finishes an introduction and people begin to sing a hymn. "Holy holy, holy," they sing, and Span's thinking, "Well, not holy enough to prevent a double homicide, not holy enough to escape its terrible aftermath." A long, white-robed procession moves slowly forward, led by a woman swinging a load of smoky incense, followed by a large crucifix, various candles, a choir, and, bringing up the rear, a clump of grim-faced clergy. Among them is Maggie.

Somehow this surprises Span. He knew she would be speaking, of course. He didn't know she would be playing a prominent role. But here she is, passing within a few feet of him, tall, slender and dignified, her strong volleyball-player shoulders evident beneath her dazzling white alb and white stole, the sun shining through the colorful windows making dappled patterns on the whole assembly. Span had never imagined seeing Maggie in full clerical garb. To see a girl, especially one as striking as Maggie, all done up as a priest is a difficult concept for him to handle. As a not-so-proud product of Chicago's Catholic schools, he had known many priests in his younger days, and even liked and respected a few. But not many.

Span admits that his disdain for religion runs deep. Many times he had picked through the events of his childhood to try to figure out the root of his aversion, but it seemed like an accumulation of things, one piled on top of another. The event that stayed with him most clearly happened one day in perhaps the fifth or sixth grade. This would have placed it about 1960 or so at the height of the Cold War. Father Kowalsky, the school principal, gathered all the kids together for an assembly and presented them with what seemed to Kowalsky a critical question: If Russian soldiers marched into Chicago, an event that the priest seemed to think was quite likely, all the kids in the school would be lined up along the shore of Lake Michigan, he said, and the soldiers would ask each child, one by one, to either renounce "Our Lord" or be shot to death. How many, he wondered, would stand up for Our Lord? Everyone willing to die for Christ should go to one side of the gym and those who would cave into godless communism should go to the other.

Still today, Span can picture the stretch of lakeshore near Montrose Beach and see clearly his classmates, Johnny Jessup and Gary Grantham and the ravishing Penny Canari in her blue plaid jumper, and the evil, brown-clad Russian troops with their machine guns slung around their necks.

Every child, of course, got up and went immediately to the Jesus side of the gym, including Span. But the absurdity of the exercise never left him. Even at age ten or eleven, it seemed far more likely to him that Chicago would be vaporized by a hydrogen bomb long before Russian soldiers could invade and, if so, there would be no children left to shoot. Second, he wondered about the motive of a grown man, a priest no less, who would frighten children with such a preposterous story. Third, and perhaps most troubling, it seemed to him highly unlikely that he and his fellow classmates had answered the question truthfully. He knew himself and his friends quite well, and he was sure that none of them would have volunteered to be shot by the side of the lake, Jesus or no Jesus. After all, hadn't they been taught about the basic frailty and sinfulness of human beings? Hadn't even St. Peter himself denied Our Lord three times when the Roman soldiers came looking for him? Wasn't God's mercy in the face of human unworthiness the whole point? Apparently not.

More than anything, it was religion posing as a threat that bothered him most as he grew into his teen years – that and the notion that religion was an exclusive benefit for the so-called righteous and not for flawed people like his Aunt Joan, who had committed the unforgivable sin of divorcing her jerk of a husband, or like his friend Barney in the next block who hid muscle magazines under his bed and talked more like a girl than a boy, or for people around the world or maybe even in other worlds who'd never had a chance for what the priests called salvation.

But now here is Maggie, the cop turned padre, who seems to project an entirely different outlook. It isn't Maggie's brand of the Christian religion that makes the difference. In fact, if today's service is any indication, this particular take on Protestantism seems to him indistinguishable from the Catholic Mass of his teenage years. There is the Kyrie and Gloria and now a series of readings, the last of which is performed by Maggie herself, standing at the center of the congregation, flanked by candles and partially obscured by a cloud of sweet-smelling smoke. She reads from Matthew, concluding with Jesus' familiar promise to his followers: "Remember, I am with you always to the close of the age."

Then she climbs into the pulpit, Matthias Hammar's pulpit, makes the sign of the cross, and delivers a clear and comforting homily about a cosmic yet intimate God who will not forsake the people of St. A's, even in the midst of their anguish over the violent loss of their leader and friend. Later, during communion, the choir offers a stirring recital of Egil Hovland's "Stay With Us" that brings a shiver even to Span, although he doesn't want to admit it.

Chapter Seventeen

Sunday, 11:15 a.m

When the seventy-five-minute ordeal is finished, Span struggles to make his way forward against the crowd to the pew occupied by Jonas Kron. But by the time he arrives the elusive industrialist has vanished – or almost vanished. Span catches a glimpse of Kron's back as he exits a side door that opens into a hallway along the west side of the church. When he reaches the hallway, Kron is nowhere to be seen. Only twenty minutes later, as Span, coffee in hand, chats with a clump of parishioners and local politicos in a crowded parlor called the Mary-Martha Room, does he spot Kron again in a far corner talking with Gwen Gray, the loquacious parish administrator and now, suddenly, talking with Maggie Lindberg, in black clerical shirt and black slacks. She greets Kron with a handshake, not with the hugs and tears that are so abundant this morning.

As Span draws near to their conversation, he detects a bemused smirk on Kron's face, perhaps his natural expression. There's impatience in Kron's manner, as if he's preoccupied with other things. His eyes focus on a far wall even though he's plainly talking to Maggie. "I'm sorry to hear that," he's telling her. "I trust a hiatus is something that suits you."

"I'd rather stay," Maggie says. "But the bishop has his own idea about what's best for the parish at this point. And, as Gwen knows, I think the cops leaned on the bishop a little, at least that's our impression. He's got crisis specialists in mind to step in here for the rest of the summer. Without me tied down so much here, I think the cops have an idea that I can help them with the investigation. We'll see about that. I think that ..."

Maggie is surprised to see Span approaching. "Span Lokken ... in a church? No way." She gives him a sisterly hug that, for him, verges on the thrilling. Her cheek is soft against his and her blond hairdo presses against his nose and mouth carrying the aroma of apple-scented shampoo. Span recovers with a nod to Gwen, whom he met only a few days before, and then elicits a limp handshake from Mr. Kron, who regards Span is if he's some kind of insect.

"Oh yes, the reporter. Somehow I pictured you younger."

"I have the same thought every time I see myself in the mirror," Span offers, sensing that he has failed to melt the frost. "Actually I'd been hoping to catch up with you, Mr. Kron. Maybe sitting down to talk about, you know, the situation."

The two young men in business suits, Kron's silent companions, have been lurking on the periphery. Now they're stepping forward, between Span and their boss. Kron's attention, meanwhile, shifts to Gwen and Maggie. "My condolences, Miss Gray, and to you Pastor Lindberg. Afraid I'll miss the funeral. Out of town on business this week."

With that, Jonas Kron, ignoring Span, gives a slight bow to the two women, turns to hand his coffee cup to one of his young associates, then walks regally toward the doorway.

Chapter Eighteen

Wednesday, June 15, 9:10 a.m

Sunday brunch is so popular at the Island Grille that it's served every day all day, which explains why Maggie is having Sunday brunch on Wednesday. She arrives early, not expecting Span for another half hour. Ordering a leisurely glass of freshly squeezed OJ, she's thinking, *so this is what it's like to be on hiatus.*

But Span arrives early, too, sliding abruptly into her booth, relieved to see her in a blue t-shirt – not the cursed collar, thank God. By now you'd think he'd be accustomed to Maggie in priestly garb after seeing her on Sunday and then again at Henrik Piedela's small funeral on Monday and at Matthias Hammar's mega-mass yesterday.

Instead of "good morning," he blurts, "Didn't this used to be a bowling alley? Isn't this where Elaine's Lanes used to be?"

"When I was a kid," Maggie responds, "Dad would drive us all to Elaine's on Sunday for the smorgasbord."

"I remember the 'broasted chicken' sign out front," Span says, "but I never figured out what *broasted* was."

Maggie points to the far wall. "Look over there..." One remaining broasted chicken sign overlooks a single bowling lane, all shiny and preserved, like an art piece. "Pretty cool they saved some of the old place. I heard this was the last bowling alley in the city that still had pin boys."

Span tries the coffee and makes a face. "Some funeral," he says, switching gears to yesterday's extravaganza. An overflow crowd had spilled into the social rooms at St. A's and out onto the sidewalks. The ceremony was packed with impressive music and remarkable stories about Matthias Hammar's improbable life. Span had gained a clearer picture of why Hammar was so admired and why a good number of people – including the absent Jonas Kron – couldn't stomach the man. The tributes made it plain why someone like Kron might consider Hammar guilty of betrayal.

It was Kron, after all, as Maggie tells it, who had plucked Hammar from East Coast academia and installed him in the grand church that his family had built and nurtured. Hammar had come with impeccable credentials and seemingly conservative leanings, looking the part of a proper clergyman, embracing the liturgical dignity and traditionalist decorum that Kron wanted to preserve.

But almost from the start Hammar had poked a stick in Kron's eye, Maggie says. First came his plan to turn the church basement into a homeless shelter, followed by the offering of free English lessons to Somali immigrants, who came into the church buildings with their hijabs and Muslim prayer rugs – came into Kron's church, for crying out loud! Then Hammar pushed to add women clergy at St. A's, starting with Maggie. Indeed, he emerged over the years as a champion for women's rights and gay rights, both in the community and in the national church. He didn't hesitate to find creative ways to speak out, even from the pulpit, in support of almost every despicable liberal cause, from affordable housing to bicycle lanes, from climate justice to gun control, from renewable energy to "Black Lives Matter." He wanted to advertise St. A's as a sanctuary for illegal immigrants!

Worst of all, Maggie recalls, the congregation loved it. The parish began to grow again, attracting a younger, more liberal crowd, including a surge of gays and members of color. Kron's traditionalist Swedish church was harder and harder to detect. Kron's dream was withering before his eyes. Hammar was Judas.

He rarely missed an opportunity to embarrass Kron, quoting scriptural warnings against hoarding wealth and instructions to give away possessions. He often spoke of the deep socio-economic chasms so evident in his adopted city, gaps separating rich and poor, white and black. "A winner-take-all" society is how he often described Minnesota — and America.

A major fracture, Maggie says, came when the pastor declared April 15, tax day, a "Day of Patriotic Gratitude." Americans should be proud to pay taxes and grateful for generous public investments that improve the lives of so many, he declared from the pulpit. Citing a Bible passage about Jesus' followers sharing all things in common, Hammar said it was time for the wealthy, having enjoyed most of society's benefits, to commit a much greater share of their income to the common good.

Kron seethed, Maggie recalls. He made nasty phone calls, wrote hateful emails and bad-mouthed Hammar at every possible turn, most notably at the upscale Downtown Club among his other exclusive haunts. "Will no one rid me of this meddlesome priest?" he liked to quote to his friends. Kron had memorized the line, thinking that people would see him as a literary man, which he was not.

The last straw came when Hammar launched a campaign to

erect a monument in Washington, D.C. to honor all the victims of gun violence — "brave people," he called them, "who gave their lives so that others may have the right to shoot; martyrs who sacrificed their lives in the fight for gun liberty."

The sarcasm was devastating, Maggie recalls. Hammar claimed to be "absolutely confident" that the National Rifle Association would join "authentic Christians and others" in paying for such a monument. After all, he said, such a monument would celebrate everyone's right to shoot guns while also memorializing the victims. What could be wrong with that? Followers of Christ, he said, should be happy to match the NRA's generosity dollar for dollar in building such a monument.

In a later campaign, Hammar claimed to have founded A.R.M.D. — Assault Rifles for the Mentally Disturbed. "Crazy people have rights, too," he argued, with only a hint of snark. "No American should be denied the liberty of having guns and ammo. Americans have the right to defend themselves no matter their mental stability."

The genius of these campaigns was the difficulty most people had in knowing if Hammar was truly serious. Perhaps for that reason, his crusade put pressure on the NRA and drew national attention. "Good Morning America," "The Today Show," "PBS News Hour" and "CBS Evening News" all featured stories about Hammar, the gun-happy clergyman and his ideas. Stephen Colbert had him on as a guest.

"Kron went absolutely postal on that one," Maggie tells Span as her breakfast arrives. "I'll never forget the fight they had. Jonas Kron is not the kind of guy who yells. He simmers. He fumes. The veins stick out on his forehead. But this time he was like a volcano erupting. It was loud."

"This was where?" Span asks.

"In Matthias' office. Door closed. But everyone heard it.

Never heard Matthias answer back, though. Easy to imagine him just sitting there with that wry smile on his face, that twinkle in his eye. Probably made Kron even madder."

More than before, Span recognizes that Maggie, because she knows these people so well, because she knows the mentality of both St. A's and the island, might have a better chance than anyone of getting to the bottom of this mess.

With the brunch check paid, the two are walking now, down Evergreen, taking a left by the church, crossing the Franklin Bridge over the west channel of the Mississippi River. The sky is hazy and the breeze uncommonly absent. There's barely a ripple on the dark and indifferent river below. At this pace, Span is wondering how long it takes for a drop of water to flow from Hennepin Island to New Orleans.

Span's mind tends to wander even in the midst of a sensational murder investigation. His occasional drift is not due to any poetic impulse lurking within him, he decides. Rather, it's a mechanism he uses to avoid the gloominess that might overtake him if he were to bore down too heavily on the malevolence of human nature, on the depravity that generated a crime like this.

Maggie is silent, too, as they walk, approaching now the turnaround point, the place with the big sculpture of the fur trader and the Indian guide paddling the canoe. A black Lincoln Navigator idles nearby. It's the kind of car a cop notices. The driver's door opens and a husky uniformed man wearing sunglasses approaches. Over the man's shoulder, Span and Maggie can see another man sitting in the back seat of the SUV talking on a cellphone. That man is Jonas Kron.

"Excuse me. My name is Robert," says the husky man. "Mr. Kron noticed you two walking as we drove across the bridge. He asked me to stop and deliver a message. He would be pleased to have you, Mr. Lokken, and, if you wish, you too Pastor Lindberg, as his guests tonight at his home at 9:30. Is that agreeable?"

Span is stunned. After being turned away by snarling dogs, after suffering Kron's dismissive attitude toward him at St. A's, after waiting in vain for the return of a half-dozen calls, now suddenly he has been granted an audience with the great man? Kron wishes to speak? There's a long moment of silence along the bridge, the only sound the whoosh of passing traffic.

"Delighted" is the only word Span eventually manages to utter – and then to Maggie as Robert climbs again behind the wheel, "Well, that was easy."

Chapter Nineteen

Wednesday, 9:32 p.m

It's past 9:30 when Maggie leans out her car window to ring the bell beside the big iron gate that leads to the Kron family compound. No response. Only the chirping of crickets fills the gathering darkness, no voice coming over the speaker, no buzzer buzzing them in. Only eventually a click, and the gate slides open revealing a massive three-story, multi-gabled house with steep slate roofs and multiple turrets.

Over in the passenger seat, Span is thinking, wow, thanks to his reporting career, he's been a guest in some impressive homes – the White House, for one, along with several governors' mansions and two or three elegant Park Avenue apartments occupied by rich executives along with an amazing retreat in Greenwich, Connecticut, with rolling lawns and gardens that seemed never to end.

There's no grassy lawn here. Kron's house is short on shrubbery with only a small cobblestone courtyard and an ominous stone wall to separate it from the stately old Kron Industries headquarters building – the one with the creepy clock tower –

and the other buildings and sheds in the sprawling complex, most of which are warehouses and sawmills long abandoned, and rickety docks that haven't loaded a barge in decades. The last stone was cut here thirty years ago as the Kron company shifted emphasis to its global construction business.

Maggie has never been inside these gates either, despite Jonas Kron's prominence at St. Ansgar. She has only heard stories about Kron, the history buff, and about this old mansion, thinking that the stories were probably exaggerations. She has heard about Kron dressing up as a knight in armor from time to time and doing battle re-enactments out in the woods, sometimes here, sometimes in Europe. And his house? People call it a museum. But then the whole south end of Hennepin Island is a musty museum of sorts. The whole Kron complex carries an aura of faded glory.

It surprises them that the massive front door opens before Maggie or Span can knock, and there is Jonas Kron, in person. No butler answering, no servant or assistant. Just Kron, slender and casually elegant in gray slacks, a pink summer-weight sweater, open-collar white shirt and highly polished tasseled loafers. He looks like a rich, aging preppy at leisure, his gray hair expertly clipped, his face tanned, his preoccupied smile that of a man who really wants to be doing something other than welcoming these particular guests on a Wednesday night.

"I'm so glad you've come," he says, sounding polite if not quite sincere.

Span's first impression is of a house of considerable volume: tall ceilings, a massive central staircase, lots of intricate dark woodwork, but none of it particularly well lighted by modern standards. This is not an opulent, showy house in the way you might expect. The chandeliers – there are many of them – are more austere than glittery. The rugs on the unpolished stone and creaky hardwood floors are Persian and magnificent, but worn and a bit faded. This is less a palace than a castle.

"Permit me to show you around," Kron is saying. And he's off on a forty-five minute monologue describing his impressive collection of slightly dusty tapestries and paintings, and dozens of artifacts dating to the Middle Ages. Span flicks the *record* function on his cellphone hoping to pick up the details because his head is quickly overloaded with names of Viking swashbucklers, early Swedish nobles and crusaders, and powerful Swedish kings who established what Kron refers to as *the empire.* Neither Span nor Maggie has heard of a Swedish empire. They trade glances to let one another know that they consider the idea vaguely amusing, later sharing the admission that the only such empire they can imagine consists of meatballs, furniture stores and gloomy, subtitled movies that go on and on.

But Kron is fully absorbed. Quite suddenly he has become an effervescent child, bubbling with enthusiasm over his collection. He's almost charming.

"This goblet (he hoists it as if offering a toast) is from an eleventh-century Norse settlement on the tip of Newfoundland, the first Viking village in the New World," he announces. "This sword and this battle ax (he points at two weapons affixed to a wall) were recovered from the bloody invasion of Alexandria in 875. The ax is said to have been swung by the infamous Bjorn Ironside himself, and to have inflicted the first terrifying Viking blows on the African continent." He points to a mannequin encased in a suit of armor posed atop a pedestal. Kron beams with obvious pride. "This armor was worn by a Swedish soldier of Pope Celestine III in the gruesome campaign to Christianize the pagans of Estonia and Latvia in the late 1100s."

Next he delivers a detailed narrative on a succession of kings (each named Gustav something or other), heaping praise on the military tactics of Gustavus Adolphus, pointing out a series of paintings depicting glorious victories over Russia, Poland and Denmark in the 1600s. "We were a pivotal player in the Thirty Years War," he declares, smiling widely.

Kron leads his guests across a hallway into a library with large south-facing windows looking out over the lighted back gardens, swimming pool, tennis court and guest quarters. He poses next to an unlit fireplace big enough to walk into. "Observe what happens when I press against this wooden panel," he says, standing to the side of the fireplace. "This secret door (it pops open as if by magic) is for servants to transport food and beverages up from the kitchen and wine cellar below." The opening reveals a steep concrete stairway leading down to a scullery and kitchen on one side and a large bunker-like room on the other.

Carefully, the party makes its way downstairs and into the bunker. "This is my workshop," he explains, showing his visitors a half-dozen tables upon which dozens of artifacts are being repaired or restored. Of special interest is a child-sized suit of plate armor resting upright on a small pedestal. "My favorite!" he announces. "This magnificent piece dates to the late 1500s and was crafted by an Italian metal worker exclusively for young Prince Gustavus Adolphus. He, as you must know, became Sweden's most celebrated warrior king. Legend has it that the boy prince never paid attention to the armor until he became king at age 16, but by then he had outgrown it. It's thought to have been worn only once."

"How did you acquire it?" Span asks. "And how much did you pay?"

"It came into my possession in 2007," Kron says, but declines to divulge its price.

Nearly an hour has passed since the lecture began. The three of them have come full circle, standing again in the front parlor. So far, Kron has offered no reasonable opportunity for

Span and Maggie to ask the questions they came to ask, questions about the envelope in the killers' luggage, questions about his grudge against Matthias Hammar. With the time approaching 10:30, the delusional Kron is only now beginning to summarize the geographic extent of his imperial Swedish dreamland. "The empire stretched from St. Petersburg in the east to Poland, Germany and the Norwegian coast in the west, and even across the Atlantic to the New Sweden colony along the Delaware River in what is now Pennsylvania and New Jersey – and, of course, eventually to Hennepin Island in Minnesota."

Curiously, Kron's mood has shifted. He's no longer a bubbly child. Triumphalism has given way to resentment. Heroes have been replaced by traitors. "The Swedish 'imposters' have betrayed the empire again and again," he grumbles, sounding as if he, himself, were the primary victim of lost empire and diminished glory. "The turncoats took charge in 1709 and they're still in power today." A fog seems to have descended over his bluish-gray eyes.

"Now the whole world laughs at us," he says. "We deserve it, of course, because we're so pathetically gullible and naïve. You go back to Sweden today and it's so sad. They've left the gates wide open. Everybody gets in. The dregs of the earth. The streets are filled with immigrants speaking jibberish, foreign women with babies, lots of them. Everybody's looking for a handout. Nobody wants to work anymore. Not even the real Swedes. The imposters I call them. They don't get married anymore. They're all fat and tattooed. They depend on the government for everything. Mosques are everywhere. Churches are a joke. They're empty. Our history, our culture is pretty much gone. The polls say that forty percent of the country doesn't even know the king's name."

Maggie sends a glance toward Span, mystified by this darker turn.

"We, that is my company, used to do business over there. Not anymore. Too much regulation, too much red tape. Costs are outrageous. Taxes take your breath away. So, they drive us out, just like they drove Saab out of business and now Volvo they've driven into the laps of the Chinese. There's a long line of traitors who sold our country and our culture down the river. I can recite a short list if you'd like."

Maggie and Span obviously don't want to hear it, but they fail to speak up. Kron is on a roll and unlikely to be deterred. He starts with somebody called King Charles XII "who got outsmarted by Peter the Great at the gates of Moscow" and ends with a few more contemporary names that Span recognizes, although he's dumbfounded about what possible ingredient could make these people so vile. Greta Garbo and Ingrid Bergman? Gunnar Myrdal and Dag Hammarskjold? Bjorn Borg and ABBA?

But Kron's arsenal of animosity peaks when it comes to Olof Palme, the socialist prime minister who was assassinated in 1986. Span remembers clearly. Palme, who often walked around without bodyguards, was gunned down at close range one night in downtown Stockholm while walking home from a movie with his wife. He remembers it not only because of the story's shock value but because a freelancer friend of his, a woman he was dating in New York at the time, was assigned to do an American reaction piece for Swedish TV. She was trying to do man-on-the-street interviews on Fifth Avenue, but nobody had heard the news, and if they had they didn't care. People had never heard of this guy, Palme. She did the piece anyway, of course, saying that Americans were shocked and saddened at Palme's murder, especially in a place so peaceful and safe as Stockholm.

Kron, with a sharp look at Maggie, now adds a final unrecognized name to his list of contemporary traitors, then realizes the need to clarify: She's the female archbishop of the Church of Sweden, he says. "She doesn't stand up to anything. She just caves in. She's a toady to the European Union and the powers that be. She's part of the ultra liberal elite that made our country soft and turned it into a laughing stock. Sadly, there are a lot of Swedes on that list, Swedish-Americans, too."

"Matthias Hammar?" Span interjects. "Is he on your list?"

An awkward silence envelops the room. Kron peers down at his shiny loafers, a vein popping at his left temple. "I'm supposed to say the polite thing," he says, "that Matthias' unfortunate death was tragic, a gruesome and cowardly act. Maybe it was. But let's face it. The Reverend Hammar's Swedish blood was running a bit thin. He was, shall we say, a disappointment. He was supposed to help me restore this small slice of empire, this island, this colony, if you will. But he forgot who he was. Thanks to his complicity, this once honorable piece of New Sweden is headed down the toilet."

"What do you mean down the toilet?"

It's Maggie asking the question, Maggie who wants so badly to see Hennepin Island as a cozy refuge for her and her daughter. To Span's ears, too, Kron's depiction of a "lost colony" headed down the sewer seems more than a little crazy. To Span's way of thinking, this island, if anything, is not headed anywhere. It's main characteristic, in contrast to the rest of a rapidly changing city, is its forgotten-ness. The island is stuck in a time warp, neither climbing nor falling, neither gentrifying nor deteriorating. Until the events of the past few days, the island seemed like a place where everyone had quietly agreed to just stop and call a timeout.

"Let's just say that this island is like the frog in boiling water," Kron says. "Every day we're losing a little more of our heritage, our identity, our specialness. Every day we're becoming more, let's say, mongrelized. More like every place else."

"So, you're not unhappy that Matthias Hammar was murdered?" Span asks, returning bluntly to the point.

"I'd expect a question like that from someone like you, Mr. Lokken. Let's put it this way. Everything happens for a reason. Surely you noticed that the Reverend Hammar died on the sixth day of the sixth month in the year 2016 at the age of sixty-six. How could that be a coincidence? If you know your history, then you know the significance of the number six."

"Must have slipped my mind," Span says, whispering to Maggie: "He died on the fifth."

Kron continues. "The police, when they interviewed me, seemed totally unaware of these facts."

"Police? When did you talk to the police?" Maggie asks, the tone of her voice letting Span know that this is a surprise to her, that Bender, in his daily consultations with her, had neglected to tell of any interview with Kron, that Maggie apparently isn't quite the full investigative partner that she was led to believe.

"Last week. Friday," Kron answers. "They came to my office first thing Friday morning."

"Was it Bender?" Span asks.

"Bender and a younger detective, can't remember his name."

"What did they want to know?"

"My history with Matthias, my opinion of him, if we had had any fights, let's see ... where I had been on the day of the murder, whether I recognized the pictures of two gentlemen, the suspects, whether I recognized their names, that sort of thing."

"And did you?"

"Did I what?"

"Recognize them."

"Of course not."

"And where were you on the day of the murder? I don't remember seeing you at church," Maggie asks.

"At my home on Lake Vermillion."

"And what else did Bender and the other detective want to know?" Maggie asks.

"They wanted to check out my bank accounts."

"Really."

"I guess they figured that I must have hired these two gentlemen and paid them off."

"Did you?" It's Span who's asking.

"Again, that's the kind of question I'd expect from you."

"Didn't they ask you about the envelope found in the suspects' luggage in Frankfurt," Span asks, "the envelope from Kron Industries Employees' Credit Union containing five-thousand euros?"

Kron tugs at his pink sweater, then drops his hands into his pants pockets. "They may have mentioned something about that."

"And what did you tell them?"

"They wanted to see some of my company records related to the credit union."

"And did you show them any records?"

"I showed them the door," Kron says. "And I gave them my attorney's number. Oh yes, and I reminded them about the significance of the number six."

"Which is what?" Span asks.

"Let's just say that soon everything will be revealed. Let's just say that six was Matthias' perfect number."

Part Two

The Walrus

PROLOGUE

Stockholm, Sweden
Friday, February 28, 1986, 11:30 p.m. local time

After the film ended, the prime minister and his wife paused on the sidewalk outside the Grand cinema to mingle with friends. Olof Palme was a complex man, both affable and enigmatic. Born into Baltic nobility, his politics were curiously slanted toward the underdog. He sided with labor over management, with social democracy over capitalism, with rebel insurgents over colonial powers. He deeply distrusted the motives of powerful nations, especially the United States and the Soviet Union. Sweden, he thought, despite its relative obscurity, provided a sane example for other nations to follow, a lucid "third path" between the absurd extremes of the major Cold War rivals.

Even so, he reserved the bulk of his contempt for the Apartheid government of South Africa, and sought for Sweden a special relationship with the activist leaders of that country's black underclass. Palme's views had been shaped largely by extensive travel, both in the developing world and in the U.S. As a young man he had hitchhiked through America and had been appalled by its wide economic, social and racial disparities.

As the gathering in front of the cinema began to break up, the Palmes started their stroll arm-in-arm south along Sveavagen, a major commercial thoroughfare. The air was crisp. Shops were closed. Traffic was sparse. There was no notice of the hefty man in the gray overcoat who reappeared, joined by a younger man in a dark jacket, both following at a short distance. Three blocks south of the cinema, the Palmes stopped to admire something in a store window. That's when Jaan, the younger man, a pistol in his jacket pocket, caught up with them. That's when it happened.

Chapter Twenty

Thirty years later
Minneapolis, USA
Wednesday, June 15, 2016, 11:20 p.m.

Surveillance is something robots do better than humans. It's a realization that frustrates Feliks who finds himself yet again behind the wheel of a rental car, lights off, ignition off, a small carton of McDonald's French fries limp on his lap, a paper cup of coffee tepid in his hand.

The only interesting thing about tonight is the baseball match on the radio. Feliks loves the sound of baseball on the radio at night, the languid hum of the crowd, the occasional crack of the wooden club against the hard leather ball, the easy banter among the commentators. This is the most foreign of sporting events, which makes it all the more attractive to Feliks. Baseball challenges his prideful knowledge of English idiom. Players are not literally *stealing* bases, he has learned. No one is really *flying out* or *coming home*. There are no cattle in the *bullpen*.

The names of the baseball sides fascinate him, too. The local side is named after a genetic abnormality: Twins. Who can say why? And Twins are playing *extra innings* in Cleveland tonight against Indians. Only Americans would name a baseball club after a people who were conquered, subjugated and humiliated. Truth is, he likes working in America because of the many riddles and contradictions that America presents. Surveillance is dull. America is not dull.

Just now Feliks sees headlights shining on the inside of the Kron castle gate and the gate beginning to slide open. He turns the key, hears the annoying cadence of bells reminding him to fasten his seat belt, flicks on his headlights and slips the rental car into gear as Maggie's clunky old Volvo, the blue-gray color of a postman's uniform, makes a right turn out of the gate onto eastbound Lake Street. Feliks' rental car makes a left and follows. The Volvo shifts lanes and turns left onto Evergreen northbound. The rented Toyota follows at a distance. Traffic is light. It is approaching midnight.

Ten blocks ahead, the Volvo makes a right onto Franklin just in front of the big church. Both cars are now eastbound before turning north and pulling over in front of what Feliks has already identified as the journalist's row house. The rented Toyota drives on past, circles the next block, flicks off its lights and stops at the corner, a hundred meters from the Volvo, which still rests by the curb, lights on. This foxy lady priest, Lindberg, and the corrupt journalist, Span Lokken, are still, as the Americans say, *yakking*. But yakking about what? Feliks can only guess. He left behind his listening gear. Perhaps that was a mistake. He would like to know what Kron had told them. Perhaps he told them some of the fantastic tales that Feliks' young associates in the Gaswerks had invented: that Somali warlords had grudges against Hammar, that homosexual revenge led to Hammar's death, or that Hammar's feud with his estranged son had boiled over into murder. Americans are gullible. Under the right conditions, they will believe anything. It is their greatest weakness.

Whether this Lokken or this girl priest Lindberg can lead Feliks to his targets, that's the central issue. He has been in town less than forty-eight hours. He's had time only to read what the Gaswerks has supplied: emails and phone transcripts from the top police official on the case. What's his name? Bender? Only now is Feliks contemplating the help that Jonas Kron could offer. This is not yet a crisis. Considering the IQs of his targets, this should be what the Americans call a piece of cake. The pros are not yet fully involved. The FBI has only begun to sniff around. Mostly it's just the locals – the Barney Fifes, as Feliks calls them.

The Big Man allows his head to fall back against the car seat. He sighs, stifling the urge to open the door and stretch out his bulky frame. He has roughly the size, strength and agility of a linebacker in the brutal American game of football. Other than that, he's not much to look at. He knows that he lacks the necessary manners and taste to be fashionable. His comb-over hairstyle is a failure. His wardrobe is a joke. Yet he has become, over time, a thoughtful and reflective man. Certainly he doesn't regret his posting to America because America has given him the freedom to ponder his regrets, or perhaps it's better to say that America has given him the *perspective* that makes regret possible.

To be still in the field at his age is testimony to his remarkable physical condition and reliability. Maybe he no longer gets the top assignments. Maybe his phone doesn't ring as often. Maybe he no longer dreams his favorite dreams. By now he imagined he'd be a high official pushing papers at the embassy in

Washington or at the United Nations in New York or in Miami or some other glamorous posting with dazzling nightclubs and women draping themselves on his broad shoulders and admiring him in the way they admire James Bond in the movies, but, of course, that has not happened. He doesn't own a tuxedo. He tends to scare women more than attract them.

What drew him to the trade thirty years ago, working mainly in Germany, as well as in the Baltic countries and Scandinavia, wasn't the glamour (there was none) or the pay or the patriotism. Certainly it wasn't the politics. What attracted him was the technique, the purity of the task, the precision required. Somebody upstairs would send a message about a target that needed to be erased at a particular hour and place, and by a particular means, and Feliks would accomplish the work flawlessly. This happened perhaps a hundred times in his first ten years.

His identity then, of course, was not Dobervich, Feliks Alexakov, age fifty-five, unmarried, of Portage Park, Chicago, owner of a small bakery shop, but someone else, he's almost forgotten who, of Leningrad, soon to be renamed St. Petersburg, age twenty-six, divorced, no children, with a whole adventuresome career ahead of him.

Never did he ask the question, why? Never did it occur to him to wonder if pulling the trigger was really necessary. But his tour in America had changed him. The culture of America was confident enough to allow self-examination. It was OK for doubt to creep in. Those second thoughts were inevitable when the old Soviet order dissolved and the new Gaswerks came in. He and others of his generation missed the ideological clarity and the blunt cruelty of the old regime. The new Gaswerks was more nuanced, more sophisticated. These people were not ideologues but cynics and gangsters who tapped into a reservoir of hope that now, in discarding the old polyglot empire, a new nationalism could be found, a pure Russia for Russians. This appealed to Feliks. But he couldn't adjust to the new, more complex management style. You never knew where you stood in the new Gaswerks. As he aged in place, Feliks felt increasingly neglected, passed over, shoved aside. It was clear that to gain attention he had to do something spectacular. So when this particular job, this church thing, came along he devised a bold plan that was sure to get him noticed.

Selecting Richard Reznik and Duane Hajinlian had seemed the right thing at the time. They were idiots. But he knew them. He trusted them. They were loyal to him. They were top performers in an off-the-books loan business he ran out of the back of his Southside Chicago bakery shop. Somebody got behind on their payments, Richard and Duane would talk with them, convince them to pay up. They even did some minor stick-up work for Feliks when he was going through particularly desperate times, times when the cards weren't hitting right or the horses weren't running as fast as they should.

Richard he'd met at a casino in Aurora, Illinois. They sat side by side at a blackjack table, both losing, both drinking, both drowning in their runs of bad luck. Duane came later. He'd done time with Richard up in Wisconsin. Together, they'd trained hard for the church job, their skills as dockworkers paying off in executing Feliks' unique plan. Feliks had chuckled at the brilliance of his crucifixion idea, a stroke of genius that would mislead the authorities and get Feliks noticed at the Gaswerks, maybe elicit rave reviews. Feliks needed rave reviews.

He never counted on his two hired scholars to fuck it up the way they did. For Richard to go off in the priest's mouth was more than a little extreme. And then came the fiasco at the airport. All these retards had to do was make their plane. Anybody can do that. Feliks stood to harvest a tidy sum at the other end. But, apparently, boys will be boys. Feliks cursed the thought.

On that terrible Monday in Frankfurt, when they didn't show up, when Feliks waited nervously in the baggage claim area, that was the low point. That's when he spit on the floor and pronounced them the Two Stooges in sarcastic honor of his favorite American comedy team. Moe, Larry and Curly never ceased to amuse him, although facing the consequences of real-life stoogery was sobering, and now terrifying. The church thing was a high-priority job, something that had come from the very top. Somebody at the very top had placed his trust in Feliks. Feliks had executed a brilliant plan until the stooges went off script. Now it was imperative that Feliks clear his name, tidy up the mess, make things right. His career depended on it. And maybe his life.

Two possible paths lay ahead. On one path, Feliks finds these morons and puts them to sleep. On the other, the local police find them, arrest them and prosecute them, leaving the *why* question wide open. Richard and Duane have no knowledge of why they erased Hammar and Piedela, except to enhance their own incomes. The real reason? There could only be conjecture, and Americans love conjecture. The new Gaswerks thrives on it. Feliks' Moscow colleagues, especially the younger ones, are masters of conspiracy theory, fake news, alternative facts, and the chaos they breed. On either path, Feliks can't lose. He tells himself that he feels confident. When, after all, has he ever failed?

As for the care and feeding of Jonas Kron, well, Feliks has thirty years of experience dealing with Jonas. He is good at it.

Still, his confidence is a bit shaky because, let's face it, his career has been, in retrospect, disappointing. More than three decades of stellar service and this is where he ends up? A flea bag motel in a second-rate city? Driving a tiny rented car?

Eating bad food? Having to leave the comforts of his Chicago operation (never mind its off-the-books profits) for cold coffee and surveillance? Truth be told, comparing Richard Reznik and Duane Hajinlian to a comedy team is just a device to keep Feliks from falling into despair. Feliks' coating of confidence is thin. Despair lives close by.

The sudden sound of a car door slamming arouses Feliks' attention. The journalist Lokken is out of the car now, turning to wave at the old Volvo and climbing the steps to his porch. The Volvo makes a one-eighty and heads south. Feliks' rented Toyota is in motion again. By now it is after midnight.

The Volvo soon slides into a parking spot across the street from Lindberg's row house on Connor. She takes long strides to quickly cross the street and ascend the steps of her lighted porch, then unlocks the door and disappears inside. Almost immediately another woman, short and stout, with close-cropped hair, departs the house and climbs into a car. Employing his night vision equipment, Feliks punches in the license plate number. Out pops Gwendelyn Delores Gray, born 1965, of 5959 Crawford Avenue South, Minneapolis. She is obviously, as the Americans strangely call them, babysitter.

As the house goes dark, Feliks once again feels the creep of boredom, like rising water about to cover his head, when he catches a glimpse of sudden movement on Lindberg's porch. A dark figure is scrambling to get free from what might have been a hiding place. The figure is jumping off the porch now and walking quickly away. This is a slender man who, by his movements, appears to be quite young — and quite familiar to Feliks. Feliks grabs his long lens and adjusts the focus. The man's face is obscured by shadow and by a wide-brimmed, floppy hat, the kind worn against the sun at the beach. But it is never worn at night. Moreover, the figure is wearing sunglasses at midnight. Feliks recognizes this strange figure by its profile and jerky movements. What remarkable good fortune! This figure is almost certainly Richard Reznik.

Feliks smiles. He will be back home in Chicago in no time. He could finish with Richard now, of course. But Richard will lead him to Duane, and the three of them can have a nice reunion. It will be tidier that way. The two stooges can simply disappear without a trace. Or, better yet, their bodies can be discovered with evidence that feeds conjecture, conspiracy and mystery. Feliks will leave those details to his friends at the Gaswerks. The priority now is to follow stooge number one.

The man who might be Richard Reznik hurries beneath the streetlights toward Evergreen Avenue. Feliks' rented Toyota, headlights off, eases away from the curb and into the street. At the corner of Evergreen and 26th, Feliks sees the floppy-hat man duck into a brightly lit liquor store, emerging a few moments later with a small bag. He pauses on the deserted avenue, seeming to look up and down the street for the trolley that stopped running at midnight. Now he's walking across to the Sheraton Island Inn where two taxis await, the drivers chatting under a streetlight. The floppy-hat man is climbing now into the backseat of the first taxi, the driver finishing his conversation and joining his passenger. After a lengthy pause, the taxi makes a U turn from the curb and heads north on Evergreen. On the side street, Feliks' Toyota comes to life and follows, destination unknown.

Chapter Twenty-One

Thursday, June 16, 1:10 a.m

Duane Hajinlian is slumped on the floor beneath booth number five at the back of Lucky's Nordeast Lounge, not moving, except for the slight up and down of his chest. Marla Kusik, the proprietor and occupant of the upstairs apartment, is sweeping up, fixing to close early on a slow night. She almost forgets about Duane, seeing as how he's been passed out since maybe 9 o'clock.

"Duane! Hey, Duane!" she repeats. "Get your fat ass back downstairs!" She kicks him in the head. Duane stirs briefly before resuming his slumber. It had been a difficult day.

The first thing entering his head when he awakened this morning was where the fuck is Richard? The chipped linoleum floor of Marla's basement apartment held two dirty mattresses. And Richard, he wasn't on the other one. Duane's second thought was projectile vomiting, which he did into the filthy toilet around the corner and then thought about a cigarette and breakfast. There was an already opened box of Cap'n Crunch on the battered table and a dirty bowl in the sink, but when Duane opened the fridge looking for milk he was almost floored by the smell. No milk in there anyway, only a few beers and a bottle of strawberry vodka. Turns out that strawberry vodka wasn't all that bad over cereal.

What was really bothering Duane was his missing medication and the probability that Richard took it. What time was it, anyway? The sun was streaming in under the pulled shades. Almost 2, according to Marla's cellphone, which Duane found in the pocket of his jeans. How Marla's phone ended up in Duane's jeans is anybody's guess. What happened to the wad of folding money was the bigger question that got Duane to wondering again where the fuck is Richard? He thought about what was going to happen to Richard when he returned, like maybe his skinny ass gets stuffed into one of Marla's trash barrels along with some gasoline and a match. Poof! No more King Richard.

In hopes of spotting Richard, Duane then pushed open the metal door and squinted into the alley lined with single and double garages, some of them coated with dirty gray stucco, others built of wood and needing paint, all of them connected by chain link fences and smelling of dog shit. Duane's head was foggy but he was pretty sure this wasn't Germany. If this was Germany he'd remember his first airplane ride, which he doesn't.

In the alley there was a side door to the upstairs, which was Lucky's Nordeast Lounge, so he dragged his fat ass up the stairs and inside where he was greeted by cool darkness and the urge to smoke another cigarette. Marla said never to come upstairs during business hours, but whatever. Right away he saw Marla behind the bar. She was wearing a white sleeveless t-shirt showing tattoos on big arms that looked like she'd been lifting.

Her stringy blond hair hadn't been washed in a while. There were maybe six old dudes at the bar and a couple more at tables in the lounge part, which consisted of a row of plastic-covered booths along one wall. Some country song was playing.

"You seen Richard? Cocksucker ran off with my stash and my cash," Duane told Marla.

"Yeah, and my goddamn cellphone," Marla said, pouring Duane a big glass of Canadian Club which went down pretty nice. "Can't operate here without my goddamn phone," she said, gazing up at the TV where horse races from around the country were happening. The afternoon was taking on a nice warm glow for Duane. Turning from the TV, Marla was staring at a blank spot in Duane's bushy black beard, down low on his right jaw. "What's that?"

"What's what?"

"Blank spot, looks like a bullet hole."

"Oh that. My old lady, the first one, she shot me in the face with a slick little twenty-five I gave her. Bullet came out down here in my neck," Duane said, showing the scar. "Messed up my dental. Cost a shitload. VA picked it up. Sweet."

Marla poured another CC double, figuring that Richard would be back sooner or later, probably with money, and she'd be getting some cash out of him one way or the other.

The debate at the bar was vigorous, Duane sensing that it was about this girl Sandy Hook who, according to several of the geezers, "never happened." Sandy's name sounded familiar to Duane, but he couldn't place her.

It was hard for Duane to remember how long he and Richard had been slumming in Marla's basement. Maybe a week? But he knew why they were stuck there. Something to do with what happened at the church. Now *that* he recalled quite clearly.

The assignment was to show up at 1:30 and unload the shit. Then after it happened, load up the van at 2:30 and make for the airport. That's where things got all fucked up, thanks to Richard. They got through security fine but Richard kept saying he had to take the edge off. They were well supplied with prescription bottles in their carry-ons. So Richard said why not? Duane didn't like the idea, thinking pills might complicate the trip.

"I ain't ever flown before, man," he protested. "I don't wanna get paranoid or nothin."

Richard shot him that superior look, the look Duane hated. After they swallowed a bunch of pills in the latrine, they spotted this cocktail lounge right across the hall, which was perfect. Two sophisticated international travelers with time to kill before their flight. What Duane remembered was frosty glasses of bourbon and this girl with amazing tits that Richard took a shine to and started sweet talking, and the next thing he knew they were in fucking custody. Well, not quite custody. Somebody got a little rough at one point, probably it was the airport security. But pretty soon they were down on the floor, and then they were down on the baggage concourse with nowhere to go but back outside. It was like totally unfair because they hadn't done nothing. But they were fucked.

See, it was supposed to be fifty now and fifty at the other end. So Richard, being totally smart, insisted on stashing forty-five in the luggage and keeping five for walking around. But then the luggage became, what you might say, unavailable. They had the five grand to split, but then things got foggy.

Only lately had it occurred to Duane that he was almost broke. And then it became plain that Richard had split with his last two hundred. Compare that to the cash that they'd stashed in their bags and the cash they were going to get in Germany — that's thousands gone forever — and the future looked pretty fucking bleak thanks mainly to dickhead Richard.

"This ain't going too well," Duane had told Marla as she poured another CC double. If Richard was to walk in the door at this moment he would run the risk of getting fucked up pretty bad.

* * *

What Duane didn't know was that Richard had, as he put it to Marla day before yesterday, "put on his thinking cap."

"Fat Duane lacks the intellectual capacity to get us our money back," Richard told her. "Bastard sleeps all day." Richard, on the other hand, was up at the crack of 10 working on a fiscally responsible economic recovery plan.

Before the church job took place, there had been the stakeout phase, which lasted about a week. For Richard it had meant sitting at the bus stop across from the church every afternoon just to see who came and went and which doors they used. The only thing he remembered – and this was a key factor – was this tall blonde with the ponytail and the really long legs. Every day between 5 and 5:30, she came out and waited for the Evergreen streetcar. This was an extremely exciting moment for Richard, a moment that he looked forward to day after day. She came out, passed through the iron gate, turned right at the crosswalk, then crossed Franklin and waited.

One day she had a kid with her, a fine-looking young girl with curly dark hair, maybe nine years old. They crossed the street hand in hand. This fact that Blondie was apparently a mom did nothing to dampen Richard's appreciation of her. But the details that were most intriguing to him were, one, that funds were running low and, two, that Blondie had a kid with her.

So, what happened this morning was that Richard got up while Duane was still in dreamland and immediately launched his investigation. In a pile of Marla's crappy stuff he found a floppy hat and an old pair of sunglasses. Perfect. Then he climbed out of the basement and walked over to University Avenue to hop on a bus. Stopping at Sunny's to take the edge off with a drink and some of Duane's medication, he looked at the TV over the bar and saw a clip of Blondie and a rich guy name of Jonas Kron III sitting side by side offering a hefty reward of like fifty grand leading to the whereabouts and apprehension of the church murder perpetrators, Richard knowing that the Kron dude was fabulously wealthy because he asked his fellow customers and they confirmed it. And it occurred to Richard that Blondie, knowing this rich Kron dude, had access to money, which is exactly what he lacked. Getting his money back was the only fair way to proceed.

Then, riding the 63 bus past the big canoe statue by the Franklin Avenue Bridge, riding with his sunglasses on and his hat pulled low, suddenly, holy shit! There was Blondie, in person! She was walking across the bridge with some dork.

Off Richard jumped at the next stop and started back-tracking along the bridge, tossing his cigarette over the side, reaching in his jeans for a couple more of Duane's pills just to stop the tingling. Pretty soon, at the far end, he spotted Blondie and the dork standing next to a big black SUV talking to a dude in a suit. The dude jumped back in the SUV while Blondie and the dork turned around and walked back across the bridge toward Richard.

Richard didn't panic. Being cool, he just kept walking, looking straight ahead, not making eye contact with Blondie or the dork as they passed on the bridge. After a few minutes he turned around and saw them both still heading back toward the island, her with the very long legs and incredible ass. He followed at a distance of maybe a quarter block, lighting another cigarette. At Evergreen she and the dork stopped to talk, then they separated. She crossed and waited for the streetcar. It screeched to a stop and Richard saw the driver hopping out and walking to the other end so he could drive it the other way.

The bell rang. Blondie got on in front. Richard waited until the last second, then tossed his cigarette aside and climbed into the back. Off they went, lurching and screeching down Evergreen, headed south.

Richard tried not to look at her, but it was hard not to look. Maybe the dark glasses helped to disguise all the attention he was giving her. He wondered about her hair, what it must feel like to touch. What does it look like when it's not tied up in back? What if she grew it out like really long? When she rose from her seat he couldn't help but zero in on the curvature of her haunches and the magnificent semi-tightness of her jeans. This was amazing. He couldn't help but think back to all those months he and Duane were at the facility fanaticizing about these kinds of opportunities on the outside, and wow, here he was, living the dream!

At 26th she got off and crossed the street going east, talking on her cellphone. Richard followed. Suddenly it was quiet. This was a part of town Richard had never seen. It gave him the creeps. Too many front porches, too many trees and flowers, too many sets of eyes, too much quiet. He wished it was dark. He wished he was in a car.

She walked straight maybe four blocks then turned left on Connor and went up to the second row house from the corner, the one with the two females sitting on the front porch, one an adult, the other a little kid, the same curly headed kid he saw with Blondie before. Up a few steps she went, bent down to hug the smaller girl, got mail from the box, fumbled for keys and, wham, Blondie and the girl were through the door while the other one was off the porch and heading the other way down Connor. If it was dark, Richard was thinking he'd be up for looking in some windows, trying to see something exciting. But it was still daylight. Maybe later he would be back.

Chapter Twenty-Two

Thursday, 1:12 a.m

Richard Reznik ducks into the shadows trying to stay out of the streetlights, walking briskly along 26th Street, away from Blondie's house, all the while thinking what a fucking genius he is.

Fat Duane lacks the brains, the initiative, the capacity to solve the fiscal problem because for Duane to haul his fat ass beyond Marla's basement would constitute a supreme effort. This operation, which Richard has now named Operation Economic Recovery, aims to restore some semblance of justice to the situation. The way Richard figures it, they were screwed out of one hundred large – the fifty they were taking to Germany and the fifty that was supposed to be added to their account on the other side of the pond, but which isn't there and therefore totally sucks.

But there's a plan. Richard is resourceful enough, despite being hunted by every cop in the city, to disguise himself, step onto a bus, head back to the island, spot the long-legged blonde who, from her appearance on TV obviously knows the rich dude, Kron, and follow her to her house and gather valuable intelligence about her and her kid, the last of the intel gathered from his position of advantage behind a large planter on her porch. All this he has accomplished in one day's work.

The next logical step is to drop into Island Package Liquors on Evergreen. This is rather urgent because it closes at 2 and because the streetlights have turned into dragons spitting fire down upon Richard's head, and nobody is allowed to mess with Richard's head. Even as seen through his dark glasses, the beasts are carving sharp slits into his brain, just in front of his left ear. It's a stabbing, metallic pain, like the unpleasant experience of chewing tinfoil. Richard's teeth are killing him now. But help is coming soon.

Island Package, although painfully bright, is all but deserted as Richard slips through the door and slaps down his last eight bucks plus change for a pint of CC. Only after he's out on the sidewalk does it occur to him that he's broke and, as reflected in store windows, he's looking conspicuous at night wearing a sun hat and dark glasses.

With no streetcar in sight, Richard has little choice but to take a taxi. Two cabs are parked across the street at the Sheraton Island Inn, the rag-head drivers standing on the curb making no sense in some foreign language. He steps into the first cab, quickly twisting off the bottle cap and washing down the last of Duane's pills.

"Where to?" says the cabbie, sliding into the driver's seat, a slight, wiry guy wearing a kofia and a short-sleeved yellow shirt.

Richard's thinking how uncool it would be to go directly to Marla's. Besides he forgets the actual name of her bar and he can't recall the street it's on. The only landmark he can think of is the Ferris wheel.

"Take me to the Ferris wheel."

"Ferris wheel? Sir, the fair, it is not currently operational.

Later it comes. In September," the driver says in an accent so thick that Richard thinks seriously about pulling him out of the cab and smashing his face.

"No, stupid, the Ferris wheel, you know, at the bar by the bridge that's all lit up in bright colors, the bar with the miniature golf and the rides and shit."

"You are describing Betty Danger."

"Yeah, whatever. Take me there."

Betty Danger's Country Club is an ultra clever place that's pretty much the opposite of a country club. It's basically a pink and white hangout for artists and hipsters, complete with an indoor-outdoor miniature golf course and a Ferris wheel that offers cheap cocktails and a view of the skyline and the Mississippi River. To get there the taxi takes the freeway loop around downtown and descends into "Nordeast," an unglamorous quarter of old houses, shabby taverns and eastern European social clubs.

All the while, Richard is working out in his mind the details of next week's financial plan, a plan that involves trading Blondie's young girl for cash. The plan germinated when he observed Blondie and the fabulously wealthy dude, Kron, appearing jointly on TV. Then, from his hiding place on Blondie's porch, he learned about the tennis lessons and the possibility of grabbing the girl en route, so to speak.

From the taxi's back seat, Richard sees up ahead the flashing neon. It's not the Ferris wheel, not yet. It's a cluster of corner bars. "Stop!" he blurts. "Up here on the corner." One of the joints is called Norbert's and it looks quiet. The "b" in Norbert's sign has gone dark but the Grain Belt beer logo is all lit up.

The taxi pulls over. "I gotta get out here for a minute, pay the bartender money I owe. Be right back."

Richard jumps out of the cab before the driver can protest. In he goes. Maybe a dozen old men in the darkened room, bartender turning to face the funny looking guy in the floppy hat.

"Gimme a Grain Belt tap," he says, despite this being almost closing time. "Where's the men's?" Bartender points to the back. Two minutes go by. Into the bar comes the Somali cab driver, looking uncomfortable and a bit frightened, eyes darting side to side, asking the bartender about a man in a funny hat, bartender pointing to the men's room in back.

Richard is waiting inside. The instant the driver opens the men's room door Richard drives his fist clear through the cabdriver's jaw. Crack! The guy goes down easy, like a girl, blood oozing from the left side of his mouth and nose. He's out. In a flash Richard is into his pockets, pulling out a fat wad of bills and the car keys. Then he's opening the men's room door and walking nice and easy back through the bar, slapping down a five for the beer and heading out the front door, his knuckles stinging with pain.

Richard never saw himself as a cabdriver, but that's one of the benefits of his chosen profession. He gets to be a lot of things depending on the situation. Growing up on the Iron Range, Richard was attracted to the transportation industry, figuring he'd like to work the ore boats that steam through the Great Lakes out of Duluth. But never in his wildest dreams did he imagine himself driving taxi in Minneapolis.

The cab is flying westbound now, down Lowry, through the Central Avenue intersection, Richard seeing the dancing lights of the Ferris wheel and the sizable bridge on the dark horizon.

His thoughts are playing leapfrog. Taking a piss is one urge he can't defer any longer. He never had a chance back at Norbert's, thanks to the raggedy ass cabdriver. So, when he sees a big church coming up on his right he pulls over onto a side street, jerks to a halt and walks unsteadily over to the edge of the building, unzips his fly and waters down the side door. Feels great, plus there's the symbolic satisfaction of pissing on something that needs pissing on, considering everything that churches have done to him in his life. "Drink ye all of it!" he yells, not sure if the voice is coming out of his throat or someone else's.

The abuse started when Richard was ten, one of the rookie altar boys. Father offered to help him with his homework over at Father's apartment after school. Treats like Cokes and cookies were offered, too, followed by an afternoon nap on Father's bed, both of them needing a break. The naps turned into exploratory games that Richard promised not to tell anyone about. These were secrets to be held tightly between Father Ed, God and Richard, and while Richard is a lot of things he's not a rat. And on this, he never will be.

Getting back to the taxi isn't so easy, Richard's legs going wobbly on him, his vision taking a violent spin. The incessant chirping of crickets assaults his ears as he fumbles for the car door and manages to start the engine, turning the cab around and getting back onto Lowry, now reconnecting to the dancing lights of the approaching Ferris wheel and seriously considering giving a free ride to any young poontang still hanging around. This idea makes him smile. A sizable roll of cash has fallen recently into his possession, he recalls. He tosses the cabdriver's wallet aside but is too busy to peel through the bills to count them, figuring that they must add up to hundreds of dollars.

The cab is inexplicably swaying from side to side now, the glare of oncoming cars breaking Richard's concentration. A horn sounds from somewhere and the whole sequence goes to slow motion, Richard feeling intrusion from the right side, hearing a deafening *blam!*, seeing glass shattering, hearing metal grinding, feeling the car twirling like a fucking carnival ride. Shit! Then darkness.

Next thing Richard knows, he's outside, lying in some

bushes, seeing steam rising from a pile of crumpled metal, headlight beams poking in stray directions, wheels spinning, somebody's motionless body sprawling on the street. Richard's first thought is to call out for help but then he reconsiders, thinking instead about running away. But when he tries to get up, the pain in his right knee and elbow is so piercing he can hardly move. Only with heroic effort is he able to crawl deeper into the dark thicket of bushes and ground cover. In agony, he sees, as if in a dream, the flicker of slowing traffic and hears the distant sirens drawing closer, but fading, slipping away. Then nothing. Nothing.

Chapter Twenty-Three

Thursday, 1:45 a.m

Somehow Feliks is not all that surprised to see Richard swerving into oncoming traffic and setting off the *boom!* and the twirling spectacle now happening before him. He pulls over sharply to the right curb and waits. Other drivers are pulling over, too. Most of them are getting out and walking forward, toward the steaming wreck, most of them, silhouetted against the glare of headlights, walking swiftly with cellphones to their ears. Not Feliks. He's staying in his car. The prospect of approaching sirens and flashing police lights fails to comfort Feliks. So much of his plan depends on Richard leading him to Duane, and the three of them having a nostalgic reunion, ending with the demise of the two retards. Now that won't happen, at least not right away. Did Richard survive this crash? Difficult to assess without getting involved. Whether Richard is dead or alive, Feliks knows his mission has just become more difficult. More patience will be required of the Gaswerks. Feliks knows its patience is already running thin. He knows he has entered dangerous territory.

Chapter Twenty-Four

Friday, June 17, 8:15 a.m

In a far corner of an almost empty newsroom, feet propped on his desk and a barely warm cup of coffee at hand, Span flips through the texts on his phone, then taps into the Star Journal's news feed, paying scant attention to an overnight item. *"Police Search for Runaway Cabdriver after Crash in NE"* reads the headline over a photo showing a smashed taxi at a darkened intersection.

Seems as though the taxi, westbound on Lowry, ran a red light, swerved, and hit an SUV headed south on University. The SUV's driver is in critical condition at North Memorial, while the cabdriver apparently fled the scene. There were no passengers in either vehicle. Cops want to charge the missing cabdriver for blowing the light, but can't find him. He was not a regular employee at Doyle Checker but rather a moonlighter identified by an empty wallet found in the wreck, and by one of the company's regular drivers, as Asam Alawi, an East African man of about 40. Police sources speculate that Alawi may have fled because of "questions over his immigration status." Doyle Checker has no comment on that.

The item means nothing to Span. He's content to sip cold coffee and exhale at the completion of his interview piece on the wealthy but lonely industrialist Jonas Kron III. The story ran this morning with Kron's deflections when asked if he'd hired the killers of the horribly murdered Lutheran clergyman Matthias Hammar, as well as vivid descriptions of the Kron castle's stark interior and references to Kron's Swedish-nationalist fantasies, including his notion that Hennepin Island is a fading colony of the once robust Swedish empire.

It's a nice read. But truth be told, the bigger story, after almost two weeks, seems to have stalled, especially with Kron all gagged and lawyered up. Span is tempted to muse that, if this were a movie or an airport novel, the clues would keep tumbling in at a frantic pace until a crescendo was reached and the bad guys revealed. But this is real life. Span and his colleagues have milked every possible angle. And the renegade blogosphere, along with local talk radio, has produced a scary array of "alternative facts," leading to a conclusion that Hammar was murdered by fellow liberals to make him a martyr for their devilish causes.

The level of frustration at police headquarters is said to be palpable. Maggie reports that Bender threw a wastepaper basket clear across his office yesterday. And even Maggie seems to have lost momentum. "I'm getting the impression that the police aren't telling me everything they know," she told Span on the phone yesterday. "I get the feeling that Bender is shutting me out, that maybe he doesn't trust me as much as he says he does."

As the volume of useful information in Maggie's pipeline contracts, the time Span spends with her expands. They see each other almost every day, sometimes for hours. There's less talk about the case and more chatter about, well, whatever friends chatter about when they're just hanging out.

Friends? Is that what he and Maggie are?

Time with Maggie has made Span wonder if people he once thought of as friends were really not friends but something far less. Contacts perhaps. Sources maybe.

"I've got a lot of friends," he once told her. "I know a lot of people in this city."

But did he really know these people? Or, had his life as a reporter made him a perpetual spectator, someone looking constantly from the outside in, evaluating, assessing, looking for an angle, trying to find a narrative? Maybe it's the only way he knows how to be. It occurs to him that he might be sitting with a gathering of people he thinks of as friends and be *among* them but not really *with* them. Yes, he's passionate about voicing his concerns for their problems. But is his empathy real? Does he truly share their anxieties? Does he suffer and exalt with them? Or are these "friends" really just props in the chronology of his narrow, selfish life?

He enjoys sometimes imagining himself as a character in a movie, usually a black and white B movie from the 1940s. There's a comfort in seeing his life in sharper dimensions, as a reporter in a bygone newspaper drama, wearing perhaps a fedora and suspenders, smoking a cigarette, pounding out a story on a real typewriter in an old-time newsroom, sipping rye from a bottle in the bottom drawer of his desk, trying as best he can to bring truth to a miserable, misinformed world.

He's not that character, of course. He's not even a modern version of that character. But pretending otherwise sometimes gets him through the day. Actually, he's quite ordinary and not all that hardboiled. His childhood was painfully idyllic, experienced mainly within the confines of his north side Chicago neighborhood. His aging parents still live in the same house. He delights in calling them every Sunday.

"You don't come across as a self-centered person," Maggie told him when he confessed his film noir fantasy. That was last night. They were sitting in wicker chairs on her front porch.

And it had occurred to him that maybe he wasn't even a major player in his so-called life but rather just a vessel for other people's stories, stories told and quickly forgotten. Maggie had led him into thinking these thoughts.

"Who do you confide in?" she had asked. He was stumped. Why would he need to confide in anyone? What would he confide? His annoyances with Her Majesty, Carla? His disdain for the digital age in general and social media in particular? His harsh and judgmental feelings toward religion?

"I tell Max everything," he told her, intending to make a joke until he realized it was true. He did confide in a dog. Pathetic? Maybe.

"Were you ever in love?"

Maggie's question hung in the air.

Not knowing what to say, Span began to tell a story about his childhood, about growing up as an only child and how that made him an oddity at his parochial grade school, the point being that he had no sisters, or brothers for that matter, to teach him about peer affection and peer intimacy. Not even his father took him aside to deliver the obligatory birds-and-bees speech, perhaps because his dad's own father had not been around during those delicate years when boys needed to learn about the mysteries of girls.

For Span, going to an all-boys school from the seventh grade on hadn't helped either. There was plenty of talk about sin and guilt, but, aside from the elusive concept of loving God and neighbor, almost nothing was said about intimate human love, devotion and relationship. All the while, the hormones raged.

He and his high school pals chased girls and had "dates" with the young lovelies from St. Kate's and other Catholic schools on the north side of Chicago, and occasionally there were sweaty one-on-ones with heavy panting during which he got his hand under somebody's bra or inside her panties and somebody got her hand on his goodies. He and his buddies discussed these encounters in great detail, Span figuring there were more than a few tall tales being spun, but the point is that he, perhaps more than most of his sidekicks at Jesuit High, thought of girls less as people than as wonderfully mysterious creatures who were objects of conquest.

"Just at the age when they should have been teaching boys and girls to be friends, they put them in separate schools and taught them to be strangers," he told Maggie. "Then there was the hypocrisy part, the part I never found out about until later. And that was that a few of my teachers were *schtupping* each other and, who knows, molesting little kids on the side."

Maggie said nothing, looking down at her feet.

"My first year at Northwestern was a lot like high school," he told her, "but then that changed. One day, I think I was a sophomore, I was in Deering library on a Saturday morning because I must have had a project or something due the next Monday. There's hardly anybody in the place, so it's easy to notice this girl. We're sitting at this really long table, and every time she gets up to check on something or go to the drinking fountain, she comes back and sits closer to me. She's wearing this sweatshirt and jeans and, being a guy, I'm checking out her body, which looks very impressive to me. But she's not what you'd think of as, you know, good looking in the sorority girl sort of way. She's got this ratty brown hair in a kind of ponytail and she's got these big glasses — those were the days before designer frames, you know, when girls would do anything to avoid being seen wearing glasses.

"So, after a couple of hours she's now sitting almost across from me and it's, like, almost noon. So, I ask if she'd like to grab a bite. And she says she's got a bucket of KFC at her apartment, and that's sounding pretty sophisticated to a dorm rat like me. When we go into her place, I remember she drapes her arm around my neck and kind of nuzzles up against me, pushing her, like, ample breasts into my ribs. So, just to be friendly, I put my arm around her waist and give her a small peck on the temple, or something like that. What I really remember, though, is I'm sitting on the sofa and she cracks a beer and when she brings it to me she kind of straddles me. And, whoa, I'm thinking this is pretty sweet because no girl has ever done that to me. In fact, girls have never paid much attention to me at all.

"So, one thing leads to another and pretty soon, there in the early afternoon, neither one of us has a stitch of clothes on, and I've never imagined anyone like her. She's aggressive and she has absolutely no inhibitions whatsoever. She's talking about all her body parts, and mine, and she's exploring every mix and match possibility, plus spreading around the grease from the fried chicken we're eating. And I'll just summarize by saying that I forgot completely about my homework.

"This went on all weekend because both of her roommates were gone, plus it continued in briefer sessions for, like, the next two months before she lost interest in me.

"My point here isn't to tell a titillating story but to confess to you that this is what I thought love was. I thought I was in love with this girl, Mitzi Stallings was her name. We never really did anything together outside of her apartment, like, maybe we went out to eat a few times or went to a movie, and she was really smart and funny and everything, but we never really got to know each other outside of small talk and these amazing wrestling matches that we had, but I thought we were in love. I didn't know any better."

Maggie just stared at Span, a slight smile on her face.

"The only other time I think I was in love, I actually *was* in love. And that happened later when I was maybe thirty, working on the paper in Madison, Wisconsin. She was a high school English teacher. And we were together, off and on, for maybe two years, and I think it was the real thing for both of us. I liked her family, she liked mine. We really connected in every way. She was an incredibly caring person and an excellent teacher. Looking back, I think she taught me what love really was about.

"This is going to sound strange, but she made me realize for the first time that love wasn't just about my own personal gratification, but was a truly mutual thing, that it took both of us feeling the same way about each other and caring more about the other person than about yourself. When I finally asked her to marry me she hesitated for a few days and then said no. I never really found out why."

"What was her name?"

"It doesn't matter. I lost track of her twenty years ago. It turned out for the best, really. I heard she married some guy in Chicago. This is the first time I've thought about her in years."

The kitten flashed though Span's mind, but he didn't tell Maggie about the kitten thing.

What had happened was that K., the English teacher, his would-be fiancée, had a new kitten — tiny, furry and gray. Span hadn't seen the kitten asleep in the sun on the carpeted stairway as he helped move heavy boxes down from the attic. But he felt and heard the terrible crunch when his work boot came down on the poor creature. He had put down the heavy box, but seemed paralyzed, immobilized by the pathetic sight of the little fur ball all misshapen, whimpering and still moving her legs. K. screamed at the sight, but she knew exactly what to do, this smart and pretty Wisconsin farm girl sprinting to the garage, retrieving a shovel, scooping the crushed kitten off the stairway, taking her out to the driveway and smashing her again and again with the shovel until she was dead, then dropping the shovel and putting her arms around Span, sobbing.

There he was, Span Lokken, the budding hardboiled newspaperman. He had never felt so inadequate, so enfeebled. Maybe someday he'd have the courage to tell Maggie this story. But moving away from all this personal talk about his personal life seemed more and more urgent. So, he did what he always did when he felt discomfort coming on: he began to ask questions, he began to interview her, he tried to turn the tables.

"I know you've been in love," he said to Maggie. "You have a daughter. And you had a marriage."

Maggie, with the ball in her court, was less than enthusiastic when it came to telling her personal story. Still, Span could tell she relished talking with him. She even said so, sort of.

"Why are you so easy to talk to, Lokken?" she complained, failing to hide a smile. "I absolutely hate you for it. You make me want to tell you all my secrets."

"Must be my natural charm," he said.

"You have charm? I never noticed charm," she said. Then, brushing aside a lock of hair from her forehead, she confessed that Span was easier to talk to than anyone she could remember, except maybe her dad, back in the days before the shooting, before he turned bitter and crazy and not at all like the man he really was. Maggie tried with all her might, she said, to keep a special picture in her mind and a special place in her heart for the real Pete Lindberg. But the old version of Dad was more elusive every day.

Her weekly visits with him in Excelsior never really go well. She confers with her sister and sometimes her brothers in California about his condition. Sometimes she takes Petra to see him, most times not. Sometimes, on trips to California, she visits her mother's grave. Sometimes she sees her husband, Petra's father, sometimes not. After more than six years of separation, she still hasn't divorced James. But he is more and more remote from her life, and from Petra's.

James Rincon still works as an L.A. County deputy sheriff, stationed now in the relatively quiet sanctuary of Lakewood, away from the frenzy of Compton, where the two had first met on a joint task force aimed at tracking down a notorious gang leader and drug dealer. Even in uniform, the two cops had made a striking couple, Maggie, the tall, athletic girl with the Nordic features, and James, with his Latin good looks and witty, outgoing personality. They were an item almost from the moment they met.

"I loved James," she said, trying to answer Span's question, avoiding his eyes. "I still love him, but obviously not in the same way I did. I feel sorry for him. I'm sorry that he was unable to climb out of his ... selfishness. I'm sorry he was unable to share himself with Petra and me. He talked a good game. He said the right things. He was the most fun, entertaining guy I ever met. It could have been so good. But his actions were different from his words. He had no sense of the fifty-fifty deal that a two-career couple needs, especially when there's a baby on the scene."

Maggie fiddled with her bracelet, something she often did when she was nervous.

"He loved to go out with his friends, for poker, football, whatever. Fine. But if I wanted to go out with my volleyball girls, he hated that. He didn't help around the house, he didn't spend time with Petra."

"Why not, do you think?"

Maggie hesitated. "James comes from a very traditional, very conservative Mexican family. Don't get me wrong. I loved his family. Still do. But they're old-fashioned. A real man doesn't, you know, do women's work. And a real wife doesn't complain about having to shoulder the whole burden. And she doesn't complain either about her husband's violent mood swings and his demeaning comments about why wasn't his dinner perfect or why was the house messy or why was I wearing clothes he didn't like."

There was a long silence before Maggie continued.

"People need to sacrifice when a child comes into the picture. James wasn't into sacrifice." A baby at home made him even more stubborn, more self-centered, more interested in being out with his boys and *not* being at home, she said.

Maggie was on a roll. Span had never heard this kind of prolonged monologue from her.

"I was a problem, too, I admit it," she said, sounding suddenly more like Maggie. "I had this rising-star, woman-homicide-cop thing going, and I liked it. But he didn't like it, because I held it over him, I know I did. I turned myself into a martyr, complaining all the time that I was having to handle the pressure of maintaining my quote '*stellar career*' while at the same time being a mom and a housewife, too."

"Was he abusive?"

"You mean physically?"

She wondered whether she should answer, but finally said yes. "Mostly the abuse was, you know, emotional, just his selfishness, his not wanting to take part, his overwhelming need to stroke his own ego by being one of the guys."

More silence.

"He hit me only twice," she said, finally. "The first time I forgave him. The second time I didn't. He moved out. It surprised me that I was OK with that. I'm still OK with it. I don't think James will be back. I'm sorry about it. But I don't think I want him back."

Maggie then recounted the other events that happened as her marriage was disintegrating: the sudden death of her mom, from a heart attack, and then, five months later, the shooting of her dad and a bystander, and the turmoil in the department over the incident, culminating in her resignation from the force.

"Everything came crashing down," she said.

"And you quit because ..."

"I couldn't stomach the cover up."

"Cover up? What cover up?"

More silence.

"Span, I've never told this to anybody," she said. "You can't print this. This is just you and me, okay?"

Span nodded.

"They told the public that it was the bad guys who shot my dad and the guy in the liquor store, the one who died later. It wasn't. It was cop bullets. They said it was the bad guys who started all the shooting. It wasn't. It was a police ambush. We opened fire the second the bad guys came out of the place. The brass lied because it turned into a fiasco and they wanted to protect their poster girl. That would be me. They wanted to make me a hero, no matter what."

Span rocked in his chair, saying nothing.

"I was no hero. Yeah, I did the intel," she said. "I set it up, the stakeout. But I didn't know it was going to go down like that. I thought we would just move in and arrest these guys. I didn't know we had some cowboys on the scene who were going to start shooting. But I'm the one who's mostly responsible for the nightmare and the killing of the clerk and the wounding of my dad."

She paused for an awkward moment, searching for words.

"The department put me in an impossible position. I couldn't bring myself to live with their lie. But I couldn't tell the truth either about what my fellow officers had done. I wasn't willing to break the code. I didn't have the guts to be a rat. The only way out for me was to quit.

"I was in a no-win situation. They wanted a hero. But I knew I wasn't one. I was what? Twenty-eight? The only thing I knew was that I was a screw-up. A lot of my fellow officers knew I was a screw-up. How could I live with that? How could I bask in the glory under false pretenses when I knew I had caused so much damage? I was in real agony because I loved the job. But I had no real choice but to resign. I waited two weeks before handing in my badge. I needed to come up with a reason for quitting. I told them I had decided to go to law school. But I never did."

"During the ambush, did you do any shooting?"

"Not really. I think I fired two rounds into the car where the getaway guy was firing back at us. It was all like a bad dream. I was appalled by what was happening. But I never objected. I never spoke up. Dad knows the truth. I think he knows. I think he blames me. He should blame me. I walk around with the burden of that every day of my life. It doesn't go away."

"What did you do after you quit?"

"One day I went over to the law school at Loyola. I had an appointment to ask some questions about getting in there, but I was early, and somehow I ended up in this little chapel on the law school campus. I don't know why. Maybe I was feeling desperate, but something drew me in there. It wasn't like I had been going to church. I hadn't been a regular churchgoer since maybe high school or younger. I just must have felt that I had nowhere else to go. Maybe it was a kind of last resort.

"I was like, who can I lean on? Not on my husband, obviously. Not my friends on the force. My dad, he wasn't in any shape to help me. By then I had no mom to confide in. My brothers and sister were supportive, but what could they really do? To me it seemed like I was all alone, just me and Petra, and Petra was barely three at the time."

Maggie said she doesn't like talking about the next part

because she doesn't quite believe what happened, but she told Span anyway. She was sitting there in the chapel, all alone, not praying really, just staring at the altar when she felt the presence of others around her, and these people were real enough for her to recognize: her dead mother was there, and her grandmother and grandfather.

"It was creepy, but not in a scary way. It's not like I *saw* these people but I *felt* them and I recognized who they were. And it occurred to me that I wasn't alone."

Span raised his eyebrows.

"Span, please don't think I'm nuts. I was astonished that this happened, or seemed to happen. I never saw it coming. Was this some kind of spiritual experience? I don't know. Maybe it was just my imagination. But it gave me the shivers. It still does. And it gave me an insight that, what? I didn't need to be afraid any more. These others were with me. I was a continuation of them, my family. They were an anchor for me. Does that make any sense? Or does it just sound weird?"

"Weird."

"O.K., I agree. I haven't felt that same thing since – not in that same sort of vivid way. But that day I decided that Petra and I would get away from L.A., come back to the island, back to, you know, our foundation."

"So, when did you come back?"

"It'll be ... six years ago last April. I got this job at a nonprofit 'Ready for K.' It's an advocacy group for early childhood learning. That's where I found out that James wasn't the only self-centered person I know. I found out about myself. Working with poor kids and mothers opened me up to a new way of thinking. Not just thinking, but *being*. This verse from Matthew kept running through my head, the one where Jesus says something like 'He who loses his life for my sake will find it.'"

"I thought we had agreed to a moratorium on Bible thumping," Span said.

"Sorry, my fault. Think of it as an anonymous piece of philosophy: If you lose yourself in the act of helping others, then you'll find your own real life, your genuine life. That's what sent me to seminary. That's how I got this vocation, this job."

The two were silent for a moment.

"That's how I got from there to here," Maggie said. "What if Petra and I had been hanging around the church on that Sunday afternoon, like we often do? I assume we would have been swept up in the slaughter along with Matthias and Henrik. I think about that a lot, Span. I never would have teamed up with you. Now I'm stuck with you, for better or worse. Mostly worse, I think."

When their eyes met, Span noticed she was both smiling and crying. He reached across for her hand, then looked wistfully away at some distant object.

Chapter Twenty-Five

Friday, 5:30 p.m

Span is driving when he hears the news. It's a WWTC all-news radio "exclusive report" from an authoritative baritone named Skip something:

"The reclusive Minneapolis billionaire Jonas Kron has upped the ante. Named by police as a 'person of interest' in the spectacular June 5th church murders, Kron today doubled the reward he's offering for information leading to the capture of the suspects to ONE HUNDRED THOUSAND DOLLARS." (Then came Kron's voice.) "I won't rest until these criminals are arrested and convicted of this brutal crime." (Skip's baritone resumed.) "Kron emphasized that he's PERSONALLY putting up the reward. His offer comes on the same day that the Star Journal linked KRON, HIMSELF, to the crime, reporting that a money-filled envelope with Kron's corporate logo had been discovered in the luggage of the two murder suspects. The suspects remain at large.

" In other news ..."

Span pulls onto a side street and parks. He picks up his phone. "Stephanie? It's me."

"Hello, Spaniel. Long time no talk."

"You hear about Kron doubling the reward?"

"Part of his new public relations campaign, thanks to you."

"What do you mean, thanks to me?"

"You spooked him, Spaniel. Your story this morning about the cops finding his name in the killers' luggage and the cops now calling him a 'person of interest.' Scared the shit outta him. He calls Olyphant, all shook up. I shouldn't be telling you this."

"Please don't stop. I'm panting." (Span knew Stephanie was referring to Clarence T. Olyphant, senior partner in her law firm and a sage in corporate circles.)

"Ollie tells him the secret word: *public relations.* Start putting his name out before the public in a positive way. Feed hungry kids. Build a new wing at the hospital. Make contributions to charity. You get the picture."

"You're kidding. Kron? Polishing his image? When did this call happen?"

"This morning, first thing. Get this. Ollie tells him to call Lionel Redding."

Span knows Lionel Redding as principal owner of the Minnesota Twins Baseball Club. "Why Redding? His PR problems are worse than Kron's."

"Maybe. But, Kron calls Lionel and, shazam! Kron is actually making a short speech at the game, and, listen to this, *throwing out the first pitch!*"

"When?"

"Tonight!"

"No way! Instant gratification for rich guys? I gotta see this."

Span's next call is to Maggie.

* * *

Tonight is one of those rare nights of summer perfection. Span and Maggie sit in the lingering sunshine near the end of one of summer's longest days and watch dusk creep in slowly from the east. The setting sun still blazes on the glassy skyline beyond the right field grandstand, but night will soon envelop the ballpark, its lights casting a spell over the players, the green grass and the sparse crowd. It's still eighty-one degrees according to the scoreboard, hardly a breeze, the stands barely one-third filled, a foul ball hit in Span's and Maggie's direction rattling around for awhile amid the empty seats before some kid trots over to pick it up.

Jonas Kron's speech had been short and a bit awkward. He stepped to a microphone near home plate and recalled the horrors of the church murders, then announced his doubling of the reward plus a generous new gift – in his name – to the Twins' Minnesota Fund to help support after-school activities for disadvantaged kids. He then bravely trotted to the mound, removed his jacket and tossed a one-hopper to the Twins' catcher before trotting back to the microphone to cry, "Play ball!"

Tell the truth, Maggie, Span and most of the spectators aren't paying much attention to the game, perhaps because the talent-challenged Twins, despite trying hard, are already buried hopelessly in last place.

Span is accustomed to last place having grown up in the shadow of Wrigley Field in an era when the Chicago Cubs endeared themselves as lovable losers while turning weekday afternoons into magic for him and his friends. They cared less about winning than about experiencing the atmosphere at Addison and Clark: the organ music getting louder as they approached, then, once inside, the cadence of the vendors, the smells of ballpark food and the marvelous sight of expansive greenness of grass and ivy.

The Twins' new ballpark is sleek and stylish but lacks the decades of anguish and false hope embedded into Wrigley's every brick. Still, it's the perfect place to lose oneself for a few hours. Span feels lost in a different way, too — as if he has lost his bearings on this case, lost the boundary between the story itself and his swelling attraction to his ballpark buddy, Maggie Lindberg. There is supposed to be a sharp line between the journalistic and the personal, but he can no longer see it.

What have they become over these last ten days? Allies? Partners? Companions? Certainly.

Friends? Absolutely.

Lovers? He can't imagine that. Well, he can imagine it, but not realistically. It's uncomfortable for him to contemplate. Better to bury the thought.

His discomfort and restlessness might be reasons he's decided to leave town for a few days. Tomorrow morning he plans to drive north to begin digging more deeply into the backgrounds of the two suspects, talking face-to-face with people who went to school with Richard Reznik and Duane Hajinlian, people who worked with them, did time with them. Maybe he'll find motives for their crimes and even, perhaps, clues to their whereabouts. Even Carla has offered her thin enthusiasm for the trip.

Now, suddenly in the fifth inning, Bender's number is vibrating in Span's pocket.

"How nice to hear from you Captain Bender, sir."

"Cut the shit, Lokken. You up north yet or still in town?"

"At the ball game."

"Yeah, right. Listen, before you leave town you might want to drop by my office. It'll make your day. First thing in the morning, 8 o'clock."

"Tomorrow's Saturday."

"No kidding. I know it comes as a surprise to you, Lokken,

but your police department is on the job twenty-four-seven, three sixty-five."

"Isn't that going to mess up your tee time?"

Span doesn't press him. Bender sounds almost giddy. He never sounds giddy. He never cares about making anybody's day but his own. If anything, Span would expect him to be extra annoyed because the FBI has begun sniffing around the case, and nobody hates the FBI more than Bender.

There's suddenly a slight commotion at the ballpark. Someone has apparently hit a home run, pulling the Twins ahead of Baltimore. The crowd's reaction is modest, expecting that the lead won't last long. Maggie and Span watch the replay on the big screen in left field, then change seats, moving to an even quieter location. Again the game fades to the background.

Maggie is talking again, and in a way Span hasn't heard before. She's talking about Petra and how, despite the recent tragic events rattling their sense of security, she and her daughter are fortunate in relative terms. They have each other in ways than many mothers and daughters don't. She reaches back to her cop days, telling of a woman by the name of L'Donna who brought her three-year-old child to breakfast one day in one of those ubiquitous southern California diners to discuss the day's activities with a girlfriend. Between cups of coffee they decide on a series of stickups in nearby parking lots. The plan is for L'Donna's friend to show citizens her gun (She shows it to L'Donna under the table) as a way to scare people into handing over their money. The proposed activity is so attractive to L'Donna that she and her friend immediately depart this particular restaurant and begin working the nearby parking lots. This goes on into the afternoon until Maggie and her partner pull up to make the arrest. Only then does L'Donna remember her three-year-old is still in the booth back at Bob's Big Boy. She flies into a panic. What bothered Maggie more than these women doing stickups was the scene back at Bob's, where L'Donna raced to her child, berating her and cursing her for causing her to worry so much. "I'm gonna whip your raggedy ass raw," she screamed at the child.

"I keep thinking about that little girl," Maggie says, "and wondering whatever became of her. What kind of a life could she have? Where is she now? She'd be about Petra's age." Maggie sighs. "I'm not saying I've been a perfect mother, far from it. But Petra has had so many advantages that that little girl could never dream of having. Even now, with what's happening to us."

"Life isn't fair, right?" Span says.

"No, it's not."

"You might expect God to make a fairer world," Span blurts, immediately regretting his bringing the Almighty into the ballpark. Span is always uneasy talking religion, especially with Maggie. He tries to recover. "What I mean to say is that I admire you people for having strong beliefs, even in the face of evidence to the contrary. I admire that you people know something for sure. Me, I don't know anything for sure."

Maggie laughs. "What do you mean, *you people?*" she says.

"I guess I'm talking about Christians. You *are* one, I hope."

"You're an ignorant man, Span Lokken," she says, still smiling. "We deserve all the crap we get because we have so many hucksters out there peddling religious belief as some kind of absolute, something you either have or don't have. Either you're 'saved' or damned. But I don't know any Christians who think like that."

"You're kidding."

"Actually not. We talk less about belief than about faith, which is hoping and trusting that something is true. Having faith is not the opposite of having doubt. Actually, they're close relatives. Everyone has doubt. We think God has given humans the capacity to question. So, what could be wrong about questioning God's existence?"

"I'd rather talk about why the Twins' pitching is so shitty," Span retorts.

"Me, too," she says, her tone suggesting that she regrets her theological outburst.

Span understands. Who can blame Maggie for reaching for her faith in a time of crisis? So here, along the third base line, of all places, Span finds himself leaning over to put his arm on her shoulder and plant an innocent kiss on her cheek.

Chapter Twenty-Six

Saturday, June 18, 8:01 a.m

Span fidgets in the reception area of Bender's office, sipping this morning's first cup of bad coffee and chit-chatting with Officer Cyd O'Donnell, the luckless rookie tapped as the first secretary ever assigned to the newly captainized Larry Bender. Despite her tender age, O'Donnell carries the stoop-shouldered fatigue of a much older woman. Span's guess is that Bender is running her ragged.

This being Saturday morning, and at an hour when Span should still be in bed, he's feeling a little ragged, too. Ragged and suspicious. What could be so gawdawful important that Bender insisted he be here now, and why did he sound so giddy? Five minutes go by before the captain himself sweeps into the office wearing what looks like a finely tailored new suit — a subtle gray check. His dapper appearance clashes with the drab décor of police headquarters, and clashes, too, with Bender's famously unrefined personality.

"Coffee, Cyd," he says cheerfully, then seeing Span in the green chair, downshifts his mood. "Oh, Jeez. And I thought this was gonna be a good day. What the hell you doing here, Lokken?"

"You're the one ..."

"OK, OK," he says, cutting Span off, putting on a show for his secretary. "Everybody knows you got newspapers to sell. Whatcha got for me today, hot shot?"

"Utter contempt, captain sir."

"Get in here, Lokken," he says, then to Cyd as she hands him a paper cup of lukewarm black liquid, "Hold my calls."

"You get calls?" Span says as Bender shuts the door behind them.

"I get plenty of calls, asshole," he says as he motions for Span to sit on the worn leather sofa, taking a chair for himself and pulling it up close enough for Span to smell his cigarette breath.

One thing Span knows about Bender: Bender doesn't do anything that's not mainly for the benefit of Bender. If he's got something for the paper, which he obviously has, then it's probably because he wants to stay ahead of Mel Thurber in the battle for public attention. Ever since the luggage leak and the tie to Kron, more and more media hits have been going to Thurber and the FBI. But, like Bender told Span at the outset: This is *his* case. If he tells Span something, then he'll get two news cycles out of it – Span's story and all the other stories that have to follow it up, all quoting him. Anyway, that's Span's guess for Bender's motive.

"You weren't really at the ballgame last night like you told me, were you Lokken? Probably off in some dark hotel room knocking the bottom outta my blond, long-legged consultant."

"God, Bender, doesn't your mind ever leave the gutter? I know you cops get a sordid slant on things from all the lowlifes you got to deal with every day, but, for God's sake, this is a mother and a minister of the Gospel."

"Yeah, whatever. Listen, Slick. I got something for you before you head up north."

"I'm all ears."

Bender rises from his chair, walks to his desk, unlocks a bottom drawer and pulls out what looks to Span like an evidence box, breaks open the seal, reaches in for a small, amber-colored plastic cylinder and tosses it to Span.

"Nice catch."

It's an empty pill bottle. Span squints at the label. Made out to none other than Public Enemy Number Two, Duane Hajinlian. Span jots down the name of the drug, which he recognizes as a notorious opioid analgesic, a painkiller popular with the rural criminal element. He also takes down the name of the drug store and the prescribing physician, then tosses it back to Bender with a quizzical look.

"Hear about the car crash up in Nordeast last Wednesday night?" Bender asks. "Taxi runs a red light, gets T-boned by an SUV. Cabdriver thrown from the vehicle and apparently gets up, dusts himself off and flees the scene. Somali. What a surprise. Substitute driver. Anyway, first report is that this driver didn't have passengers. But then we check the trip sheet. Turns out the driver had picked up a fare on Hennepin Island twenty minutes before the wreck and was taking this person-of-interest to Betty Danger's when 'boom!" So we search the cab top to bottom and out rolls this little bottle with Duane's name on it, and fingerprints all over it. Guess whose prints?"

"Duane's?"

Bender makes the sound of a buzzer. "Incorrect-o! Prints belong to Duane's best friend, the one and only Richard fucking Reznik."

"But Reznik could have been in that cab any time that day, or even before and dropped the bottle."

Bender again makes like a buzzer. "Wrong. So this being a

wreck, the crime lab boys do a full workup of the interior, with special emphasis on the front seat, where there's considerable blood and other bodily fluids, and guess whose blood type and DNA comes up?"

"Wild guess: Richard Reznik."

Bender nods.

"But he wasn't at the crash scene. So where did he go? How bad was he hurt?"

"We looked for a blood trail, but it rained that night. We canvassed the blocks around the wreck. A lot of neighbors came out to look at the crash. Two think they remember a man with a limp, white, slender, 30s. But it was dark and nobody asked any questions, and nobody remembers where the guy seemed to be headed."

"So, where *was* he headed?"

"We're knocking on every door in the neighborhood, showing pictures, seeing if anybody has seen these two creeps hanging around. Might take a while. Nothing so far."

On his way out Span thanks Cyd for not offering him any more coffee. She gives him a puzzled look. Next stop for Span is a better cup of coffee and a quick walk with Max back on the island, then downtown to the paper. Another story to write. His trip up north? It'll have to wait a few days.

Chapter Twenty-Seven

Tuesday, June 21, 12:05 p.m

Even a fast driver like Span finds it hard to cover the ground between downtown Minneapolis and the Mesabi Range in under three hours. But now, fully down-shifted and moseying along East Harold Street in Ferris, Minnesota, Span sees his trip as surprisingly complex. Yes, he has driven a hundred and eighty-five miles, but he has also traveled back in time by several decades, from a city of sleek glass towers and bustling streets to a tired mining town that, by the looks of things, could use a transfusion. He's guessing that somewhere along this street of sad-sack brick buildings there's a modest cafe where he can grab a bite while soaking up some local flavor.

There's plenty of flavor to soak up on the Range. It's a storied region with a gritty history both tragic and heroic, its cast made up of Ojibwe hunters, French fur traders, hardy lumberjacks, wealthy robber barons (John D. Rockefeller and Andrew Carnegie, among them) and thousands of immigrant miners who struggled against bitterly cold winters to dig and crush the iron ore essential for making steel. Up here, it's an article of faith that the nation could not have won World War II without the Iron Range. And it might be true.

In its natural state, the region is a dense pine forest stretching upward beyond the north shore of Lake Superior to form the sharp northeastern point of Minnesota. Nature took a decisive detour in the 1890s, however, when several rich veins of ore were discovered and the forest gave way to huge open-pit canyons, ton after ton of their reddish, rocky contents scooped up and loaded onto rail cars and then onto ships bound for the steel mills of the eastern Great Lakes, the ore eventually becoming cars, trains, tanks, bridges, refrigerators, washing machines, and all the stuff of modern life.

One of the world's largest iron mines abuts the northern edge of Ferris. The town itself had to be moved beginning in 1919 to accommodate an expanding pit that now measures three miles across and almost six hundred feet deep. The quality of the ore in Ferris and throughout the Range has diminished over the years, along with the numbers of miners required to extract, process and ship it. But the industry hangs on, along with the Finnish, Slavic, Italian and other ethnic cultures that characterize the Range. The region has produced an impressive lineup of talent — Judy Garland and Bob Dylan on the plus side, Richard Reznik and Duane Hajinlian on the minus.

It's Reznik and Hajinlian who occupy Span's attention as he settles onto his stool at the lunch counter in the Sportsfan's Bar and Grill on East Harold. Maybe a third of the seats are filled, mostly with guys in workingman's clothes and ball caps, average age fifty. The floors are linoleum, the fixtures are 1950s, the walls are plastered with flat-screen TVs and various sports jerseys, mainly hockey and football, although there's a hallowed place for Hibbing native Kevin McHale's bright green #32 Boston Celtics.

None of this surprises Span. What surprises him are the waitresses and the menus. Span's waitress is twenty at most, skinny with spiky black hair, a silver ring through her lower lip and both arms generously tattooed. Her pink t-shirt reads "Loves animals, hates humans." The menu – she hands it to him with routine indifference – is shocking. Steak frites, croque madame, onion soup, sandwich coq au vin and salade Niçoise are listed alongside the expected burgers, all at reasonable prices. Span's a sucker for spaghetti carbonara, so that's what he orders. It comes promptly, and it's delicious. Span begins to see Ferris through a whole new lens.

Lingering over coffee as the place empties, Span begins chatting with the young waitress and two older gents at the counter. Turns out that the once obscure Reznik and Hajinlian are sudden celebrities in Ferris. Everyone knows them, or knows someone who knows them or someone who remembers them.

"My oldest sister's best friend says that, like, one of 'em was in her class," the waitress allows. Which one? She can't remember. "I think it was the fat one with the beard." Without Span asking she refills his coffee cup. "You don't think they're here, do you? You don't think they're hiding out around here?"

"This is probably the last place they'd run to," Span says. "People here know them by sight."

The two older guys aren't so sure. They're thick with theories about Reznik's and Hajinlian's whereabouts, their motives for murder, and their capability of performing such a gruesome and theatrical crime. And they're brimming with gossip about the killers' past lives in Ferris and how they took a wrong turn. "I heard somebody saw Reznik the other day over in Hibbing but the cops wouldn't do nothing," one man tells Span.

"They better not come by my place," says the other one. "Because if they do, I'm ready," he says, forming his fist into a gun and pulling the trigger.

By the time Span makes his way up and down the street and in and out of stores, it's clear that people are in two camps: those disgusted, embarrassed and horrified that these two killers are local men and still on the loose; and those fascinated by them and eager to make them local legends. As for motive, a half-dozen people mention revenge, speculating that Richard was abused as an altar boy, a theme common in the media.

"But the pastor they murdered wasn't even Catholic," Span tells one woman.

"Well, Richard never got nothing right," she retorts.

Span, himself, has tried several times to elicit comment from church officials in Ferris and at the Duluth diocese, but without success. St. Leo's, the parish Richard, his mother and sisters are said to have sporadically attended, still stands three blocks from Richard's childhood home. But it was closed in 2014.

He's frustrated, too, that, while Richard and Duane are well-known in Ferris, no one he's talked to really *knows* them. All they know is just the community chatter.

All that changes later in the afternoon when Span talks with the high school's long-time guidance counselor. They've talked on the phone, and Doris Peterson is eager to meet with Span at the school library where they can plow through old yearbooks and recall which students might have been close to the town's most notable miscreants. This being summer, Ferris High is empty and stuffy — but it's nothing like Span expects. Built in 1921 in the Tudor Revival style, the four-story structure is astoundingly lavish, with Belgian cut-glass chandeliers, brass stair railings and a large pipe organ. Doris explains that the mining industry built the school to appease the townsfolk for relocating the town. The school is on the National Register of Historic Places, she tells him.

The soaring architecture apparently did nothing to inspire the academic pursuits of Richard and Duane, however. Photos of a skinny, pimply-faced Richard appear in his ninth and tenth grade editions with no mention of extra-curricular activities. Doris remembers Richard as a sullen teenager who was bored with school and obsessed with cars and motorcycles.

She confesses to have dug around in her old files for information about the two boys when they were identified as suspects in the church murders. Richard apparently dropped out of school after his sophomore year. His grades were dismal, as was his disciplinary record: four suspensions for fighting and one for habitually cutting class in the company of Curtis Winger, another hard case who eventually dropped out after being caught with drugs. Doris is sure that both Richard and Curtis had juvenile records, although the school was denied access to any details. Curtis Winger, by the way, still lives in Ferris, Doris announces.

"He pretty much turned his life around, I guess. I see him at the dealership when I get my car fixed."

Doris barely remembers Duane. Doesn't remember if the two boys hung out together, or even knew each other in high school. Consulting her folder, she tells Span that Duane transferred in as a sophomore from the Milwaukee public system, tried football but quit, and stuck around long enough to graduate near the bottom of his class. Photos of Duane show a dark-haired, smiling, chubby-faced kid. His junior yearbook lists him as a member of the Art Club. But that's all. Doris thinks the Hajinlian family has left Ferris.

After a short drive, Span finds Curtis Winger at the Chevy dealership where's he's just finishing up his day. Span expects Winger to be suspicious, even hostile. Instead, he smiles and calls home to check with his girlfriend before inviting Span for a beer at a tavern out on the highway. Curtis (his mechanic's work shirt identifies him as "Curt") is a bubbly, sandy-haired bantam who struts more than he walks.

And he's eager to reminisce about his former best buddy, Richard Reznik.

"Ain't seen him in ten years, and I guess I'm glad about that," Curtis says when the beer arrives. "But me and Richard go way back. Him and me were a dynamic duo when we were kids. You wouldn't believe the shit we did."

Curtis launches into a series of stories going back to fifth and sixth grades. In one, a man named Grobie had two big apple trees in his back yard that Richard and Curtis used to raid regularly. Grobie would come out swinging a baseball bat and yelling at them, which they hated. So one night Richard got a can of gasoline and they burned the trees down.

"I thought it was kind of stupid, because there goes our apples," Curtis recalls. "But Richard was totally serious about it. Made him feel good."

Another story involves several Fourth of July holidays when Richard got his hands on fireworks, which somebody bought for him in Wisconsin. The two boys hung around a slough where there were hundreds of frogs. Richard loved catching a frog, stuffing a firecracker in its mouth and lighting it. The frog would hop away until BOOM! Pieces of frog everywhere.

"Richard loved that," Curtis recalls. "We did it over and over."

Stakes got higher in their teenage years. They stole bikes and eventually cars. They broke into houses. They started fights with younger kids and took their money. Eventually Richard got his hands on guns and they started flashing them around. "I'm coming across as the reluctant one who just went along with Richard. But I was just as bad," Curtis says.

By tenth grade, Richard was driving his own car even though he wasn't old enough to have a license. "Nineteen-eighty-five Pontiac Firebird V-8, two-oh-five horses, yellow, beat to shit," Curtis remembers. The two boys always had money to spend and they had the coolest, latest video games. "It was a thrill type thing for both of us," Curtis says. "Flying high."

Things changed a little for Curtis when they got high one night and stuck up a gas station and got arrested and hauled into juvenile court. "Richard was pissed and totally defiant, but I admit I cracked a little. Looking back on it, I think I saw that all this shit we were doing was cool and thrilling and, like, nothing but a bunch of pranks. But Richard took it serious. I think he liked the idea of being a criminal. It came natural to him. It was like the only way he knew how to be. He was a good guy in a lot of ways, and he wasn't stupid. But I think deep down he was like the song says, you know, bad to the bone."

Eventually, Curtis joined the Navy, got his G.E.D. and got trained as a mechanic. Richard took up with Duane Hajinlian, a quiet kid who was always hanging around the fringes. After Duane did a short stint in the Army, they both moved to Milwaukee, back to where Duane came from. Curtis heard that they made occasional side trips to Chicago, engaging in various felonious exploits that finally landed them in the Wisconsin state facility in Racine. "I don't know what they were in for, or how long," Curtis says, "but obviously it wasn't long enough."

It's twilight by the time Span and Curtis arrive at Richard's old house, the one he lived in as a child with his mother and three older sisters. It's a small frame house on a patchy street of similarly modest homes punctuated by weedy vacant lots where other houses once stood. There's no light inside, no car at the curb, no sounds except for a barking dog somewhere on the block and the low purr of a switch engine on a nearby siding. "I think his ma still lives here," Curtis says. But there's no answer when he knocks.

Span asks about the family backgrounds of Richard and Duane. Curtis shrugs. "We never had nothing. None of us," he says. "I never heard Richard mention a father. His mother worked at the cafeteria at the hospital, I think. Duane, his old man did something at the mine, drove truck or something, I don't know. None of us had a silver spoon in our mouth."

As they walk back to their cars, Span asks about Richard possibly being abused by a priest. "He never said nothing about that," Curtis says. "Nothing."

"Did you ever hear any talk about Richard or Duane being connected in any way with Jonas Kron?"

"Who?"

"Jonas Kron. A rich guy up on Lake Vermillion. Ever any talk about Richard and Duane being up there?"

Curtis shakes his head. Span has a vivid imagination, but one thing he can't imagine is how two dirt balls like Richard and Duane could ever cross paths with Jonas Kron. Yes, there's the Kron envelope and the money in their luggage. But there's something fishy about that.

Back at the motel, Span runs through his emails. Maggie reports that she has been talking to a prison shrink who evaluated Richard and Duane as inmates. The cops, meanwhile, have been scouring the internet for clues about religious nuts with grudges against Hammar — and there are plenty, she says. Lots of comments about him getting what he deserved.

Span also read a response from a guy he knew from his days on the Madison paper. The man has long since retired as a parole system supervisor. But as a favor to Span he got hold of some D.O.C. records of interest. Looks like Richard and Duane each did thirty-two months at Racine on two counts of auto theft, plus twelve months parole. That puts them basically out of circulation between 2008 and 2012. Richard got himself arrested again in 2013, this time for aggravated assault. But the charges were dropped.

While in the slammer, Richard took a course in accounting (did poorly) and one in auto mechanics (slightly better) but got into fights with other inmates on four occasions and twice had to be isolated from the general population for short periods of time. "Anti-social behavior persists despite counseling," said one notation on Reznik. "Extreme self-centered personality." Maybe this is some of the same stuff Maggie got from the prison shrink, Span thinks.

Duane's behavioral reports were better but his psychological file was lengthy, noting "deep mood swings" and "contempt for authority" and "unpredictably quick temper." What got Span's instant attention were Duane's two suicide attempts. Twice he was transferred to a mental health unit for evaluation (depression, low self-esteem), then returned to the general population, where he worked without incident in the commissary.

Neither inmate received much mail or had many visitors. The most frequent visitor to both was an F. Dobervich who listed his vocation as "baker" and his address as Chicago. Span takes down a quick note but doesn't think much of it. He's tired. He opens a bottle from the minibar and scribbles on his pad: "Need more on Duane."

As he drifts toward sleep, a vision creeps over him that he can't easily erase. He's standing in front of Richard's old house in Ferris. And he sees a little kid – Richie, perhaps – toddling his way through weedy vacant lots and playing in rubble alongside the railroad track. And he realizes that, from the beginning, Richie never had a chance.

Chapter Twenty-Eight

Wednesday, June 22, 7:52 a.m

Richard Reznik is not by nature a patient man. After two days of practice-walking and drug-taking his leg is feeling better and his confidence is high. And it's time to put his Economic Recovery Initiative into action. Getting Fat Duane out of bed is a major undertaking, but they're both alert now and primed for action, Duane piloting Marla's Shitcar Chevy eastbound on the 94 freeway over the Mississippi River, past the University District and across the city line into St. Paul. The morning traffic is heavy and the sun is devastating as Duane, squinting and leaning right, turns onto the Cretin Avenue ramp. Richard checks his watch. Right on time. Practice makes perfect.

The Riverside Town & Country Club sits just across the river's east channel from Hennepin Island. The golf course hugs the Mississippi. The tennis courts are next to the big stucco clubhouse. Duane tucks the Shitcar Chevy into a spot in the employee parking lot, the same spot they've had in the practice runs. At 8:10, right on schedule, the skinny college kid in the white golf shirt retrieves the little green bus. It's like one of those miniature rental car buses you see at small airports except that it has the club name and logo painted on the side. He starts it up and begins filling out some paperwork on a clipboard that he leans against the steering wheel, not noticing that Richard has walked across the parking lot with a small satchel in his hand and entered the bus, as if to ask a question.

Duane, from his vantage point, can't see exactly what happens next but pretty soon he sees Richard standing in the doorway of the bus wearing the white golf shirt with the Town & Country crest on the pocket. Richard's now driving the bus over to the dumpster. Again, Duane can't see what Richard is doing but he knows he's supposed to be hauling the unconscious, tied-up kid to a predetermined location in the trees behind the dumpster. Then both Duane and Richard, in separate vehicles, drive out of the parking lot, past the clubhouse and tennis courts. Duane turns left. Richard turns right, crossing the Lake Street bridge onto Hennepin Island.

At the second right Richard turns the bus onto Connor Street. Soon he spots Blondie looking super fine in t-shirt and shorts standing on the curb with the small, curly-haired girl who's wearing a backpack and toting a tennis racquet, both of them smiling at the little green bus. This is the bus's first stop. The girl gets a hug and a kiss from Blondie and jumps on board. Blondie notices that the driver is different but apparently thinks nothing of it. The bus turns left at the end of the block. Twenty other kids won't be getting their tennis lessons today. Richard Reznik, just as he planned it, has the bus and eight-year-old Petra all to himself.

Chapter Twenty-Nine

Wednesday, 8:36 a.m

When Fat Duane reaches the rendezvous point, he checks the time on the cellphone he lifted the other night from Marla's upstairs apartment back at Lucky's Nordeast. 8:36. About twenty minutes it has taken him to drive the Shitcar Chevy from the fancy ass country club to this godforsaken mudhole next to a swamp in a town that the map calls Lillydale, which appears to be somewhere on the damp, smelly underside of St. Paul. Duane can detect no evidence of a town, just cottonwood trees, tall grass and the looming Mississippi River. He can't actually see the river through the trees. But when he rolls down the window he can smell it — a putrid mixture of chemicals and the organic stink of rotting death.

Opening the window is a mistake, he quickly decides, not just because of the stink but because of the swarms of bugs that quickly invade the car. Rolling up the window and sweating is the better option.

Duane's thumping headache doesn't help his faltering

mood. All his life he's been pushed around, and lately Richard has been on a pushing jag. Richard, for no good reason, thinks he's the brains of the operation. Richard giving orders. Richard constantly picking at him for everything. His driving, his sleeping, his eating, his farting, his breathing. Richard even blames him for the trouble at the airport, like when they missed their plane. Christ Almighty! Missing the plane was Richard's fault! Richard is way too wired. Way too uptight. He needs to relax. He needs to treat Duane with a little fucking respect, you know, like he promised when they made this deal fifty-fifty. It has never been close to fifty-fifty. It was, after all, the Big Man, not Richard, who drilled them on every detail. Duane remembers *nothing* about the Big Man putting Richard in charge. Maybe the Big Man's English wasn't so good, but he never appointed Richard boss.

Nearly ten minutes go by before another vehicle approaches, Duane spotting it in his rear view mirror and instinctively reaching for the thirty-eight tucked somewhere below the bulge of his damp midsection. But it turns out to be the country club's little green bus bounding over the rutted road with Richard bouncing behind the wheel.

Duane climbs out as Richard pulls alongside. "Where is she?" he shouts above the rumble of the bus's motor. Richard points to the back, Duane leaning in to inspect the package. The curly-haired little girl lies across the rear seat, her arms and legs crudely bound by duct tape, a small yellow ball inserted into her mouth, her flushed face and wide-open eyes telling Duane one thing: she's terrified.

"Hoo-eee!" Richard yells. "Just like I planned it! Smooth as fucking silk!"

He turns, then, to hurl the bus keys into the woods before he and Duane haul the kid out of the bus and into the Shitcar Chevy for the half-hour ride up to the motel.

Chapter Thirty

Wednesday, 10:30 a.m

A knock on the door is something Feliks Dobervich is not expecting. His efficiency apartment has been selected carefully to reduce his visibility to almost zero. His comings and goings are obscured by a large spruce tree on one side and a series of dumpsters on the other. The sixties-style architecture provides overhangs and shadows that help, too, not to mention the fact that his room is on the far backside of the complex.

All this was essential during the training process. Richard and Duane could park in the Costco lot – always busy – then thread their way behind the Costco, down the hill and through the trees almost to Feliks' door without being noticed. Plus, Feliks had waved some cash at the desk clerk who promised to safeguard his low profile. And the maid had been instructed to clean only on Fridays. So a knock on the door today? Extremely suspicious.

Maybe Feliks will get lucky and it'll turn out to be Richard and Duane coming home to papa, coming home to the place where they had spent so many happy hours training. Such a Richard-Duane homecoming would solve all of Feliks' problems. It's the best-case possibility. The worst case is that it's the Gaswerks at the door. But that's unlikely. The Gaswerks doesn't knock. Feliks knows from experience that if the Gaswerks is close, you won't hear them coming.

So, he draws his pistol and cautiously approaches the door, peering through the peephole, seeing a face he doesn't recognize. This is a large woman, mid-thirties, not fat really, but big arms with tattoos, blond stringy hair and a face with attitude.

"Yes! Who are you, please?" His voice is strong, firm and confident from behind the door.

"I'm looking for the Big Man. Just want to ask a question. Name is Marla. Marla Kusic. Friend of Richard. *Used to be* a friend of Richard."

Feliks unlatches the door, motioning with the gun for Marla to come inside.

"You ain't that big," she says, trying to smile at the Big Man's face while staring at the gun, Feliks responding with a blank expression.

"You know whereabouts of Richard and Duane?" he says, getting right to the point.

"Don't I wish!" Marla says, walking over to the fridge like she owns the place. "Fuckers took my car and my cellphone. You still got beer in there?"

Feliks gives her a look. "Beer? You been here before? How do you know this place? How do you find me?"

Marla, hands on her hips, says, "Listen, the issue here is where the fuck is my car? And where the fuck is my cellphone? And where did Richard and Duane run off to? I need my car. I need my phone! I got a business to run! I call my phone, nobody answers! So, how about you put that gun away?"

Instead of putting it away, Feliks sticks the barrel up against the side of Marla's head. "*I* ask questions! *You* give answers!"

Marla says nothing.

"When are you here before? I never see you."

Marla's bravado has shriveled. *Silence.* Followed by, "I was like over here partying and whatnot with Richard and Duane like one time, maybe a month ago. You must have been out for awhile. Like overnight."

"They show you this place, Richard and Duane? They invite you?"

"Yeah."

"Where are these imbeciles?" Feliks demands. "You tell me."

"I don't know, man! They was staying with me until like two, three days ago. Then my phone disappears, my car disappears, *they* disappear, pfft!

A chill runs though Feliks. Richard and Duane are stupider than he thought. Inviting this woman to their training site? Into this hidden place where Feliks sleeps and resides? Into a place that he had instructed again and again must never be revealed to anyone? Feliks' first inclination is to rage against these two morons.

Then he has a second thought, making a new calculation. Two people looking for Richard and Duane are better than one. He's already composing in his head a new transmission to the Gaswerks. He's thinking: *momentum, finally!* These past days he's been trying to reassure Moscow that he's hot on the trail, but his reports have lacked specifics and he suspects Marshkova and his other managers are losing patience. But now he has a specific! Marla Kusic. Tenuous, perhaps. But, unbeknownst to her, she's now part of a global network working digitally and literally to find and track down the two naughty boys.

For his report, Feliks will have to conduct a modest

debriefing of Marla. Where did she meet Richard? What kind of car is missing? What kind of cellphone? What's the number? Who else knows Richard and Duane are in town? Where do they hang out? Are Richard and Duane armed? If so, what do they carry? And Marla, without a car, how did she get here today? What taxi company did she use? Does she have a receipt? And so on.

An hour later, these two new friends climb into Feliks' car and drive to Lucky's Nordeast Lounge where Feliks, never telling Marla his name or his business, scours the basement apartment looking for bits and pieces.

"Hey Big Man," she says at one point. "Who are you anyways?"

Chapter Thirty-One

Wednesday, 1:30 p.m

If Feliks could pace, he would pace. If he could stop sweating through his snug-fitting knit shirt, he would. But he's trapped in his car on a hot afternoon, waiting. Waiting for a return transmission from the Gaswerks. His request had been simple. Could they plug in Marla's cellphone number to their satellite database and trace the whereabouts of her phone and thus the whereabouts of the miscreants who stole it, namely Richard Reznik and Duane Hajinlian? Should be a piece of cake. He knows it's, what? 10:30 p.m. in Moscow, but the Gaswerks never sleeps.

So Feliks waits, pawing at the air conditioning controls and flicking on his music. Out pours the first strains of Dmitri Shostakovich's Eighth Symphony. Ordinarily Feliks sticks to American music. He admires Miles Davis and the jazzy tunes of the late '50s and early '60s sung by the likes of Sinatra and Ella Fitzgerald, but sometimes, when he's extra nervous or wants to sink deeper into his melancholy, he turns to Shostakovich.

He identifies with the composer's struggle against rigid authority and the cowardly accommodations that an artist in those times had to make in order to survive Stalin's purges. Yet, there were times when the composer had shown courage and defiance, too, especially with the Eighth Symphony. Stalin wanted it to celebrate the glorious victory of the Red Army over the Nazis, but Shostakovich had instead written about the violence, horrors and suffering that the war had inflicted on the Soviet peoples.

There is something in this terrible tension between master and artist that Feliks feels deeply. He lives with a similar tension every day, he realizes, even if his pursuits are comparatively trivial. He lives those tensions even at this moment.

His life could have been so different if only he had made better choices when he was young. Now it is too late. Like Shostakovich, he has no choice but to walk the tightrope, no choice but to make the best of reality.

Reality makes it imperative that he finds Richard and Duane as quickly as possible, finds these two wayward contractors who seem to have gone into business for themselves. Surely the Gaswerks is impatient in this matter.

Still, any details surrounding the deaths of Richard and Duane must be carefully considered. Do their bodies simply disappear, as in the old days? Or is there a narrative that should be concocted to serve Russia's greater interests? This is the new emphasis. Maybe they could be murdered by an immigrant group, or by Black Lives Matter, or by Islamic terrorists. Luckily, deciding on the best story won't be left to Feliks. The Gaswerks has specialists who know how best to manipulate American public opinion. He's heard rumors that the Gaswerks may even be in the process of selecting America's next president! Now, that would impress even Feliks.

Suddenly he hears the ping he's been waiting for and a

coded message comes trickling across. Quickly Feliks dials into his way-finding program. A little blue blip shows up on the map, moving northward along White Bear Avenue. Feliks slips the rental car into gear and makes for the freeway.

Chapter Thirty-Two

Wednesday, 1:35 p.m

Gwen Gray has no idea how people talk about her the way they do, like, how many times can you say her name in five seconds? Gwen Gray, Gwen Gray, Gwen Gray. She wouldn't understand the humor. What she does understand is how to run a church office. Even in a crisis, St. Ansgar runs like a dream. Few human beings have the poise under pressure that Miss Gray possesses, and she knows it.

She's proofreading the weekly newsletter before taking her two o'clock coffee break when her telephone rings.

"St. Ansgar Church. May I help you?"

A man's voice. "I'm looking for the tall, blonde female who works there, the one with the kid. I forget her name."

"Are you referring to Pastor Lindberg? Margaret Lindberg?"

"I guess."

"I'm afraid she's on hiatus. Perhaps someone else on our staff can help."

"I don't think so. What's her number? I need to call her."

"I'm afraid I couldn't give out her number. Maybe you could tell me the nature of your problem."

"My problem? I ain't got no problem. She's got the problem."

Gwen pauses. "Perhaps I could have Pastor Lindberg call you."

"No, you give her this message, and I'm only going to say it once, because I'm going to destroy this cellphone as soon as I hang up. So you take this down. Ready?"

There's another pause before Gwen Gray says, "Yes."

"We got her little daughter. She wants her daughter back, she leaves a hundred grand cash small bills in the blue recycle bin on the side of the road at — you got this so far?"

There's a pause. "Yes."

"Leave a hundred grand in small bills in a paper shopping bag at 12074 Cedar Grove Avenue North in Circle Pines tomorrow at noon. In the blue recycle bin. You got that?"

"Yes."

"Read that address back to me."

Gwen reads it back.

"No cops find out about this. No cops! You listening to me? Blondie comes alone. This place is in the open. We can see if she's playing games with us. She plays games and the girl is dead meat. She don't show up with the money, the girl dies. We'll have the girl right close by. Got it? This is tomorrow I'm talking about. Simple business transaction."

"Where can ...?" Gwen manages to ask before caving in, before giving the caller Maggie's number.

What to do now? Call the police? Call Captain Bender directly? But this man said no police. Call Maggie? For now, calling Maggie seems the best bet.

Gwen is surprised that she's shaking as she presses Maggie's number on her speed dial. Maybe she's not as cool and calm as she thought. Poor little Petra! She and Petra have a special bond. Petra is that darling daughter that Gwen never had. She buys Petra gifts. She loves hanging out with her, showing her how the office operates, taking her on walks through the park and along the river. Whenever Maggie wants her to babysit for Petra, she cancels her other plans. Gwen doesn't know if Petra feels the same way about her. Probably not. Eight-year-olds don't understand how important they can be in the life of a lonely, unmarried adult. Petra is the soft spot in Gwen's rather stoic, efficient, utilitarian existence.

Maggie's phone is ringing, but goes quickly to voicemail.

Chapter Thirty-Three

Wednesday, 1:40 p.m

Maggie, sitting at her kitchen table with a cup of hot coffee and a huge stack of police reports, has just hung up from a chat with Bender who wants her downtown for a 3 o'clock meeting. That means that after tennis lessons, the little green bus will have to drop Petra off not at home but at Nori's house. So Maggie is quickly calling her daughter's new cellphone to leave her a message.

But instead of her daughter's voice or her daughter's precocious recording ("This is Petra, you know what to do and when to do it."), it's a man's voice on the other end. This must be a wrong number. But no, it can't be. Probably it's one of the tennis coaches, Maggie thinks, Maggie hopes, trying to calm herself. But this man doesn't sound like a coach at a country club.

"Yeah?" he says.

"Petra? Where's Petra?"

"Who the fuck is this?"

A chill runs through Maggie's body. Her throat starts to

burn. Her ears begin to ring with a panic that's impossible to suppress. This is a mother's ultimate nightmare, calling her child's cellphone and getting some ... somebody else.

"Isn't this the cellphone of Petra Lindberg Rincon?" Maggie hears her own voice as if from a distance.

"Maybe it used to be her phone but it ain't no more," Fat Duane says with an uncertain chuckle. He's suddenly confused about how to proceed. When Richard drove off for what he called his "business meeting," he hadn't left instructions other than to keep the kid in the motel room, and keep her quiet.

"Who the fuck are you?" he says.

"I'm her mother! Petra's mother! Where is she? Why do you have her phone? Is she all right? Let me talk to her!"

"Hey, Blondie! Is this you?"

Maggie has trouble swallowing. How does this man know what she looks like, who she is?

"You supposed to be talking to, um, Richard, right? He ain't called you yet? He ain't given you the pitch?"

"Pitch? What pitch? Who are you? Hand the phone to Petra."

"Relax, Blondie. Everything's cool. This here is just a business thing. I told Richard I was like against it because it sounds like, you know, I hate to even say the word, like kidnapping, and that's like the last thing we need right now is for the feds to get into our shit. But Richard says, no, it ain't like that. This here's a business proposition, pure and simple, he says. Part of the Economic Recovery Initiative, he says. We get the money, you get the kid."

"What! Who are you? Where are you? Who's this person Richard? I want to talk to my daughter. I want to talk to her right now!"

Maggie realizes now that she's pacing frantically up and

down the length of her house. She grasps also that she is totally forgetting her police training. Calm? No way! Police training never included having your own child abducted, never included your own child as a hostage. Still, she takes a deep breath. In a calmer voice she asks, "May I talk with Petra? Is she there?"

Fat Duane looks over at the girl with the small yellow ball in her mouth and the terrified look in her teary eyes. "It's your mother," he says, and then into the phone, "She's here but she can't talk right now."

"Why is that? How do I know you've got her? I need proof. Tell me what she's wearing," Maggie pleads, fearing for the first time that maybe these assholes have stripped off her clothes, maybe they've assaulted her, maybe they've killed her.

"OK, she's got on white shorts and a green shirt that says, let's see, Town Country Tennis Camp, and white tennis shoes, and there's a blue ribbon thing in her hair."

"But how do I know she's alive?" Maggie cries, losing her composure again. "This is my baby!" She begins to sob quietly.

There's an incoming call on Maggie's cell, a number she doesn't recognize. But she can't risk losing the call she's on. She can't!

"Tell me she's OK! Tell me she's alive! Tell me how I can get my girl back? Tell me what you want!"

"She's fine. Nobody's gonna hurt her. I mean, for sure, I ain't gonna hurt her. About getting her back, I can't help you there. See, I'm not, shall we say, authorized. There's somebody else who has to say those things, somebody else who knows the pitch. This is a business thing."

"Who? Who is this other guy I should talk to? Is it this Richard you keep talking about? Where's he?" Maggie pleads, realizing for the first time that one of the suspects she's hunting is named Richard, Richard Anthony Reznik.

A call is coming in on Maggie's phone, again. Same number

as before. It occurs to her that she has her daughter's cell number, a number she could call at any time.

"He was supposed to call you by now," Duane says. "He needs to call you."

Maggie picks up the other call. "Richard? Is this you?"

"How the fuck you know who this is?"

"I was talking to this other guy who claims that you two have kidnapped my daughter."

"You were what? Who were you talking to? That fat ass shit for brains! What did he tell you?"

"Like I said, that ..."

"Yeah, OK, we got your kid, but she hasn't been kidnapped! She's just, you know, our guest at corporate headquarters until you can scrape together an investment."

"You mean money? I haven't got any money!"

"You will by tomorrow. Like I saw you on TV acting chummy with some rich dude who's offering a reward, so I figure you can easily get, you know, a hundred thousand cash from him. You put it in a shopping bag, deliver it ALONE at noon tomorrow to an address I'm gonna give you. ALONE, just you, Blondie. No cops. You call them, I'll know about it. You get your kid back tomorrow noon. After I get the cash. A hundred thousand."

"What? You're insane! You better not hurt my child. You touch one ..."

"Hey, ma'am. I hope you aren't threatening me. Is this the polite way to conduct business? I don't think so. This is going to be a proper transaction. So, don't threaten me. If you do, then something bad might happen. If you stray off the path of, you know, fiscal responsibility, somebody might get hurt. You fulfill your fiduciary responsibility and you get the girl back. Got the picture?"

Maggie is trembling uncontrollably by the time Richard

disconnects. She has scribbled down the address he gave her. She's already thinking about how to approach Kron for the money. Her mind is racing. This can't be happening, not on top of everything else crashing into her life. She almost calls Bender, but finds herself dialing Span instead.

Chapter Thirty-Four

Wednesday, 1:45 p.m

Richard is back in the Shitcar Chevy hauling ass, heading for the motel, not in the best of moods. Sweat runs down the sides of his face. His head is bursting and throbbing. All his careful fucking plans! Who's the one who found the obscure motel? Who found the deserted house out in the open with the recycle bin out front? Who set things up for tomorrow in a way that's perfecto! All this careful work about calling the church, then forcing the church lady to finally give him Blondie's number! All that precision-type work! And then shit-for-brains Duane has already *talked* to Blondie? Already *told* her? Already placed in jeopardy the *whole fucking works?* And now that great big tub of pig shit thinks he's gonna get his full fifty grand? *Never - fucking - gonna - happen!*

Chapter Thirty-Five

Wednesday, 2:10 p.m

Feliks dabs his considerable chin with a paper napkin to mop the grease left by one of the sliders he lifts from a bag of several, the bag resting on the passenger seat of his car parked in front of the White Castle on the road known as Old Highway 23.

As he chews, he gazes out on the not-so-magnificent sight of the adjacent Snooz Pines Inn. Long past its prime as a roadside attraction, the 1960s motel, with the drooping sign, the crumbling asphalt parking lot and the two dead willow trees, still manages to hang on, even though the interstate took away its regular trade decades ago.

Feliks knows the motel's history, not because he has studied this particular place, but because he has observed the fascinating layers and cycles of renewal and rot that constitute his adopted country, his beloved America. He knows how you can go into a city, any city, and, like an archaeologist, study the overlays – the new buildings and new districts that go up over the old ones and the other old ones that always get left behind. This strip of marginal fast-food joints, dated motels and off-brand gas stations has clearly been left behind.

In a more immediate sense, Duane has also been left behind at the motel with a kidnapped child and Marla's cellphone. Richard, meanwhile, is out and about, driving an old Chevrolet. Feliks casually glances at his computer screen, which shows him a map with a blue dot that's still miles away but now moving rapidly again back toward the motel, back toward Feliks' own stakeout location. This blue dot would be Richard, his wayward boy, coming home to papa. The youngsters at the Gaswerks had solved the problem, figuring out Richard's cell number by matching calls going into the church with calls going into Marla's number, then planting the GPS tracking code into Richard's number. Indeed, for the last hour or so, Feliks has been able to locate Richard in real time and record his conversations.

Feliks was listening as Richard promised the church lady that he would destroy the phone, but Feliks knew he would not. Later he had heard Richard threaten the church lady into providing Margaret Lindberg's number, and then heard, in real time, the amusing conversation between the female pastor and Richard, who is clearly — how do the Americans say it? — coming unglued. Something very soon must be done about Richard. The blue dot is moving closer. Feliks calculates that within ten minutes, Richard should be back.

Feliks contemplates entering the motel room now and ending it for Duane — and then waiting for Richard. But he doesn't want to risk traumatizing the child and creating the bigger problem of what to do with her. Too messy now, especially if there might be ample time later this afternoon to deal with the two fuck-ups alone, or ample time for the Gaswerks to concoct an effective narrative to feed the public, a narrative about how these two unfortunate boys departed this vale of tears.

Chapter Thirty-Six

Wednesday, 2:19 p.m

Fat Duane slides a big slice of yesterday's pizza out of the motel room microwave and opens another can of beer, but not without guilt, sensing the obvious hunger in the little girl's eyes. Taking a bite and popping another slice into the oven, he steps lightly across the room to take the ball from her mouth, then, bending to untie her hands and feet, noticing for the first time that her shorts and legs are sopping wet with urine.

Petra makes no sound, but stretches the muscles around her mouth before quickly gobbling the slice of pizza and draining the cup of tap water her generous host has provided.

"I want my mom. I wanna go home," the girl says weakly, having trouble forming her words.

"Just eat. No talking."

"Why did you tie me up? What's going on? You were talking to Mom on my phone? What did she say?"

It's clear to Duane that Petra isn't going to scream, isn't going to cry, isn't going to try to run away, isn't going to be a pain in the ass. She and Duane share a basic human problem: They're hungry. So both together are attacking the remaining slices of pizza. "Your mom is worried about you, but there's nothing to be worried about," Duane tells her. "You're gonna go home tomorrow. We just gotta take care of something first."

"Take care of what?"

"You don't have to worry about that. Just relax."

"I'm wet."

"I know. I'm sorry. Can't be helped."

Finding a kind of rapport with the child, Duane tells Petra about his own little girl, five years old, he says. Name of Kristal. "Haven't seen her lately," he says. "Her mom don't want me around, don't want me to see her. Not fair, huh?"

Petra doesn't answer. "I like to go fishing," she blurts inexplicably. "Sometimes I go with my mom. I've caught a walleye several times."

Duane folds a pizza slice and takes a giant bite. "I used to fish when I was a kid," he manages to say between chews. "Lake Michigan."

Duane's recollections of childhood aren't all that pleasant. Unlike Petra, he was never tied up or held hostage. But he and his brothers often went hungry. His mother had a job working on the line at Harley-Davidson, but on payday his father would come by to take his cut, sometimes pushing her around or slugging her to get what he wanted, then disappearing for another two weeks. She, in turn, took out her frustrations on the four boys, especially on Duane, the youngest, fattest and stupidest.

Fast forward to now and it's Richard who's always pushing him around. Duane is about fed up. Look at the way he has treated this little girl! Even in his anger at Richard, Duane is surprised that his heart goes out to her. No kid should be treated like this. She keeps talking about fishing. Fishing wasn't a recreation for him when he was a kid. It was about getting food for him and his brothers. When the fish didn't bite, the boys would fan out to shoplift groceries. They made it a contest. Who could get the most? Duane was proud to be the master shoplifter. It was something he could do well, using his portliness to hide cans of Dinty Moore and pints of ice cream, among other items.

"I wasn't good for much," he told her. "But shoplifting, I was real good at that. The best!"

Petra gives Duane a puzzled look. "I don't like to catch bullheads," she says. "They got a lot of 'em in the river. They have whiskers and look kinda ugly."

"I got whiskers," Duane says, showing off his beard. "Kristal, she don't like it. Says it's scratchy."

"My dad, he ..."

Wham! There's the sound of a car door slamming out front. Must be Richard coming back, Duane thinks. The motel room door swings open sooner than Duane expects, and Richard storms in, the mood instantly transformed from almost tender to super tense.

"What the fuck, dude!" Richard screams, launching a profane tirade about all the things that have gone wrong for him this morning, all because of fucking Duane. The girl being untied and ungagged, for one, and Duane's utter general stupidity for another, especially the fact that it was Duane, not Richard, who had made first contact with Blondie! And Duane, well shit! Who knows? Duane might have botched the whole brilliant business deal that Richard had so cleverly planned. It's only by luck that Blondie seems down with the deal, no thanks to fat, stupid, shit-for-brains Duane who doesn't deserve his cut of the ... "You ain't getting shit, dude!" Richard shouts.

Turns out, those are Richard's last utterances. The thirty-eight caliber bullet enters his forehead just above the right eye, Duane not remembering pulling the pistol from his belt, not remembering squeezing the trigger from his seated position behind the pizza slices now glazed with coagulated grease and still resting on the table between him and the girl.

The release of horrible tension is happening so fast and, yet, almost in slow motion. There's no denying what just happened. There it is! The gun in his hand! And his ears ringing to beat shit! And the acrid scent of gun smoke rising to his nostrils! And the concussion waves from the terrible bang filling the motel room and bursting out into the world!

Chapter Thirty-Seven

Wednesday, 2:33 p.m

The sound of the shot propels Feliks out of his car in a flash, his fluid movements like those of a big cat. Now he stands poised on the crumbling surface of the White Castle parking lot assuming the ready position, legs braced, arms out in front, keen eyes scanning his field of vision. No other pedestrians in view, no cars pulling to a halt because of what their occupants might have seen or heard. Feliks focuses now on the motel door no more than fifty meters away. This is a situation, obviously. His training calls for immediate evaluation and immediate action before any citizens, or especially any police, can get involved.

He sprints to the edge of the window on the front side of Unit Fourteen. Then he moves gracefully toward the door. It is ajar. There in the doorway, on the floor, he encounters his wayward pupil, one Richard Anthony Reznik, sprawled on his back, motionless, eyes open, blood oozing from a good-sized hole in his forehead. Across the room, sitting at a small table wedged between the beds, is Duane Clyde Hajinlian, his more obedient client, chewing on a slice of the large pepperoni that sits in a pizza box on the table. And in the corner stands a small, dark-haired girl with hands over her ears and horror on her face. Of Feliks' greatest interest is the thirty-eight revolver resting on the table, near the pizza box.

"What!" says Duane, his eyebrows rising. "Big Man? What the fuck you doing here?"

"We must go now," Feliks says quietly, calmly.

"But I ..."

"Now! *Bistrye, bistryre, bistrye!*" Feliks says slowly but firmly, stooping to pull a gun and a cellphone from Richard's limp body, then focusing again on Duane. "Leave on the table the gun. And the pizza also."

Maybe it's the mind-bending surprise of the Big Man's magical appearance. Maybe it's that Duane is in some kind of shock. Maybe it's that Duane feels somehow beholden to the Big Man for giving him a chance at the big time and the big score. Probably it's the Big Man's pistol pointed directly at his abdomen.

Whatever the reason, Duane abandons the pizza, the gun, the girl's cell phone, Marla's cellphone and, as it turns out, Marla's Shitcar Chevy. He steps over poor Richard's corpse, glances at the car, and ducks around the back of the motel, now walking with the Big Man slowly, nonchalantly, toward his rental car, Feliks behind him with his pockets stuffed with guns and cellphones, a small girl tucked like a loaf of bread under one arm, the girl frozen with fear, wanting to scream but unable to utter a sound even as Feliks places her gently into the car's trunk.

As Feliks and his new passengers drive south on Old Highway 23, back toward the city, they meet two screaming cop cars and an ambulance headed north toward a possible crime scene. Somebody has seen something.

Chapter Thirty-Eight

Wednesday, 3:00 p.m

As Span pulls to the curb in front of Maggie's house, he sees her pacing end to end across the front porch in obvious agony. The two embrace at the top of the steps, Maggie's cheeks wet with tears, her body trembling. Barely has she had a chance to blurt out the kidnappers' demands when her cell chirps. It's Bender. Maggie presses speaker so Span can hear Bender's breathless pronouncement.

"Richard Reznik is dead."

The cadence of his words and his heavy breathing make it clear that Bender is running, probably to his car. "One shot to the head," he gasps. "Nobody else on the premises. No Duane. No Petra. Snooz Pines Motel. Room Fourteen. One-oh-one-zero-six Old Highway 23, Circle Pines."

It occurs to Span that events are suddenly moving at the speed of light. One minute Petra is snatched and held for ransom. The next minute, one of the kidnappers is killed. By whom? We don't know. Maybe by the other kidnapper who's now on the loose with Petra, who's presumably still alive. One minute Petra is a meal ticket for two losers. The next minute she's a hostage, perhaps, for the survivor of the pair, probably a more desperate, dangerous survivor.

Despite her police training, it's hard for Maggie to think of the situation in law-enforcement terms. For her, this is solely about Petra and her safety. This is about her baby, her daughter, the person she loves more than anyone in the world. The murders at the church were personal. This is more personal. This bores a hole into the soul of Margaret Lindberg.

Among reporters Span is known as a fast driver, and he sets an overland speed record getting Maggie from the island up to the desolate stretch of strip malls in Circle Pines. It's a roughly fifteen-mile trip. Maggie hardly speaks all the way up. They pull into the motel's cratered, weedy parking lot, joining a fleet of squad cars from various jurisdictions. For maximum public effect, all have their motors running, their lights flashing, their doors flung open.

Between them, Maggie and Span have visited hundreds of crime scenes, but none quite so intimate as this one. Not even the fiasco in L.A., the liquor store robbery that cost Maggie her career and her dad his mobility and sanity, can measure up to this one because this one involves Petra. Never having been a parent, Span knows he can never fully comprehend Maggie's anguish as she ducks under the yellow tape, showing her police credential and trying to balance her impossible trinitarian role of cop, priest and mother — with mother sucking out all the oxygen from the others.

She's giving cool professionalism a really, *really* hard try, consulting other officers, taking notes, drawing a rough diagram of the room. But when you see up close the shit hole that your daughter has endured, when you step over Richard's body, his blood pooling in the doorway, when you duck into the stuffy room smelling the smells of urine and body odor, stale beer, cigarette smoke and day-old pizza, when you see the stained chair she sat in and the tape that bound her, that's when the cool professionalism begins to melt away and dread takes over.

Span, he can hide in his disguise as a newspaper reporter. He can tell himself that he's just assembling the facts, you know, just setting the scene, just arranging the paragraphs in his head, just placing the events in context, just imagining his finishing lines about the cops looking high and low for Richard's killer and about the FBI turning over every trash can in town looking for Petra and the fat but elusive Duane. But even for Span, it's all a diversion. He realizes that he's far more emotionally tied to this case than to anything he's ever written. He has spent a career pretending to care deeply about all kinds of misfortunes that befall people. Now, finally, he *does* care deeply. He *is* this case. He's no longer a fraud.

He remembers vividly his first crime scene. He was a kid just up from Madison. Corky Goodyear was the veteran crime reporter on the Star Journal in those days. He took a shine to Span. "What you doing?" he asks him one horribly hot afternoon as they stood panting on the sidewalk outside the newspaper building.

"Not much," Span says.

"C'mon," he says. They jump into a company cruise car and drive up into the north side. On the way Corky, between puffs on his well-chewed cigar, tells Span that neighbors have been complaining about a terrible stink in the back of a house at Emerson and 26th. They pull up behind a cop car parked at the curb and a couple of sweaty uniforms lead Corky and Span through some tall weeds into a junky backyard. There's a rusty old car back there baking in the afternoon sun. One of the cops has a crowbar, and he proceeds to pry open the trunk. The smell gets suddenly worse, so bad that Span struggles not to vomit. No one present, not the cops, not the circle of neighbors now gathered for a peek, wants to breathe this putrid air. The body in the trunk is bloated and liquefied. It looks like black jello. It's hunched up and bound by ropes.

Span quickly retreats to the edge of the yard, grabbing a handkerchief to cover his nose and mouth. Later, Corky tells him there's a slug in the back of the head. The story Span writes describes the execution of a popular seller of narcotics. Later stories document the revenge killings of other young entrepreneurs trying for a monopoly on a lucrative street corner. As far as Span remembers, none of the murders was ever solved. Perhaps the neighbors were more eager to get rid of odors than to finger possible suspects. Perhaps the cops weren't all that eager to solve cases in the black sections of town. Corky even offered in one of his stories an off-the-record quote from one of the investigating detectives – something to the effect that he didn't mind that these bad guys were killing one another, he just wished they would do it someplace else, like out in the country where nobody else would be in the line of fire.

Span isn't sure why he thinks of this now, except perhaps to remind himself that maybe he hasn't really been such a fraud in seeking some level of detachment in writing about these tragic events. If every story were personal, then reporters would risk not seeing the bigger picture, not finding the broader perspective. Even on this crime scene, for example, he's tempted to give in to personal emotions and write about Petra when the real story is this: After two weeks of futile searching by police, the church murderers finally revealed themselves in sudden and sensational fashion. First, they kidnapped the daughter of an associate pastor of the same church, demanding a ransom. Next, one of the kidnappers, or perhaps someone else, gunned down the other for unknown reasons, escaping with the captured child. Finally, the police have mounted a massive search for the fugitive and the child, but so far they've come up empty. Again the authorities and the public are left frustrated.

These events prompt a number of questions for puzzled readers: Why have two petty criminals from outstate Minnesota zeroed in on one large church in the city to carry out their crimes, which have so far left three men dead and one child kidnapped? How have Duane and the child been able to elude the police on foot, without a car? (The suspects' car was left in the motel parking lot.) Are there other unknown suspects involved?

Maggie tells Span that there's one sketchy report of a "third man" who might have driven Duane and the child away from the scene. But the witness cannot describe the driver or the car and can't say which way the vehicle might have traveled.

Maggie sighs. After twenty minutes of trying as hard as she can to be official, she has begun to crack a little. "Span, can we go back to the car?" she asks.

So, they do. Span expects her to feed him more details about what the cops are thinking. Motive? Means of escape? Likely whereabouts? Instead she falls into a kind of panicky trance, wanting to talk about Petra. So he lets her vent. He hears a mother talking about a much-loved daughter. A special child, she says. Everybody says so. They say she was born wise, like maybe she had lived before. They say she's the family's most mature member, clearly more mature than her dad, a crack that always brings laughter. She's a child who's hard to punish because she has this look about her that says, "Mom, I know you feel this is necessary but, really, I'm seeing right through you."

Maggie's mind is racing. Petra was a happy baby who cried very little, she says, nervously. As she grew older she got along particularly well with adults – could repeat their conversations, even if she didn't really understand them. She loved her dad, even if he wasn't around and even though she rarely asked about him. She had good friends but was happy, too, to spend time alone reading or playing games or watching TV.

Maggie is talking a mile a minute. She sees Petra as proving a point of one of her favorite books, a book about the "disappearance of childhood." The premise was that while adults get sillier, more gullible and more childlike, kids, no longer shielded from adult "secrets" about sex and violence, lose the "enchantment" of traditional childhood and become more like adults. Petra had seen close up the continuing friction between her parents. One way she coped was to take delight in "disappearing" behind disguises or in hiding places. She loved to play dress-up and to wear costumes. Her favorite holiday was Halloween, and not because of the candy. Once in her hiding place she could stay motionless for long periods of time.

People said she was a pretty child, slightly plump with sparkling dark eyes and curly dark hair. She had the good looks and darker skin tone of the Rincons, but the serious disposition of the Lindbergs, people said. She was the perfect amalgam of the Latina and the Nordic types, they said.

It strikes Span that Maggie is drifting toward shock. She's sounding way too philosophical for the situation. Too detached, in a way. She's speaking of Petra in the past tense. It's heartbreaking to listen to her ramble. As a cop, she must know that the longer a hostage is in the clutches of a desperate, armed criminal, the less her chance of survival. Raw fear seems to have gripped Maggie despite her police training, despite her religious faith. The best moments of her life, Span realizes, have been spent with her precious daughter.

Chapter Thirty-Nine

Wednesday, 3:00 p.m. (23.00 hours in Moscow)

When her day began, the sky was blue and the forest was green outside her window at the headquarters of Sluzhba Vneshney Razvedki – SVR – the foreign intelligence service in Yasenevo, on the southwest edge of Moscow. Now, sixteen hours later, the shades are drawn against the darkness but still Colonel Yelena Marshkova sits chain-smoking at her desk. If there were papers on it she would be shuffling them furiously. Instead she's clicking, clicking, then pausing before clicking again on her keyboard. An already troublesome case has taken another wrong turn.

Reports from the American Midwest tell of a child being kidnapped and then, only moments ago, a contractor of the service being killed in the line of duty. These events do not reflect well on the future prospects of Colonel Yelena Marshkova.

Why not? The brutal truth is that the man with the infamous blue-eyed stare cares deeply about this otherwise obscure case. No one knows why, but he does. And no one wants to disappoint the man with the infamous blue-eyed stare. It is said that within months, perhaps by September, the man will appoint Sergey Naryshkin to lead the service. Naryshkin is a wealthy man and a strong patriot. And he has made certain promises to Colonel Marshkova – that when he rises she will also rise. Let us just say that it is in Colonel Marshkova's very best interests that this case is resolved smoothly, without further problems. Her future depends on it.

Looking back, she regrets giving the file to Code Name *Morzh* – Walrus. When she had met him in Helsinki, he had impressed her as capable. He was a big man, perhaps a brutal man, not polished, not stylish, yet trustworthy and straightforward, a serious man. Most notably, her decision rested on the fact that Walrus, years ago, had been a close colleague of the man with the infamous blue-eyed stare, back when they were both KGB stationed in Leipzig. Perhaps it would impress the blue-eyed president if he knew that his old colleague, this Walrus, this Feliks Dobervich as he calls himself today, is still a capable operative.

But, most embarrassingly, he is not. Despite Colonel Marshkova's best efforts, Walrus has fumbled the task from the beginning. Yes, the targets in the church were hit, but in a method that raised far too much commotion. Then the contractors failed to meet Walrus in Frankfurt upon completion and instead went rogue. Now one of them appears to be dead. And Walrus has not responded to inquiries. Walrus has gone missing. And Colonel Marshkova's patience is nearly at an end.

She stands now, engulfed in a cloud of blue cigarette smoke, a slender woman of medium height and short brown hair, wearing a finely tailored blue suit. She walks gracefully to a small table and pours herself a glass of hot tea.

Already she has asked for a new mental evaluation of Walrus from the SVR *Psikhologiya* Unit, a team of psychologists specializing in stresses and neuroses common among those engaged in secret work. His last evaluation in 2014 noted worrisome signposts for a man of Walrus' age and station. He may, for example, glorify the past as superior to the present. Indeed, Walrus continues to refer to the SVR as the Gaswerks, a pejorative German term once popular among KGB veterans who belittled the motherland's newly intellectualized intelligence service as more vapor than steel. Perhaps after the U.S. elections this fall, the old timers will have a higher regard for the SVR's new emphasis on cyber warfare, conspiracy theory and disinformation.

Also, an agent of Walrus' age and station may resent those whose careers have eclipsed his, suffering depression as a result. Or he may begin to overreach, taking chances in hopes of producing spectacular results but risking grave failure. What we appear to have here is grave failure.

Colonel Marshkova knows the clock is ticking, both for Walrus and for her. Unless she hears from him soon, she may have no choice but to drop the hammer on Walrus. That would be tragic, she muses, but necessary.

Chapter Forty

Wednesday, 3:30 p.m

Crossing the city line, Feliks cuts left into a hidden alley behind a seemingly deserted trucking terminal, stopping the car and retrieving from his backpack what looks like a large blue fountain pen, leaning over now to show it to Duane. Fat Duane, sitting silently in the passenger seat, has been silent during their short ride, his mind racing over this sudden turn of events, yielding to the shocking appearance of the Big Man bounding in out of nowhere to replace Richard as the alpha figure in his life.

Duane stares at the pen for a second, thinking maybe it's a gift. Then he lets out a yelp as Feliks jabs its sharp point into his thigh. Almost immediately Duane's head slumps to the side, his eyes glazing to white.

The magical glow of a summer afternoon has overtaken the shabby landscape of weedy empty lots, low concrete buildings and a dozen trucks parked in a row, temporarily silent. There's no living soul in sight, no movement that Feliks can detect, just shadows stretching toward the east as the sun falls lower toward the horizon. Feliks pauses for a moment to reflect on his situation, to evaluate his next move. Then, noticing the pen still in his hand, he opens the car door, pops the trunk and retrieves the sweaty, petrified girl who squints in the sudden sunlight but hasn't a chance to say anything before she, too, is jabbed and fades quickly to unconsciousness. Feliks transfers her to the back seat before resuming his customary position behind the wheel. There he sits, pondering.

Perhaps twenty minutes pass before he hears a door slam and the growl of a truck coming to life. Quickly he reaches for his backpack. Then he's out the door and up the weedy incline to the patch of gritty pavement where the trucks and trailers wait. A door slams again as the driver climbs down and saunters back to the terminal, leaving the motor running. Feliks makes quickly for the back of the trailer, noting its Texas license tag. Out of his backpack he removes Marla's cellphone, his official cellphone, his battery pack, his digital tablet and a role of duct tape and quickly goes to work. As Feliks finishes affixing his pieces to the trailer's undercarriage and placing Marla's soon-to-be-crushed phone under one of the trailer's giant wheels, the driver reemerges and climbs once again into the cab, testing the brakes, shifting the gears and finally pulling away from the loading dock. Feliks scrambles back to his car, back to his snoozing companions.

Again he sits behind the wheel, this time for perhaps an hour. Finally he reaches a third time into his backpack, this time for an unauthorized, renegade cellphone tucked into a zippered compartment. He hesitates, then punches in a number.

Six times it rings before a man's familiar voice answers, "Yes."

"Jag hater Jesper," Feliks says in badly-accented Swedish. My name is Jesper.

Jonas Kron greets him warmly. "What a pleasant surprise!" he says. "Where are you?"

"I visit Minneapolis only briefly," says Feliks, now suddenly Jesper. "Just passing through, as you Americans say. I have in possession, my dear Jonas, an artifact you will want to see. I will say only that it is Swedish and it is a sword with remarkable beauty and history."

"You've definitely got my attention, Jesper. Unfortunately, I'm up at my lake home. But I can be back to see you, say, Friday morning. I would be delighted if you would stay at my place in the city, on the island, for a few days."

"I am afraid, Jonas, that I travel with two associates, and this may be a burden for you."

"Nonsense. Robert will take care of everything."

"Also it is vital that the artifact and my associates be treated with utmost discretion. I hope I am not being overly mysterious."

"Anything you need, my friend. You may trust Robert completely. I look forward to seeing you and your artifact Friday morning, say 11?"

Arrangements are quickly made. Feliks disconnects, opens the car door, hikes up his backpack and escorts a drowsy, compliant Duane into the backseat next to the girl.

Thirty minutes later they cross the Lake Street Bridge onto Hennepin Island, turning right into the private gate of the Kron castle. The gate opens. Robert emerges to welcome the guests.

Chapter Forty-One

Thursday, June 23, 12:05 a.m. (08.05 hours in Moscow)

After four hours' sleep, the colonel is back in her office, no longer clicking on her keyboard but pacing, pacing and digesting the latest transmission. Overnight, her colleagues closed in on Walrus. Satellite data placed him driving south on the Interstate Highway Number 35 north of Kansas City, Missouri, heading perhaps for Texas and then Mexico. But when they caught up with him at a truck stop, it was not Walrus but rather his tablet and cellphone taped to the underside of a truck.

"*Svoloch!*" Colonel Yelena Marshkova utters, slamming the report onto a table and exhaling a cloud of cigarette smoke. The bastard Walrus has either been compromised or he has gone into business for himself. Either way he leaves her no choice. The hammer must fall on Feliks Dobervich. She walks to her desk, stubs out her cigarette, and picks up her phone.

Chapter Forty-Two

Thursday, 5:15 a.m

Feliks opens his eyes to a pre-dawn glow hanging over the Mississippi River, forgetting for a moment where he is. His surroundings are luxurious, at least for now. Kron's well-appointed guest quarters are in a separate coach house tucked into a back corner of the castle grounds. To the front of the guest house is a lovely garden and swimming pool. To the rear, with the river as its backdrop, lies a stark contrast – the dreary, abandoned south section of Hennepin Island.

This lower tip was once much larger, receding gradually over the first eighty years of the twentieth century as rocky chunks were hauled away on barges and rail cars. These chunks were some of the finest amber-colored limestone in the world – Kronstone – used in some of the world's greatest works of modern architecture. The last barge departed in 1981. Now, the docks lie rotting, the cranes are rusted hulks, weeds overtake the riverbank, and the quayside's framed buildings slump in despair.

A faded sign on the closest frame building reads "Harbormaster." If Feliks could see through the grimy windows, he'd recognize a scene out of the 1940s: a non-working ceiling fan, a Formica countertop, a large wall clock stopped at 9:41, a prominent chalkboard showing the long-ago arrivals and departures of barges, and several oaken desks fitted with musty manual typewriters. The window air-conditioners were yanked out years ago. One wing of the building included a dormitory where barge crews slept, ate, played cards, told jokes and picked fights.

Feliks closes the blinds to the glaring sun and mentally checks the locks on the two adjoining guest rooms where he has stashed Duane and the girl. Feliks knows this arrangement can't last. He knows he must make something happen, and soon. Accustomed to following orders, he's slowly getting used to the idea that he's on his own, freelancing, improvising. He knows also that Moscow will be looking for him.

The more he thinks about his new situation — and he's thought about almost nothing else these last fourteen hours — it was the gunshot that killed Richard yesterday afternoon that marked the turning point of his life. There's no going back. He remembers clearly observing Richard's swift arrival at the motel parking lot, his slamming the door of that decrepit car and striding toward Room Fourteen. He remembers the sound of the shot and his own dash to the motel doorway, his nine-millimeter pistol drawn. He sees himself stepping over Richard's still body and taking dead aim at Duane's forehead. And then ... he stopped. Everything went to slow motion.

Why did he stop? Never before had he stopped, or even hesitated. Was it the small girl with the petrified expression and hands over her ears standing in the corner? Perhaps. Was it his actual *liking* Duane, as opposed to hating Richard? That was unlikely. He'd executed many targets over the years, even people whom he had liked, or at least tolerated. And he'd used many methods.

A sampling of victims now flickers before Feliks' eyes. There's the arrogant Israeli agent in Tallinn who wants to fight Feliks with his hands, the man's eyes glowing with self-confidence, his manner brimming with the conviction that he's some kind of impervious master killer. Feliks uncoils his body, shifting his considerable weight from right foot to left hip, hitting him with a short powerful pop, so hard that the left side of his face caves in, Feliks feeling as if his big fist is passing clear through the man's head. This is back in about 1983, back when Feliks is perhaps at his sharpest and most efficient, fresh from the KGB's personal combat school. Feliks sees in his mind the man dropping in a heap, sees himself leaning on the body but finding no pulse. He can still feel, all these years later, the exhilaration and the pride in a quick, clean kill. It's perhaps his favorite moment.

Most of the others aren't as poetic. The dissident journalist in Budapest who thinks Feliks is a repairman coming to fix his phone, the man dying at his desk, an ice pick inserted into the base of his skull. The reactionary politician in Krackow who, despite no history of coronary disease, dies of a sudden heart attack a week before the election. The woman in Dresden who never gets an opportunity to testify at the mayor's corruption trial because she is struck with seizures and dies within a few days. The German family on holiday in Jamaica whose fishing boat is found adrift at sea, the bodies, including those of three children, age six to thirteen, never found.

Feliks does not consider himself a sniper, but there is one long shot he savors, delivered from a rooftop in Dayton, Ohio, into the parking lot of a shopping mall and through the left temple of a disloyal Russian novelist who was spending the academic year lecturing in America.

Altogether, Feliks has used, on maybe two hundred enemies of the Russian state, his hands and fists, various guns, knives, needles, pills, cigarettes, vapors, saps, and even a car. He's also employed his considerable powers of persuasion to issue threats or to hire and train others to do certain delicate jobs.

He thinks, for example, of his careful and patient recruitment of a sixteen-year-old black kid from Chicago who, following Feliks' instructions, expertly mugged and murdered a criminal Russian businessman who had betrayed his country and his president. To the cops, the assault looked like an ordinary street crime. Last Feliks heard, the kid, now in his twenties, is doing life downstate.

Then there's the matter at hand, the one involving his befriending of Jonas Kron many years ago. Isn't it fitting? he muses. Tomorrow, when Kron arrives, there will be a reckoning. Their long relationship will come full circle.

Chapter Forty-Three

Thursday, 9:30 p.m

Night is creeping into the city as Span steps out of the Star Journal building and makes for police headquarters five blocks away. The lines of cars and busses that four hours earlier had jammed the streets have thinned to a trickle. Pedestrians, even on a warm and pleasant summer evening, are few in this part of downtown, allowing Span to ignore the walk/don't walk signs and slip quickly into the spacious art deco lobby that once passed for elegant. But two decades of police occupation have erased all the vintage charm of a building constructed originally as the Perpetual National Bank, an institution that turned out to be neither national nor perpetual.

The cops took out the teller windows and inserted a massive and battered plywood check-in desk flanked by cheap bulletin boards and kiosks littered with official municipal fliers and postings. They unhooked the stately chandeliers and put in harsh floodlights that make visitors feel ready for immediate interrogation. Once the metal detectors and security fencing went up, the

Historical Society let out a collective sigh and gave up on saving the building.

Span finds Maggie on the third floor, in the homicide bureau. She's standing tall and slender at the far end of a long, dimly lit bullpen, near the entrance to Bender's office. With her are three men talking and gesturing forcefully. Bender is one. Thurber, the FBI field office's chief investigator, is another. The third man Span doesn't recognize.

Maggie turns slightly, her eyes locking into his. As Span weaves his way through the mostly empty desks, she moves towards him, still locking in, Span noticing as she draws nearer the tears welling in her green, green eyes. As they halfway embrace, Span kisses her gently on the cheek, fearing the worst.

"Anything new?"

"No," she whispers.

Late yesterday afternoon, after racing with Span up to the motel where Richard Reznik's corpse lay sprawled in the doorway of Room Fourteen, and after grasping the reality that Petra had probably witnessed his violent death, Maggie and Span had ridden together back downtown, Span jumping out at the paper and Maggie driving his car straight to the chapel at St. Ansgar, where she spent the better part of two hours on her knees, pleading for the life not only of her beloved daughter but for the lives of damaged children everywhere. By the time Span finished writing, Maggie was back with the cops who had set up a command center in a large conference room next to Bender's office. Twenty-four hours have passed, and they're still here.

"I don't have to tell you," Maggie says, "that the odds get worse the longer we don't hear anything."

"Too early to worry about that," Span says, taking her hand, trying to reassure her. "Every cop in the city is out looking and the FBI is finally on the job. And don't underestimate the public. Shouldn't be hard to spot a fat man and a kid – on foot."

But Span's words seem not to console her. He's never seen her so agitated, her hands trembling, her shoulders heaving, her eyes darting around the room. The remarkably calm professionalism she had shown since the church murders, the ultra strong Maggie that had so amazed him is suddenly vulnerable, almost fragile. The reality of Petra's kidnaping is sinking in, he gathers, in a kind of delayed reaction.

"Oh, Span!" she finds herself whispering, hearing her own words as if they're coming out of another body. "I've never felt so helpless. Petra is all I ..." She stops abruptly as a shadow moves across their conversation.

"Who you supposed to be?"

The voice comes from the man Span doesn't recognize, good-looking guy, dark hair, medium height, solid build, mid 30s, Latino maybe, and coming at Span with attitude.

As politely as possible Span introduces himself, explaining perhaps awkwardly that he has information to discuss with Pastor Lindberg.

"You gotta be the hot shit reporter she likes to talk about," he says, sizing Span up and down, not impressed by what he sees. "I'm the husband, Petra's father, Jimmy Rincon."

They don't shake hands.

"I'm so sorry for this awful situation," Span manages to say, glaring at the guy.

"Well, at least the FBI is on the case. All we can do now is wait."

Turns out that James, as Maggie calls him, has flown in from L.A., landing a few hours ago. Maybe it's Span's wishful thinking, but Maggie doesn't seem all that grateful, all that happy to see him. His comment about "all we can do is wait" seems especially irksome to her. Span sees it in her eyes, detects it in her body language.

"Lokken! How the fuck did you get in here?" It's unmistakably Bender. He's walking toward them as Thurber turns and heads into the first interrogation room off to the side, the one where detectives seem to be constantly coming and going. "Officer Rincon," Bender says to James, "you may not know it but you're in the presence of greatness, you're looking at God's gift to journalism." He turns an upward palm toward Span. "We get a lot of scumbags in this room, and we lock up most of 'em, but this one here keeps coming back for more."

Bender throws his arm around Span's shoulder. "Come with me, asshole," he says, leading him into his office, closing the glass bubbled door behind them. Once inside, he bellows for all to hear, "Christ Almighty, Lokken! This is a fucking homicide investigation! We got a kidnapping here!" Then he lowers his voice and steps to within a few inches of Span's face. Span smells the familiar blend of cigarettes and Juicy Fruit.

"Did we have some fun up north?" Bender asks. "Get laid, did we? Learn anything about our two upright citizens?"

"Boy Scouts, both of them. Merit badges galore. Classmates voted them most likely to succeed."

"Yeah, whatever," Bender says. "Listen, Genius, out of the goodness of my heart I got two things for you. You ready?"

"Shoot."

"The lab finally sorted out the DNA thing. The sperm in the dead priest's mouth belongs to guess who?"

"You, probably."

"Not likely. Belongs to our recently deceased hero, Richard Anthony Reznik. Thought you should know that it wasn't the janitor and wasn't our fat friend, Duane Hajinlian."

"So, when was this deposit made? Before or after Hammar's death?"

"Good question. Don't know. Lab can't tell," Bender says. "Duane is the only one who can help us with that one, and he's not available for comment, not yet anyways."

"Number two?'

"Yeah, number two. We found a car and two guns at Richard's homicide scene. First gun, not very interesting. Nine-mill automatic under the seat in the jalopy parked out front. Gun stolen in 2011. Richard's fingerprints on it. Hadn't been fired recently. Second gun, a thirty-eight revolver, the one that put Richard to sleep. Had Fat Duane's greasy fingerprints all over it."

"No surprise there. Everybody figured him as the shooter."

"Bingo. But it wasn't the same gun that whacked what's-his-name, the janitor at the church.

"Henrik Piedela."

"Right. That weapon hasn't turned up. But here's the thing about this particular gun. We ran a trace on it. And we ID'd the owner." Bender stops abruptly to gaze out his window onto the darkened square below. He checks his watch. "That's about all I can say about that for now."

"What do you mean, all you can say?"

"Listen, Slick. I'm giving you a break here. I give you a lotta breaks."

"I know, Captain sir. And don't think I'm not grateful. But don't leave me hanging on this one. Please!"

"The reason I can't tell you is that my tall blond consultant can't know about this. Not yet. She finds out she'll go hysterical on us, and I don't need no more of that around here tonight."

"You know something about Petra you're not telling her?"

"Maybe." He fumbles for his pack of Camels, forgetting the city's indoor ban on smoking. "OK, you cannot, repeat *cannot*, tell her this. And I don't wanna see this in the paper tomorrow. Not even any of your 'sources speculate' bullshit. Capeesh?"

Span nods.

"The car and the nine mill belong to Marla Kusic. K-U-S-I-C. Age 32. Piece of work. Interesting tattoos. We got her in

Interview A, next door. Thurber and some of my boys are in there working her over, thinking she maybe knows the whereabouts of the kid and Duane."

"Why would she know?"

"Funny thing. She runs this bar in Northeast. Lucky's at 27th and Arnold. Turns out to be three, four blocks from the site of the taxi crash I was telling you about last week. So, we get a warrant to search the premises. Downstairs in a basement apartment we find all kinds of shit belonging to Richard and Duane, along with their fingerprints and some of Richard's blood. One idea is that either she gives the gun to Fat Duane or he takes it. Also, looks like, from premises analysis, our two genius boys had been staying there maybe a week."

"So, this is what? A hideout?"

"Seems to be," Bender says. "Turns out Marla and Richard went to school together up on the range."

"Co-valedictorians, no doubt."

"Huh?"

"OK, so you got her, right?" Span says. "She's part of a what? A conspiracy, an accessory after the fact, aiding and abetting, harboring fugitives? You're gonna arrest her, right?"

"Actually, we want to be friends with Marla."

"You what? You gonna flip her?"

"Let's just say lawyers are now involved. Our people are talking to her people."

Chapter Forty-Four

Thursday, 10:10 p.m

As Span emerges from Bender's office he sees something he's never seen before: Maggie unhinged. She's not quite yelling at her estranged husband, but she's gesturing wildly and speaking in what parents might call her "outdoor voice." Her vocabulary is not of the sort usually associated with the Lutheran clergy.

"What do you mean I can't get in there?" she wails. "I need to find my daughter!"

The essence of what she's demanding is entrance into Interview Room A, the room where Marla Kusic is being questioned about Petra's whereabouts. Right away, it's clear to Span that somebody has spilled the beans, somebody has told Maggie about Marla's role, probably one of the cops told James about it and he spilled it to Maggie. And now she's desperate to get in on the interrogation.

It's up to Bender to cool things down. "This is something I don't need right now," he shouts to the warring couple as he approaches. "Officer Rincon, I wonder if you'd do me a favor and run into the ops center and check on the latest radio traffic. Come back in ten minutes and give me a rundown."

Once James is gone, Bender zeroes in on Maggie, who's visibly trying to calm down and looking more than a little embarrassed. She's taking deep breaths and stretching her arms and shoulders. "Margaret, I obviously have never been a mother so I don't have a clue about what you're going through. But I hope you remember that we got a partnership, you and me. You agreed to help me out on this case and you've done outstanding. But now, this shit is getting a little too delicate and a little too personal. It's not what we need right now. As former police, I know you can see that."

She looks down at her shoes.

"Listen," he continues, "we have our best people on this. And Thurber, despite him being FBI, he's got a lot of talent on this type of thing. He knows kidnapping upwards and down. What I want you to do, what I *order* you to do, is get the hell out of here, take a break for the rest of the night, try get some sleep, or at least some rest."

"I can't leave this building until I know what's happened to Petra," Maggie says, softly.

"OK," Bender says, sighing. "Look, I got this key." He holds it up. "I'm gonna open the evidence room over there." He points to the far side of the bullpen. "You know where it is. There's a big sofa in there. I'm gonna put you in there for a couple hours so you can get some rest. We'll be close by. Anything breaks, we'll be in to tell you about it, OK?"

Normally evidence is kept in a central vault in the basement of police headquarters. Access is carefully controlled. In big cases like the church murders, select evidence is sometimes moved upstairs to a smaller vault in the homicide bureau, providing easier access to detectives working the case. Maggie has been in this vault a dozen times over the last two weeks.

Hearing the click that locks the door behind her is almost soothing. Maggie's brain is still racing, her muscles still tense. But at least in here there's silence. There's no James to torment her, no radio chatter, no Bender shouting orders, no detectives moving in and out of Interview A, no chance whatsoever for her to participate in the interrogation of this new *person of interest,* this Marla Kusic. Maggie's religious training has taught her about the freedom and release that can come from silence, solitude, contemplation, meditation, prayer. So, she almost accepts her predicament, turning the lights lower and stretching out on the big, well-worn leather sofa.

She's horizontal now, but her mind churns and tumbles with images and memories of her daughter. Petra's first birthday parties back at the old house in Redondo, Petra with chocolate cake smeared all over her face, Petra's first trips to the beach and the look on her face when she first dipped a toe into the cold Pacific, her thrill at going off to pre-school like the big kids, at kicking a soccer ball, at going to Disneyland with her cousins, at reading stories and snuggling up at bedtime, just the two of them, mom and the dear child she calls Cubby. Love is supposed to be life's ultimate gift. But love is the most terrible thing imaginable when the one you love has gone missing, is in danger, is being tortured perhaps, raped, maybe even killed. And there's nothing you can do about it.

Faith. She reaches for her faith. That's all she can do. It's all she has left. There's perspective in faith. After all, you're not the only one. Others have suffered, too. They suffer this very moment. Disease, pain, injury, poverty, war, destruction, fear, anguish, hunger, death. What's so special about *her* fears? *Her* anguish? The brother she knows as Jesus was supposed to have taken care of all that anxiety. Erased it. Blotted it out with his own blood and suffering. He kept saying to people, fear not. He said it over and over. That was his central message, perhaps. But is it really possible for flawed humans not to be afraid? She's a police officer. Or was. She had courage. Or once had.

Does courage help? Maybe. Maybe she'd feel better if she felt less helpless. If she were more active, more involved in finding Petra, more invested in getting to the bottom of this terrible string of events. To say Petra is missing is a strange way to put it. She's missing from Maggie and from her other loved ones. But she's not *missing*. She's not *invisible*. She's someplace. She won't be found by just wishing and hoping.

Maggie's eyes scan the opposite side of the room. Evidence boxes with labels are stacked on metal racks. She has been through most of them. One contains Matthias Hammar's bloody vestments, shoes, and other clothing. Several others hold items from his home and office; letters, diaries, calendars, photos, recordings, computer hard drives, cellphones, statements from friends, enemies, relatives, colleagues, anything that might supply the police with a motive for his mutilation and murder.

Other boxes labeled for Richard and Duane contain, as she recalls, high school yearbooks, military records, airline reservations and unused tickets, license plates from a stolen van, statements from airport employees and from the German police. There are separate boxes for various community figures with whom Matthias Hammar clashed openly, including one for the National Rifle Association, one for Grover Norquist and other anti-tax agitators and one for F.A.I.R. and other nativist groups. One box was labeled for Jonas Kron, and contained a recent police interview with the reclusive industrialist with whom Hammar had feuded. But in the dim light, Maggie caught sight of one box she'd never opened, never even noticed. It was labeled Henrik Piedela.

Chapter Forty-Five

Thursday, 10:30 p.m

The first thing Maggie notices about Henrik's box is its lack of weight; it's a feather compared with the others. At the top there's an itemized inventory of the stuff found in his church-basement apartment and in his gray 2004 Toyota pickup. Among the items on the list that stand out to Maggie: a collection of paperback Westerns, in English, by Zane Grey; a large assortment of DVDs, including six seasons of Andy Griffith and four of Seinfeld, plus two dozen old Western movies with three or four porn titles tossed in for good measure.

There's also a thumb drive inside an envelope labeled "Summary of Personal Records." When Maggie slips it into her laptop, up pops Henriks' job reviews dating back to the 1980s (They glow in praise of his janitorial skills.) along with other records and a folder of receipts showing something peculiar: For nearly thirty years, Henrik's salary has been paid not by the parish but by annual gifts from the Kron Family Foundation. Why in the world, she wonders, would Jonas Kron be paying Henrik's salary?

Another remarkable item is a plastic package containing the clothes and shoes Henrik wore on the day he died. Blood had oozed from the holes behind his left ear down onto the collar and sleeve of an otherwise spotless white shirt. The sight of it sent a chilly quiver through Maggie, overtaking the thick protective shell that cops – and clergy – develop to help them cope with the routine, and sometimes the horror, of death.

What got to her more than anything was the familiar aroma of Henrik's shirt, his special blend of male sweat and sweeping compound, and maybe a hint of floor wax. Oh yes, and cigarettes. Henrik was one of the few people she knew who still smoked, not inside the church, of course. That wasn't allowed. But outside, furtively, in the back courtyard, during breaks. Every time she ran across him back there taking a few puffs, he smiled awkwardly, looking more than a little guilty.

She loved Henrik, loved his easy-going vulnerability. He was a slender, aging, melancholy, intensely private man but with a happy veneer, always a smile for her, always a joke, some of them a bit off-color but who cared? They shared something that no one else on the staff shared. What was it? Maybe they, without words, acknowledged that they, unlike, say Matthias or Gwen Gray, weren't far removed from peasant stock, that they were just ordinary flawed people who lived life without much pretension — Henrik especially. She surprised herself by openly crying at his small funeral. Sobbing actually. That was rare for her. She feels the tears now welling again in her eyes, her throat constricting and burning. "Petra, where are you?" she whispers. "Where are you my Cubby, my beautiful little girl? My baby!"

Minutes pass before Maggie, red-eyed, resumes her dig toward the bottom of the box. Suddenly there are photos, a sheaf of them, showing Henrik as a younger man on horseback in front of what must be a dude ranch, the gate saying simply "The Lazy L, Prescott, Ariz." There are other shots of what appear to be Henrik shading his eyes in the glare of the sun on the Las Vegas strip, Henrik with sagebrush and buttes in the background, Henrik with the bartender and some of the patrons at Sunny's bar down the street from the church. Then there are Henrik's wallet with several hundred dollars in cash and a Minnesota driver's license but no credit cards. Here's a bankbook, showing a savings account with a hefty balance of $639,774.16. Wow! He didn't have to live as simply as he did, rent-free, in a small dark apartment, in a church basement. But she finds no passport. No Social Security card. No citizenship papers.

At the very bottom, there's a plain manila envelope with a simple notation: "To Matthias Hammar." The seal had been slit open — by the police no doubt. There's a small post-it note acknowledging as much. Whoever looked inside — an officer Naulty, according to the scribbled note — must have simply given up when he saw foreign writing on a yellow legal pad. There is no hint that anyone had tried to translate it.

Maggie scans the document. It is hand-written in blue ink. Its pages carry a headline: "*Jag erkänner*".

When she pulls out her phone and clicks into Google Translate, it's clear what Henrik has written to Matthias:

"I confess."

This confession, if that's what it is, goes on for four pages. Maggie scrutinizes the first page looking for words she might recognize. She sees *Gud* quite a lot, expecting that it means God. She sees *Jesus Kristus* also, supposing that it means the obvious. *Polis* also catches her eye, leading her to conclude that the police are involved in whatever Henrik is confessing. Most intriguing are the two yellowed newspaper clippings attached to the last page of the document. They are from *Aftonbladet,* which Maggie also Googles, discovering that it's a Stockholm tabloid. The stories are from March 1986. The headlines scream with words like *död* and *skott* and *kaos*. (Dead, shot and chaos, she guesses.) Photos show badly lit nighttime scenes of police officers roping off the crime scene on a Stockholm street and stock photos of the dead prime minister Olof Palme and his wife Lisbet, who apparently survived the attack of an *ensam skytt,* a lone gunman.

But what could this have to do with Henrik? Why was this part of his confession?

A quick glance at her cellphone tells Maggie that it's almost midnight. Late, but not too late on a Friday night. She clicks into St. Ansgar's member directory looking for Ken Petersson, the Nordic languages professor at the U. He's probably still out at some dreadful faculty dinner party, she guesses. But she finds him at home sounding a little yawny.

"Margaret?" he answers, obviously surprised.

"I hope I didn't wake you up."

"No, just reading. Maybe dozing."

"I have a big favor to ask. I want you to translate something. Just a few pages."

"Well, sure. Happy to ..."

"Trouble is I need it now. Can I drop by?"

There's a pause on the line. "Give me a half hour?"

"I'll be there in twenty minutes."

"Margaret?"

"Yeah."

"This has got to be about Matthias' murder, right?"

"Maybe. Look, Ken. This has to be completely confidential. I mean, it's like you never saw this piece of paper. Ever. Is that OK with you?"

"Well, I guess," he says, his curiosity surging.

Guilt is eating away at Maggie as she steps out of the elevator toward her car. She has removed evidence from police headquarters without authorization. She's got the pages stuffed in her bag. That's the kind of thing that could get her into big trouble, not to mention hurting Bender and the whole department. It could jeopardize everything they're working on. It could jeopardize Petra.

Then there's the part about the confidentiality of a confession, if that's what Henrik's document actually is. She knows that her employer, her church, like the Roman Catholic church, strictly prohibits the sharing of a confession with any third party. Confessors act as connections between the penitent and God, she was taught, and they have no right to break the seal that protects this sacred communication.

Maggie? Breaking the laws of both church and state on the same night? Just goes to show her mental state, she says to herself. She's trying hard to concentrate on something other than Petra. She's confused about Henrik's confession, if that's what it is. Did he ever confess it to Matthias in person? If so, why did he write it down? Or did he send a copy to Matthias? No way to tell. Nothing like this was found in Matthias' stuff, as far as she knows. What are her obligations now as Henrik's pastor? He's dead, after all. Must whatever he wrote still be a secret? What about the fact that the confession wasn't meant for her eyes? She discovered it by chance. Maggie's mind is scrambled as she drives through the darkened city.

T. Kenneth Petersson, PhD, lives in a tall narrow condo building in Prospect Park, near the U. When Maggie presses the buzzer next to his name, the front door clicks open leading her to an elevator that stops on the eleventh floor. Stepping off, she sees Ken standing halfway down a narrow hallway, in front of 1123. He's a tall man in his sixties, bald, bearded, wearing khaki pants and an untucked polo shirt. Despite the warm summer night, it's absolutely frosty in this building, someone having jacked up the air conditioning to ridiculous levels. Turns out that Kate, Ken's wife, is out of town and that Ken has brewed some hot coffee and even flipped on the gas fireplace. They sit at the dining room table, Ken pecking away at his laptop as he translates Henrik's document. This goes on, mostly in silence, for about twenty minutes. When he's finished, Ken throws Maggie a worried look, then clicks "print." The familiar hum of a machine spitting out paper comes from an adjoining room. With two copies in hand, he refills his coffee cup, and Maggie's too, and they both retreat to seats by the fire, Maggie starting to read before her butt hits the padded chair.

8 October 2015

I Confess

I did a very bad thing many years ago. This thing did not trouble me at the time because, for doing it, I was paid many thousands of dollars — and it was promised to me that my family in Estonia will not be harmed.

It's about here that Maggie realizes, despite her emotional bond with Henrik, how little she knows about his background, except the few things he told her: that as a young boy of ten or twelve he came alone to Stockholm from Estonia — from outside of Talinn, she thought — joining an uncle or a cousin who worked on the docks. This would have been in the late 1960s. He attended school and learned the language, although never lost his Baltic accent or identity. It wasn't clear to Maggie whether the boy had arrived legally in Sweden, or whether he ever went back to Estonia, it having been absorbed more thoroughly into the Soviet Union by that time. In any case, he must have left a family behind that he cared about deeply. And, by the 1980s, the family must have been in some kind of danger if Henrik felt they would be protected only if he agreed to do something bad.

Oh, God in heaven, if you are out there I want you to know that I experience again that terrible moment, again and again, day and night. And as time goes by it is harder and harder for me to make excuses for myself. I did this ...

After several minutes of silence, Petersson interrupts Maggie's reading. "Most of this is a straightforward translation from Swedish, but the writer has some phrases in here in another language that uses some idioms I don't quite understand."

"Estonian?" she asks.

"Maybe."

Maggie continues her reading, slowly, methodically, page by page, getting finally to the last sentences.

O God, I don't know if I believe in you, or in Jesus Christ, but I'm hoping so hard you can remove this from my shoulders. I am sorry and ashamed that this happened. I should say that I am sorry and ashamed that it was me, and me alone, who made this happen, who did this terrible thing, who shot a man, who killed a man, an important man, who shot a woman and injured her, who enjoyed the money I was paid. But I cannot any longer enjoy it. If there is such a thing as forgiveness, I beg you for it.

After she finishes, Maggie sits for a long time by the fire, closing her eyes, saying nothing. Finally, she decides that, until she can sort everything out, she must keep Henrik's confession secret. It's her sacred duty. She has taken a vow before God. She won't tell Bender. She won't even tell Span. Maybe there will come a time when the police or the public will benefit from knowing what she knows. Maybe. But not now. Not yet.

Chapter Forty-Six

Friday, June 24, 9:30 a.m

Feliks awakens with the sensation that he has overslept. And that he has been dreaming, reliving, actually, a childhood memory. He is a boy of ten or eleven back in Smolensk. There is snow on the ground outside his apartment building and the morning is cold. His mother has sent him into the nearby grove of trees to check the traps. Only one has captured a rabbit. This one is still alive and struggling to free itself. Ordinarily Feliks would obey his mother's instructions to bash its head with the garden shovel he is carrying. But the rabbit looks Feliks in the eye with such a fluttering fear that Feliks cannot do it, at least not right away. He sees the eyes of the rabbit so vividly now and feels the fear that the rabbit felt. It's an odd sensation for Feliks. He has not been afraid, truly afraid, in a long time. And he has not felt helplessly trapped until now.

Kron's walled compound offers safety, yes, but for how long? Today is an important day. Today he will reunite with Mr.

Kron and he will be obliged to tell him a story — the whole story — and he will make Mr. Kron an offer that cannot be rejected.

Yet, even after these things are accomplished, the fear will not recede. Feliks understands that he has crossed a line and that there is no going back as far as the Gaswerks is concerned. He knows they have read the headlines by now: One of the kidnappers shot dead, the other one and the kidnapped girl on the run. He sees shadowy figures now recovering the electronic gear he taped to the truck. He sees them ransacking his small apartment. He sees them all around.

Still, looking back on his life, Feliks cannot say that he has regrets. Ultimately he did kill the rabbit, and his family enjoyed the stew. And, in his life's work, he executed many targets flawlessly with precision, skill and self-satisfaction. Until Wednesday. On Wednesday he had aimed the pistol at Duane's head, and then failed to follow through.

Why? It is a puzzle. Perhaps he no longer believes. After so many years in Chicago, Feliks has to admit that he no longer hates the West, not in the way he was trained to hate the West. Its decadent culture seems to reward the freelancer, the entrepreneur. Running off the usual track is celebrated here. So why cannot Feliks run off the track? Has not the Gaswerks been an unwitting partner? His young colleagues have been taught that their craft is more art than science. They are encouraged to concoct false stories and to spread them in the media. This more subtle warfare is aimed at dividing an enemy, corrupting it from within, employing creativity rather than muscle to expand the motherland's influence. But those things are not in Feliks' repertoire. He pulls triggers.

And so, when the rare occasion arose, when the church operation presented itself, he may have overstepped, he may have allowed his own clumsy creativity to careen out of control. Richard and poor Duane may not have been his best choices.

But the Gaswerks is not without blame. Its new emphasis on creativity does not always bring the best solution. Feliks is, in some sense, a victim.

Over the years, he often thought of the question: Could he be turned? He never imagined that politics could turn him. Politics were not that important to him. He was like the British people he had read about in a book about the Great Patriotic War. They climbed out of the bombing rubble to offer shot-down German pilots a cup of tea. It infuriated Mr. Churchill that the English did not hate the Germans enough. Perhaps he did not hate the Americans enough.

Likewise, he could never imagine that women could turn him. He was no James Bond, after all. Women feared him far more than they loved him.

Money, on the other hand, might do the trick. In his current predicament, travel money was a top priority. Mr. Kron appeared to be the likeliest source. The ninety-five grand Feliks had hoped to *divert* from Richard and Duane would have made a nice down payment on his future life, a life spent, perhaps, on a remote island. But Kron has more money than that, much more. Hundreds of millions, at least. Two million is the sum that Feliks regards as a reasonable share for himself.

With upcoming travel in mind, Feliks feels a sudden need to take a quick inventory. On his bed he empties the contents of his sleek, black backpack. There's one shaving kit, one extra pair of socks and set of underwear, one rain jacket with hat, one Mayak SPS automatic pistol with silencer and three clips of nine-millimeter ammunition, seven passports from six countries, each providing a different identity. There's also seven packets of matching driving licenses, identity cards and bank cards. There's one portable listening kit with earbuds and miniature cameras, one notebook with several pens, one renegade cell-phone loaded with American show tunes and Russian symphonic pieces, one key chain with two keys, and one drug kit that includes chloral hydrate in both capsule and hypodermic versions.

Feliks' thoughts are quite suddenly interrupted by the sound of a motor splitting the morning silence. A boat? Peering again out of his window and into the dawn, he sees a twin-engine floatplane touching down on the river. The motors get louder as the plane splashes its way toward the decrepit docks down below the harbormaster shack. As the propellers go still, a man steps out of the cockpit to tie up the plane. This is perhaps the pilot that Feliks will need for his escape and his trip to paradise. This pilot closely resembles Robert, although at this distance it's difficult to tell. Minutes later, Feliks sees another man, his old friend Jonas Kron, step out onto the dock, handing the pilot a small overnight bag, then walking briskly toward the castle. Mr. Kron is back in town.

Part Three

The Castle

PROLOGUE

Stockholm, Sweden

The first bulletins hit the wires minutes after the official announcement at 00.06 CET on March 1.

00.46 01 MAR 86
URGENT

SWEDEN PRIME MINISTER ASSASSINATED

LONE GUNMAN SOUGHT AFTER SHOOTING ON STOCKHOLM STREET

STOCKHOLM (INS) – Swedish Prime Minister Olof Palme was shot and killed on a city street moments after he and his wife attended a cinema on Friday night.

Palme, 59, was felled by shots from a handgun on a street corner in central Stockholm. Witnesses said he was hit in the torso. After an emergency vehicle transported him to Sabbatsberg Hospital, he was pronounced dead at 00.06 local time, Saturday.

Witnesses said the prime minister, walking with his wife

and without bodyguards, fell onto a snow-covered sidewalk along Sveavägen, a main commercial artery. A taxi driver told police he had seen the shooting but was unable to provide a clear description of the assassin. Palme's wife, Lisbeth, 56, was apparently grazed by a bullet but not seriously injured.

Police cordoned off several blocks around the blood-pooled scene and established checkpoints on main roads, at airports, at rail and ferry stations and at border crossings. King Carl XVI Gustaf cut short a ski holiday in the north to return to the capital. Acting Prime Minister Ingvar Carlsson, Palme's deputy, called the shooting "a blow not just to the Palme family but to Sweden as an open society."

For two decades, Palme had been prominent in the Social Democratic Party, credited with expanding social welfare and education programs. First chosen as prime minister in 1969, Palme emerged as a global player in the Third World's battles against colonial powers. He was a sharp critic of U.S. involvement in Vietnam and Apartheid in South Africa.

Born 30 January 1927, into a family of Baltic nobility, Palme was proud of his association with the working class, often emphasizing his devotion to "freedom, equality and fraternity among people." He was often seen on the streets without a security detail. Ulf Adelsohn, leader of the opposition Moderate Party, saw the slaying as an end of innocence, adding, "Sweden will never be the same."

Said Thorbjorn Falldin, Palme's predecessor, "This must be the work of a lunatic."

ENDIT 00.

Chapter Forty-Seven

Thirty years later
The Quetico, Ontario, Canada
Friday, June 24, 2016, 11:30 a.m.

When you imagine a lodge set beside a glassy lake in the pristine southwest corner of Ontario, you don't picture Ducksie's Docks. True, the landscape is a glorious carpet of evergreen and birch generously dotted by crystalline waters with rocky shorelines. But Ducksie's is the human scab on nature's perfection. It slouches along the edge of a swiftly moving creek that merges into the Rainy River which, for two hundred fifty kilometers, constitutes the Canada-U.S. border, not as a linear demarcation but a meandering series of remote lakes with an invisible boundary somewhere out there in the middle.

In the late 1960s someone told Brian Duck, when he inherited the ramshackle resort from his suddenly dead father, to paint the whole place yellow to make it stand out against its forested surroundings. Good for business. So he did. Fifty years later, the same paint is chipping and fading. And Ducksie's dreamy lodge is a random pile of shacks and house trailers, routinely avoided by even the most rustic tourists.

So, anticipating yet another slow weekend ahead, the sound of a vehicle crunching on his gravel parking lot in late morning startles Ducksie to the point that he quickly hides the bottle of Jim Beam he's been working on since sunrise and steps to the screen door to investigate. It's a late-model Jeep Cherokee with two very large men slamming the doors and heading his way. Looks to Ducksie like a couple of goddamn make-believe fur trappers all decked out like fucking peacocks in new gear purchased no doubt from some high-design outfitter in Toronto or Winnipeg.

Turns out these two are more foreign than Ducksie expects, barely speaking English. Still, despite their poor language skills and his own wooziness, it's plain what they want. When the slightly less massive one, the one with the beard, shows a stack of crisp American bills, maybe five centimeters thick, Ducksie's eyes refocus and his duty becomes clear. These gentlemen want to go on a quiet, one-way canoe trip to Minnesota. Ducksie figures they've come to the right place.

Slipping undetected into the U.S. isn't all that hard from the Quetico, Ducksie's place lying just outside the western boundary of the Quetico Provincial Park which, when combined with the Boundary Waters Canoe Area on the U.S. side, forms a vast wilderness paradise where no motorized travel is allowed. Backpackers and canoeists spend days, sometimes weeks in the woods and on the water without seeing another human.

Ducksie is normally a curious sort. Not today. He's taking at face value the explanation that these guys — they don't offer their names — are tourists from Finland looking for, as the bearded one explains, "some nature adventures." The man shows a map of where they want to go. Ducksie asks when? The man says, how about now?

Ducksie is pretty soon down at the dock tinkering with the big canoe, the twenty-footer, the one rigged with three seats, three life jackets, various lights, fishing gear, bug spray, dried food packets, pup tents, bedrolls, water and a cooler with beer and an extra bottle of Jim. He hasn't bothered to spruce himself up, still wearing the three-day beard, and the haggard look of a skinny, rapidly aging man whose luck has run out. But his eyes dance at the thought of the cash he has just stashed away in the floorboards beneath his cot up at the cabin.

Two hours later they're on the water. Ducksie has placed the biggest guy in front, instructing him briefly in the art of paddling. The middle guy takes charge of the cooler and the two identical backpacks – black, unmarked, streamlined jobs that Ducksie has never seen before. He is, of course, in the back, acting as rudder and tour guide. They're moving along quite nicely, thanks to the up-front paddler who, while an obvious novice, has an impressive stroke due largely to brute strength. Must be a body builder, Ducksie assumes, never before experiencing the feel of a canoe hurtling with such power over the tops of the waves.

They're westbound on the Namakan River now, just beyond Lady Rapids. At this rate the trip will take less than five hours. Ducksie's plan has him dropping off his guests in Minnesota sometime before dusk, with him continuing alone to the Burnt Island campground, arriving around sunset. For now, he feels obligated to point out to his companions some of the sights along the way. A pair of loons draws his attention.

"Do you have loons in Finland?" he wonders.

No response. Undeterred, Ducksie holds forth on the fish species available in these waters, describing in detail the much-admired walleye – both how to catch them and how to cook them. He has his own recipe for deep fried fillets in beer batter. His passengers seem uninterested.

An hour goes by. No other signs of human habitation appear. The sun is getting lower. A hawk circles overhead. Aside from Ducksie's narrative, the only sound comes from paddles hitting water. Ducksie moves on to geology and history, telling about how the glacial ice retreated twelve thousand years ago leaving these astonishing rocks and lakes, six hundred of them in the Quetico alone, and how the Ojibwe and French trappers once roamed these waters and woods, and how the Canadian and U.S. governments came in with all these bullshit rules and regulations, but with Mickey Mouse enforcement that almost never happens.

"Might see a chopper up high once, twice a week," he says. "U.S. fucking Border Patrol. Might see a Canuck inspector's boat checking for permits and papers once a month, but that's about the extent of it."

Again no response from his tourists, who, despite the spectacular beauty all around them, aren't bothering to snap pictures. In fact, he's seen no evidence of a camera or a cellphone.

After two hours, Ducksie steers the canoe toward a sandy spot between two giant rocks on a small island, jumping out knee deep in water and dragging the canoe partially onto the shore. Time to take a piss break and change paddlers, he says. The two big guys step out onto the tiny beach and everybody stretches. Ducksie can't help but notice again how large and athletic these men are, a little intimidating.

The bigger one is blond and silent with transparent gray eyes. The other one, the one with the beard, is a bit darker and seems to take the lead in communicating with Ducksie. Ducksie is just about to direct him to the front of the canoe to take over as lead paddler — the bigger one is still back in the woods doing whatever he needs to do – when just behind them there's rustling in the bushes next to the giant boulder. Ducksie turns, expecting to see the big guy, and immediately recognizes Sandy. Sandy is a tail-wagging yellow lab with a distinctive red collar and a pleasing disposition. Wherever Sandy goes in the Quetico, Julie O'Connor won't be far behind. Sure enough, there is Ontario Conservation Officer Julie O'Connor stepping sideways through a thicket and onto the narrow beach, a smile on her face.

"How's it goin,' Ducksie?"

Julie is fortyish. Her brown ponytail sticks out the back of her green baseball cap with the official provincial conservation patch on the front. She's wearing her tan, short-sleeved uniform shirt today with green vest, sidearm and radio strapped to her waist, olive-green khakis and black boots down below. Sunglasses hide her eyes.

"Oh, Julie!" says Ducksie. "Hi! Things are goin' pretty good. Didn't know you were here."

"Yeah, well, just the other side of these rocks. You probably couldn't see my boat. Me and Sandy needed a break. Who we got here?" she says, gesturing toward Ducksie's newest friend and benefactor.

"Oh, he's one of my guests," Ducksie says, shooting the guy a look that seemed to say, "Don't worry; I got this."

"From Finland, actually," Ducksie says. "Doesn't speak English too good. We're not fishin' or nothin' today. Just pokin' around, learnin' about canoeing."

Officer O'Connor never takes her eyes off the guy, husky, tall, bearded, decked out in new outfitter garb.

"Welcome, sir. Sorry, but gotta check your passport and permits."

The man turns, leaning into the canoe to fetch his sleek backpack, fishing around for papers, coming up with a red-covered passport labeled "Europeiska unionen Suomi Finland Passi."

Julie steps to the man's side to peer around the bottom of his enormous shoulder, reaching out to page through the document, concentrating on it as Ducksie notices the bigger guy with the empty gray eyes emerging silently from the woods, walking calmly toward Julie's back. Seems to Ducksie like he's going to give Julie a friendly hug, wrapping his massive left arm around the back of her neck, then twisting slightly to the right, Ducksie hearing a snap, Julie going limp. Before she hits the ground, the man bends gracefully to scoop her up in both arms and carry her into the trees. Sandy, her tail no longer wagging, follows along, the three of them disappearing from Ducksie's view. He hears a bark, a whimper and then nothing.

Ducksie's mouth is gaping now, his heart pounding, his breathing heavy, his brain addled. Just seconds ago, he was chatting with his long-time friend. Now something very bad has happened. Ducksie isn't exactly terrified. That might come later. But he's dumbfounded.

"What?" he hears himself saying. "What?"

The bearded man stares calmly into Ducksie's eyes for a terrible moment, then his friend emerges from the woods carrying Julie's radio and pointing Julie's pistol right at Ducksie. The bearded man utters a few words that Ducksie doesn't understand. The bigger man uncocks the gun and sticks it in his pocket.

"We go now?" says the bearded man, stuffing the passport back in his pack, gesturing Ducksie to the back of the canoe. They're off once again, heading south, Ducksie's travelogue going silent, his arms shaking. They slip past the backside of Burnt Island and into Sand Point Lake. It occurs to Ducksie that he might not have much time left to live, that he probably won't get to enjoy the money he's so busy earning, figuring that it adds up to maybe five grand U.S. The trip to Vancouver he was dreaming about may never happen. He wanted to see his daughter and the new baby somebody said she had several months ago. But now it's, shall we say, up in the air.

"Where is United States?" It's the first time Ducksie has heard the bigger one speak. Ducksie points to the distant shore on the right, steering the canoe in that direction, to the southwest.

It's not altogether clear just when they pass into U.S. waters. But a half hour later, they enter King William Narrows and then float gracefully into their destination, Crane Lake, Minnesota, a remote body of water bordered by impressive rocks and a thick layer of pines. Checking the map, the bigger man sees the lake's East Bay and the point that marks their small, sandy landing spot. As the canoe glides into shore, he breaks into the cooler, pulling out the extra bottle of Jim Beam and three paper cups. Standing now on the beach with his friend and Ducksie, he pours three stiff drinks, expertly slipping a tiny white tablet into Ducksie's cup without anyone noticing.

Ducksie's hand trembles as he accepts the drink. He needs it, and downs it enthusiastically. Without a smile, the three men toast their arrival on U.S. soil. Ducksie awaits his fate without a word. The end is near, he says to himself. The men are methodical, grabbing their backpacks and stiffly shaking Ducksie's hand before turning and heading into the woods. A blue SUV awaits them on a dirt road, a quarter mile up the slope. It will take them four hours to reach Minneapolis. Locating the man, codename Walrus, and his one remaining stooge shouldn't be a problem.

Ducksie is left standing on the tiny beach expecting a bullet from the trees at any second. He thinks about the wife who left him twenty years ago for a better prospect, and a daughter he really never got to know, and a granddaughter he'll never see.

But there's no sound, no bullet. When it doesn't happen, he turns to gaze out over Crane Lake. Ducksie trembles. A fine summer day has turned to evening. A mist gathers at the edge of the far shore. A jetliner, very high in the sky, leaves a vapor trail as it moves off to the northeast. The lake is calm, like glass. Ducksie figures to make the Burnt Island campground by sunset. But, of course, he won't make it. Within a half hour, Brian Edward Duck, age sixty-eight, will suffer a fatal heart attack. His body, slumped in the bottom of the big canoe, will be discovered two days later drifting on Rainy River.

Chapter Forty-Eight

Minneapolis
Friday, 11:30 a.m.

Feliks has barely finished his inventory when there's a knock at the carriage house door. It's Robert in a white tunic with a tray, the midday sunshine flashing over his shoulder. This is the same ubiquitous Robert who is also the pilot, and who moments ago had ushered Kron from the float plane up the hill and into the castle. On the tray there's a light breakfast for three – bagels, cream cheese, jam, coffee and juice in paper cups.

Robert politely issues a formal invitation for later. Mr. Kron is back in the city, he announces. And he'd be pleased to see Feliks for lunch at 1.

"I'll come fetch you," Robert says.

Ninety minutes later, there he is, leading Feliks toward the castle. The day is fresh and sunny. The garden behind the castle is one of the most beautiful Feliks has ever seen. He neither knows nor cares much about flowers, but they are colorful and everywhere – in beds, on trellises, in pots, large and small.

Robert leads him over curved walkways of blue flagstone (past a shimmering lap pool) to a table set with white linen, white plates and crystal champagne glasses. The contrast between the rotting south end of the island and this patch of green splendor is nothing short of stunning. No more than fifty meters separate the two worlds.

"Mr. Kron will be down shortly," Robert says, pouring Feliks a steaming cup of coffee. Moments later, Feliks spots his old friend coming his way. Perhaps his hair is grayer, but otherwise Jonas Kron hasn't changed all that much in twenty years: tallish and slender with an aristocratic face and a confident gait, wearing a white polo shirt, dark slacks and sunglasses. Feliks stands, stepping to the side of the table and offering his big, meaty hand, smiling.

"Jesper, my old friend," Kron says in his hardiest voice. "How long has it been?"

The two sit, shaded by an arbor. Robert, still in his white tunic, pours more coffee and sets down a basket of croissants and an ice bucket with a bottle of Prosecco. Kron knows his old friend only by a previous alias, Jesper Szabo, and by a previous cover occupation — mechanical engineering consultant working in the glass industry in Dresden. They jump quickly to reminiscing about their first meeting more than thirty years ago outside Leipzig where both were taking part in a re-enactment of the Battle of Breitenfeld, a victory for Swedish Protestants midway through the gruesome Thirty Years War. Feliks (né Jesper) had greatly admired the authenticity of Jonas Kron's helmet and sword. For his part, Kron recalled his fascination with meeting an actual Russian national who spoke both German and English and who displayed a deep knowledge of the Swedish empire of the seventeenth and eighteenth centuries.

Kron had always been under the impression that this had

been a chance meeting of like-minded history freaks. But, of course, it hadn't been.

Lunch arrives: omelets, sausages and fruit salad. Conversation turns toward the present. Kron explains that he was at his northern home on Lake Vermillion when he got Feliks' desperate call. What he doesn't explain is that he was up there frolicking with his latest boy, Martin, a local 19-year-old specimen, whom he thinks of as his young lumberjack. But then Martin will be around next weekend; Jesper turns up once every twenty years.

The two had never stopped corresponding, first by letter, then by email and phone. The Swedish empire was always the topic, with Jesper continually offering news about artifacts that Kron might like to acquire or re-enactments he might like to attend. It might be said that Kron, who generally felt obliged to no one, came to feel a keen obligation to Jesper for keeping him in the loop, for providing him with inside information about their arcane obsession. So, Kron hadn't hesitated in responding to Wednesday's call from Jesper saying he was in town and would love to show Kron his latest acquisition – a jeweled sword authenticated as belonging to Gustavus Adolphus himself, the king's initials having been engraved on the handle. So, early this very morning, after a day's delay, Kron had packed a small bag, hopped into his twin-engine floatplane, and had Robert ferry him back to his castle.

"I hope my guest quarters are satisfactory for you and your mysterious companions, Jesper," Kron tells him, poking at his omelet. "And your artifact? You can't imagine my curiosity."

As the Americans like to say, the ball is now in Feliks' court. He pauses before answering, taking a long tug at his coffee, summoning the more ruthless side of his persona, and looking straight into Kron's pale eyes.

"My companions. Well, one of them is small girl. Unfortunately, she is kidnapped."

"What?" Kron's smile weakens. He looks suddenly puzzled, a bit amused, as if this were a game.

Feliks continues calmly. "The other companion is criminal, name of Duane. I am afraid police are looking, as you say, high and low for both of them."

There is a long, awkward silence, Kron calculating the likelihood that his old friend may have a mental problem. "Well, that can't be the case," Kron says.

"I am afraid, my friend, there was third companion as well, but he is shot dead. Not here. At another location."

This sudden turn in the conversation has left Kron grasping for any handle on reality. He's suddenly perched on the edge of a cliff with no place to go. Whatever is happening is happening on his own property, in his own kingdom, in a place that he alone controls and governs.

"Jesper! Why are you saying these things? Tell me this isn't true! You're harboring fugitives on *my* property? How could you do this to me? This is a total breach of our trust, a total breach of our friendship!"

"I am afraid, my dear Jonas, that we are not friends after all. May I smoke?" Feliks lights a cigarette and exhales a blue stream.

Kron feels a tightening in his throat. His heart is thudding against the wall of his chest.

"First," Feliks says, "you should know that my name is not Jesper Szabo. I am not engineer. I do not work in glass industry. I am not enthusiastic for history, or for Swedish empire, or for Thirty Years War. These do not concern me."

Kron feels himself sliding toward shock. Fear replaces bemusement on his face. "Who the hell are you?" he blurts, adjusting his shoulders, trying to re-gather himself, trying in vain to portray the confident business executive, trying to retake control of a situation that's obviously slipping away.

"Let us say that I am like contractor," Feliks tells him. "For thirty years you have been my subcontractor. This has been true for large portion of my career, since I was young man, since you were young man. I selected you."

"*Selected* me? Selected me for what?"

"I tell you story," Feliks says, leaning back in his chair, his eyes staying squarely on Kron's.

"Once upon a time, there lived in Dresden, in what you called East Germany, a Russian young man, let us call him Jesper. In same office was young colleague name of Vladimir, also Russian. This boy Vladi, as the Germans called him, was very friendly, very smart, very ambitious. Everybody wants to be like Vladi. He comes to me one day, it is 2 March 1986, and he says to me that boss wants to see us. So, we go.

"Boss congratulates Vladi on success of *Severnyy Olen'*, which is, in English, Operation Reindeer. But there is problem for making Reindeer complete. Vladi tells boss actually no problem. Jesper can solve. In fact, I had already solved. Solution involved you."

Kron's head swims with confusion. He feels himself sinking. Feliks continues.

"Operation Reindeer began a year before, in 1985, operating out of office in Dresden. There was in Sweden a troublesome man that was roadblock for our glass company. This man must disappear. One task for me was to arrange transport out of Sweden for another man, young man who must hide in safe place. To do this I looked at list of foreigners coming to eastern Germany in spring time 1985. On list were people coming for re-enactment of big battle in Thirty Years War. This occasion was to be in Leipzig. One name on list stands out. He was young industrialist from United States name of Jonas Kron, whose uncle runs fleet of cargo ships based in Sweden. Perfect says Jesper. This Jonas Kron is big enthusiast for Swedish empire and for Thirty Years War and for Battle of Breitenfeld from 1631, which is to be re-enacted. So, when Jonas Kron comes to Leipzig, Jesper becomes good friend. Tells Jonas Kron he, too, has great interest in Swedish empire and in Thirty Years War. Uses friendship to arrange with Jonas Kron to remove particular young man from Sweden on ships owned by uncle. Jesper pays Kron generous fee to transport young man and get him job in Canada or U.S. Tells him this young man is to be known as Henrik Piedela.

It's about here in Feliks' story that Kron begins to understand who Feliks really is. He isn't exactly a con man, not in the way Kron had first suspected. He isn't a criminal in the usual sense, although maybe he's Russian mafia. Maybe he's a spook, a foreign agent, a KGB man, or whatever the Russians call their secret people these days. Feliks never really acknowledges as much, but Kron is not a stupid man. Feliks' choice of words gives him away. Operation Reindeer? His admission of using a cover identity? His desire to sneak someone out of one country into another? And now his clandestine game of hide-and-seek involving a kidnapped girl and two criminals, one of them dead? Kron is half intrigued and wholly terrified.

"Jesper?" he interrupts. "Are you a spy?"

Chapter Forty-Nine

Friday, 1:45 p.m

At the most basic level, the struggle for power comes down to physical size and strength. Fans of American football know this. Dexterity, strategy, speed, trickery – they're all important. But brutality is the main element. Imposing superior bulk and power at the point of attack wins games. This is the case at the Kron castle as well.

From his island compound, Jonas Kron controls a vast global enterprise. The mere inflection of his voice causes ripples around the world. Maybe the company hasn't the profile it once had. Maybe its headquarters buildings aren't quite up to date. Maybe its methods aren't the most modern. But Kron Industries is still one of the world's largest general contractors with projects going up on three continents.

Yet over the last forty-five minutes, Jonas Kron's status has gone puny. At a slender six-one, one-sixty, the sixty-two-year-old Kron doesn't measure up to Feliks Dobervich's rugged, more impressive physical presence, and that's what it comes down to. That and the verbal rocks that Feliks has been hurling.

Humiliation is a new thing for Kron. Rising from the table and standing next to Feliks in the garden, Kron is clearly intimidated. He's looking up at Feliks, his mind tumbling with questions about the true identity of Jesper, or whoever the hell he is, and questions about the murders of Henrik Piedela and Matthias Hammar, and about his own role in delivering Henrik to his Hennepin Island hiding place, and about the roles of Duane and somebody named Richard, and about the little girl whom he now understands is the daughter of Margaret Lindberg, the kidnapped girl he read about in the paper the last two mornings. It's a lot for Kron to absorb. Already, Feliks has forced him to lock Robert in an upstairs room with this man Duane and the small girl. There's no one else in the castle.

"I will tell you now what I need from you, my friend," Feliks is saying, back downstairs in the garden, staring down at Kron. "Number one is money. I will need from you two million dollars. This is not in cash but in numbered account. I will tell you how to establish. This can be done today because of the people you know. Number two, I need airplane and pilot. Robert is pilot. He will take me where I say to go. It is tomorrow that Robert and I depart."

Feliks reaches into his pocket and withdraws his nine-millimeter pistol, not to point it at Kron, just to show it to him. Then, in a more ominous tone, he continues: "There is number three also. Number three is not what I want. It happens only if number one and number two fail to happen. If, for some stupid reason, there is no money and no airplane, then I tell interesting story to media. Story involves you, my friend."

"You're threatening me?"

"Such an unfortunate term," says Feliks. He motions for Kron to again sit at the table. Kron feels as if he's sinking into a bottomless hole. Feliks, still standing, continues his tale.

"Let us begin in 1985 when there is Operation Reindeer. It

is executed by young KGB officer in Dresden name of Vladimir. What is this Reindeer? Biggest part is, shall we say, liquidation of prime minister of Sweden, name of Olof Palme. You remember this man."

Kron stares at his tormentor.

"Why do this terrible crime?" Feliks asks rhetorically. "Palme, as Americans say, is bad apple, double-crosser, betrayer. He betrays Moscow in many ways. One thing he does is interfere in Soviet plan to build what you call power base in south of Africa. Also he is making trouble for Soviet Union in Europe by creating strong socialist solution outside Soviet sphere. Palme is cowboy. Too big for britches. Even when Moscow demands Palme to stop, he does not stop. So Reindeer is initiated.

"Plan is for Vladi to recruit young man to shoot Palme. Then, as diversion, plan is to get police to arrest likely local suspect as real assassin is sneaked out of Sweden. To do this, Vladi asks Jesper to help. I find possible assassin on docks. Show him how to shoot. Pay him money. I also find gullible American industrialist with uncle who has Swedish shipping line. This American, name of Jonas Kron. Kron helps to sneak young assassin out of Sweden."

Kron looks for a hole to climb into.

"Name of young shooter we decide to call Henrik Piedela. Jonas Kron even finds job for assassin in American church, finds hiding place for him in church basement, even pays for apartment of assassin."

Kron sinks deeper into his crater as Feliks continues. "Years pass and everyone forgets Reindeer. One day, however, it is necessary to erase all evidence of Reindeer and some other KGB — what to call them? — *activities.* This is because Vladi says to erase. Vladi is by now famous. He has become president of Russia, then prime minister, then president again. But there is now what you call social media, which has potential for wild, inaccurate stories about KGB past. These fairy tales have potential to embarrass Vladi. So, suddenly, as part of erasing Reindeer, there is sensational murders in Minneapolis. Everyone thinks priest is primary target. Not true. Primary target all along is janitor Piedela. This activity becomes urgent when Russia intelligence learns that priest and perhaps janitor have contacted FBI. FBI cannot learn about Reindeer.

"So, this is story of how American industrialist Jonas Kron becomes stooge of Russian espionage. Sensational story. Not good for Kron. Not good for Kron business."

The blood seems to have run out of Kron's face. "Jesper, my God, you're insane. You know I had nothing to do with the Palme thing. I didn't know what Henrik Piedela had done – if he did anything, that is. Who in their right mind would believe a story like this?"

"Oh, I have papers to prove," Feliks says. "Papers show name of Jonas Kron on Soviet documents. American journalists love these documents. They will wet their pants."

"This is blackmail, Jesper! I will not be blackmailed! How dare you?"

"This blackmail is such a harsh word. I do not wish to hurt you, my friend, or spoil your business. I do not wish to shoot you. Think of this as business opportunity too good to pass up."

Chapter Fifty

Friday, 4:01 p.m

Feliks wants to stay sharply on the task at hand, but his mind wanders. Again it is off on a detour, this time to Moscow, where they are talking about him, saying unkind things about him. Feliks is sure of it. They're saying he has gone rogue, that he has betrayed his country, that he is a chaotic disaster. None of this is true, of course. Feliks may have drifted off the main road. But he is no traitor. And he is certainly not disorganized. Far from it. He is totally in charge here at the Kron Castle where things are perfectly sorted out, über-organized.

Always Feliks has been organized. Even as a child, his notebooks and pencils were lined up in perfect order. At age ten, when his mother proudly enrolled him in the Young Pioneers, he set an example for the older children. "Notice how this boy has organized his knapsack," the leader had said. "Try to emulate this boy in the way he has so neatly packaged his camping gear," another had admonished. Feliks had taken the Pioneer motto to heart: *Vsegda gotov!* Always prepared!

To this day he remains prepared. In his right hand he holds a large wire-cutter secured from the tool room in the castle basement. Tucked in his belt is a leather case containing keys for every door in the castle. Thus equipped, he is touring every room, starting at the top and moving down.

Now he has worked his way to the main level, to the kitchen, where he snips a land line and flings the telephone across the room where it collides with a stack of pots and pans setting off a clatter. In one drawer he finds a cellphone and attacks it decisively with a meat cleaver. He reaches over a countertop to lock two windows, preventing what could be an easy escape. In one corner there is a laptop computer that Duane now disconnects and smashes against the side of a granite countertop. Duane has been deputized to help with Feliks' meticulous task. Soon the castle will be in complete lockdown, cut off entirely from the outside world – except for Kron's cellphone, of course, which Feliks has tucked safely in his pocket.

Why trust Duane to help him? Duane is not, as the Americans say, the brightest light on the porch. But Duane is deferential toward Feliks. Duane respects Feliks. Feliks likes it when Duane refers to him as "the Big Man." Loyalty should be rewarded. It is part of Feliks' management style.

The others? Feliks has now locked each of them in a separate room. Kron has been simultaneously fearful and defiant all afternoon. The contempt in his gray eyes is obvious. But when the time comes — and that time will come soon — Kron will make the calls that Feliks tells him to make, even if a gun must be put to his head.

The girl? Feliks has locked her in his own room. If complications arise, she will be an important safeguard to Feliks' clean getaway. She is his shield, his ticket to a peaceful, secure retirement in a remote tropical paradise of his choosing.

Robert? As the airplane pilot, he is an essential cog in the getaway operation. None of these three, not Kron, not the girl, not Robert, is expendable, at least not in the near term.

And what about Duane? Well, loyalty deserves a reward, doesn't it? Fat Duane is special. With the kitchen wrapped up, the big man now ushers Duane up the stairs and toward his room, apologizing for locking him in. "I do not like this, my friend," Feliks utters as he turns the key.

Just across the corridor is the bedroom suite of Jonas Kron. As Feliks steps to the doorway he adjusts the pistol in his belt and retrieves a notecard from his shirt pocket. Then he turns the key and enters.

"Jonas, my dear friend! What are you doing?"

He finds Kron frantically raising and lowering his window shade as if to signal someone on the outside that there's trouble in the castle. But Kron's window overlooks the west channel of the Mississippi River. The far bank is hundreds of meters away and covered by a thick belt of trees. Beneath the limbs there is a parkway and a bicycle trail, but it is highly unlikely that anyone notices Kron's frantic ups and downs.

Kron turns and bellows, "You are preposterous!" Feliks approaches with a drawn pistol aimed at the industrialist's slender midsection.

"Let us make our phone call, shall we?" he says, calmly.

Kron, his face red, his pale eyes raging, his chest heaving, screams at Feliks. "You are the lowest snake that crawls on this earth!"

Feliks chuckles and motions for Kron to sit at a small table in the alcove that serves as a parlor adjacent to his bedroom. He fishes from his pocket Kron's cellphone, places it on the table and sits next to the defiant executive. With one hand he holds the pistol, with the other a notecard. Then, reading the card, he punches seven numbers and tilts the phone toward Kron, turning on the speaker function.

After two rings a voice comes on. "This is Karen."

"Karen, this is Jonas Kron. I want you to do something for me." Jonas' voice is shaky.

"Yes, Mr. Kron."

"I want you to move some money out of my personal numbered account, the one in the Caymans. Move everything except two million to our corporate numbered account."

"But sir, it's getting late in the day."

"I know the hour, Karen. But you can do this online. You have all the codes and passwords. Call me back when the funds have been transferred. Remember, everything goes over except the two million."

"This is extraordinary, sir."

"Sometimes business opportunities arise very suddenly," Kron says abruptly, looking into Feliks' eyes and feeling the nearness of the gray steel pistol that Feliks holds near his head.

"Yes sir, I'll call you within the half hour."

It stands to reason that Feliks, too, should be nervous about this transaction, agitated about it, anxious to get going. Actually he is quite calm. He holds no grudge against Kron. He pities Kron's weakness, his self-loathing in swallowing Feliks' feigned fascination with Swedish history and all his other tales. Kron may bellow and scream, but Feliks knows that his anguish is aimed not at Feliks but at himself. Self-loathing is not a pretty thing to watch, really. If it is possible to feel sorry for a delusional billionaire, then perhaps that is how Feliks feels. That Feliks feels anything at all is quite remarkable. He's not accustomed to feeling.

Again his mind drifts away from Jonas Kron toward the two million and how he'll spend it. Travel, of course, is the answer. Urgent travel. He and Robert must get underway tomorrow at the latest. He senses danger approaching. But if they are coming, and if they are from the Gaswerks, then he has little to fear, really. He will never hear them coming, never see them coming. It will be over in an instant. He will not feel a thing.

Still, he must give his undivided attention to planning any future that he and Robert may still have. Where will that future be? He and Robert will not be filing an official flight plan, that is for certain. He remembers once meeting a commercial pilot at a lunch counter at O'Hare. The two got to talking. He asked what was the pilot's favorite place in the world. He was surprised by the response. Saipan. Saipan? Feliks knew this was an island somewhere in the Pacific. He had seen it in the newsreels from the Great Patriotic War. American marines were fighting Japanese holdouts in a hellhole of rocks and shredded palm trees, using flamethrowers to roust the poor wretches from their caves. Favorite place? Unlikely.

Not so, the pilot had said, describing sunny days, sandy beaches, gently swaying palms, crystal waters, lovely people, mild temperatures. And remoteness. Lots of remoteness. "The perfect place to get lost" is how the pilot had described it.

Feliks feels another bout of dreaminess coming on. He yawns. His ears crackle. Why do they do that? Fiddling with Kron's phone, he looks up the distance to Saipan and calculates the range of the Twin Otter. Distance? Six thousand, nine-hundred miles. Range? Eight-hundred and eleven miles. That's about nine or ten refueling stops by Feliks' quick math.

His trance is interrupted by the chiming of Kron's phone. Feliks punches the speaker and hands the phone to Kron, who has retreated to a lounge chair, his face the face of a sulking child.

"Yes, Karen," he says.

"It's done, Mr. Kron," she says and gives him a transaction number, which Feliks jots down on the notecard. She also recites instructions for setting a new password and retrieving several other new codes for the account.

* * *

After a short nap, with his prisoners locked away for the night, Feliks is strolling now through the gardens, hands clasped behind his back. The afternoon sun has fallen behind gathering clouds, but still the day is warm and thick, the flowers fragrant, the insects busy. The laziness of the early evening envelopes Feliks like a blanket. American show tunes loop through his brain... *My Rio, Rio by the sea-o. Got to get to Rio and we've got to make time.*

He pictures Fred and Ginger dancing on the wing of an airplane. He's breathing easier now that he knows two million smackers are only a few keystrokes away. Gazing down at the river, beyond the garden, down at the docks, he sees the Twin Otter poised and ready for a trip.

Chapter Fifty-One

Friday, 6:30 p.m

Bender considers Ronnie Saperstein a "greasy little puke," which makes him a perfect fit as Marla Kusic's court-appointed attorney. But for all his faults, especially his wardrobe, Ronnie is showing off the few brains in his head and the last drop of integrity in his soul by urging Marla, actually begging Marla, to make a deal with the cops.

"Spill your guts to Bender and you get probation, maybe even you walk," he tells her. "Otherwise, you got a good chance of serious jail time as an accessory to murder — three murders — which, believe me, is something you don't want. So, go ahead and spill the whole works. Remember, Richard Reznik is dead. He's no threat to you no more. Fat Duane? He probably did Richard, no doubt. And he did him with *your* gun. That's gonna be hard to explain. But you know Duane. You know what he's like. He ain't no freaking Richard. He ain't coming after you. They're gonna put Duane away for a long time. There's a federal warrant on him, remember. Kidnapping ain't nothing to sneeze at, especially considering whose kid it is."

Marla tells Ronnie she'll sleep on it.

Her sister Glenna is waiting back at Marla's cruddy apartment above Lucky's Nordeast Lounge. Glenna has the same blond stringy hair, but way fewer tattoos on account of her arms being so thin. Glenna is a slender person and a heavy smoker, given the number of butts that have accumulated in Marla's kitchen ashtray. It doesn't take long for the two of them to start in.

"You totally promised to be back by 5," Glenna shrieks, gesturing toward the clock over the stove. "Me and Troy were going out, but now he calls and says forget it. So I'm sitting here waiting for you while Clem has been a freaking pain in the ass." Clem is her baby who's stripped down to his diaper and crawls on the dirty floor toward the stairway that leads down to the bar. Glenna blows a stream of blue smoke and crosses her legs.

"Troy?" says Marla. "You and Troy? And *he's* the one to say forget it? What a freaking loser! Forget that shit face, baby sister."

"At least Troy is working."

"Where is Troy working? Who exactly would give his sorry ass a job?"

"Down at the casino in Red Wing, Treasure something."

"Shit, Clem!" Marla howls, dashing suddenly to her left, bending to scoop up the baby just as he begins to fall down the steep stairway. "Some mothers don't pay no attention to their kids. Drives me ape shit." Clem starts to cry, Marla reaching for the sixteen-ounce bottle of Pepsi with the nipple stretched over the top.

"Troy might be a loser," Glenna says, "but he don't hold a candle to Richard in the loser department, him being dead and all." There's an awkward pause. Glenna stubs out her cigarette. "You decided what to do?"

"My attorney says spill my guts to the cops. Tell everything.

Says I'll get probation. Says not to worry about Fat Duane. I told him I'd sleep on it."

"Tell everything? Seriously?"

"I'm thinking I'll say that Richard done everything, that Fat Duane was just along for the ride, or maybe that he wasn't even there, you know what I'm sayin'? I mean he's just a big baby. None of this is on Duane. He had a bad upbringing. He follows Richard around like a puppy. He's got a good heart, Glenna. I even thought about calling him to let him know I wasn't gonna rat on him, you know, to feel him out on me saying that like him and me were like getting it on when some of that shit went down."

"Marla, you always was the creative one."

"Then I remember him or Richard stole my freaking phone."

Glenna and Clem leave a half hour later, after each sister has drained a couple of beers and "Wheel of Fortune" is over.

Chapter Fifty-Two

Friday and Saturday, June 24-25, overnight

For the two Finnish tourists, the drive from Crane Lake goes well enough for the first hour. Their Chevy Blazer hurtles down a series of narrow two-lane roads pinched on both sides by forests of thick pine. Bugs splatter against the windshield as dusk turns to night. High-beam headlights reveal an alarming number of animal eyes lurking in the ditches as the SUV presses southward toward Duluth. Once they arrive there, an Interstate freeway will deliver them swiftly to the Twin Cities by the target hour of 1 a.m.

But for now, the roads are narrow, and, even at this late hour, fraught with obstacles. Pokey logging trucks can hog the highway. Old men driving campers or towing boats can move at a pace far too slow. A brief rain shower can slicken the pavement and distort visibility. But the driver, the larger of the tourists, the one with the pale, blank eyes, blasts past the slow pokes, unafraid of consequences. This is one well-oiled machine piloting another, a single-minded mission leaning forward, ever forward, hurrying toward its objective.

But suddenly a thump. The car quivers and veers into a violent spin. Only the driver's uncommon strength keeps the vehicle from skidding into a ditch and rolling over. Quickly the car stabilizes, sliding along the damp shoulder, slowing slightly, giving the tourists the opportunity to absorb what has just happened.

"*Olen*'" is all the driver says. Deer.

The car has struck a young buck, its antler protruding just above the right headlight, its body embedded in the grille. The Blazer slows briefly to a crawl, but does not stop. Now it picks up speed, the deer carcass sloughing onto the side of the road, the car's right headlight sending its beam upward and off to the side at a cock-eyed angle.

Once the tourists clear Duluth their speed accelerates and actual words are exchanged. One of the four destinations that the Yasenevo headquarters has provided has dropped off the mission. The signatures from Walrus's cellphone and laptop, placing the target near Kansas City, have now been characterized as a diversion. Three objectives remain. The first is the East Side motel/apartment where Walrus is officially registered as Feliks Dobervich. The second is the apartment upstairs of a place called Lucky's Nordeast Lounge, which serves as the residence of Marla Kusic, a known associate of the recently deceased Richard Reznik. Kusic, Yasenevo instructs, may know the whereabouts of Walrus. The third objective is the impressive residence of Jonas Kron III, the industrialist, and a known associate of the elusive Walrus.

The bearded tourist, the one riding shotgun, turns and leans into the backseat to double check the two sleek leather backpacks. Affirmative, their position is still being transmitted to the satellite. Affirmative, they are still on target to reach the first destination on time. Affirmative, their primary weapons are loaded and ready.

Chapter Fifty-Three

Saturday, 6:35 a.m

Jonas Kron III sits on the side of his four-poster bed facing his east window, squinting into the sliver of early morning sunlight just now peeking in from between a clump of nearby buildings. These are *his* buildings. This is *his* compound, *his* house, *his* castle, *his* island, *his* colony. Jonas is feeling defiant this morning. It's a delusion, of course, running up against the hard reality that he's a prisoner in his own realm. If he stood right now and walked to his massive bedroom door, he'd find it locked. Even if he could somehow breach the door, he'd encounter a man with a gun. Not just any man, but an imposter, a traitor and a despicable creature that he once trusted.

Kron has slept hardly at all despite an impressive volume of alcohol consumed in the hours before bedtime. His overnight hours had been filled with dreams, or perhaps visions, things he saw happening while not being quite asleep. These were pleasant, vengeful things, willful fantasies, perhaps, continuous loops of righteous indignation aimed at Jesper, the turncoat, the deceiver known also as Feliks.

In one loop, revenge came with the army of New Sweden arriving on horseback and in wagons, soldiers clad in gleaming armor and bearing the blue and yellow banners displaying the three Swedish crowns. Stout men, all marching in good order, were singing the old songs with gusto as they marched across the bridge and onto this island, this Lost Colony.

The restoration was swift and decisive. The traitor Feliks was captured and tortured. Soldiers tied each of his limbs to muscular horses, prodding them to pull strenuously in four directions and, pop! Feliks was left bloody and limbless, screaming in the town square. Kron was then handed a spiked cudgel and given the privilege of pulverizing the gory head and torso, a task he undertook with relish, swinging with abandon until the thing stopped twisting and screaming, after which the crown was returned to Kron's head as the armies cheered lustily.

In another loop, the armies arrived in stealth, clad in the form-fitting camouflage of modern commandos, equipped with Kevlar helmets, night-vision goggles and compact automatic weapons. Dark helicopters swooped low, just over the horizon, just over the Mississippi, hovering over the island, over the Kron compound, dropping ropes, the commandos rappelling down into the parking lot while other troops arrived silently in armored personnel carriers streaming over the bridges, securing the island without a shot fired. They found the coward Feliks squirming and whimpering in a hole dug at the edge of the parking lot. As crowds of Kron corporate employees gathered and gawked from behind the ropes, the commandos pulled Feliks out of the hole, tied his hands behind his back and brought him to Kron for interrogation. The big man was quite suddenly smaller and fatter, his comb-over more pathetic, his body a quivering mass of fear and dread.

"Why have you betrayed the colony?" Kron thundered. "Why have you conspired against the Swedish nation, and even against your own country? Vladi will not be happy with you. I am not happy with you!"

In his first act as restored monarch, Kron ordered this public menace, this Feliks, to be taken out to the large balcony overlooking the parking lot where all the inhabitants of Hennepin Island joined the Kron employees to witness the execution. Vendors had erected tents to sell commemorative T-shirts and key rings.

Soldiers had placed a tree stump and, next to it, a cushion on which Feliks could kneel. His head would be forced down onto the stump by soldiers holding a long iron bar at each end. But before they could proceed, Kron stepped to the microphone. He was dressed in his favorite pink cotton sweater over a fashionable white sport shirt. His starched and pressed khaki pants broke perfectly just above his highly polished tasseled loafers. His stylish gray hair was newly clipped. He motioned to the orchestra to stop playing. It was an all-white big band reminiscent of Lawrence Welk's ensemble, each player dressed in a baby blue tuxedo. They had just leaned into an upbeat Latin number that sputtered to a halt as Kron began to speak into a microphone.

"Testing one two. Testing one two," he declared as a hushed silence overtook the square. "I know you feel privileged to be with me here today to say 'so long' to a rat who deserves far worse than he's going to get in just a few moments. So, without further ado, I want to ask Feliks here if he has any last memories to share. Feliks? Any memories?

Feliks was silent. "OK then," Kron continued, motioning for the soldiers to force Feliks' head to the stump. Then, to a smattering of applause, Kron gratefully accepted the battle axe, the orchestra's drummer began his roll, and Kron lifted the axe. He came down hard, right on the dotted line where the Sharpie had marked Feliks' neck for severance. Kron had expected more resistance but the razor sharp blade sliced through Feliks as if he weren't really there. The orchestra responded with a brassy ta-dah! as Kron hoisted the bloody head and threw it down into the cheering throng.

These happy thoughts propel Kron into the shower, after which he shaves and slips on fresh clothing. He takes cheerful confidence in the fact that this Feliks, now in possession of two million of Kron's dollars, will be motivated to depart the castle and the island. Maybe today life will return to some semblance of normal.

For confirmation, Kron flips on his TV. Sure enough, Mike and Angela are telling viewers that temperatures in the metro dropped to fifty-six in the overnight, and that traffic is moving smoothly at this hour.

It's after nine when the lock finally turns on Kron's bedroom door. The girl, Petra, is red-faced, quivering, and sobbing quietly as she enters the room. Duane stumbles in behind her. There's a large blue welt on his left cheek, and his eye above is swollen nearly shut. Feliks enters last, feeling the need to explain that Duane, trying to flee with the girl, regrettably squared off against him in a fistfight last night that ended quickly and decisively, but, alas, not in Duane's favor.

"Our disagreement is over, I am pleased to announce. Duane and I are once again friends," says Feliks.

Duane doesn't look so sure. As for Petra, Feliks explains, "I am afraid she is suffering from a bout of homesickness. But this will soon be over."

Feliks, by contrast, is looking well-rested. His hair is combed. His pistol is in his belt. His mood is jovial. "Robert will soon bring breakfast," he announces.

Chapter Fifty-Four

Saturday, 4:00 p.m

Feliks' stroll through Kron's backyard garden ends at the hammock, which is artfully strung between two large trees beside the pool. A brief swim and then a nap are concepts that strike Feliks as good ideas for a humid afternoon. Already he has released the other guests from their rooms for an hour of fresh air, if this is what passes for fresh.

All are poolside. All are under Feliks' watchful eye and in range of his automatic pistol. The girl is squatting in a shady corner sobbing quietly. Duane and Robert are busy with some kind of card game. Kron is hunched in a deck chair sulking. As for Feliks, it seems to have slipped his mind that today is getaway day, the day that he and Robert are to fly away to a hidden tropical paradise. Is this no longer the plan? Has Feliks forgotten? He's not saying. Perhaps he's thinking that he's already living the dream, that he has already achieved his island paradise here at the luxury Kron Palms hotel and resort. He enjoys the other guests, after all. He enjoys hanging around with his old friend Jonas. He's not such a bad fellow, even if he does seem to be a bit grumpy lately. Earlier they had discussed Broadway musicals, Feliks having discovered amid all the medieval artifacts in the castle Kron's impressive collection of vinyl albums, heavy on show tunes.

"We have not these musical theater shows in Russia," he told Kron, who seemed both bored and agitated. "Many years I have been big fan," Feliks said, going into surprising detail about his favorite numbers, especially from "Guys and Dolls" and "Damn Yankees."

But now, in the midst of these gauzy recollections, why are Kron and the others so sullen? Why from across the pool does Kron stare at him with such contempt? Probably he doesn't like his new life as Feliks' manservant, but Feliks has always wanted a servant. Well, he really didn't want one in the communistic days when it would have been improper to admit wanting a servant. *All* people back in those days were servants for the common good. But now, in the new individualistic Russia, each person can be a czar if he shows the proper initiative, which is what Feliks is now showing.

Does he want a swim to cool off a bit? Why not? This hotel's lap pool is especially inviting, surrounded as it is by palm trees and tropical shrubs. Who needs a swim suit? Even at his age Feliks is not ashamed of his bulky body or his unsuccessful comb-over. The water is cool. It refreshes him, surrounds him, caresses him, makes him desire a woman. There are always alluring women in the classic Broadway musicals, women with amazing contours that are a delicious blend of soft and firm to the touch. He pictures himself as Emile, the plantation owner in "South Pacific" with the hots for the spunky, curly-haired American nurse, Nellie Forbush. "There is nothing like a dame!" Feliks belts out the tune. "Nothing in the world! There is nothing you can name that is anything like a dame!"

More relevant to the current situation, perhaps, is Jason

Bourne, tucked away with his tasty German girlfriend, Franka Potente, on a sultry remote island where they'll never be found. And even if they are found, so what? Isn't this a better life than Feliks ever had before? The thick groves of palm trees surrounding the pool give testimony to that. The tropical breeze cools things down as it flows in off the ocean.

Climbing out of the pool with his full manhood on display, a display that's either impressive or repulsive depending on your point of view, Feliks retrieves the gun he had placed within easy reach at the edge of the pool and searches in vain for a towel, finally settling for a roll in the grass before slipping back into his dirty clothes. He makes a mental note to ask Robert to wash them and to find others for him. Something tropical. Perhaps the hotel gift shop has something that will fit.

But a nap comes first. Feliks didn't sleep well last night. He climbs into the hammock, finding the process harder than he expects. Swinging back and forth, drifting toward slumber, it occurs to Feliks that his life has become a mathematical equation. On the one side there is duty and tradition. He was trained and served nobly as a Moscow Center operative, a surgical specialist, as it were. He took great pride in the precision of his work. He had nothing else in his life.

When the KGB and the nation transitioned to new entities, well, that was difficult. But he saw the change as an inevitable acquiescence to human nature. People are selfish at their core, even if they profess to care for the whole of humanity, they care mostly about themselves. Once you discover who humanity really is, do you actually want to be together with them? Do you really want them on your side? Do you want to nurture them, care for them, trust them? Not really. Do you want to drink with them? Dine with them? Have sex with them? The Russian people came to understand the perils of a polyglot society. They came to understand what the Americans have always understood. What is the American expression? Looking out for number one. Being stationed for so long in America has made Feliks appreciate the authenticity of this natural order. Yes, he feels deeply the surge of nationalism that Vladi is trying to instill in the new Russia. He's even able to push aside the sad fact that mafia criminals have taken over the new apparatus.

On the other side of the equation he has come to appreciate what the Americans call freedom. You don't have to fly the flag if you don't want to. You don't have to pledge your allegiance to it. You don't have to pay attention to politicians, or show up to vote, even. You are released from caring about the collective whole. That is where Feliks finds himself now. Not caring. For him, that is the heavier end of the see-saw. That is the side of the equation that draws him in. Every man can be an island if he wants to be one, and Feliks wants to be one, preferably one that's far, far away, where the tropical breezes blow gently and the palm trees sway and nobody cares about the petty ideologies that ruin your life. What, after all, has political allegiance ever done for Feliks Dobervich? What has his old comrade Vladi ever done for him? Except, perhaps, betray him. A posting to the American Midwest, the land of the Dollar Store and the meat raffle? They don't make James Bond movies about that.

Once one has slipped into sleep it's hard to recognize what exactly wakes one up. But this time Feliks is pretty sure it is the sound of a motor starting up, first one motor and then another, each of them driving the distinctive flapping sound of an airplane propeller. How long has he been dozing? The bright sunshine of afternoon has turned to early evening. Clouds have gathered. It occurs to him that he never got his poolside drink.

He rises unsteadily, managing to adjust his balance on his way to the railing at the edge of the pool, the palm trees swaying and hissing all around him. When he looks down at the dock he sees that someone has started up the Twin Otter. Instinctively he reaches into his pocket for his gun. Why? Because the situation has changed, that's why. Peering down at the dock, into the lengthening shadows, he sees in silhouette three figures moving toward the floatplane. Looks like two men, one skinny, the other fat. And there's a child clutching what looks like a stuffed animal.

These are tourists, obviously. But why are they checking out? Why would they depart a paradise like this? Perhaps he should investigate, especially since one of the passengers resembles his manservant Jonas. Are these tourists just arriving at the hotel? Or are they checking out? Departing? Feliks *needs* his manservant. Left all alone, who will bring him dinner? Who will serve him drinks?

Pushing off against the railing, Feliks stumbles down the stone stairway, then along the plank walkway that leads to the docks. He sees his thin manservant unlooping the ropes that secure the floatplane to the dock. He sees the other two moving quickly toward the four-step stairway into the aircraft. Meanwhile, carefully avoiding the roaring portside propeller, his manservant, Jonas, now begins to untie other ropes as the young girl and the fat man step into the plane.

Feliks is an excellent shot. Even from this distance of forty meters he's confident that he can sever the fuel line that runs along the underside of the left engine. No one hears the muffled shot above the sound of the motors, but Jonas Kron feels the plane quiver and sees the stream of fuel shooting outward as the engine sputters, pops and slows to a stop. Feliks now readjusts his sites to the cockpit's open window where Robert now appears, leaning out, looking back over his shoulder, trying to discern why his portside engine has suddenly failed. Behind Robert's aviator-style sunglasses Feliks detects a quizzical expression. Now, just over Robert's left eyebrow a red spot appears, Robert's head slumping downward, coming to rest at the bottom edge of the open window. Feliks suffers a sudden pang of regret, a sudden spasm of remorse. Was this really necessary?

His mother stands alongside him on the walkway now, leaning with him against the railing. It has been, let's see, nearly fifty years since he last saw her. She's wearing her apron and hairnet from the kitchen where she works at the People's Hospital No. 4 in Smolensk. She is a tall, sturdy woman but has a sweet and kindly manner. Feliks (he had another name then) and his brother Pavel never doubt that she loves them deeply. When the other boys tease and bully Feliks because he is slow and fat, his mother comforts him with stories of hefty heroes. Feliks is never sure if the stories are real or if she makes them up. She has a phonograph, too, and her boys spend hours sprawled on the apartment floor listening to recordings of the Red Army Choir and of Kirill Kondrashin conducting the Moscow Philharmonic. When the orchestra performs a free concert in Smolensk to commemorate the death of the city's greatest hero, the cosmonaut Yuri Gagarin, his mother takes the boys.

Never is their father mentioned. When Feliks or Pavel ask about him, her answers are short and she's quick to change the subject. After the gas explosion at the hospital, the lives of Feliks and Pavel, both teenagers, go into the toilet. Pavel eventually joins the army. Feliks never hears from him again. Only now does Feliks realize how much he misses his mother. He aches for her. Seeing her now brings tears to his eyes and a burning sensation to his throat. There's so much he wants to tell her. She certainly is finding it hard to believe his luck at ending up here in this Pacific paradise, a place so remote that they'll never find him. Perhaps she will soothe him over this thing that has now happened to poor Robert. Maybe Robert was, as the Americans like to say, in the wrong place at the wrong time.

Chapter Fifty-Five

Sunday, June 26, 10:15 a.m

Maggie watches through the blinds, seeing Span turning and walking with Max down the steps, away from her front porch, down to the curb, into his car and then disappearing around the corner. This plunges Maggie back into her inner storm. When the doorbell first rang, she peeked through the window, catching a glimpse of man and dog. But she couldn't answer the door. Just couldn't. The morning is pleasant enough, sunny, cool, the leaves stirring slightly in the green canopy that covers Conner Street. But in her chest, in the pit of her stomach, and in the back of her neck, this is just another stormy day.

James is back. Their daughter's disappearance brings them suddenly closer. Maggie has to admit that there's some comfort in that, some security in having a man in the house again. He doesn't fill the agonizing hollowness of Petra's absence. But he is their little girl's father. He does care about her. He is where he should be in these terrible days. Maggie can't barricade herself against the old feelings seeping in from the times when James and she were a new couple, and when they were all a new family, the three of them. There are plenty of bad memories from those days, but some good ones, too.

In the space of only two weeks her life has flipped over. On a normal Sunday morning she'd be at St. A's helping her people to abide in the divine, and, she hoped, helping the divine abide in her people. But now there's an oppressive new normal imposed by murder and kidnapping that she never saw coming. Despite the comforts that her faith is supposed to offer, she suffers deeply this cruel separation from her daughter, this unthinkable terror.

Her police work offers no real therapeutic diversion. Neither does her partnership with Span. All yesterday she had ignored his incessant calls because she couldn't decide whether to tell him about Henrik's confession – or whether she could tell anyone about it. Still, don't the police deserve to know the true circumstances that led to the murders of Henrik and Matthias? And shouldn't Span know? Shouldn't they all be told that Matthias, just weeks before his murder, had called the FBI, had wanted to talk to Agent Thurber. That phone call is what got them both killed, Maggie imagines. Someone knew about that phone call.

All through last night these questions roiled her mind. James must have sensed her extra anguish, telling her again and again not to get involved, not to screw it up, as she had in L.A. Those weren't his exact words. He was kinder than that, but the message was clear and it shattered her confidence. When she overstepped in L.A., she lost her dad. And now it's Petra's life on the line. Let the FBI handle it, James said again and again. They know how to deal with these situations.

But the clock is ticking, and not in Petra's favor. Maggie feels it. So, on Thursday night, when Maggie saw Marla Kusic being led into the interrogation room at police headquarters, and when Bender wouldn't allow her to take part, and when it was suggested to her that Marla might know something about Petra's whereabouts, well, since then it's been like there's a bomb inside of Maggie. She can't just sit on the sidelines. Not any longer. If Marla knows something, then Maggie deserves to know it, too. And now with Bender calling yesterday to say that Marla has decided to cooperate with the cops, and that she'll be giving a deposition at noon today, Maggie can't help herself.

"James, I've got to get out of the house for awhile. I'm going down to Whole Foods and pick up some stuff."

"We don't need anything, Baby," he says.

"I know, but I need to go out. I'll be back in a few minutes."

When Maggie drives her old blue Volvo past the market, she doesn't stop. She gets to the freeway, drives past downtown, gets off on University Avenue and heads into Northeast Minneapolis, toward Lucky's Nordeast Lounge, toward Marla's upstairs apartment.

As she expects, the door to the bar is locked. Too early to be open. She walks around to the side of the shabby stucco building, weeds growing up through the cracks in the sidewalk. She's about to knock on the side door, but then doesn't bother. It's open. Broken open, by the looks of the cracked and splintered doorjamb. Maggie steps in. There's a stairway on the right.

She calls out, "Ms. Kusic?"

No answer.

"Marla! Are you home? It's Margaret Lindberg."

Silence.

The stairs creak as Maggie climbs slowly up. About when the second floor reaches eye level, Maggie catches a whiff of stuffiness — with highlights of rotten garbage and stale cigarette smoke. The linoleum floor is dirty and littered. Sunlight streams through a smudgy east window, showing scattered paper plates, beer cans and two ashtrays overflowing with butts. Maggie tries a bathroom and a closet. Nothing. Only silence. Stepping to the back of the main room she presses on a half-open bedroom door.

This is apparently Marla, lying face down on her blood-soaked bed, clothed in panties and a sleeveless t-shirt, her big, tattooed arms spread wide, her greasy blond hair tossed to one side, a trickle of drying fluid coming from two dime-sized holes above her right ear.

Maggie sighs. "No sign of a struggle" is all she says.

Chapter Fifty-Six

Sunday, 10:45 a.m.

It's not that Span has any hope of being in the room when Marla sings, but he can't pass up the opportunity to hang around in the D.A.'s outer office to describe the scene and interview the participants as a way of showing that, if nothing else, the Star Journal was there. Besides, Carla insists. He's stuck now at a stoplight three blocks from the Hennepin County Courthouse when his phone chimes. It's Stephanie Levin.

"My dear Spaniel. Don't you love me anymore? We haven't chatted in days. I feel left out."

"Just been busy."

"So I've been reading! Looks like you've got the competition inhaling your exhaust."

"Hope so. How about you, Stephanie? Taking the summer off, I assume. Up at the lake catching your limit? I know you're an outdoors girl. Hiking, camping, trapping small furry animals, singing dirty songs around the campfire in your Armani short-shorts."

"My favorite is gutting fish and swatting black flies."

"My favorite is climbing into the pup tent with you at night."

"Ooo! Repulsive!"

"What's up?"

"Haven't been reading much about crazy Jonas Kron lately," she says. "Off your radar, is he? Was talking just now to one of the partners at the firm — won't say who — who calls asking for a detail or two for Karen Crawley, who's, you know, Kron's right-hand girl when it comes to finance. Karen says Kron is moving fifty-some million out of his personal account in the Caymans, leaving two million behind. This is totally out of the blue, he says. And Kron's needing new passwords and codes for the leftover two mil."

"OK," Span says slowly as the light turns green and the car glides forward. "And your point is?"

"The point is, why does he need two million dollars all of a sudden, with us, his top attorneys knowing nothing about it and getting no explanation. Word is that everybody working at the castle this week, like the maid and the yard guys and the pool guy and the cook, they all got sent home on Thursday. No reason given. And nobody knows for how long. And when you call the castle all you get is a busy signal. And when you call Kron's cell, all you get is no answer. Not even a voice message. But people still saw lights up there last night and his airplane is there at the dock. And through the gate you can see his car in there by the house. So W.T.F?"

Span is silent as he pulls into a loading zone near the courthouse parking garage. "Thanks, Stephanie," he says. Then he disconnects, just sitting there behind the wheel. He checks his watch. He's way early. 10:55. Sixty-five minutes to wait on a lazy Sunday morning? Why not check it out?

Chapter Fifty-Seven

Sunday, 11:00 a.m

Maggie, careful not to touch anything in Marla's apartment, descends the stairs, pushes open the door and heads toward the street while reaching for her cell. Bender has to know about this. But just then, a gray unmarked police car pulls to the curb in front of Lucky's. Officer Cyd O'Donnell hops out from behind the wheel, opening the back door for Bender and his companion, a short swarthy man in a yellow sports jacket.

"Lindberg! What are you doing here?" says Bender when he sees Maggie emerging from the side of the building.

"I'm wondering the same thing about you."

"We came to get Ms. Kusic for her deposition," says the man in yellow, reaching out with his right hand. "By the way, I'm Ronnie Saperstein."

Maggie nods. "I'm afraid you guys are too late. Marla has nothing to say."

Chapter Fifty-Eight

Sunday, 11:04 a.m

Six hours after their sortie into Lucky's Nordeast Lounge, the Finnish tourists are on Hennepin Island motoring back and forth on Lake Street studying the private entrance to the Kron compound. Finally, they slide their blue SUV into a parking slot on a side street and approach the castle on foot. This being broad daylight, they probe the perimeter in a casual, relaxed manner. They are tourists, after all. Perceiving no vulnerabilities at the front gate, they work around to the fortress' west side where the wall is almost hidden by a thick grove of lilac bushes and a clump of tall spruce. The stone barrier looks to be three meters high with a one-meter iron fence at the top. The whole setup provides leafy cover for anyone hoping to surreptitiously scale the wall and penetrate the property.

From his backpack, the bearded tourist produces a small flashlight-type device, aiming it at the alarm system that runs along the top of the fence. After checking a reading on the device, he exchanges it for another instrument that includes a pulley and a slender nylon rope with a hook at one end. He uses the device to shoot the hook and trailing rope over the top of the fence. Two minutes later both men are standing inside the private, residential portion of the Kron compound next to a lap pool and adjacent to a patio surrounded by trees. No alarm has sounded. The time is 11:13, Central Daylight.

Chapter Fifty-Nine

Sunday, 11:08 a.m

Span's drive from the county courthouse to the south end of Hennepin Island takes less than fifteen minutes. Crossing the Lake Street Bridge, the Kron complex glides into view on the right, the imposing clock tower impossible to miss. Span turns left onto a tree-lined residential street. He parks in the shade. Reaching for his cell, he speed dials Bender, but the call rolls over to message.

"It's Span Lokken. Was planning to meet you at Marla Kusic's deposition, but I might be late. Want to check out something strange at Kron Castle. Hoping you can fill me in on what I miss."

Now on foot, Span heads for the smaller of the two gates that form the entry point to the compound. This is the same gate he and Maggie entered for their personal tour of the castle. Stepping onto the cobblestone driveway, Span peers through the iron grille. Kron's black Lincoln SUV is parked in the driveway. He rings the bell and waits. No answer. He tries the intercom button. No reply. He scans the mansion's windows, but sees no sign of movement.

Traffic behind him on Lake Street is sparse and quiet. He leans into the iron fence to listen. A mourning dove coos, coos, coos. Leaves rustle slightly in the trees. Nothing else. And then … a faint, distant cry. A sobbing, perhaps. The faraway cries of a child. Not loud, but loud enough. A child in Kron's castle? Not likely, Span thinks. Sobs descend to whimpers. And then … quiet. Staring intently now at the mansion, Span sees on the second floor the profile of a side window cranking shut.

In his younger years Span was known as an adventurous reporter. He knocked on doors in dangerous neighborhoods. He rode a helicopter into the mouth of a smoldering volcano. He dodged FBI agents to interview a militant American Indian activist who was wanted for murder. He posed as a customer to break up a notorious heroin and prostitution ring. Never had he been ordered into a combat zone overseas, but he would have gone had the paper asked.

But not now. Now he did most of his work on the phone, most of his interviews in public places, most of his investigating in libraries. Danger was not on his gentle, downward glide path.

But this is a definite situation. Big stakes. A child crying in the Kron castle? Petra missing? Maggie suffering? This is not about journalism. This is different. This is personal.

He walks cautiously now along the high stone wall that surrounds the compound, walks along Lake Street back toward the bridge, toward the point where the wall turns south along the riverbank. At the corner he stops to scan the castle's west wall partially obscured by trees. Abruptly he freezes in his tracks, astonished to see what he sees. Not more than a hundred feet away, a dark-clad man, a large man, is nimbly pulling himself up a rope and, aided by a another man already on the wall, reaches the top. Both men then disappear behind tree branches, the rope coming up behind them. Quietly, Span threads his way along the bottom of the wall, through the trees, toward the spot where the two men had been, his heart pumping faster. This is a secluded place, hidden by groves of spruce and a few tall oaks and maples. As a kid, Span was a champion tree-climber. There might be some older trees on the north side of Chicago that still bear his initials high in their branches. He eyes a tall maple with sturdy-looking branches that hang over the top of Kron's wall. He grabs onto the trunk but immediately realizes the folly of trying. He's no kid.

Breathing faster now he quickly retraces his steps back to the car. He drives west, again crossing the Lake Street Bridge, then turns left on West River Parkway, making another left after two blocks into a boat landing operated by the city parks system. Minutes later he's in a small rented fishing boat, rowing across the river's gentle current toward Hennepin Island. Three hundred yards ahead he sees a twin-engine floatplane moored at one of a half-dozen docks that were once part of Kron's shipping operation. The cranes are idle and rusted. The plane, by contrast, looks new, its white and red fuselage glistening in the midday sun.

"Didn't know Kron had an airplane," Span whispers to himself. "Should I be surprised?"

Minutes later, he climbs onto one of the rotting wooden docks and ties up the boat. He scans the backside of the castle. All quiet. In the foreground there's a lush garden, a swimming pool and a coach house. Also quiet. Closer yet there's the float-plane – a sensible place to start, perhaps. But as Span draws nearer he sees a man slumped in the cockpit, his head hanging partially out the window. There's a trickle of drying blood beneath the man's aviator sunglasses and a small round hole in his forehead. Span is quick to understand that this man has been shot dead. But when? He has heard no shot.

And where are the two dark-clad men? He doesn't see them. He doesn't see anyone.

The immensity of his mistake is now creeping over him. Coming to this compound was a very bad idea. High-tailing it back to the boat and making quickly for the far shore seems like his best choice. Or calling Maggie? Or calling Bender? Or calling 9-1-1? All are good options. But when Span begins a frantic search of his pockets he comes up with – no phone! Where is it? Back in the car, probably. Often he leaves his cell-phone in the center console. A cold nausea invades the pit of his stomach. A sourness overtakes his throat. Then he hears it. It's coming from an open window on the second floor of the castle. Music.

Chapter Sixty

Sunday, noon

Feliks realizes that locking Jonas Kron and Duane Hajinlian in the same room last night was not the best idea. Through the night they screamed at one another and made violent sounds (throwing things, sounded like) hindering the sleep of other guests, namely those in the next bedroom. The little girl Petra clutched her stuffed rabbit most of the night, and Feliks himself got little rest, believing now that the resort's management should take a more active role in screening its overnight customers. Whose idea was it to place a pretentious capitalist in the same room with a dirt-ball ex-con? Feliks' apology to Petra about the sleeping arrangements brought on a bout of crying and sobbing "Mommy! Mommy!" again and again, which Feliks did not like to hear. She finally quieted down a few minutes ago when Feliks cranked shut the window and gave her a look.

Now, she is propped in her bed, tears in her eyes, clutching the purple rabbit, staring at Feliks, saying nothing. Those eyes! What is she thinking? Feliks has not the foggiest idea. He does not know children. There are millions of them in the world, yet he has had almost no experience with them, cannot understand them, cannot relate to them. Yes, in musicals there are children. Oliver! comes to mind, as well as the one about Siam. But the ways of children are mysterious to him.

Memories of his own meager childhood in Smolensk are vague. Was his an actual childhood or was it just a grim hardship to be endured? It is a question, perhaps, to ask his mother. As for his professional life, only once does he recall receiving orders to, shall we say, include children in a termination package. The German family in the Caribbean comes to mind. There may have been two or three *kinder* involved on that one. But it was a clean job. "Brown paper packages tied up with string," Feliks hums, "These are a few of my favorite things."

He fails to understand why his three companions seem so unhappy. He, by contrast, possesses an exceptionally sunny disposition, and why not? Are these not posh, tropical surroundings? Are these not the best of friends enjoying time together? Are these not joyful, festive tunes he is belting out?

The trouble started yesterday afternoon immediately after Robert was taken ill in the cockpit of the Twin Otter. His three passengers — two men and a small girl — stepped back onto the dock with their hands in the air. It was a posture that Feliks considered overly dramatic and totally unnecessary. On their way up through the garden toward the castle, their hands still in the air, Feliks overheard Kron telling Duane, whom he called "Shit-for-Brains," that he, Duane, was, quote, *a dead man,* prompting Duane to answer, quote, *and you ain't?* Duane then proceeded to tell Kron that he didn't appreciate his condescending attitude toward him, although he expressed it more directly. "Don't fuck with me, Slick" is what Duane actually said. Normally Duane was on the quiet side. But his taciturn nature was misleading. True, Feliks had thoroughly vetted both

Duane and the late Richard for the church operation. He found Duane to be generally non-aggressive. But if somebody pushed him too hard, humiliated him, teased him, bullied him, then he might erupt without warning, without regret. Poor Richard found out the hard way. Jonas Kron, Feliks thinks, does not know that he is, as the Americans say, "skating on thin ice."

Feliks understands from his training that tight-knit groups, such as these dear vacationers traveling together, always develop rival alliances. In this instance it is Petra and Duane versus Kron and Robert. But now, with Robert dropping out, Feliks calculates that Kron feels isolated and helpless. Always in his life he has been in charge. Not now. This new circumstance may cause Kron to cast about in search of someone inferior, someone to pick on. Duane fills the bill. To Kron, Fat Duane is a repulsive figure. Feliks knows from his preparation for the church operation that Duane had been urged by his sisters to become a hair-care professional, a career he rejected in favor of the Tastee Freeze followed by One-Hour Martinizing where, it was said, he could not handle the pressure. During the vetting process, Feliks recalls one of Duane's sisters saying that her brother started going totally downhill after hanging around with Richard when they were both in the facility down at Racine.

Feliks' thoughts are interrupted by a buzzer that Robert will surely answer. Someone is trying to get into the front gate. And why wouldn't they want to? There's a pool, a patio, a putting green, a terrace, a tennis court and so on, plus palm trees and sea breezes. Still, the buzzer is terribly annoying. Feliks makes a mental note to disconnect it.

The slight distraction, however, cannot overcome the splendor that surrounds him and his strangely somber fellow guests. They show not the slightest appreciation for the show tunes and dance numbers that Feliks is blaring on the sound system. Feliks notes that the musical themes fit perfectly the atmosphere."I have often walked down street before," Feliks sings boisterously, "but pavement always stayed beneath feet before." And then, in the next number, "Don't let be forgot that there was once spot for one brief shining moment – Camelot!"

Still, the most appropriate lyrics come from South Pacific, the sounds flowing out the hotel's open windows into the trade winds. Soon, Feliks realizes, there will be no need for the loaded gun tucked in his belt. It is unfortunate what happened to Robert. "Did you know my mother has come for holiday?" Feliks had told the group last night. "Have you not met her?" With that, he had launched into a bedtime story, a *skazka na noch,* an incomprehensible tale about a boy, a black cat and a wicked witch.

Now, glancing at his watch – past noon – Feliks unlocks the bedroom doors to gather everyone in the library for his midday presentation. Duane emerges from the other bedroom looking better than yesterday. But Kron is limping severely and showing a swollen, discolored face with multiple bruises and a deep laceration on his left cheek, apparently a product of last night's altercations.

"Jonas, you must be more careful," Feliks instructs.

As he begins to outline the brunch menu, he realizes that Robert won't be available to cook or serve. As if seeking reference, he glances out the second-story window toward the Twin Otter still resting by the dock. Robert, he supposes, is still in the cockpit preparing for their flight. He hopes his pilot is feeling better. Leaning out the open window he looks down to notice a new guest standing at the back edge of the garden, next to the swimming pool. For a moment Feliks is alarmed. Perhaps this man has been sent by the Gaswerks. Perhaps this is the beginning of the end. But no. A Gaswerks man would not be dressed in a navy blazer and khaki slacks. He would not look so confused and cautious. He would not allow himself to be so easily seen. And so this must be a new guest. Perhaps he is as hungry as everyone else. Probably he will need to purchase tropical resort wear to overcome his obvious wardrobe deficiency.

Pulling away from the library window and refocusing on the assembly, Feliks sees the girl Petra staring at Jonas Kron's rearranged face, and who can blame her? The shades of color range from bright red lumps to deep gray blotches and pockets of yellow where pus has begun to pool. One cheek is much larger than the other while the nose seems crooked and flattened.

Indeed, the missing front teeth remind Petra of her own recent months of toothlessness and the ten-dollar bill she found under her pillow. "From the tooth fairy," her mother had said. The pillow Mr. Kron carries, however, is soaked with blood. This frightens Petra. She begins to quiver. She grabs hold of Duane's hand.

As Feliks begins his announcements, Kron takes a seat at a small table in the corner. He wears a scowl on his damaged face. As if to further taunt him, Duane, with Petra in hand, takes up a stance near the unlit fireplace, beneath the giant, gold-framed portrait of Kron's great grandfather, Andreas.

Failing to pick up on the tension, Feliks launches into his program. "Today's topic was to be volcano and how it forms Pacific island. But there is not sufficient enthusiasm for geology speech. We talk instead about why Polynesian woman is so alluring." He admits that "darker" women tend to excite his Slavic libido but confesses also a slight embarrassment, aware that his visiting mother is old fashioned and serious about her Russian Orthodox faith and, thus, might be uncomfortable with his observations on the South Seas female anatomy.

Still, he presses on, failing to see a man on the central staircase just outside the open library door. The man approaches slowly and cautiously, peering into the room where a small group is gathered, backlit against the sun streaming through the large windows, making it hard to see faces. But a large man with a comb over, dressed in Bermuda shorts and standing behind a small lectern appears to be lecturing from notes, speaking in accented English. Conspicuously protruding from his belt is the butt of a large black automatic pistol, the sight of which jolts Span Lokken into thinking, "What the hell am I doing here?" Indeed, every fiber in his body is telling him, "Run back down the stairs as fast as you can, back to the boat, get some help."

But when he peers again around the library door to take one last peek, he sees more clearly a small, curly-haired girl – Petra! – standing just to the side of the fireplace, holding hands with a husky bearded man who is unmistakably Duane Hajinlian! Then, suddenly, it's too late for Span to run. Looking up from his notes, Feliks sees the stranger standing in the doorway, the same man he saw down in the garden moments before. By instinct and training he pulls the pistol from his belt, pointing it at the stranger. "I see we have new guest," he says with a smile. "Welcome! We would like you to register, please. And your name is ... "

"Span Lokken," Span stammers.

Surveying the room nervously, Span fails to immediately recognize the disfigured Kron. But he sees more clearly the beloved child Petra, teary-eyed, with one arm clutching a purple rabbit and the other holding on to the bearded man he recognizes from pictures plastered all over the media.

"Span!" the girl cries. He returns his best and bravest version of a smile, which probably doesn't look like a smile at all.

As for the man in charge, the one with the gun and the Eastern European accent, Span can't imagine who he is. "Who are you?" he blurts.

"I am resort executive," Feliks says.

Span's eyes focus on the barrel of the gun as Feliks walks

toward him. Span freezes in place, thinking that none of this was supposed to happen on his downward glidepath. None of this would have happened if he'd stayed at the courthouse for Marla's deposition. But then there's the tenuous upside he has stumbled upon. He has found Petra! Alive! And, he has found Duane Hajinlian!

Feliks, still smiling, gestures with the gun to the rest of the room. "This is our island paradise, my good man. Do you have bags to check? Perhaps you would like to freshen up. Robert, our concierge, will come soon to help. He will find also suitable clothings.

"Oh, one thing!" Feliks adds, reaching toward Span with an empty palm. "You may leave cellphone here with me for safe-keeping."

Span's explanation of a missing phone fails to satisfy Feliks who gives him a quick pat-down before guiding him to stand near the fireplace. Petra lets go of Duane and grabs Span by the hand.

"Why don't you let this girl leave? Span says. "She should go home to her mother."

"But we are all so happy here," Feliks says. "My own mother is here to look after this girl. We are all here waiting for final resolution. We are like family. We will be together when final resolution comes."

"When what comes?" says Span.

"You will discover," Feliks says, singing loudly along with a lyric suddenly blaring on the sound system. "When you are Jet, you are Jet all the way, from first cigarette to last dying day."

"Would you like last cigarette?" he asks Span. "Would anyone like?"

No response. Kron, recognizing Span, is thinking, hoping desperately that help is coming, that Span has notified the police who must be on their way. Kron stands now and limps toward the others standing near the fireplace. Feliks, his back to the library door, looks down at his notes, searching for a place to resume, failing to notice that his audience is giving him the double deadface.

Kron's attention is now focused solely on the pistol that Feliks has tucked back into his ample midsection. If it were somehow possible for Kron to obtain this pistol, he would point it at Fat Duane and pull the trigger multiple times. To just dream about such a delightful prospect brings a crooked smile to his blood-caked lips. Duane's thoughts, on the other hand, are centered not on Feliks' droning on about South Seas "culture" but on buttermilk pancakes with maple syrup and a frosty beer. There has been no food since yesterday afternoon, which makes Duane more than a little cranky.

Petra is perhaps the first one to see, past Feliks and through the open library door, the two black-clad figures stealthily approaching. These are very large men with blond hair, the color of her mom's. Kron now sees them, too, thinking right away that these are special ops guys from the Minneapolis PD come to rescue him. Each is in a partial crouch there in the doorway. Each has a large black automatic pistol drawn and held with both hands, the barrels in a horizontal sweep of the room.

Span sees them, too. Then glancing to his right, toward the edge of the fireplace, not ten feet away, he sees the wood-paneled door, Kron's secret door, the one that leads down to his workshop, the workshop he's so proud of.

Feliks, looking up from his script, sees distraction in the eyes of his audience. He turns abruptly, facing his two assassins head on.

Kron expects Feliks to reach for his gun. But it doesn't happen that way. Instead, one of the men, the one aiming most intently at Feliks, speaks to him harshly in a foreign language. These are not local cops.

Feliks smiles broadly, speaking what sounds like Russian but in soothing tones, and then in English. "Gentlemen! No need for firearms! You can check them at front desk. Robert will take good care for you."

"Mr. Kron?" Feliks says, turning toward Jonas. "Will you be so kind as to take weapons of new guests down to Robert at front desk for safekeeping? And you may take mine, also?" he says, reaching into his pants for the nine-millimeter, offering it to Kron handle first, Kron moving slowly, cautiously toward Feliks, toward the gun.

"And gentlemen," Feliks continues, still smiling broadly, turning back toward the newest guests. "Welcome to our tropical home. I know you will be comfortable. Robert will help."

The visitors are blank-faced. But once Kron has Feliks' gun in his hand, their mood sharpens and their focus shifts abruptly to Kron, each now taking deadly aim directly at the industrialist. But Kron turns away from them and calmly points the gun at Duane, still standing by the fireplace, and, suddenly, the library explodes in sound.

Blam! Blam! Blam!

Kron manages to fire three shots, two of the slugs striking Duane square in the chest, the other penetrating the portrait of Kron's great grandfather. Simultaneously, five quieter shots, toy shots, really ... *Poof! Poof! Poof! Poof! Poof!* ... pass through various parts of Jonas Kron. Kron looks startled. He and Duane fall to the library floor together, as if in a slow-motion dance, the nine-millimeter sliding out of Kron's hand and skidding across the shiny floor, the whole house echoing with the sounds of gunfire.

As Duane falls, Span grabs Petra and dives toward Kron's secret door, crawling through it, then tumbling — the two of them — down the flight of concrete stairs, the door closing behind them.

This cacophonic eruption fails to dim Feliks' spirit of hospitality, nor does the sight of Kron and Duane slumped on the floor dampen his mood. "Would you fine gentlemen care for a beverage?" he asks the new arrivals. "Once you are settled we may chat in garden?" he suggests. "It is beautiful, sunny day. We are discussing here attributes of Polynesian female body."

From downstairs comes again the annoying buzz of the front gate buzzer, and, through the open window comes the distant whine of approaching sirens.

One of the black-clad tourists, the bigger, clean-shaven one, is now striding slowly toward the congenial Feliks, his arm and weapon hanging loosely at his side, his transparent eyes drilling into Feliks' eyes, Feliks' thoughts shifting toward the girl Petra, who seems somehow to have disappeared in all the commotion, Feliks' hospitable smile turning wistful, his lips beginning to sing softly: "Getting to know you, getting to know all about you," he sings. "Getting to like you, getting to hope you like me."

Poof! Poof!

Two shots to the side of the head is how it ends for Feliks.

Chapter Sixty-One

Sunday, 12:56 p.m

In the deepest cavern of his brain, Span Lokken flashes on a newspaper story describing his own death. Not the whole story. Not the part about the killings that just happened upstairs. Just the part about his body being found, shot, execution-style, in a storage room next to the Kron mansion's kitchen. In the majority of his brain, however, in the ninety-nine percent part, Span is simply racing through the current terrifying moment, hoping to survive the next few clicks of his life.

Hiding seems the only option.

He would like to think of a more dignified way to go, maybe even with a dose of courage. Perhaps he'd give up his life for his friend, his young fishing companion, the girl, Petra. But the harder truth is this: When two steely assassins are going room to room looking for you, all you're thinking about is yourself. It's true what they say — when you die, you die alone.

In their desperate scramble to avoid bullets, Span and Petra had come out of their tumble down the narrow concrete stairway with scrapes and bruises they barely noticed. Their choice at the bottom was either kitchen or storage room. Kron's storage room is a dimly-lit chamber with his survival gear neatly stacked in one corner, but dominated by piles of various Swedish artifacts – goblets, shields, tapestries – in various stages of cleaning or repair. His prize possession, as he'd shown Span and Maggie during their castle tour, was slumped against a wall: A child-sized suit of armor crafted in the late 1500s for young prince Gustavus Adolphus.

It's the clang of plate armor against the tile floor that shifts Span's attention from himself to Petra, who's gamely trying to climb into the suit. Immediately Span sees the suit as a brilliant hiding place. Turns out that an eight-year-old girl is more resourceful than he is, and braver, too. He dashes to help her disappear into the metallic costume, then crouches behind a stack of shields that only partly obscures him. He trembles now and listens. Intently. There are footsteps for sure. Upstairs, probably. Then maybe on the narrow servant's stairway. The one just outside this door. Maybe. Louder now. Approaching footsteps for sure on the concrete stairway. And now nothing. Quiet. Seconds go by. Now the latch on the door clicks. The door opens. A dark figure enters.

"Mom! Mom! I'm here."

The dark figure pivots. And over there, less than ten feet away, amid an impressive jumble of medieval artifacts, a diminutive suit of armor begins to move and a hand lifts the visor on the small helmet. Petra's familiar face materializes, all smiles, dimples and tears! "It's me, Mom, I'm here!"

Span finds it hard to control his emotions as the darkened figure becomes Maggie, turning and lunging to embrace her daughter, managing simultaneously to hug her tightly while peeling away the metal coverings one by one. Maggie then scoops Petra up into her arms, carrying her quickly out of the room, up and out the front door of the castle, into the courtyard. There, a medical team ushers mother and daughter into a waiting ambulance, Span following and watching from the doorway, waving to Maggie as the ambulance begins to move away.

"Don't look so worried, Lokken. You'll make page one."

It's Bender, of course, standing behind Span as swarms of special ops cops methodically sweep through the rooms and corridors of the castle.

"Follow me, Sport," he says. "I got a lotta questions for you."

He grabs Span forcefully by the arm and up the main staircase they go, Span still struggling to recover from the sudden turn of events.

"I'm the one with questions," Span protests. "I have a deadline."

"Listen, asshole. We got a shooter on the loose. This is police priority. I got to know what you know. I got to know it quick."

They're at the top of the stairs now, at the entrance to the library, the spacious room with high ceilings, vast musty bookcases, a few statues, and above, big chandeliers hanging over a shiny stone floor. It's the floor that draws most of the attention. On it lie three still bodies.

Near the fireplace lies a dark-bearded fat man with tattooed arms and two slugs in his chest. "Here lies the former Duane Hajinlian," Bender says. "Breaks your heart to see this fine specimen of American manhood shot down in the prime of his miserable fucking life," he says, grinning ear to ear.

"Can I quote you?" Span asks.

"Why not?" he replies.

Next to Duane lies Jonas Kron III, his face discolored and misshapen, his blue eyes opened wide in fright. This is not a dignified end for a wealthy international businessman. Three feet from Kron's body lies a scary-looking black handgun.

Bender ID's it as a German-made HK nine-millimeter semi-automatic pistol.

Near the middle of the room lies a third body that no one seems to recognize. This is a bulky man, age maybe sixty, dressed in a flowery shirt and Bermuda shorts. His feet are bare. There's a small tattoo on the left arm. The hair is grayish-blond and thinning. Two bullet holes are prominent above the left ear. Blood flows from the nose and mouth. An open notebook lies near the body, its pages face up. The writing is in a neat hand, although the words are written in what appears to be Cyrillic script, a clue that English may not have been this man's first language.

"Where are the bad guys?" Span blurts. "Where are the two big guys dressed in black?"

"There's two?" Bender says.

"Yeah."

"We're looking for 'em," Bender says, his view of Feliks' body suddenly obscured by a police photographer stepping in to snap rapid-fire photos of the corpse, soon to be known in police circles as "Mystery Man."

Bender pulls Span toward the tall windows at the back of the room, Span spilling out everything he remembers. The man in shorts had a big black gun and spoke with an accent. Inexplicably he handed the gun to Kron after two black-clad intruders appeared in the doorway, Kron taking the gun and shocking everybody by shooting Duane. As more bullets began to fly, he and Petra made their desperate plunge down the servants' stairway. That's all he knows. Oh, and there was another dead body, the one in the cockpit of the floatplane down at the dock. White male, about forty, brown hair, big bloody hole in his forehead.

"Gimme a description of the two intruders," Bender demands.

"Very big, lots of muscle, blond hair, dressed all in black.

Had guns. Didn't know they had guns when I saw them climbing over the wall to get into this place."

Bender shoots a look at Span, a look intending to make Span feel stupid. Maybe he is stupid.

"Busy day on the island, right Bender?" Span says, looking the policeman straight in the eye.

"Stay available, Lokken," Bender says, poking in his pockets for a pack of cigarettes.

By mid afternoon Span is back at his desk downtown. Before composing his story he dashes out a cryptic outline based on what he just witnessed and what Bender and others had told him. His hands glide over the keys.

4 shot dead at Kron castle, 1 in N.E.

Jonas Kron III among shooting victims

Also among them, the remaining fugitive wanted for murder in last month's St. A church killings

Kidnapped girl found unharmed

Also safe Star Journal reporter who was present during shooting spree

Police searching for two unidentified suspects

Related shooting earlier Sunday resulted in death of a N.E. Minneapolis bar operator

City police and FBI working to untangle who responsible for 8 violent deaths in past 3 weeks.

Summary of victims, Sunday, June 26:

- *Jonas Kron III, president and CEO of Kron Industries, shot five times by unknown assailant or assailants for unknown reasons, in Kron mansion library.*
- *Duane Hajinlian, wanted for murder in June 5 church killings, shot twice by Jonas Kron for unknown reasons, also in mansion's library.*

- *Robert Storen, aide and companion to Kron and licensed pilot, shot once by unknown assailant for unknown reasons in floatplane docked outside mansion.*
- *Unidentified male shot twice, execution style, by unknown assailants for unknown reasons, also in the mansion library.*
- *Marla Kusic, N.E. Minneapolis tavern operator and associate of the church killers, shot twice, execution style, by unknown assailant for unknown reasons in apartment above bar.*

Earlier victims:

- *Richard Reznik, wanted for murder in the June 5 church slayings, shot once by fellow suspect Duane Hajinlian for unknown reasons Wednesday, June 22, at suburban motel. Two guns recovered, including murder weapon.*
- *The Rev. Matthias Hammar, pastor of St. Ansgar Church, tortured, crucified and executed for unknown reasons, Sunday, June 5, near the church altar, presumably by Reznik and Hajinlian. Weapon not recovered.*
- *Henrik Piedela, church sexton, shot twice, execution style, Sunday, June 5, at church's baptismal font, presumably by Reznik or Hajinlian. No weapon recovered.*

Police believe this was sequence of deaths: Piedela then Hammar on June 5. Reznik on June 22. Storen on June 25. Kusic, Hajinlian, Kron and the unidentified man on June 26.

Police believe they know killers of four victims. Results from fingerprint and ballistics tests — expected tomorrow — might help ID other assailants. Motives are much harder to determine. Cops think that church killers were hired talent, but don't know who hired them or the nature of their motive against Hammar. Motives for other killings? No solid clues have emerged, although possible international connections of Kron and unidentified victim drawing special attention from FBI.

Chapter Sixty-Two

Thursday, June 30, 9:00 p.m

When stripped to its essentials, journalism is about answering five questions: *who, what, where, when* and *why?* The first four have been pretty much covered by the cops and by Span's stories. Ballistics, fingerprints, video recordings and interviews with Span and Petra helped Bender fill in the blanks on who killed who — and when and where.

The *who* question hasn't been fully nailed down, of course, but Bender and Thurber at the FBI have turned up important clues on the victim labeled "Mystery Man." Petra thinks she heard him referred to as "Felix." Among several travel documents found in a backpack in one of the castle's bedrooms was a Russian passport assigned to a Feliks Alexandrov Dobervich. Six other passports also carried Dobervich's likeness attached to other names and nationalities. The backpack contained additional items that the police and the FBI would not tell Span about. National security, they claimed.

Thurber studied Feliks' body and face at great length, and

was particularly intrigued by a series of numbers jotted down in a notebook and copied into a notation on Feliks' cellphone. After conferring with Kron's financial secretary, Karen Crawley, he told Span that the numbers were codes for accounts in offshore banks. Still, it will take cooperation from Swiss, Bahamian and other authorities to solve a puzzle that may never be fully explained. That the German police had recovered five thousand euros plus forty thousand dollars in cash from Richard's and Duane's bags checked to the Frankfurt airport added confidence to the FBI's conclusion that the clergyman, Hammar, had been killed by assassins hired and trained by a foreign power, or foreign business interests, and that Feliks may have been the unfortunate handler of two overly enthusiastic but bumbling assassins.

And so there is momentum to answering the *who, what, where* and *when* questions. But the *why* is a gaping hole, a chasm so wide that Bender and Thurber may never make the leap. There were eight connected and violent deaths on or near Hennepin Island with no apparent explanation. Thurber, more experienced in these matters, is more comfortable with ambiguity. Bender is frustrated as hell, but eager to move on to his next big case.

Span is the most troubled by the absence of motive. He's usually OK with ambivalence. Big questions about the universe, for example, might not have answers knowable to humans, he thinks. Yet, he's stuck with the newspaperman's boundless curiosity. These events happened in his community. Like a bomb they shattered the innocence of Hennepin Island. The motive *is* knowable, he tells himself again and again.

It doesn't help that Bender keeps whispering in his ear, trying to lay doubts about Maggie not telling everything she knows, a detail about Hammar's life, perhaps, that she should remember but isn't remembering, or prefers not to remember.

So over and over Span runs though the progression of killings, trying to put the puzzle together. Why do the Russians want to kill Hammar? Why is Kron involved? If Feliks supervised Hammar's murder, then why was he still hanging around three weeks later? How does the still-missing Somali cab driver fit into the picture? Why do mysterious professionals dressed in black show up suddenly to kill everybody?

Four days have passed since, as one headline put it, *"Epic Spasm of Violence Rocks City."* Tonight is gorgeous and peaceful by contrast. Span, having worked almost straight through for the last seventy-two hours, is dozing on his screen porch in front of a 1940s film noir, something starring Dana Andrews. A ping on his phone causes him to stir. A text from Maggie:

Cumover?

It takes him less than ten minutes to get there, and that's including time spent shaving, splashing his face with cologne and putting on a fresh shirt.

Pulling up to the curb the first thing he notices is the absence of James Rincon's rental car. A good sign, he thinks. Then, illuminated by the porch lights, he sees all the yellow ribbons, scores of them, tied to the trees and shrubs, to the porch railings and chairs, to the front door. And a banner hanging over the stoop proclaiming: "Welcome home, Petra!"

"I'm a little embarrassed by all this, but what can I do?" Maggie says as she greets him at the door. "It's from neighbors and friends and parishioners, and really it's what they feel in their hearts, so ..." Then she leans in to kiss Span on the cheek. "You never smelled this good before," she says.

"Maybe I'm trying to impress you."

"I think it's working," she says. "Truth is you never impressed me before."

"No?"

"No. But now I'm changing my mind. It's totally the perfume you're wearing."

"Cologne," Span corrects her. "A very manly scent."

"Whatever," she says, smiling and turning to lead Span through the kitchen and into the backyard. The lighting is indirect and tasteful. The chorus of crickets and frogs is deafening. On the flagstone patio there's a small table and two chairs with a flickering candle, a frosty bottle and two glasses.

Petra is up in her bedroom asleep, Maggie explains. She had spent Sunday night in the hospital, a precautionary measure, Maggie by her side the whole night, James there for a few hours. On Monday the team of doctors, psychiatrists and social workers proclaimed Petra a "miracle kid." Not many children could have gone through the experience of seeing what she saw, hearing what she heard, feeling the fear that she must have felt, suffering the anxiety of separation that she suffered without major and lasting scars, they said. But Petra emerged almost as if the nightmare never happened. Maybe there will be a delayed reaction at some point, they warned. Probably there will be. But for now, her ability to cope and recover is nothing short of remarkable.

Span bends sideways to take a beautifully wrapped little present (the store wrapped it) out of a small shopping bag and set it on the table. "For Petra," he says, straight-faced. "A diamond bracelet, two-carat."

Maggie shoots him her skeptical look.

"OK, maybe not. Maybe it's the Minnie Mouse Birthstone Necklace from the Disney Store."

"She'll love it!" Maggie says, surprised and smiling.

They're sipping their Absolut now, enjoying the night sounds and the stillness of the air. Span has to say Maggie's looking more relaxed than she has in weeks. He doesn't think he's ever seen her in a dress, but she's wearing one of those long, sleeveless shifts that falls almost to her ankles. Her feet and shoulders are bare. She's wearing dangly earrings, another first. And she's ditched her frequent ponytail and her rounded wire-rimmed glasses.

She notices that Span is admiring her, so Span feels compelled to say something. "Um, you're looking kind of spectacular tonight."

"Must be the vodka talking," she says.

That leads into a long, awkward pause interrupted by the distant groan of a riverboat's horn from somewhere south of the island. That's when Span notices she's ditched something else: her wedding ring.

Span tries not to let her see that he's noticed. But the reporter in the man can't help but blurt out the first thing that comes into his head. "So where's James?" he hears his idiot voice saying. "I thought he'd be here."

"Went back Tuesday morning," she says.

More crickets. More frogs. More sipping of vodka. Span studies the cheese and crackers. He's thinking they're both a little drunk. It's an observation she confirms by finally breaking the silence.

"I have to admit, I had a few drinks before you got here," she says, smiling again, pausing for another sip. "Span, can I tell you something?"

"Of course."

"I hope it's OK if I tell you this."

"It is."

"I've missed you the last few days ... missed talking to you. You should know, um, that all through this entire mess you've been very ... important to me. You don't know how much you've kept me going."

Her eyes glisten. Again she tips the glass to her lips, still looking Span in the eye.

"I want to say thank you," she says. " I want to ... and I've thought about this a lot. I want to give you something."

Span's mind races. His heart thumps. He admits to himself that his lower regions are tingling, and that his head swims a few strokes. Not often is he speechless, but....

Maggie rescues him by standing and saying, "Come with me."

A little wobbly on his feet, Span follows her willowy form into the kitchen, then the dining room. He's thinking she's heading for the stairs when she turns and takes a manila envelope from the top of the buffet and hands it to him. Then she sits at the dining room table, her amazing green eyes locked into his. Span exhales, peeling open the envelope, not knowing what to expect. He finds several pages of yellow legal pad with writing he can't read, followed by several typed pages in English.

"What's this?" he says.

"It's something I found in police files," she says. "I'm afraid I pinched it from the evidence vault ... but I had a good reason."

"I hope so."

"I found it in Henrik's file, in an envelope addressed to Matthias. The cops had looked at it. But they never bothered to translate. It's in Swedish."

"What is it?"

"It's a confession. A confession from Henrik. Don't know if Matthias ever got it. Don't know if he ever read it. Don't know if he ever heard a verbal confession from Henrik. Anyway, I had it translated."

"But you're not supposed to ..."

"I know. I realize what I'm doing. I broke the law when I took it out of the evidence room. And I'm breaking my vows by showing this to you. But, God help me, this is a secret I can't keep any longer. Like I say, I've thought about this a lot. I've struggled with it. Now I want you to read this. Please. Before I change my mind."

Span sits down next to Maggie, his eyes skipping over the yellow pages to the typed translation:

8 October 2015

I Confess

I did a very bad thing many years ago. This thing did not trouble me at the time because, for doing it, I was paid many thousands of dollars — and it was promised to me that my family in Estonia will not be harmed.

Here, Maggie has penciled in a note at the margin: Didn't know about Henrik's family in Estonia, didn't know about danger.

Oh, God in heaven, if you are out there I want you to know that I experience that terrible moment again and again, day and night. And as time goes by it is harder and harder for me to make excuses for myself. I did this. I pulled this trigger. I can no longer hide it. I cannot erase it. I am told that your son Jesus Christ, through his own suffering, has already made me a clean man. But the feeling of regret and guilt will not leave me. I need to be released from all this terrible weight that I carry, every day. As I get older it is worse and worse. By myself I do not know if I believe in you, if I believe that you actually exist. But the people all around me do believe it and they are a better kind of people than me. So, I am trusting them to speak up for me because I am not worthy to do it.

If you, God, are who you they say you are, then I do not have to tell you what happened in those dreadful days. You already know. But, for me, I need to say it anyway. A man came to me in a bar near the waterfront in Stockholm one day after my work shift was finished. He was a big man who was not a Swede but seemed to be a Russian. He did not give me his full name, but said I should call him Feliks. We drank vodka and ate sand-

wiches. Feliks paid. He was there in the bar the next several nights. This was in February 1986. I was 29 years old. I was working on the docks for more than ten years. Feliks knew a lot about ships and said he came from a long line of merchant sailors. He said he helped manage a shipping operation in Gdansk, and was visiting Sweden for business. One night he offered me a job with his company for a very big bonus — the equivalent of about $100,000 for one week of work. I thought maybe he was drunk. We were drinking a lot of vodka. I was suspicious and did not believe him.

When I said I was not interested he told me the names of my family in Estonia and where they lived. He named my father and mother, and my brother's three children and where they went to school. He named my sister and where she lived and where she worked. It was at this point that I no longer saw Feliks as a friend, even though he kept smiling at me. He then reached into his pocket and took out a fat envelope. When I looked inside I never saw so much money. He said it was 90,000 kronor, which was at that time about $10,000. I was, you might call it, thunderstruck. He said I could keep it and that there would be ten times more when I finished the job. I drank up my vodka and put the money in my pocket. We walked out to the street and got into his car. From under the seat he took a paper bag and handed it to me. It was heavy. Inside there was a pistol and some bullets. Have you ever used one of these? he asked me. No, I said. The only time I shot a gun was in army training and that was a rifle. Well, he said some practice would be necessary. I was scared. But the next night we left the bar and drove into the country. It was cold. We drank vodka and shot the gun at some targets. At the time I thought it felt good to shoot. Feliks told me I was a talent for shooting.

Back in the car Feliks told me that a very bad man, an assassin, wanted to kill him and his business partners and steal the business away from him. Feliks told me that the man had even raped his young daughter, from which she never recovered. He declined to tell me this man's name, but described to me how he looked and showed me a picture. They tried to stop him in the courts and every other way, Feliks said, but he was very rich and privileged. The only way to justice was to shoot him. Feliks could not do it himself because his hand shook, he said. And yes, out in the country on those nights, he was a very bad shooter.

Feliks said the next five days I should keep available at night. We drank more and more vodka. One night this Feliks was more excited than before. The man he called Mål X was at a cinema and maybe will walk back to the subway after. We meet on Sveavågen, which is a busy commercial street in Stockholm, at about 10 o'clock. We drink more vodka and walk around waiting for film to be over. At 11:15 people come out and we spot Mål X talking to other people, then he and a woman begin walking down toward the subway. We are on the other side of the street. After passing in front of a big church we see they are crossing over to our side of the street. Feliks took the gun out of his pocket and put it in mine. He didn't say anything, but he walked away down a side street. I followed the two people for a while, then I ran up and shot the man, who fell down. When the woman screamed and looked at me, I shot her, too. Then I ran or walked, I cannot remember. I went down a side street, the newspapers said it was Tunnelgaten. Feliks was there, in the back seat of the car I got into. He took the gun from me. Somebody I didn't know was driving. A man. We saw many police cars but they were going the other way.

Another pencil note in the margin: Henrik uses some phrases that are not Swedish, maybe Estonian, translator says.

After drinking more vodka I must have fallen asleep. I woke in the morning on board a ship in a harbor. I couldn't tell exactly where we were. It wasn't Stockholm. I was there for maybe a week or ten days. That's when I read in newspapers and saw on TV that the Prime Minister of Sweden had been shot in the back and his wife was wounded. This happened on Sveavågen. That's when I understood fully that I was tricked by this liar, Feliks. I was extremely frightened. But he was on the ship, too, and he assured me that all was OK. He gave me a number and told me that I could draw money from it wherever I was in the world. He also gave me some papers and a new name: Henrik Josef Piedela. Until that day I had been Jaan Mihkel Talvik.

Another pencil note: Astonished! Henrik not who he seemed to be. Maybe trying to forget past life.

One day Feliks was no longer aboard the ship. Other men, I didn't know their names, put me on another ship, a bigger ship. We were on the water for many days. We came finally to Canada where I was then put on another boat, an iron ore vessel on the Great Lakes, then later a very small boat, then a car and soon I was at a big log house with many luxuries. It was in the woods on a big lake. There, I was met by a very rich looking businessman who turned out to be Mr. Jonas Kron, an American who spoke Swedish. He told me I would have a free apartment and a job taking care of a large church in a big city.

This, O God, is a thing I want to say. If I was in America working on the docks like I was before in Sweden, then I would not be confessing this. I would not feel pain of what I did. I would forget that terrible moment I pulled the trigger. Or deny that I ever did it. But since I am working at this church I see things in a different way. People are all both good and bad. That includes people in this church. The difference is that people all around me at this church admit their bad parts and find peace for themselves and for those around them and then they have a motivation not to care so much about themselves but to help other people even if those people don't deserve help. Like me. This new kind of life is what I need. This is who I want to be. More like them.

Maybe I'm just getting older, so I think more about these spiritual things. Maybe I'm not smart enough to figure it out. In school I was taught that religion is a bad thing, a kind of drug that makes people think only of heaven and not about solving problems in the world. I am no longer so sure about that.

O God, I don't know if I believe in you, or in Jesus Christ, but I'm hoping so hard you can remove this from my shoulders. I am sorry and ashamed that this happened. I should say that I am sorry and ashamed that it was me, and me alone, who made this happen, who did this terrible thing, who shot a man, who killed a man, who shot a woman and injured her, who enjoyed the money I was paid. But I cannot any longer enjoy it. If there is such a thing as forgiveness, I beg you for it.

Henrik Josef Piedela

Chapter Sixty-Three

Stockholm, Sweden
Friday, September 9, 7 p.m.

The most popular attraction in Stockholm is the Vasa Museum, an emblem of Sweden's wry ingenuity in making triumph out of blunder. *Vasa* was one of the world's most formidable warships when launched with much fanfare in 1628, loaded with so many heavy guns that she promptly sank to the bottom of Stockholm harbor. There she stayed for three hundred years until she was raised and towed to shore, and a museum was erected around her. The museum opened in 1990. Maggie and Span plan to visit *Vasa,* but it's not their top priority.

First on their list is finding the exact spot where, in a sense, they began.

It's evening by the time they check into their hotel, get settled, find the Café Tranan, have dinner, drink more than a few drinks and then hop in a taxi for the short ride to the Grand theatre on Sveavägen. They arrive a bit early, about 11:15 local time. So, they stand around talking about movies. Even jet-lagged, Span can talk at length about film noir, and tonight he's telling Maggie about a movie in which a reporter tries to expose a corrupt prosecutor by framing himself for murder only to find himself — the reporter — convicted of the crime and sentenced to death. Maggie's patience and good humor let him go on and on until she raises a more interesting topic: movies you admire but cannot bear to watch again. She names two films that are so deeply sad to her that she avoids them: "Saving Private Ryan" because of the cumulative suffering on Tom Hanks' face, and "Ordinary People" because of Mary Tyler Moore's "veneer of denial" in grieving a dead son.

Span and Maggie are grieving, too, in this pilgrimage.

But they're also celebrating their ... what can we call it? Span hates the word relationship. It's not quite a relationship that Maggie and he have, not in the sense that most people use the term. Friendship? Well, yes. But it's more than that. There's really no word in the language to describe what they have. At least that's the way Span sees it. He's not sure how Maggie sees it. She's of the generation that accuses his generation of over-analyzing everything. So, let's just say that they enjoy each other to the point that they cannot be apart for very long. And, so far, neither of them has been able to knock the enjoyment off track.

The trip was her idea, and Span tends to think that all her ideas are good ones. Aside from Mexico and Canada, she'd never been outside the United States. Span, he'd been to Europe several times, but never to the Nordic countries. From what he can tell, Stockholm is spectacular.

Together, they concocted reasons for coming here. Maggie convinced her bishop that, in light of Hammar's death, she should reaffirm the special ties between her parish and the "mother church" in Sweden. And so, a meeting with the Swedish archbishop had been arranged. As for Span, he'd been struck by disturbing similarities between the U.S. presidential campaign now underway and the white nationalist, immigrant-bashing politics of Europe. Not that he was overly worried about the American outcome, but doing some interviews over here would be helpful for a piece he was planning. Actually, of course, the trip was about something else.

At 11:30 they start walking the walk they've come here to make, down Sveavägen toward the subway station. They walk arm in arm, touching sometimes at the hip, both of them wearing running shoes so that Span comes almost up to her height, able to see eye-to-eye and touch nose-to-nose. It's light-jacket weather. This is a major commercial street, but not many people are out walking at this hour. Auto traffic is light. After passing the lush grounds of a big domed church, the Adolf Fredriks Kyrka, they cross over to the east side of the street. At the end of a long block they come across one of the Stockholm's three Urban Deli locations. This is a glassy, well-lit bar/restaurant/market combination with a rooftop garden. To Span it has the look of a hipster hangout, tattooed young people coming and going. Embedded into the sidewalk out front, near a scrum of parked bicycles, is a surprisingly small bronze plaque. People walk past not noticing. Maggie and Span are the only ones to stop and read:

PÅ DENNA PLATS MÖRDADES
SVERIGES
STATSMINISTER
OLOF PALME
DEN 28 FEBRUARI 1986

(Murdered on this place Sweden's Prime Minister Olof Palme on February 28, 1986.)

They stare at the plaque for longer than seems necessary. When Span looks over at Maggie, he's surprised to see tears streaming down her cheeks. She dabs at her eyes with her jacket sleeve and starts to laugh. "I'm thinking of the last joke Henrik told me," she says. Every day he had a new one. This one he told me in the hallway just before Mass on the day he died."

The story, Maggie recounts, is about a Norwegian arguing with a Swede and a Dane about who has the most endurance. So they decide to find out who can last the longest in a stinky pig barn. After five minutes the Swede has had enough. He comes out. After ten minutes the Dane comes out. After fifteen minutes all the pigs come running out.

She laughs again and sniffles a little. They both look around, neither of them saying the words they're thinking. What they're thinking is that this is the spot where Henrik, of all people, ran up from behind and shot the prime minister of Sweden in the back and, as he fell down to die, Henrik shot and wounded his wife, and then over there, around the corner, he hurried away to meet Feliks Dobervich. And they're thinking that this is where the long chain of events started that ended in a big puddle of blood on Hennepin Island thirty years later.

But, considering everything that happened, everything that emanated from this place, including for Maggie the murder of two friends, the kidnapping of her daughter and the loss of innocence on what she thought was her island refuge, they are both underwhelmed standing here on this sidewalk.

Perhaps this place is deliberately minimalist. Perhaps it was designed in the tradition of Scandinavian understatement. Perhaps there was fear that a more elaborate monument would become a tribute to the act of assassination. Whatever the reason, Maggie and Span can't help but feel a little let down.

Then they tell each other: Maybe the emotional power of this place is in its ordinariness. That the murder of a prominent figure did, indeed, happen on this mundane corner, and that people now go about their lives barely noticing. Maybe that is the intended lesson — that life goes on.

It's midnight. This has been a very long day. They are

exhausted. Span wipes a few remaining tears from Maggie's cheeks. She throws her arms around his shoulders in a tight embrace and exhales. They look each other in the eye but can't find words to say. There are a few taxis lined up at the subway station across the street. They take one of them back to the hotel and ride the elevator up. They're sharing a room, but not a bed. That's the arrangement they made before they left. It's an economy move, they told themselves, and a sensible move, all things considered. She gets the bathroom first, emerging in a T-shirt, long bare legs and fuzzy socks. She's tucked in with eyes closed by the time Span turns off the bathroom light and slips quietly into the other bed.

Silence. Minutes go by before he hears a voice in the dark.

"Span? Are you asleep?"

EPILOGUE

SVENSK INTERNATIONELL NYHETSTJÃNST

SLT IUPN TI MON CNN

BREAKING NEWS ALERT

AFTER 34 YEARS, SWEDISH OFFICIALS CLOSE THE BOOKS ON PALME ASSASSINATION

EVIDENCE POINTS TO STIG ENGSTROM, WHO DIED BY HIS OWN HAND IN 2000

STOCKHOLM (SIN) 10 June 2020 – Shrouded in mystery since 1986, the killing of Prime Minister Olof Palme has been officially laid to rest, judicial officials said on Wednesday.

At a news conference here, the prosecutor Krister Petersson described "reasonable evidence" that Palme's assailant was Stig Engstrom, a graphic designer who worked at an insurance company. Engstrom, 52 at the time of the assassination, killed himself in 2000 at the age of 66. Since the suspect is deceased, there will be no court case to decide guilt or innocence, Petersson said.

Petersson said he could not rule out the possibility that Engstrom had been part of a larger conspiracy. He did not elaborate.

Palme was shot in the back shortly after leaving a cinema with his wife, Lisbeth on a cold winter night in 1986. His prominence as a social idealist who opposed perceived injustices around the world made him an attractive target for international intrigue. Spy agencies from Chile to South Africa to Israel were said to have grudges against Palme.

A prime architect of Sweden's social welfare system, Palme advocated for a "third way" in the cold war competition between the Western democracies and the Soviet system.

(ENDIT 15.01 EDT)

Afterword

Like many contemporary novels, "Lost Colony" is a blend of actual and imagined events, places and people. Any writer, while immersed in telling a tale, can easily conflate the real and the unreal, leaving the reader justifiably confused. This afterword is meant to set things straight.

First, as you probably know, there *was* a Swedish prime minister named Olof Palme who was assassinated pretty much as described in these pages. And, yes, the police were baffled by the crime. After three futile decades they officially closed the case in 2020 without definitively naming a suspect or a motive. Not surprisingly, the case generated waves of conspiracy theories. This story *should not* be added to the list. *It is purely fiction.* There's no convincing evidence, after all, that a foreign power was involved in Palme's death. None of the main characters portrayed in these pages is based on an actual person.

As for the story's setting, Minneapolis is obviously a real city, although it is not configured quite as the author imagines. Likewise, Hennepin Island is a real place. But it's a tiny dot in the Mississippi River at St. Anthony Falls in downtown Minneapolis that functions mainly as a hydro-electric plant. It is *not* the Hennepin Island depicted in these pages. The fictional island is much larger, more populous, more eccentric and more intriguing — and the author situated it two miles downstream from the real island.

About this book's title, Lost Colony usually refers to Roanoke Island, a failed attempt to establish a British outpost in what's now coastal North Carolina in 1585. By 1590, the colonists had mysteriously vanished. Another lost colony, dating to 1638, was New Sweden, a string of Swedish settlements along the Delaware River in present-day Delaware, Pennsylvania, New Jersey and Maryland. The colony was "lost" to Dutch control in 1655 and eventually absorbed by the British. In this novel, the delusional Jonas Kron envisions Hennepin Island, in Minnesota, as a colony of his imagined Swedish empire.

Also, it must be said that the Minneapolis described in this story was the city of 2016 — still ascendant and bustling. In the wake of the pandemic and the riots that followed George Floyd's murder in 2020, many of the city's central districts are, as of this writing, struggling to recover.

Finally, the writer confesses to being an extreme slowpoke. The idea for this book first emerged in the 1970s following a sensational double-murder in Duluth, Minnesota. But before work could begin, there were thousands of newspaper stories to write and two kids to raise and several new houses and cities to move into. After that there were two non-fiction books to write before the author dared to try fiction. Even then, nearly a decade passed between this book's first and last sentences. As he often explained, "It's hard to make stuff up."

Thank you for reading "Lost Colony." I hope you will consider leaving a review wherever you buy books.

— Steve Berg, 2023

Acknowledgments

Without the persistent encouragement of Dixie Rollins Berg, my wife, this book would not have been written. Nor would it have been completed without the expert coaching of Alex Rollins Berg, an accomplished screenwriter and director, who's also our son.

Alex was my writing partner throughout the project, offering valuable insights on plot, organization and character. Learning from your children is a wonderful experience. Whenever I grew impatient or discouraged (which was often), Alex was there to pick me up.

Dixie, a gifted communications specialist, stepped in as a copy editor extraordinaire. She caught dozens – maybe hundreds – of mistakes, inconsistencies and blunders in the manuscript and patiently suggested fixes.

I'm indebted, as well, to David Zucchino, Stephen Nelson and Vinton Rollins who read early versions of the project and encouraged me to continue.

About the Author

Steve Berg interrupted his love of film noir for a career in journalism. He was a Washington, D.C.- and Minneapolis-based reporter and editorial writer for the Minneapolis Star Tribune before writing two architecture books on sports stadiums. His educational credits include the University of North Carolina - Chapel Hill and Stanford University. *Lost Colony: The Hennepin Island Murders* is his first novel. Steve and his wife live in Asheville, N.C.

Learn more at www.steveberg.org.

Also by Steve Berg

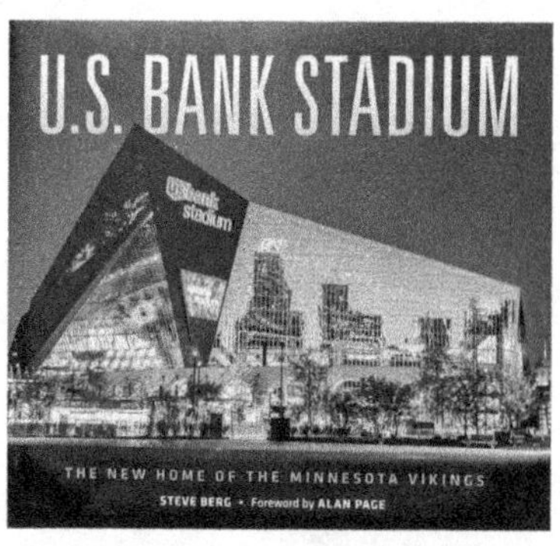

"U.S Bank Stadium: The New Home of the Minnesota Vikings," 2016

"Target Field: The New Home of the Minnesota Twins," 2010

Printed in the USA
CPSIA information can be obtained
at www.ICGtesting.com
LVHW051336111123
763517LV00030B/249

9 798988 363712